*Love, Betty*

**Laura Kemp** writes tender but hilarious romantic comedies which are unashamed love letters to the everywoman. She is a journalist and has written for the *Guardian*, *Daily Mail* and the *Sun* amongst others. Laura lives with her husband and son in Cardiff, where she pretends to be a domestic revolutionary, so she doesn't have to do the ironing.

Follow all her book news at facebook.com/Laurakempbooks or on Twitter @Laurajanekemp

*Also by Laura Kemp*

The Year of Surprising Acts of Kindness
Bring Me Sunshine
Under a Starry Sky

For the Babas, my very own golden girls

# Before

## Betty

I shoot my target smack bang in the chest, then turn my back on the cry for help.

'Really sorry, lovely,' I say over my shoulder because I don't want to be rude.

It's just that I'm on a call, chasing a meeting buffet that's gone AWOL, and work comes first.

'The street menu for twelve, including gluten-free, halal and vegan options,' I say to the caterer, 'it'll be there in ten?' If not, there's no need to panic. I may be in a hideout of stacked tyres during a corporate team-building paintball session but nothing is beyond me and my phone – there's always Deliveroo. But it's good news. 'Lush, thanks!'

Job done, so I go back to my victim who is splattered in a kaleidoscope of orange, yellow and purple, which makes a gorgeous clash of colours against the issue camo-combat gear.

'Betty Hopkins! You savage!' It's Sami, my firework of a best friend and colleague who is currently fuming and holding me to account with an arched and perfectly groomed black eyebrow. He takes off his goggles and looks like he's been face-painted by Jackson Pollock. 'I've got a date tonight! If I get a bruise ...'

I

'Get some ice on it and then foundation,' I suggest as I dial the boss. 'How did you know it was me, by the way?' I look down at my spotless uniform.

'The hair and make-up, of course.' If I'm going to stick out as a redhead I may as well go the whole hog with scarlet lips. 'The wedge trainers.' I can't do flats, I'm too short. 'You've got an earbud in and you're working. As usual.' I could protest but, to be fair to him, he's spot on.

'Well, your uncle has to eat!' I explain, before confirming to Ahmed that food is on its way, and then reloading my weapon with a satisfying click.

But Sami is still looking daggers at me. 'You could've at least aimed for my legs. Why do you have to be so ... efficient?'

Clutching his throat he stalks off back to base.

It's a dramatic exit but he's a flamboyant designer at the family fashion empire. Once upon a time I had some of that strut and passion but there's not much call for it when you're the personal assistant to the managing director, his decision-maker by proxy, available twenty-four-seven, and on it at all times. It's not my fault that my preparedness, focus and organisation overlap in a 'what it takes to be a cold-blooded sicko' Venn diagram. Which reminds me, I'm still in the game with no hits and eight kills under my pink belt.

I get to my knees and crawl along the concrete of the East London activity centre's vast industrial wasteland, shadowing scaffolding, camouflage nets and huge steel pipes, beneath the scudding clouds of the February sky in search of new cover. I spy a breeze block hut just as crackling loudspeakers announce there are two active players left, there are fifteen minutes to go and whoever is last back will be crowned Survival of the Fittest champion.

Only two? I could win this! Not bad for someone who was asked to come at the last minute 'to have some fun for a change' when Jax from sales called in sick. I wonder if my nemesis is from the office; every group has been bundled into this last session for an 'everyone versus everyone' finale. I'd prefer a stranger because I've already shot Matt from marketing in the nuts and that'll make our next departmental meeting awkward.

I hot-foot it into the lean-to and realise with a jolt that I've got company.

'Gotcha!' I say, staring down the barrel of my moving rifle tracking through the gloom, like they do on *Line of Duty*.

But as my eyes adjust to the dark I see a six-foot-plus man waving a handkerchief. Instantly I think, what kind of a weirdo carries one around these days? A mummy's boy or a bounder?

'Take me, I'm yours,' he sighs in an amused, deep voice.

The suspicion and adrenalin slip away and a smile slides onto my face. 'Goddammit! I wanted to take you down in a blaze of glory, not via a surrender hankie.'

'You still can; tell them we had a dog fight,' he says. I laugh because his weapon is on the floor. 'No one needs to know that my strategy right from the start was to sit it out. So if you know anyone who's looking for the next James Bond ...'

He's as dry as a bone. Not to mention very easy on the eye, so I size him up properly through the cross hairs. It's not strictly necessary to scope him out because there's nothing threatening about him; I trust and like him immediately. But I can't pass on the chance to use my

3

advantage to get a decent look. It's shameful, it really is, but it's been a long time since Jude and I broke up and the work catwalk is full of sculpted boyish smooth skin whereas this one looks manly.

He's leaning casually against the wall with muscular arms crossed and his fatigue jacket is undone enough to reveal a very naked olive-skinned chest. Classically handsome, he has wide eyes, full lips and a strong, stubbled jaw, and it's all framed with dark bed hair which stands to attention because his goggles are pushed back on the top of his head. Dear God, this man is impossibly attractive even with a pair of goggles on the top of his head.

My body reacts with a shiver, then a warm surge washes over me. He's completely disarmed me so I drop the gun but make out I'm just following the rules of engagement.

'It's against the Geneva Convention to attack someone no longer involved in hostilities.'

He laughs and my inner thermostat cranks up to hot.

'Curious,' he says with a raised eyebrow.

'What?' I say, hungrily. What has got into me?

'You know your military stuff and yet that pink belt isn't regulation wear. Are you a renegade?' he says, his accent pure Home Counties.

I snort because the truth is less exciting. 'It's to stop my trousers falling down.'

He gives a belly laugh this time. Suddenly self-conscious, I pull my goggles off and shake out my hair. I get a moment of acute self-awareness as if I'm doing it to look my best because I fancy him. And then I realise I am and I do. I make a lame effort to take back control.

'Right, so … I can capture you or you can surrender. Or we can call it a truce.'

'It's entirely up to you; depends how much you want to win.'

I surprise myself by hesitating. What do I want? My head demands first place but my heart throbs with 'whatever it takes to keep us here for as long as possible'.

'In the meantime, killer queen,' he says, just as a square of sunlight comes through the door and I see he has dark-chocolate eyes, 'would you like a G and T in a can?' By way of explanation he adds, 'I'm on a stag do.'

I gasp because I'm technically at work. I let off a lot of steam when I'm out, but when I'm on, I'm one of those committed-to-the-job people – or, as Jude put it, 'married to your bloody phone'. I get a rush of rebellion that makes me want to prove I'm not.

'Go on, then.' And I start to gabble to justify it to myself. 'Because I'm off for a week when this ends; I'm going to Italy, so I might as well start as I mean to go on! Shall we just be joint winners?'

I'm a walkover; I'm so not usually a walkover. He throws me a tin that he's produced from his pocket and it comes with a waft of his delicious lemon scent.

He takes one more from the other thigh, cracks it open and takes a slug. I pop mine and predictably it fizzes up into my face.

'You may as well use my surrender hankie.' Credit to him, he resists sniggering at my beard of bubbles.

I take it, dabbing myself dry, and then wonder what to do with it, I can hardly hand it back like a child.

He sees my dilemma. 'Keep it. Like a war trophy.'

It's a soft pink, emblazoned with the words The Repair Guy in a red circus-style font and patterned with little spanners, hammers and jigsaw puzzle pieces.

'That's me, Guy, that's what I do. I fix stuff – repairs, restoration, replacing missing bits and pieces – in the workshop down in Tunbridge Wells.'

So that's why The Repair Guy rocks goggles. He's naturally handy and wholesome, the gin is lively and lovely and pleasure descends on me as we sit down in the sunlight.

'What about you, then?' he asks. 'Who are you?'

'I'm Betty. I'm in fashion—' I draw breath to expand but he cuts in.

'Ah! I would've guessed something creative. The way you look. The – er – hair.' He stumbles over his words and looks shy, which makes my pulse race. 'And, of course, the belt and your—' he conjures it up with his hands – 'spirit.'

He clears his throat, which I guess is because he thinks he's been too familiar, as if his veins flow with the reserve of an English gent. I'm not phased by it, I'm a Welsh girl and my DNA hums with speaking one's mind. In fact, I'm pleased that he doesn't see me like everyone else does: as a walking spreadsheet. I channel my imagination at work to find solutions for problems. At home it runs riot in my statement walls, quirky lamps and fireplaces full of plants, in my wardrobe, which is stuffed with clothes I customise from charity shops. And when I get the time, I love to explore what the city has to offer. I give him a little reassuring nod.

'So, if it's Italy you're going to, would that be Milan?' he says.

'Close! Venice. On my own; first time I'll have been away by myself!' The trip was booked last year for Jude and me. I've always wanted to go and see the festival and its carnival of masks. So I thought, what the hell, I would.

'Cool! I've never been, it looks amazing, like a labyrinth.'

My phone vibrates.

'Excuse me, I need to take this.'

'Do you?' He says it doubtfully. But he doesn't know I've never had a pay rise refused and this is the price.

It's someone asking if the boss really needs the figures by the end of today, it's the weekend tomorrow, surely he won't look at them until Monday? Oh but he will, I say. Then I have to go because the call is interrupted by another – it's HR informing me the application process is officially open for a new position, head of sustainability, which has been my idea, my baby, to make us greener.

I come away beaming, but Guy is bemused.

'What?' I ask.

'You head of Versace or something?' He's teasing me – people don't tend to because of my role – and a fizz in my stomach rises up into a giggle. I can't remember the last time I felt giddy around someone.

'Not quite. I work at Banta, the lads' online label?' He looks blankly at me so I quote our slogan 'Oi oi, load your cart and check the hell out'.

'I'm not the skinny joggers type. More cargo shorts with glue on them. But still, you're in the fashion industry!'

'I'm a secretary. I do the boring but essential stuff.'

'Doesn't sound like it.' He still looks impressed and it's very flattering.

'Well … I do love it. It wasn't what I originally wanted to do. I went to fashion college but took an office job to give myself an in, hoping I'd dazzle them with my designs.'

His intense listening sparks something in me. Out of nowhere a gap opens up in my chest and things tumble out as if I'm in a confessional. 'I've always wanted to have my own brand – nothing global, more slow fashion rather than fast. Maybe one day, back home.' To prove I was better than my failure of a father.

'You should!' He says it as if it's that easy.

'I'm in no rush to leave London. I'm thinking ahead, maybe ten years or so, when I'm done with the rat race.'

There's another buzz in my pocket. I look but ignore this one.

'Not going to take it?'

'Nah, it's not important. Just my sister.'

Guy's eyebrows furrow and while I don't usually feel the need to explain myself, I find I want to.

'I don't do personal in business hours. It's different to Wales, the Valleys, where I'm from.'

'Yeah, I clocked that. My granny's Welsh. But we don't like to talk about it.' He pours on the well-spoken posh-boy act for the gag.

So I whack up the intensity of my lilt. 'Yeah? My third cousin on my grampy's side, he's English and we don't like to talk about it either.'

He guffaws and I grab the chance to move the chat away from me. I want to know about him.

'The stag, then ...' It has to be him. He'd never be single and he seems incredibly buoyant and happy.

He gulps at his can.

'Yep. It's me,' he says, as if he's surprised by it. 'Last-minute thing, hence the paintballing ... I didn't want to do anything really but my best man wanted me to have a send-off.' He pauses and then adds, 'Apparently nerves are normal.'

'Of course they are!' I sing. Although I have no insight – and never want to.

'It's excitement too.' He grins. 'I'm going to be a dad, next month. We wanted to do what they call The Right Thing, all a bit of a shock, to be honest, but the best one of my life! Once we're settled in, probably around five, six months, I'm hoping to take extended paternity to be the main carer.'

'Ah, that's lovely! Life is full of surprises. You'll make it happen.' And I bet he'll make a brilliant dad. He is ecstatic and I bask in his glow. Until a klaxon goes off and it's all over.

'You've won!' he says, delighted for me, showing off the most perfect teeth, and I always notice a set because of the gap in mine.

'We both have!' I say, as we get up. And in the most natural of movements we put our arms around each other. It's only a short cwtch of a hug, but how it feels takes my breath away, not least because it goes against my standard stand-offish London posture. In that brief embrace, when my head rests against his towering body and I lose myself in his citrus smell, when his hands wrap me up and he holds me tight, I go somewhere deep and dark that leaves me light-headed. As I said, it's been a long time. We come apart without any embarrassment and agree to share our victory on the walk back to HQ where the crowd cheers us inside.

Swallowed by his stags, Guy mouths 'goodbye' and I wave farewell to this charming man whom I'll never meet again. That thought ends up flitting around my tummy. But I bat it away because, never mind if it was effortless and tingly, and that in itself is so very rare, it was just a random moment. With a taken man, I hear my sister say in my head. I delete him from my mind but the unexpected effect he had on me remains: that he saw me as someone more than the person I see myself as. It's something I'll think about, I know it, but not now – I need to act sharpish.

'Time for a quick one, Bet?' Sami's sulk has vanished – he loves a celebration.

'I wish but I've got a plane to catch.'

We kiss goodbye and I head to the changing room where I stuff my bits and pieces into my satchel, get into my latest favourite outfit – a green vintage jumpsuit I've tarted up with emerald sequin epaulettes, chunky jewellery and a peacock-blue beret and a big camel-coloured teddy coat. I grab my wheelie suitcase then nip out onto the street where people, cars, bikes and cabs weave in and out, merry on Friday vibes.

All the while my phone is crying for my attention. As I walk, I tie up the loose ends of the calls, emails and messages, responding to diary queries, sending out reminders, and I promise myself I'll get back to my sister once I'm past passport control.

I'm at a zebra crossing, I check it's clear left and right, then step into the road. I'm halfway across and am about to stick on my out-of-office automated response when my ears fill with screeching tyres and blaring horns. I feel an enormous sickening thud on the side of my right thigh, my legs leave the ground and I'm being carried on the bonnet of a car. My head hits the windscreen and I'm thrown into the air, which smells of burning. The sky comes at me then retreats, all the while my fist has refused to give up my phone, until it is knocked out of my hand when I crash down on the road.

And then everything goes black.

# I

## Betty

Baking sunshine streams through the lounge window of my mother's terraced house so I pull the curtain and sink back into the sofa.

I'm meant to be working up to a walk by myself for the first time since the accident, that's the goal I've set myself this week. But it won't happen while we're having a heatwave. The sun will burn down on me like a spotlight, picking me out as that 'poor girl, terrible what happened to her'.

It's bad enough when Mam is with me, when sad eyes and hushed voices tell her I'm 'awful pale' and 'nothing like the Betty we know', as if I wasn't there. They mean no harm – the village that is named Pant Bach, or 'small valley' where it nestles beneath the South Wales mountains, holds its own dearly and where else could I go that was safe and soft enough to recover? It's been a weight on me, though, squeezing the air from my lungs, making me pretend I'm much better, thank you. Now I need to start believing it because I've become a burden.

Yet the thought of going out makes me want to hide behind Mam's nets and the waves of fear that haunt me and hover on the horizon start to come in at me.

'Cup of tea, love?'

She's in front of me. I blink hard to clear my gritty, tired eyes. She's holding one of her bone-china mugs for best, depicting a watercolour of gambling lambs, and a plate of pink wafer biscuits, my favourites when I was little. It's officially elevenses time.

'Sorry, I was miles away.' I make an attempt to slow down my breathing and swallow back the nausea.

'Sign of a good carpet, that is.'

'What is?'

'That I could creep up on you! Always worth getting the best carpet you can afford.'

In the furthest reaches of my mind hovers a comment about important life advice but I don't have the energy to grasp it. It'd be too late anyway, as Mam has already moved on, pulling out the smallest of her nest of tables and laying down two coasters before disappearing then returning with her own drink. Everything she does, she does with gusto. I used to be like that. Now I'm exhausted just watching her.

'When you were miles away, were you somewhere nice?' Mam says, plumping a tassled cushion before sitting down next to me and switching off the daytime telly I wasn't watching on ITV. 'I'd ask you that when you were in pigtails. You'd always say something funny, like you were at an underwater circus!'

Her eyes shine with hope as if she's lit a match to ignite my soul. She's trying to remind me of the person she says she knows is still in there somewhere. But my imagination has been sealed off; where I'd once go to find inspiration, where it was Technicolor and infinite, has become a dense, suffocating and matte pit of oblivion. And any talk of being away from these four walls, of being in the open,

14

makes my chest tight. It comes quickly and completely. A howl escapes me and I cower into a ball, hugging my legs through my cotton nightie. This happens a lot.

'Oh, my love, my darling girl,' she says. I loathe myself for bringing her pain because that's what's in her voice.

Mam pulls my shaking body into the comfort of her embrace. I stay there until my hot and fast breathing subsides.

'I hadn't gone anywhere. I don't want to go anywhere. I don't want to be anywhere.' It's strange how I can be upset and numb at the same time.

'This is all normal, remember? That's what they said, this'll happen, it's part of the process.'

How is this normal? How is this a process? Nothing has changed since February and now it's July.

'Little steps, that's all you need to take.'

'I know and I want to, but I feel like I can't move.' That's not strictly true. I can walk. The lingering limp from the pelvis fracture will go. But some days I have a mental block and my body has phantom aches: there's thick, banging all-over pain, sore armpits and shoulders from the crutches, my mouth still detects weeks of bitter medication and I'm unable to move, stuck in fog. 'All I want to do is sleep. But then the nightmares ... I'm frightened and I've had enough.'

'This'll pass. It will!' She says it as if she means it has to. 'You had a shower yesterday, didn't you? You've washed your hair.' She strokes it and my body goes rigid. Once my best feature, my bob no longer bounces but has grown straggly and hangs down my back as if it's given up on me too. I can smell a sourness about me. I haven't cleaned my teeth today and yesterday's deodorant has lost the battle.

'A shower? Is that what you call a victory?' I know it's unfair to rage at my mother but she's the only real safe person I have. I cling on to her and cry harder. 'When is this going to stop? When?'

'I don't know when, but it will. Listen, let me get you a cold drink,' she says, getting up. 'I'll come on a walk if you want?'

Her intention is to soothe but I get a surge of fury – not at her but at me.

'I need to do it by myself,' I yell, smacking my balled fists on the settee.

My mother doesn't flinch. She's used to this.

'Stop being so hard on yourself, Betty. You've got to be kind. And if you can't, then I will. And I will do whatever it takes, give you whatever you need to get through this.'

Her calmness makes me seethe.

'Look at me, Mam, I'm thirty-six, I'm back in my childhood bedroom, I'm scared of cars and crowds. I can't cross the road. My world is literally this street. I hate the dark. I haven't got a job, I haven't got a life. I can't even bring myself to use my mobile.' My hands are in the air with desperation. 'Thirty-six. I'm meant to be in the prime of my life.'

'I know how hard this must be for you.' Mam is so patient. Gentleness radiates from all over her.

'Everyone treats me with kid gloves, like I'm an invalid. Like I can't do anything for myself.'

I see her reach for the back of one of the dining chairs behind her. We both have cornflower-blue eyes; mine lost their sparkle long ago. I search for the vitality in hers to protest that I can look after myself but they're dull. When has that happened? She's stooping slightly too. Since when has she needed to support herself on a piece of furniture? Her arm is thin and where her sleeves are rolled up, I can see a bruise, the type she says she gets as a result of ageing, when she finds marks of green and purple and doesn't know how she's done it.

She looks weary too, her wrinkles seem deeper and the henna of her hair has become grey at the roots. They're subtle differences in the mother I know but they signal she isn't the invincible force I've always had in my life.

A stone sits in my belly as I realise I've relied on her far too much – she's only fifty-nine, she has a lifetime left. Yet she seems much older. This woman, Carol Hopkins, should be enjoying life – after decades of struggle, scrimping and saving, she bought our former council house home. She considers herself lucky because she only needs one job now. And she's cut her hours at the launderette not to take up a new hobby or to have more spare time but to be there for me. She has a man friend, Cliff, and I can't recall when she's last been out with him.

Her identity has faded. I've been so focused on my wounds I haven't noticed. The guilt comes crashing in. Just as it always does because, no matter what people say, I shouldn't have been glued to my phone, I should have been paying attention to the traffic. I wobble as I get to my feet but I'm determined. I need to get my life back – for her. I need to get back to London. My old job is there whenever I want it. Ahmed has cover but he's made it clear with the bouquets and offers of therapy and a phased return-to-work plan. My throat goes even drier at the thought of it; it's beyond me right now when my world has become so small and suffocating. But I can start the journey. It has to begin here, though – my flat is rented out and I need a soft re-entry into the workplace to ease me in. It's a daunting thought but my mother deserves her freedom and I need my independence.

'I don't know what I'd have done without you, Mam.'

She's been my rock. My father, David, who left us when I was five, is a waste of space with three failed marriages to cry over into his beer. He's only ever been preoccupied with himself, chasing a dream – and women – to play rugby for Wales, which he managed once. I can't put on my younger sister Nerys, who's juggling a baby, toddler and a business. And while I treasure Sami's weekly landline updates with his despatches from fashion weeks, new trends and gossip, he's miles away.

'I'm your mother, I've got no choice,' she says, kindly.

'You don't deserve this wall-to-wall misery,' I say, swaying slightly but splaying my toes to grip the floor.

'It isn't!'

We both smile ruefully at her trying, even now, to make things better. I promise myself I'll head out alone tomorrow. But right now getting back to who I was starts with what I know best of all: work.

'I'm going to do this, Mam,' I say, watching her grow visibly taller. 'I'm going to get myself a job.'

## 2

### *Guy*

I switch off the engine and allow myself a second to flop back against the head rest. It's just gone six. That makes it almost Maud's bath time. My heart swells as I think of her squidgy legs kicking on the changing mat, her quick reflexive breath as she senses the warm water and her tiny hands patting the bubbles. Her gurgles and coos as she's wrapped up for cuddles in a fluffy, hooded towel, and how she smells like heaven itself.

Unlike me, who's been on the road for eight hours on a sweaty delivery run around the tropical south-east before finally coming home to Tunbridge Wells. The evening sun is still fierce and it's blowtorching the cab of the van even though the air con is still on. Unpeeling myself from the seat, I clamber out and the door squeaks. It's like Maud's impatient yelp when she's dressed for bed, anticipating milk and a story before she drifts off in my arms. Some oil will fix the van but it can wait. Family will forever come first.

I let myself into the Victorian apartment and a delicious draught scented with honeysuckle kisses my face.

'It's only me,' I call into the dark hallway as I throw my keys on the sideboard. The chink echoes off the smooth white walls, bounces off the high ceiling and lands on the Victorian tile flooring that I restored to its geometric glory.

'In here!' comes her voice, which radiates calm and love and my throat starts to ache with emotion. But I can't let Myfanwy see me like this. Luckily, my grandmother gives me an out.

'There are some of those beers you like in the fridge, the crafty ones,' she says with a smile in her voice.

I get one, hold it to my forehead to cool myself, then go into the drawing room where she's sitting at the table with her back to me. The two-bedroom ground-floor flat is airy but not too bright; a gentle breeze through the open French doors teases the sheer-cream curtains. They remind me of muslin squares on my shoulder for Maud and the loss winds me anew, as it does daily.

'Good day, Guy?' she asks, patting the bench I've upholstered for her which she calls her jigsaw seat.

'Not bad,' I say, keeping my voice steady, taking another big gulp. 'You're right, G, these beers are crafty. They're very moreish, I'll have finished this before I know it. What have we got, then?'

I take a pew beside her and kiss her forehead.

'Fish pie and a bottle of plonk,' she says, her hand deftly sorting through the hundreds of scattered pieces laid out before her.

'My favourite! But I meant jigsaw-wise.' Granny has raised me on puzzles and it's what we do on what she calls our weekly school-night suppers. She'll start a new one and it's my job to find the straight bits before I go home.

'It's Cats on a Hot Tin Roof.' She hands me the box.

'You're not lying. There's an abundance of cats on the

roof which looks both hot and tin. Tabbies, moggies, Siamese, fat ones, kittens ...' I feel a lick on my ankle. It's Bobby the ancient black pug making a late entrance as usual; he's hampered by his poor hearing and can't detect new arrivals. 'Hello, Bob! He's sensed the enemy within. All these cats.'

I pick him up and the weight of him in my arms suddenly sets me off. A sort of strangled moan escapes me and I have fat tears rolling down my cheeks.

'Oh cariad,' Granny says, using the Welsh term of endearment for darling that she says was my first proper word. 'You must be hurting so much.'

My shoulders heave and Bobby lets me rock him as words spill out. 'He's as heavy as Maud ... I miss seeing her so much, I miss being her dad and—'

'Let it all out,' my grandmother says, softly, patiently, even though she has had to deal with my devastation for a month now.

'Just ... despite everything, I miss being a husband, having a family.'

My sorrow quickly turns to anger. 'How could she have lied to me? How could Sarah have not known?'

And how did I not know, when Maud is fair and both Sarah and I have dark skin and hair? But then I was so in love. Obsessed with her tiny fingernails, her big blue eyes, her quivering tongue as she cried.

'I would think she wanted to believe Maud was yours, so very much.'

I hear Sarah telling me how much she loves me and begging for my forgiveness and asking if there is a way we can get through it while I am falling apart from the shock.

'No wonder,' I say, sourly. 'Better to pretend you

haven't had an affair, got pregnant, and to let your husband think the baby is his.'

We were together for six years but things came to a head when I asked her yet again to move in and for us to take things forward and start a family. Sarah wanted time to think about it – I took it badly, because hadn't she had plenty already? We split up. I didn't know it until the day she told me Maud wasn't my daughter, but when we were apart she'd had what she called a moment of madness, a drunken, meaningless one-night stand, and had realised her mistake straight away. In the intensity of that, we got back together, both of us clueless that she was having a baby, until we found out and I presumed she was ours. I was so very happy and I tried to ignore that we had both had what were doubts, preferring to think our pregnancy was a sign we were meant to be. After that, I find it hard to be fair.

I put Bobby down and wonder if ignorance would have been the better option. It certainly has been when it comes to the identity of the real dad. Before Sarah could offer it up I told her I didn't want to know – I didn't want to put a face to him, to embark on obsessive online searches for his name when I was tortured enough already. While it's laughable to think Sarah acted out of decency after what she did, she was acting in the interest of the truth.

'Why did she wait four months to do Maud's DNA test? That's what hurts the most, that I had four months of being her dad, thinking she was my own flesh and blood. I was there when she was born, I saw her first smile, I was there for every night feed ... I still wake up in the middle of the night and then it hits me: I'm alone.'

'I'm here. And so's Charlie.'

'Yeah, I should call him,' I say. My best mate was there for me straight away. He always has been. But after a few too many times of leaning on him, I've backed away, no one wants to be the dreaded, draining friend, not when he's got stuff going on with his mum who is having chemo for breast cancer. 'Trouble is, I know what he'll say.'

'What's that?'

My stomach lurches at the indecency of it. But also because I know that if I say it out loud it's an option, one that I refused to entertain outright, yet one that creeps into my head in the small hours. I decide to test myself – if the words feel like shards of glass in my mouth, then maybe I'll know it's absolutely not going to happen.

'That I should try again with Sarah.'

I taste no blood and Granny doesn't scoff at me. Maybe I could get my head around it?

'Because she wants to, G.'

'And you?'

I can't bring myself to tell her I'm tempted. What kind of a fool would go back to her?

'Think carefully about what you need, Guy. But remember, people make mistakes. It's not a weakness to forgive someone.'

I drop my head and stretch my neck. The weight of all this is so heavy on my shoulders.

'Come on, let's eat,' she says, taking me by the hand like a child, pretending to heave me with all her might. She winks at me and she's the same as she's ever been. Of course she has wrinkles and white hair now but, to me, she's the youthful and playful woman who brought me

23

up after my parents died before I even took my first steps. This flat is home, although it's not strictly 'ours'. When Granny met Grandpa at training college, she moved here to be with him and they rented because she insisted they'd moved back to Wales one day.

Years on, the four walls and garden have been moulded by them, and we dine in the shade of Granny's jungle-style patio that's filled with pots of huge palms and giant leaves at the wrought-iron dining table and chairs that have been here ever since I have and listen to dusk falling.

Granny asks me to tell her about my deliveries; no one day is ever the same and it reminds her of my grandfather Robert, hence the pug's name, who taught me all I know about tinkering in the workshop. So I fill her in on the lady in Lewes who cried with joy when I returned her great-aunt's rocking horse to its former glory with a new stirrup, glass eye and a repaint. Then there was the violin that needed a varnish in Hastings and a cuckoo clock that had lost its chirp in Ashford. And my favourite of the day, a minuscule chaise longue that had one broken leg for a gentleman in Maidstone who was never allowed one as a child. I could easily have posted it, but the personal touch is my thing.

'That was perfect, G,' I say, when we finish eating. 'I feel like new.'

'Good!'

'I don't think I'll be able to drive now,' I say, with the near-empty bottle between us. 'I'll collect the van tomorrow morning. I'll knock, if you're in?'

'I have my Welsh club first thing, then yoga for old bags.'

I laugh. It's a good note to leave on so I tidy up, make Granny a cup of tea and we hug goodbye.

On my way along the leafy streets, I ring Charlie. It's time to be more than a misery guts; he's been there for me forever and I've been so wrapped up in myself I need to check in on him and see that he's OK. I miss him too – he's been the sibling I never had. Granny and Grandpa gave me everything but as an only child it could be quiet. Charlie, along with his two brothers and his parents, gave me the glorious noise and bustle and sense of belonging that comes with a normal family life. I get his voicemail so I have a go at sounding brighter.

'Mate, it's me. What you up to? Working? Sharking for the perfect woman? Or training for that ultra marathon? I've heard you can shave seconds off your PB if you shave your balls. Anyway, we need to do lunch or drinks. Give me a bell.'

I live around the corner from Granny's so it's not long before I'm back at my own grand white Georgian townhouse.

This place has been a labour of love for me. The renovations and modern touches all sped up when Sarah was growing because I wanted to make a nest for us. The wooden herringbone floor of the hall and the thick walls always reassured me. Now, as I shut the door, the bang makes it sound empty.

I wipe my face with my hands and beg myself not to go over this all over again. I head to the open-plan lounge-diner to the art deco drinks trolley that I got from an auction and see that I'm out of gin. I've been far too reliant on alcohol lately; in fact, before Sarah fell

25

pregnant, we did a lot of drinking together. But at least it guarantees some sleep.

There's another bottle in the cupboard under the stairs but when I'm leaning down to get it, I see a little stuffed toy in the shadows. It's Peter Rabbit, just like the one I had as a baby, which is tucked away in a drawer in my room. It floors me instantly – it must've fallen out of Maud's buggy, because we used to park it in here. My knees want to buckle and I have to hold onto the side. I squeeze my eyes shut – I thought I'd cleared every scrap of her out of here. I lean in and pick him up. Pressing my nose to his soft ears, I breathe in my daughter. Is it a sign that I should go back to them? Because being here in this building of bones by myself is unbearable.

I grab the bottle, twist off the cap, neck back a burning mouthful that makes me cough. I cannot stand to be in here anymore. I throw open the back door, slam it shut, get to the safety of my workshop and decide two things.

I'll sleep in here from now on, on the shabby sofa bed from my teenage days. And I'll think about calling Sarah.

# 3

## Betty

'Betty! You're up, love!' Mam sings from her pride-and-joy breakfast bar when I get downstairs.

And showered and dressed, she might as well add, but, after my performance yesterday, she knows I'm on a tightrope. I feel dizzy from the alarm; my old life was a 6 a.m. start but 8 a.m. now feels like the middle of the night. Getting ready was a shock too. On the plus side, I recognised I needed to mark my first solo walkabout with a suitable outfit. But the zebra-patterned wrap dress, which was the least ostentatious outfit of my London wardrobe, makes me feel like an imposter; I've been used to wearing supermarket – and more often than not stained – T-shirts and joggers.

'Fancy some toast?' Mam slides off her chrome stool, already at the matching bread bin. She paid for this on credit and her threadbare dressing gown hurts my heart – this is why I need to pay my own way.

'I thought I'd have something at Hoffi Coffi.'

'Oh! Lovely!' She's thrilled I'm visiting my sister's café, named after the Welsh for 'I like coffee'. I wouldn't be surprised if Mam produced a top hat and tap shoes and rattled away across the jazzy galaxy black tiles that sparkle with glitter.

27

The truth is I feel too sick to eat and this outing isn't a jolly but a necessity. My verve had shrivelled away by last night after my job search online only threw up positions a drive away. Buses from Pant Bach are sketchy, there's only one taxi firm and Phil's Cabs requires at least a fortnight's warning. I can drive, everyone can around here or you'd never leave. I was the first of my friends to pass my test, a few months after I turned seventeen. For me it was my first step to freedom; the second was my Saturday job in the Arcade and last, but not least, was getting into fashion college in London. I never thought I'd come back here to live, not then, it was too claustrophobic. I could never escape the gossip about who my dad was shacked up with nor avoid his needy attempts, when he could be bothered, to win my forgiveness for abandoning us. For now, it's practical to be here until I can get my old self back and return to Banta. But it presents the problem of getting about: I am terrified of getting behind the wheel, of being amongst traffic, and what if I had a flashback, what if that made me hit someone? That's why I have to find a job within walking distance.

The thought propels me out of the house and I give Mam a cheery wave which my hand drops as soon as I'm alone. The thud of the door matches the boom in my chest as I survey the street. It's overcast but stifling and I feel compressed by the cloud cover, my lungs working hard to gulp back air. I tell myself I've done this before so many times with my mother, and I don't even have a road to cross. I just need to follow the mental map I've laid out and obsessed over for weeks when I'd planned this. I check for cars, both ways, over and over, squeezing my nails into my palms which are beading with sweat.

It's all clear, it normally is because it's a narrow street, so I move off the doorstep, tread the three paces of our front garden and turn left onto the pavement. My feet are slow, like they're in setting concrete, and I hug the terraces, my head swivelling behind and in front to check for anyone who might waylay me – the last thing I need is a friendly neighbour telling me how brave I am. Because this isn't brave, this is normal. At the top I turn left again onto the High Street and this is where I have to pause – cars and vans are moving, they seem so fast and their engines appear to roar. But that's the blood in my ears and my pulse hammering away. I'm almost there, just a couple of minutes, so somehow I move, keeping my head down, tucked right up against the buildings, past the launderette, which blows out lavender and I imagine I'm in a field, blocking out the noise. Past the bookies, newsagent's, hair salon and post office, my adrenalin peaking as I near the Arcade. I quicken up; my sensible sandals, bought precisely for this moment, giving me confidence and, as soon as I see the peeling red paint on the iron gates, I dart inside and only then do I dare to look up.

Relief sweeps through me, I've done it! And all without a panic attack! There are eight units in here, four on either side beneath the domed glass roof, and the walkway between them is still quiet as the shops open up. I know this place of old; it was my childhood haunt and the old-lady dress shop on the right was where I got my first job. Beside it is Jack of all Fades barbers, Jones Brothers ironmongers and The Sweetie Shop. Closest to me is an empty unit, then the charity shop, then my sister's place and the greengrocer. Filled with gratitude because I've made it, the jingle of Hoffi Coffi's door sounds like a pealing bell of celebration. Thankfully, no one looks up; they're too busy eating their breakfast baps.

'Oh my God, Betty!' Nerys cries, bouncing a beaming baby Daisy on her hip. Seeing my niece makes my heart soar and I get a moment of pure joy as she gurgles at me. Nerys stops arranging buns and teacakes on the counter and dashes round to give me a huge, warm floury-fingered hug. 'It's Aunty Bet, Daisy!' Then she says, wide-eyed, 'Where's Mam?'

I feel like a child who's slipped off without asking but I can't be offended, this is how it's been for months.

'I'm on my own, first time out. Thought I'd come and see you.'

'Well!' Nerys's curated painted eyebrows shoot up. As is her way, from her thick blonde waves, full face of make-up and lively bosom, she is naturally buoyant. 'This calls for a fancy coffee, presh! Sit down! The usual but with chocolate sprinkles?'

I nod. I used to be a double espresso addict but it's decaf now because of my palpitations.

'Take Daisy, will you?' Nerys hands her over and I dot kisses all over the baby's plump cheeks and tickle my face with her soft curls. 'The childminder's sick. Lucky I've got the travel cot out the back.'

'Lily OK? Devoted Steve?' That's what I call her husband because he's such a diamond, working all hours as a builder and then willing to have his nails painted pink by their eldest, who's just started school.

'Lush, as ever.'

Nerys, who is the happiest woman I know, walks off humming to herself and I hear her rattle off the order to Maddy, her waitress.

Daisy is a beautiful little doughy dumpling with white-blonde hair, pudgy wrists and several chins who is all smiles – except now, when she sees her mother leaving her side. She starts to cry. I try to soothe her, pat her bottom, rub her back and jiggle her about but it's no good.

'It's me,' I blurt out, feeling a failure. And in the depths of me, I wonder if this is some kind of punishment …

Nerys takes her back and my arms feel tragically empty. It confirms what I have been reluctant to admit to myself: I have begun to want children, feeling an unnatural yet natural broodiness when I see Daisy. Unnatural because I had never desired kids before the accident, because I've never been serious enough with anyone. Yet this longing I feel watching her bury her head in my sister's chest is a physical instinctive pull. I know why it's happened now – my consultant warned me that my injury might make conception difficult and delivery very complicated. Nothing becomes more desirable when you're told you might not be able to have it.

'Don't be silly, she's teething,' Nerys says, pointing at her angry gums.

'Poor lamb. I can take her to Mam's, if you want? Or … if you need a hand?' I might as well seize the moment. 'It's a Friday so you might need—'

'It's fine. Maddy's got two sets of hands and eyes in the back of her head.'

She appears with my veggie sausage sandwich on buttered doorstep white and decaf latte and laughs.

'Nothing will ever compare with feeding hungry bikers in my burger van on a weekend, so I'll be fine.'

'Fab!' Nerys says, another problem solved.

31

'You're busy, then,' I say, trying again.

'Always, people got to eat!'

'Listen, Nerys, I need to work.' She nods enthusiastically. 'I need a purpose until I can go back to my old job.'

This is the first time in my life that I have been unemployed. Although I have my flat in London, my sick pay is about to end, I'm cash-poor and I wasn't entitled to any insurance payout from the accident.

'Do you have any shifts? I'll do anything. Washing up, clearing tables, scrubbing the loo.' If anyone will help me, she will. But her head goes still.

'I'm so sorry, Bet, I wish I could, but I wouldn't make anything if I took on another person.'

'Of course.' I don't expect or want her to create a role for me just to give me a break.

'Listen, there are a few things going on the noticeboard.' She springs up then comes back with a handful of postcards plus the weekly rag. 'There's a position at the charity shop, cleaning at the rugby club ... bar maid at The Prince Of Wales,' she says, flicking through them. 'But you're overqualified for all of them. The jobs' page might have something ...'

She rustles through the paper, takes one look, then shuts it firmly, folds it in half and rests her elbow on it. Nerys doesn't want me to see. But why?

'No good?'

'Nothing for you.'

I baulk at that. 'You saying I'm not up to it?'

'No,' she says, her eyes cagey.

It's the kid-gloves treatment all over again.

'Know what, I'm trying to get myself better. You could encourage me.'

32

'It's not that,' she says, sighing. 'Here.'

She hands me the newspaper. There's something going at the local primary and that's within walking distance, that could be good! I read on and immediately understand. It's for a school-crossing patrol warden, no experience necessary.

'There's no hope. I can't even be a lollipop lady,' I say, my voice catching on the words. 'Nerys, I'm sorry. I should've known.'

She puts her hand on my arm to steady its shaking. 'I didn't want to bring it back.'

But it's too late. I'm absorbed in my own world, on the phone, oblivious to the road. I hear urgent, panicky beeping and screeching wheels. The dread hits me, I know what's next, it wakes me up night after night, jolting me awake as the car juggernauts into my right thigh. It's a pain so utterly whole yet the shock takes over and I'm numb and breathless. I'm carried on the bonnet, whack my head and I bounce up and off into the air before I crash to the tarmac. But that's nothing to what happens next: coming round from concussion a few hours later, trying to make sense through a drug-fuelled haze of the biology of my pubic rami fracture on the anterior pelvic ring, which turns out to be my left pubic bone. Feeling the savage stabs of agony in the window before my next medication is due. The humiliation of a catheter and bed washes. And that is nothing compared to the exhaustion of having to start walking within days, nauseous on pills and then hearing how lucky I am. I didn't die, I didn't have a brain injury, I didn't need surgery and I was home within a week. Lucky? That just made it harder, loading on the guilt because I felt anything but fortunate. I was angry, drowning in 'why me?', isolated and grieving the loss of my independence, income and choices. I still am.

Legally, no one was at fault. It was a terrible accident: the driver of the Lexus that hit me had lost control of the car when he had a sudden catastrophic heart attack and died at the wheel. The police and pathologist learned the poor man, who was driving home from a long family lunch, had been fit and healthy, with no prior cardiac problems, and he hadn't felt unwell that day. He was blameless and so, they said, was I.

But that doesn't stop the hornet's nest in my chest – foolishly, irresponsibly, unforgivably, I wasn't looking as I was crossing. Why hadn't I just waited to use my phone? What if I'd been two seconds quicker and got to the pavement? What if I'd stayed with Jude, worked harder to reignite our relationship, got through it and he'd met me after the course, delaying my path into the road, and we'd gone to the airport together? But I'd panicked when things got serious – the irony of ending it over that when it is security I crave most. Why couldn't I have appreciated him more? Eight years younger than me, he wanted to settle down and plough back his experience as a fashion photographer into lecturing. And I could be there with him now, appreciating his calm and quiet, his love of museums and reading. We could have moved to the suburbs and got a dog, and perhaps, eventually, tried to start a family. Anything would be preferable to this prison.

My head is in my hands. I've found out that wishing for change doesn't guarantee what kind of change you get. Today I felt there was a possibility of recovery.

But as Nerys wraps herself around me, it feels as if she's the only thing holding the broken pieces of me together.

# 4

## *Guy*

As a rule, I don't tend to tinker with teddies.

They hold such sentimental value that the trained hands of a surgeon would be the safest way to operate. But when I've come as a recommendation, from a friend of a friend of Granny's, how can I say no?

Yet the responsibility weighs on my shoulders as I lay Bryn the Bear out on my worktable. So precious is this 1950s honey-coloured ted to Gladys back in Granny's home village of Bethlehem in Wales, that he arrived in the cardboard-box equivalent of an ambulance, zip-locked, bubble wrapped and cradled by polystyrene peanuts. A letter was tucked under his threadbare arm, written as if he had penned it himself, asking if I would fix him with love. That's a given. But if I'm going to repair his ear that hangs by a thread, patch his paw pads and plump him up with stuffing, I'll also have to use a needle and glue.

'This won't hurt at all,' I tell him as I carefully begin to unpick his stitches. While Grandpa taught me how to use a hammer just as he did my father, Granny didn't want me growing up to be one of those helpless types who couldn't sew a button on a shirt. My fingers tremble as I work alongside the framed glossy 1980s photo of my beaming parents on their wedding day. It's the only one I have up anywhere because I don't want to live in a mausoleum. There's a suitcase of things belonging to them somewhere that I haven't looked through in years, I accepted long ago that they're gone and my grandparents gave me their all. In truth, the picture of my mother in a puff bridal dress holding hands with my dad in a bad shiny suit doesn't feel real. I mean, I know I look like them and apparently have their mannerisms. It's more they seem like distant relatives. How can I feel more when I don't remember them? The tremble instead comes because I want to do my best (although I suspect the hangover combined with a bad night on the sofa bed may be part of it too). I pray to God that I can do Bryn justice. I have to. That's my mission on everything I do as The Repair Guy; it always has been since it started off as a hobby when I first went to work as a temp at an insurance company. I wanted to be normal and have an office job but it became clear after a year there that I only coped with being behind a desk because I had my private passion to fulfil me. I was never without work, thanks to word of mouth, so I resigned, advertised like mad, attended night classes for furniture restoration and carpentry and anything there was that would add a string to my bow. It mushroomed so now I have clients from across the country. I don't have set fees, I ask people to pay what they think it's worth – so I may get a few quid for reattaching a spout on a watering can and then much more for fixing a Teasmade because that morning cuppa is what gets someone up in the morning. Personal service is important too and I try my hardest to return projects face to face.

My phone beeps. It's a message from Charlie, who's

asking if I'm free in twenty for what he calls 'some tucker'. He's a bit of a lad but my oldest mate, who's loyal, funny, hopeless in love and, since the moment we met at school, like a brother. Mainly because we were both bullied, him for his thick glasses and me for being a lanky orphan. I was forever round his as a kid and his family treated me like one of their own. I met Sarah through him, they were friends for years after they both trained in accountancy together, so the three of us have loads of history.

Charlie doesn't need to say where to meet – it'll be our usual bistro on The Pantiles. I have a delivery around the corner so I wheel a repaired bike out of the workshop, through the garden and inside, where it seems far less lonely with the sun streaming in through the windows.

I imagine having Sarah and Maud back, here in the house which I poured my inheritance into. She had this theory that I renovated it in a subconscious way to reverse my parents' deaths, as if I was rebuilding the home I was born in, half of which came crashing down in the hurricane of 1987. A huge oak tree fell through the roof of their bedroom. They were killed but somehow, only feet away in the nursery but on the other side of the hallway, I survived. I think Sarah was trying to see if I had any underlying unresolved issues ahead of becoming a dad – it's true I've always wanted a family because I didn't have the usual childhood but my only motive was to get it ready for Maud. I see Babygros drying on the radiators, I hear Sarah moving around upstairs and I smell my homemade bread that I'd make most days. Could we just pick up where we left things? Could I handle Maud's father turning up for access? If Sarah has told her one-night stand that the baby is his, that is. The very fact that I can even consider this makes me wonder if we could. It's something I'll mention to Charlie.

Mrs Green is very pleased with the job on her ancient bicycle. Even though it was a simple tyre change and gear check she pays me over the odds – her wheels are her freedom because she can't drive due to epilepsy. Besides, she doesn't trust those trendy men in lycra at the shop and she certainly doesn't want to see what they had for breakfast, thank you very much.

Then I'm at The Pantiles, where the sunshine makes the split-level Georgian colonnade blindingly white. It's busy and it feels good to be amongst bon viveurs – there are the old school Disgusted of Tunbridge Wells colonels here but a new breed and a new attitude is growing. The touristy draw remains in the spa waters ladled out by dippers in pinnies and bonnets and in the Dickensian actors who tread in Queen Victoria's footsteps in skirts and top hats, but there's also jazz on the bandstand, craft and food fairs and independent boutiques.

I'm early so I take a seat in the sun outside La Trattoria and order myself a hair-of-the-dog beer and a pizza and a glass of sparkling water and a seafood linguine for Charlie. It's nice to take a breather and people watch. This time of day it's the suits out getting sandwiches or entertaining clients in the wine bars, restaurants and pubs. There's a gentle buzz as there always is when it's warm enough to eat al fresco. There's also the buggy brigade, and I can't deny it catches in my throat to see fathers pushing their offspring. I used to bring Maudie here; the cobbles would rock her to sleep and I could have a quiet coffee and marvel at her, the way Granny says my own dad, her son, did with me. I can see her rosebud lips and the flutter of her eyelids, and the halo of warmth above her perfect skin. It gets worse, though, because through the crowd I actually do see her looking out from Sarah's chest in a carrier. My heart bursts with joy at her little straw sunhat and wriggling bare feet, pulling at her mother's dark hair. They're living with Sarah's mum until her tenant moves out of her old flat. Both places are tiny – her mum's got a two-bed new-build that's great for her but with Sarah, Maud and all their stuff it'd be cramped. Sarah's home is in a dodgy part of town and she used to find needles chucked over the wall from the alley into her courtyard square every now and again.

My instinct is to run to Maud to see how she's changed in four weeks. I start to wonder, like I have so many times, if it's all been a mistake and there was a DNA test mix-up. That Sarah's hunch that the baby wasn't mine, which she could never explain other than a gut feeling, was all wrong. I still feel the sting, though, that now she has what I have wanted for so long. I've always been a relationship person; she hadn't been until she met me. I wanted a family because I'd lost mine; she was scared of commitment because her dad left before she was born.

I ground myself to my chair and know I should look away. But Sarah always stands out in a crowd, with her height and willowy figure, and I can see her talking to someone … it's Charlie, his bald head and aviator shades are a giveaway. I get a stab of jealousy – it's not that it's weird they're together, they're mates, both of their offices are behind The Pantiles and they often go for lunch. She's holding a coffee cup, so it looks like she's bumped into him and that's pretty typical here where everyone comes on a sunny day. I'm jealous because he has the freedom of friendship and can see Maud whenever he wants to. I turn away to take a breath and it hits me – I can have that too. Sarah had her reasons, we can put it in the past, we were so happy as parents of a newborn ... does it matter if Maud isn't biologically mine?

'Foxy!' Charlie says from behind me. It's what he calls me because of my double-barrelled surname Fox-Slater, which I dropped as soon as I left school because I wanted to be normal.

I jump up and he gives me a bigger bear hug than usual and the bond between us is there in our back slaps.

'Mate! Sorry I've gone off the radar a bit,' I say, as we plonk ourselves down.

'You've had a lot on.' Charlie moves his chair so it's under the umbrella and pats his scalp. 'Forgot my factor one hundred.'

I laugh because the sun needs to just fart at me and I go brown. We're opposites in almost everything. He's wide and buff like a squaddie; I'm tall and lean. He's a numbers man; I'm practical. He's a five-kilometres-before-breakfast fitness fanatic who measures every foot-step on Strava and I prefer a hike. But he, in his shirt and tie, seems to meet me, in my T-shirt and shorts, somewhere in the middle.

'How's things?' I lean back, waiting for an energetic self-deprecating story about a thirty-mile run that saw him caught short and crouching in the bushes, told like a stand-up, that begins somewhere and goes off in different directions until he gets to the point that will have me howling.

But he kind of deflates as he exhales.

'You all right?' I ask, leaning in.

'Yeah, yeah.' He takes a sip of his water.

'Your mum? How's she?'

'Good, you know what she's like. Nails.'

They say people battle cancer but in Pat's case it's the other way round. She mothered three boys, always made room for me at the table, kept her larger-than-life husband Barney on his toes and worked full-time as a nurse without ever taking a day off sick.

'When's her next chemo?'

'Few days. Anyway, I want to know about you.'

'OK.' I don't want to moan when we've just been talking about his mother. 'I've been thinking. About Sarah. Maybe trying again.'

He immediately puts his hand on his heart. 'You know I'd back you whatever you decide.' This is 100 per cent true.

'I've asked myself if I would've stayed if she'd had the fling but Maud was mine, and I know I would. I see her as mine anyway, so maybe I can get past it all. What do you think?'

'You'd be a better dad than the real father, that's for sure. Sarah would be lucky to have you.' He says it with absolute faith and I'm grateful. But I don't like the sound of his voice, which is hoarse. He's got bloodshot eyes too.

'You look worn out. Have you been overdoing the training?'

He shakes his head. 'Things on my mind. I've … uh … been offered a job. I'm going to take it.'

'Yeah?' He hasn't told me he's been looking for one. But then I've been preoccupied with myself and I feel terrible that I've let him down. 'That's good, though, right?'

He scratches his stubbly chin, which again I notice because he's normally clean-shaven. 'Interim chief-financial-officer position for a restaurant group.'

'Fancy! Well done! So why the long face?'

I wait for him to crack a gag about a horse. But it doesn't come.

'It's in Glasgow. I start in September.'

'Shit! Scotland? Wow …' I'm happy for him but it means I'm losing him.

'Yeah, I've been tossing and turning about it.' That explains why he looks so knackered. 'I wasn't sure. I didn't mention it, I'm sorry.' I feel for him. It must've been really hard for him to tell me this.

'Sorry? What for? It's a wicked opportunity.'

'It's miles away. I'll miss you.' I see his eyes water.

'Mate, I can visit, there's FaceTime, and if I'm going to be a dad again, well, I won't be around as much, will I?' I'm trying to make it better for him but I feel the wrench heavy in my stomach.

He nods slowly. 'I've been treading water a bit, to be honest, like something has to change.'

'I get it, man.'

He gives me a strained look and starts to tear up. 'You know I – er – love you.'

I gulp. Not out of embarrassment or discomfort because we say it every now again when we're pissed. But because something's wrong.

Our food arrives just at the wrong moment and Charlie clams up, reaching for his shades. He clears his throat, picks up his fork and then he plays with his pasta, unable to eat. This is the man who piles into every meal and finishes off everyone's leftovers.

It's then a switch in my head flicks. I wonder something, and I go over things, and it's impossible. Still, my pulse reacts. It can't be, but then things seem to settle into a row and I start to panic because they're adding up. I don't want them to, I'm swallowing hard, urging myself to calm down, so I start again but come up with the same result. It rises up inside me and jumps out and maybe it's better out there so Charlie can shoot it down and tell me it's just the damage talking.

'You're not going because you want to, are you?' I say it almost laughing, disbelieving, begging him to prove me wrong. 'You're running away.'

He stops dead. But there's no ridicule, no denial.

His reaction throws what I'd hoped were coincidences into sharp focus.

He hasn't brought up that he's just seen Sarah. He's been distant. He shaves his head because he's balding but the fuzz on his face glares ginger at me. And those eyes are the same as hers.

I see my tortured face in the sunglasses on the man who has stolen my life.

The shock makes me stand. Just one look from him, one bark of outrage, anything, is all I need.

But what confirms what I thought was madness, what tells me finally that I have worked it out, is that Charlie doesn't look up. Instead, he drops his head and his arms fall to his sides.

'You,' I hear myself say in a weirdly distant voice, 'my best mate, my best man, it's you, isn't it? You're Maud's father.'

Charlie grips his forehead with taut fingers and in a strangled voice he says, 'I'm so sorry. You'd split up; it was just a drunk thing. I never knew about Maud, I only found out a week after you, I swear it.'

'When you came round after she'd been born, you couldn't wait to hand her back to me.' I say it with utter scorn. '"Rather you than me," you said.'

'I didn't know; I'm just not a baby person.'

'A baby person? When you've got one?' I'm seething at his feckless attitude.

Charlie is shrinking before my eyes. It's pathetic but I ball it up and throw my napkin at him. How much I wish I could throw a punch instead. But if I start, I don't know when I'll stop.

I'm absolutely broken again. This man has been like blood. Now I hate the bloody sight of him. I have to take a breath, and another, but they're sharp, as if they're my own shattered pieces. And there's one, the sharpest, that cuts me most of all.

'You can do what the fuck you like, at work and in your sleazy private life, I don't want to know,' I say, my voice cold, 'but don't you dare let your daughter down.'

That's when the adrenalin hits and I start to shake.

I have to get out of here. I have to get away.

# 5

## *Betty*

'I'll be in touch, then, Betty. Thanks for your time.'

The interview is over and, by the tone of her voice, so are my chances. I chuck the landline down onto the bed and join it. A mouthful of duvet turns out to be useful for drowning out my wail of frustration.

It isn't just about failing to get the manager's job at the Life Goes On charity shop. It's because it took every scrap of me to apply and my show of heart still wasn't enough. Mam and Nerys thought I'd breeze it, they've long had me on a pedestal for making it in London. They'll console me with 'you're too good for them anyway' but the position wasn't beneath me because my past life feels like it belongs to someone else.

I don't blame Mrs Hughes, the charity's chair of trustees, for asking, though. Why would someone like me, who is overqualified, be interested in such a small set-up?

I was honest. I'd left London after eighteen years because of the accident. I'd come home to recover and I saw this job as a chance to get back on the clothes horse. It was local, I had plenty of transferable skills and perhaps I could bring something new to the role. I felt it was right to declare my ultimate goal – to return to my old life. But she didn't say a single thing. If I was hiring, that'd be a red flag. It must mean she has someone else lined up and is duty bound to interview every applicant. She probably thinks I'm flaky and she didn't hold back on listing the negatives: challenging volunteers, emptying endless black bags of sometimes flea-ridden donations, grimy house clearances and low pay. But the fact stands: I need this.

With a glowing reference from Ahmed – given on the condition that this was just a short-term position to get me up to speed for my return to Banta – I told her I was 'a fabulous people person, wholly dedicated, full of warmth, ideas and energy'. If only I sounded like one.

What the hell do I do now? I roll onto my back and sigh. On the ceiling there's a load of drawing pin holes from my fairy-lights obsession. The wall still has a few greasy spots from Blu-Tacked pages ripped out of *Vogue*, starring the likes of Madonna in her cone-shaped John Paul Gaultier bra and Naomi Campbell collapsing in Vivienne Westwood platforms, styled like works of art. My room was bright and colourful, never 'tortured teenager' grey.

If only I could go back and tell that girl to change direction, to avoid taking the same steps which led, one by one, decision by decision, day after day, to where I am now. So that she would never have to go through what I have gone through. She wouldn't have listened, though. She was headstrong and chopsy. And she's gone for ever. Just like my faith – I have none in her, nor in myself. Others do, Mam, Nerys and Sami, but they kind of have to, that's love and friendship. But it's unconditional and it feels tainted. What I need is conditional validation. Is there anyone else out there who does think I'm capable of getting myself out of this hole?

I turn over into the foetal position and my eyes wander across to my white MDF vanity table. All of my precious trinkets are on there. Smooth china seals from my seal period, my wind-up ballerina jewellery box and my beloved and ancient polka-dot sewing basket. I would spend hours ordering threads into colour blocks, changing what went in which compartment according to my latest obsession, whether it was feathers or sequins, and lately too, using up scraps for doll's clothes for my niece Lily, both for her satisfaction and mine because sewing has been constant in my life. My bits and bobs of adulthood, my driving licence, mobile and passport, are at the back of one of the drawers. Once I took them for granted, now they belittle me.

And then I see it – and my heart leaps at the one new addition to the table display. Pressed into a square, lying quite by itself away from the stuff of my adolescence, is a handkerchief.

It's The Repair Guy's from when my gin and tonic fizzed up in my face. Somehow, after everything, when Mam packed up my flat, this pink hankie dancing with spanners, hammers and jigsaw puzzle pieces has survived.

I find myself smiling and feeling inexplicably lighter.

I always thought I'd return it to him when Mam popped it washed and ironed onto the vanity table a few days after I came here. I remember thinking it'd be something I'd do when I was able to leave the house, when I was back to normal because, as silly as it sounds, that's what the hankie represented.

That war trophy, as Guy called it, is a symbol of a moment: when I stopped and looked up after a random encounter with a man who seemed to see the essence of

47

me and made me open up about where I was and what I was doing with my life. I liked him too, fancied him even, for his humour and decency. He lit a spark and that was the last time I've experienced a genuine spark of something. I feel my cheeks pink at how my mind is blossoming – it would be ridiculous to put any great significance to him and yet here I am feeling more alive. Maybe it's a fascination, because he isn't the usual kind of person I'd mix with? He had a class I've rarely encountered. It's entirely mad to project meaning onto a piece of cloth, of intimacy and connection, it's me overthinking again, of reading too much into something. He'll be married and a father now, for goodness' sake. Yet, if I'm feeling it, I could use it. It's a shock to think like this again – and a pressure too. Am I up to it?

I'm stunned to find that I sit up quickly and go to the table with an urgency I haven't had for ages. I shut my eyes as I hold the silky handkerchief to my nose and breathe it in. Did I just get a split second of citrus before the floral fabric conditioner kicked in? I smell it more deeply, hungry for lemons, but it had all been in my head. I'd imagined it, of course I had.

Suddenly the hairs on my arms stand up as I realise I'd imagined it. My imagination! It may have been tiny but, in that flash, I was basking in his delicious lemon scent. That meant my imagination wasn't dead. It had just been dormant! It had to mean that the Before Betty was still inside me somewhere.

I'm spurred on and scrabble around for a pen, pad and envelope and I lie down on the carpet and begin to write. I don't need to wait for recovery to return the hankie – maybe it's part of my recovery to return it. Just a short note but that's enough.

Then I fire up my laptop and google The Repair Guy for his address. Finding him online makes my heart quicken; his website has the same pink and red circus-style font and it's a carousel of quirkiness. Before and after pictures of his projects include a bird cage and a tin bath, chairs and lamps, even a tiny chaise longue for a doll's house!

Glowing testimonies speak of his professional and personal touch. He includes links to repair cafés, which is incredibly sweet considering he's running a business. But I'm disappointed there are no images of him. Just fingertips or a hand, but how clean the nails are and how craftsman-like they seem. His workshop, though, looks a tip.

Sealed and addressed, I limp-gallop down the stairs and shove on my sandals.

'Betty?' Mam comes along the hall, flushed with alarm.

'It's OK,' I say, breathlessly, 'Just going to the post office.'

I fly out the door, not even noticing the traffic or the spitting rain, buy a stamp, stick it on, and, at the post box, I wish it good luck. When I hear it land I get a surge of emotion that overshadows the charity-shop flop, for I've achieved something today.

There's a rainbow now, I see it out and proud above the oily rooftops, and there's another inside me too. If my imagination can come back then I can go back into the world again: I can find a job, return to myself, and, at the sound of a car approaching behind me, I can fight the fear. My back hunches but I tell myself to stand tall, there's no need to worry, it's going nowhere near me. The splash of tyres through puddles and an exhaust getting louder conspire in my head and I take them on even though my feet have sped up, my armpits prick with sweat and my muscles are primed. The noise is like a storm now and panic rises up and adrenalin kicks in and I'm breathing fast. Closer and closer it comes. I try to see this as exposure therapy: the car will pass and is no threat to me, just wait and see!

Yet my brain is in overdrive, nowhere is safe and no one understands. At the edge of my vision I see the lights and the bonnet and I begin to run and run, my arms pumping hard for momentum while my feet seem to be sucked back by the pavement. My heart is on fire as I get home, hammer on the door, crying for my mother.

She comes and I collapse inside.

'What's happened?' She's torn between protecting me and seeking out the danger.

'It was a car, it was coming for me,' I sob into my palms.

I hear Mam murmur and I peek through my fingers and see her waving at someone. She shuts the door.

'It was one of Phil's Cabs, he was dropping Mrs Griffiths home with her shopping,' she says quietly.

I am sick in the head. I'm aching all over. I don't move until my chest's rise and fall evens out. I want to lie here on the floor for ever. The thought of getting up is too much to bear.

The thought of going back into the world is impossible.

8 Llewellyn Road
Pant Bach
Merthyr Tydfil
CF48 1ST

*July*

*Dear The Repair Guy,*
*I'm sorry it's taken so long to return your hankie.*
*You'll find it clean and smelling of budget fabric*
*conditioner.*
*I hope you're well in jolly Royal Tunbridge Wells.*
*Scrub that, I'm sure of it.*
*Love,*
*Betty xxx*
*(the killer queen in a pink belt)*

# 6

## *Guy*

I'm woken up in the workshop by my phone buzzing at my feet.

I grope into the tangle of the sleeping bag, take one look and see it's Sarah. Again.

Five minutes after I left Charlie at the bistro, their desperate calls began. I set up a group chat, named it 'Maud' and sent them a message.

'The only person who matters in all of this is your daughter. Please, from now on, do not ever contact me again.'

Charlie stopped but Sarah has continued, leaving teary voicemails begging for forgiveness and wanting to explain.

It's been three days and she's worn me down. I figure that for her to stop I need to pick up.

'Guy?' I hear the shock in her voice that I have answered. 'Guy? Are you there? It's me ... Sarah.'

'Listen, you need to—'

'I'm outside. Can we talk?'

I'm so angry at her setting the pace of this. I don't want to see her. This is about her appeasing her guilt – why can't she respect my need for space?

'I'm alone.' It's her way of saying I won't have to see Maud. 'Please.'

Her voice cracks with emotion just as I roll over and see Peter Rabbit by my side. I end the conversation telling Sarah to wait. It's partly the shame of being a grown man who's taken a bunny to bed but mostly disbelief that I haven't returned it to Maud. The thought that she may have pined for it instantly ratchets up the intensity of my thumping head. That's what gets me up, dressed, in the house, picking up the post and opening the front door.

Sarah is as striking as ever. Her charcoal shoulder-length hair is straight and shining and she is dressed in her uniform of fluid androgynous lines, a long loose black tunic and simple sandals. Anyone else would think she looks serene but I can see that she's anxious by the slight clench of her jaw.

I say nothing, unable to marry the intimacy with which I know her and that we've shared with this frigid feeling between us, but stand aside to let her in.

She glides in with a quiet thank-you and hesitates in the hallway, unsure where to go, which room to enter, because each has its own ghosts: the lounge-diner where we would lie on the rug with Maud, the kitchen where Sarah told me the worst news of my life. I don't want her inside, so I lead her to the garden, which feels more neutral, and we sit opposite each other at the picnic table.

'I won't stay long,' Sarah begins cautiously, setting out her stall. 'You don't owe me any of your time, I'm very grateful. And—' I flinch because we can read each other and I know she's going to say her name, it has to be said, it can't be a conversation without it – 'because Maud is at my mum's, she'll need a feed soon.' I nod, knowing the routine off by heart. 'She's getting hungrier as she moves around more.' This development is a reminder that I don't know the new routine at all. I swallow back the hurt, the rage and the sorrow because I want this over with.

'I wanted to tell you who the father was but you asked me not to. In hindsight, I should've pressed on with it because it was him. But I didn't want to hurt you even more,' Sarah says to the point. 'I know now that was wrong but it was a very painful time. I told Charlie a week after I told you Maud wasn't yours; I said you didn't want you to know and I told him I didn't want him involved.'

She is reading from a script, a well-rehearsed one, yet I don't blame her for preparing; she knows she has one shot at this.

'However, he's insisting on contributing financially and I feel it's right for her future. That's what we met to discuss the day you saw him with me. He realised, of course, that we'd been seen and, well, he made a mistake in lining you up afterwards so closely. Perhaps, though, it's best it's out there now. Like you said, Maud is the most important person here and she deserves the truth. No matter how grubby and sordid it is.'

There's a tremor to her voice but she doesn't break eye contact with me once. It's her showing me she takes responsibility but I do have some pride.

'You had unprotected sex with him, then with me. Never mind the risk to my health, you were hedging your bets, just in case.'

'No, no! I was on the pill with … him; it's just I'd had a stomach upset in the days before so I wasn't covered, and—'

'So the pill stops STDs, does it?' This is an old

argument but now I know it was Charlie and I know he was seeing someone before he shagged Sarah.

Sarah holds herself together. 'I made sure I got tested. I've told you that. I came off the pill when we got back together; we agreed, didn't we?'

My fists turn white.

Sarah blinks hard to compose herself.

'I only wish you were Maud's father. I stand by what I've said, that I'm sorry, it was madness, a test, if you like, of what I wanted and I'm ashamed my stupidity took me there. I should've known all along it was you, that I was carrying around that fear that my mother had when my dad left. Her suspicion and hurt, to doubt the existence of love. And … the dithering about having a family is my greatest regret because I could still be with you now. With our own child. However, that is what I have to live with and I could never wish Maud wasn't around.'

I take it all on the chin except one thing. 'Why did it have to be Charlie? Can you imagine how humiliated, how let down I am? How much I've lost?'

Sarah looks to the side and places her fingers to her nose to stop herself from crying.

'I don't understand it now but at the time I was confused, very, very drunk, and I thought by doing it I would prove I wasn't ready to settle down. Except the second afterwards – I felt so hollow because I realised I was ready, because it felt so—' she says with a grimace – 'horrible. But please know it was me, not Charlie, who started it.'

'Oh, please.'

'I took advantage of him, Guy. He was very sweet to me, he listened, he told me I was a fool for even thinking about leaving you.'

'But he didn't say no, did he? And I bet he can't wait to get his feet under your table.'

Sarah looks down. 'We have had a conversation but I have told him there is no future for us.'

'I can't decide if I'm impressed by him finally manning up or fucking outraged at his cheek.'

'He wanted to do what you would think was right.' She lifts her eyes back to mine.

'I think he wanted to do what he wanted to do. Anyway, that's it, with him.'

'And me? And us?' Sarah says and the hope in her eyes, even after all this, stuns me. How can she even think we have a chance?

'You know, that day I found out, I told Charlie that I had been thinking about us getting back together.' Her hand goes to her mouth, she's still wearing her wedding ring. 'But how can that happen now?'

'It can, it still can.' It's the most desperate I've seen Sarah. 'Give it time. I'll wait for you, however long it takes. Please?'

'You have no right to ask ...'

A tear runs down Sarah's cheek as she at last acknowledges the insanity of her request.

Yet amidst the torture of betrayal I still feel something for her – love isn't a light switch and, while I'm devastated, it's still there albeit dimmer. What still shines bright is my urge to protect Maud and give her the best of myself.

'Going from this to where we'd need to be ... it just seems impossible.'

I realise I have Peter Rabbit in my hand, I've had him there the whole time, like some kind of man-child, and I give it to her.

'Maud will be so happy he's back,' she says, understanding her time is up. We make our way in silence through the house.

I am desperate to ask if she misses me, if she'd know who I am, but I will crumble. I am feeling like I will now.

'Give her a kiss from me,' I say, unable to help myself, closing the door.

How can life have flipped so quickly? I should be winding down my clients, getting ready to be a stay-at-home dad. I'd started looking into activities and groups that we could go to – swimming and soft play. My legs have taken me up the stairs and my hand is opening the door to the nursery. It's empty but the carpet still bears the indents from the weight of the beautiful walnut cot I did up. This is how it will always be – there will always be a trace of her in my heart.

I stagger downstairs, feeling utterly hopeless. I should be looking into a fresh start. I should be getting to grips with the paperwork of separation, getting my name off Maud's birth certificate and selling up, moving on. Apart from Granny, there's nothing here for me, and she's always wanted to return to Wales. Yet the bond with Maud hasn't faded – her absence has made it even stronger.

My head banging, I make a strong cup of tea and go through the post to distract myself while working out today's jobs. There are bills and flyers and then I get to what feels like a padded envelope, which is addressed to me with some very lively handwriting.

I rip slightly too hard at it and a letter and a square of fabric fall out onto my lap. Most of my business comes via email or the telephone but I sometimes get some interesting requests through the letterbox.

It turns out to be a handkerchief – identical to one of mine. Is it mine? It has to be. There are no other Repair Guys out there. I suddenly remember I gave one to the woman at my paintballing stag do. My jaw actually drops and I get a surge of warmth at the memory of her. Betty, that was her name. She was one of those people blessed with charm but completely unaware of it.

Curious, I unfold the A4 sheet and scan the letter.

My heart skips and before I know it my cheeks are aching. The Valleys Girl from London via Wales has returned my hankie and I'm so amazed I laugh out loud, something I thought I'd forgotten how to do.

I hadn't asked her to send it back, I never expected her to. And yet I'm unfeasibly delighted about it.

I reread the letter. It's funny, breezy and yet heart-felt – how has she managed that in just a few sentences? That was how she'd seemed to me that day. That day, she'd struck a chord, maybe because she was quite unlike anyone I'd ever met before. And her appearance, well, I would be lying if I said I hadn't found her attractive. But it wasn't just her vivacious red hair and sparkling blue eyes and that charming gap between her teeth, it was her sense of the world and her spirit.

I dissect the letter some more, my eyes creasing at the lightness of her tone. It's addressed from Merthyr, which means she's not in London anymore, and she's teasing me for living somewhere posh. I'm gulping; she doesn't just hope I've made things work out for me, she is sure I have.

She's reminded me I have power over my own life.

If only she knew how broken I am and yet I feel a burst of energy, as if I'm riding the bounce and loop of her handwriting. If that was the impression I gave her then maybe I can find that again within me and find the resolve to make a decision about what to do?

I need to act on it, to look outside rather than within. I spring up and head to town where I choose a naff sepia postcard of a Victorian scene of The Pantiles, scribble a thank you note, pop on a stamp and then put it in the postbox.

It's only when I'm back home, when I've decided to have a break from the booze and to plough myself into my work, I notice my head is clear and my heart feels strong.

Dear Betty,
Much obliged for the return of my heavenly scented
hankie. Waitrose needs to up its fabric-conditioner
game.

I'm delighted you made it back to Wales. In fact I
KNEW you would.

Best,
Guy

# 7

## *Betty*

'Mrs Hughes, it's Betty Hopkins, we spoke last week about the job.'

I'm out the back, away from Mam's hoovering, and steeling myself for one last stab at going for the manager's post at Life Goes On.

'Ah, yes. Hello, Betty. Good morning. I'm sorry I haven't got back to you yet. I was going to contact you today.'

Her polite preamble fills me with nerves but there's no room to pace them out in our narrow split-level garden. The washing line sits on the bottom and crazy-paving steps lead up to a small patch of grass. It's the same all along our terrace, exact replicas go on and on either side of us, separated only by hip-high stone walls. And it's the same above us, too, with another few layers of terraces until you reach the sweeping mountains of the valley. It doesn't feel as claustrophobic as it did when I was a teenager; in fact, I can admit that it was like a hug of safety in the early days after my accident.

'The thing is, Mrs Hughes,' I say, cringing at my interruption, 'I have to have this job. I need it and if I have to beg, then I'm prepared to do it.'

She clears her throat, which gives me a way in – it's now or never.

'I came across badly the other day, I wasn't myself. I didn't show you who I really am.'

'I see.'

I take it as permission to pitch myself to her.

'I'm very hardworking, I'm passionate, I'm up for it.' I shut my eyes, knowing I'm not speaking her language.

'What I mean is, Mrs Hughes, I have a wealth of experience. I understand it appears strange that I would wish to work in a village charity shop when I've had a career in London but I'm here now and I'd like to use those skills to benefit Life Goes On. Please forgive me, and I mean this with the highest respect, but the shop doesn't stand out. In a community like ours, where people are living and working in poverty, it should be heaving. Cheap clothes, shoes, gifts, homeware – it's all there under one roof. But it looks like a jumble sale. They're going for brand-new fast fashion instead. We need to make pre-loved feel good, not just for environmental reasons but also because it's an important message, that if something has had a past, it has value and so much love and life still to give.'

I stop, breathing fast. I've been heartfelt and that takes effort. It also means I could've mortally offended her.

'And how would you go about this transformation? Funds and able volunteers are extremely limited. Others have tried but failed. I won't lie to you, income is down and we're struggling. How would you succeed?'

'It's all in the shop already! It just needs organising and a rebranding. The window is the key to getting people in.' My brain is like an electrical storm with ideas striking fast and furiously. It's similar to how it was when I was a PA but it feels more intense. 'Our buyers had to predict trends. This is no different. So, for example, there'd be themes for summer, back to school, cosy autumn, Halloween and fireworks night, then for Christmas … say, a zero-waste Christmas, or how about The Spirit of Christmas Past, selling the idea that second-hand is special? Then there's what we can give back, maybe a happy-to-chat bench, a library of things – and of course we mustn't forget the kids.' Life Goes On is there to fund projects for children who have lost parents.

There's silence at the end of the line. I've said too much. I've judged it all wrong.

'Your managerial and retail experience isn't ideal.'

And here we go, it's the start of the let-down.

'I know I don't actually have any. But—' I think quickly – 'I've worked behind tills and with people all my life. I've had departments beneath me and I managed them fine. I'm a consumer too. I know what makes me spend money. And I understand the people; I used to spend my pocket money and Saturday-girl wages at Life Goes On, a lot of my wardrobe is from charity shops. In fact, sewing clothes for my nieces from bits my mother picked up for me from the shop has kept me going.'

'Betty, I don't wish to probe, but your enthusiasm is as if I'm putting you in charge of a department store, not a "jumble sale", as you put it. Can I ask why?'

I've blown it. Desperate is never a good look. All positivity drains from me. My shoulders sag and I flop against the garden wall. How do I tell her that four words are behind my determination?

I imagine telling the story. 'Bear with me, but I had a freak-out the other day, I thought a taxi was going to run me over. Then, this is a bit odd, but a random bloke

63

I met, I happened to mention to him that I might come home to set up my own label, well, I got a postcard from him this morning and he said, "I'm delighted you made it back to Wales. In fact, I knew you would." Those four little words, "I knew you would" – and the "knew" was in capitals – they were a bolt of lightning. He believes in me. It's ridiculous, obviously, that a stranger's faith means more to me than my own family. But it does – it means he saw me for me, before the accident, he saw the essence of me and he believes I still have it. And it made me feel alive.' I so could not tell that story.

'I need this job because,' I say, clutching the postcard with its scruffy, adorable handwriting in my dressing-gown pocket, 'I have no money, confidence or self-worth and I have nothing to get up for in the morning. I want to believe in myself again.'

I'm done. I've said my piece – I've said my truth. And my application will be marked 'mad woman' and forever filed under 'Do not employ. Ever'.

'Thanks for taking my call, Mrs Hughes,' I say, wrapping it up, because I've wasted enough of this woman's time already. 'I know you must be busy.'

'Busier now.'

Way to make me feel even more of a nuisance.

'I'm going to have to ring around the trustees and tell them I've changed my mind about the appointment.'

'Well, thanks again for considering me ...' Then I register what she's said. 'You've what?'

'When can you start?' There's no mistaking her.

'Seriously? Have I got the job?'

'Yes.' A hint of a smile is in her voice and I do a jig in my slippers. 'And the salary, you do realise that's non-negotiable?' It's peanuts to what I used to earn but what do I need masses of money for when I'm in a relationship with the remote control of the telly? 'Absolutely,' I say. Then it occurs to me ...

'Don't you want to meet me in person? Find out what I'm like?' I'm incredulous. And stupid – why give her a chance to reconsider again?

'My dear, I think I've worked out what you're like. We'll meet soon enough anyway. I'll get a contract out to you later, liaise with the manager who can show you the ropes before she leaves. Shall we have, say, a fortnight's probation period, to make sure it's the right fit? The shop is at a critical junction, the whole charity sector is, so I need someone who can turn it around.'

'Absolutely fine.' I'll take whatever she offers, even a sinking ship.

Mrs Hughes ends the call. I punch the air and, as I used to in my old life, I ring Sami to share my good news.

It goes to answerphone and I'm about to start when it dawns on me: I've just signed up for a nine-to-five when I don't normally get up until 11 a.m., after I've had around five hours of sleep disturbed by nightmares. What if it's too much for me? How am I going to handle people again? There's also the other stuff that needs doing to reintegrate myself into the world: my hair, for starters. Nerys needs to give me a trim and I have to go through my wardrobe for work wear. Even these trivial things seem huge. And yet in amongst the doubts is a flicker of joy that I haven't felt in so long. It's more powerful somehow, too – perhaps this creativity that I've unlocked is what was missing from my life. And it's down to Guy. I end the call before I speak. Because the first person I want to tell is him.

Dear Guy,

Yes, it's true. I'm back in the motherland – or, as the national anthem goes, the land of my fathers.

Talking of which, how is parenthood going?

Your postcard made me laugh: I knew Tunbridge Wells was posh, but I didn't realise men and women still paraded on The Pantiles in bonnets and top hats. Mind you, here we're all still in miners' hats and shawls, eating coal for breakfast.

Thank you for your unswerving faith in me. I've got a new project on the go. It's called Life Goes On.

Love,

Betty xxx

# 8

## *Guy*

Eric Cummings gasps when I hand over his good-as-new gnome.

'Gordon! You're back!' he says, looking not a great deal unlike his pint-sized garden companion.

Obviously, he's not in a red-pointed hat or blue trousers but he comes up to my chest, has a white beard and his eyes sparkle just like his beloved statue.

He produces a crisp £50 note and, as is my way, I ask if the job was worth such a big amount. My previous drop-off – a lengthy French polish on an antique table – yielded less but I never question it; that's just the way it goes with my policy to pay what the restoration means to the customer.

'I should say so,' Eric says, holding him tight. 'You have no idea what you've done for me. He looks so smart! Lovely paintwork, and you can't see the join at all where his mushroom broke off! As I said, this chap is almost as old as me; he was my mother's, but he's more than a sentimental thing. He listens to me, you see, we have elevenses together in the garden, rain or shine.'

Meeting people like Eric and making them happy is the best bit about being The Repair Guy. I leave him with a warm feeling, like I've had a bowl of creamy porridge. Which reminds me, I promised myself lunch in the park to get some vitamin D before I return to the dusty workshop.

The yellow wooden kiosk is an old haunt of mine. In the early days when I'd stayed over at Sarah's, I'd walk home this way and grab a breakfast roll and polystyrene cuppa. It was where Charlie and I would come for a hangover-busting bap. And even Granny is a fan – fancy fare is all well and good but the smell of sizzling bacon takes her back to her childhood.

Aleksander greets me like an old friend. 'What can I get you, mate?'

'The usual. Make it large, I'm starving.'

'Coming right up.'

We only ever exchange pleasantries, he's not a man of many words, and I like it that way because I get to watch him. It's like he's conducting an opera, the way his huge hands go this way and that from grill to worktop. He hums as he goes, ending with what would be a big cymbal clash by shaking a crisp brown paper bag open before he fills it then folds the top two times over and bows as he places it down.

I go to get my wallet and he tuts and shakes his blond buzz-cut head.

'You've been a loyal customer, this is on the house. A thank-you for your business all these years.'

I'm so touched but I'm also confused. 'It sounds like you're going somewhere. You're not, are you?'

'It's time to go home. To Poland. To be with my family.' His wrinkles smile as he says it.

'Well, that's just selfish!' I say, trying to make light of losing him. 'What will we do without you?'

'The council is buying me out. They have plans. To update and upgrade and so on.'

'Gutted,' I say. 'Why do they do that, the people in charge? What's wrong with the old, it's way more charming. It'll be granola bowls and pomegranate seeds, like everywhere else.'

'You can't stop change or time.'

There's a queue behind me now. I wish I could tell him how much I'll miss his presence – he has been part of my life, albeit on the sidelines, but he's been one of those unsung heroes of the community, part of the furniture. All I can do is raise a knuckle to him and thank him as he returns the gesture. 'Don't be sad,' he says, stoically, 'I get to go home.'

Home. It's such a small word for such a big place, so humble for what it represents: belonging, safety, comfort, laughter, love. Everything I've lost. Where is home for me now? Maybe it's time to sell up? I walk the path away from the bustle to a shaded bench to recalibrate. I shut my eyes and take in slow, deep breaths, clearing my mind so I can enjoy my last kiosk feed.

There's birdsong, rustling leaves and I start to relax. But then the hairs stand up on my arms as I hear a cry and I recognise it instantly. How is it possible to be so fine-tuned to a baby who isn't even mine? Across the grass I see Sarah pushing the buggy as she tries to shush Maud to sleep, but she's only getting louder. It hits me in the guts and I find myself willing her to pick her up. Maud has got herself worked up and when she did that on my watch, I'd rock her in my arms until she ran out of steam. Sarah spies me and she comes at me at speed. Imagine being so worn out you see your estranged husband as a source of help. Exhausted, with dark semicircles beneath her eyes, her hair is scraped back into a bun which makes her seem pinched. A panic rises in me. I don't want to be involved, I don't want to catch sight of Maud because it'll kill me. But how can I put my own needs ahead of a scrap of a thing whose only protector right now is looking at me desperately?

'She won't stop yelling,' Sarah says. 'I've been walking her for forty minutes. I've got a back-to-work thing this afternoon and I haven't even had any breakfast or a shower yet.'

'Back to work?' I stand up and take the buggy but I can't bring myself to look. 'Bacon and egg roll and tea – have it.'

Sarah is an independent person but for once she doesn't put up a fight. She looks at me instead with deep gratitude as she collapses on the seat. 'I'm finishing maternity leave early. I need to start earning properly again. Mum will have her two days a week, then I can afford nursery three days.'

'Full-time?' I gently shake the handlebar to see if the rocking will help. 'Isn't Charlie supporting you?'

Sarah is halfway through her food already. 'Yes, but childcare is so expensive. Life's expensive.'

'But isn't he helping you out with Maud, giving you breaks, doing the nappy run, that sort of thing?'

Sarah starts to sob and the baby's gone up a notch. I think I have no choice, but the truth is I could leave them both right now. But I would never do that, the thought horrifies me.

I steel myself to see Maud, turning my body away from Sarah, praying I can do this objectively. She's not my daughter. But the second I see her pink face, screwed up with her fists curled beside her cheeks, her gums almost white from the crying and that tiny tongue, she still feels mine.

'Come on, Maudie,' I say, putting my hands beneath her rigid body, feeling she's become hot, raising her up, releasing her from a blanket, pulling her into my body, where I hold her head against my cheek. Skin to skin, I breathe her in and shush her as I wander through the trees. Her fight recedes and the bellowing turns to gulps of whimpers which quieten and I lower her so she's in my arms. Her eyelashes are wet but her face has plumped out and I stare down at her, finally asleep, with so much love. Does she sense who I am? Was that why she stopped? Or was it the power of touch?

I head back to Sarah and she sighs with relief.

'She knows it's you,' she says. There's no proof whatsoever of that but haven't I just thought the same? 'Thank you, Guy. I was at my wit's end.' She pauses and then dares to ask. 'How does it feel, holding her again?' It's almost a whisper because she knows what's at stake.

I say nothing but gently pop Maud back into the buggy, immediately noticing the chasm left in me.

'You should talk to Charlie. He needs to up his game.'

That's all I can manage and I leave, which goes against every instinct. But I can't tell her how holding Maud made me feel. I don't know what good it would do admitting it to her; it might give her hope when I'm swinging madly between going back to them and finding a new path. Charlie would be my go-to but he's not there. I realise how much I miss him; not that we'd talk every day, more that we could message at any time, day or night.

He was my right-hand man, my best man, who gave the warmest, funniest speech about our brotherhood – the time we tried to become blood brothers and he fainted at the sight of a single drop, how he'd bring me a cuppa every morning when I put him up when he was going through his divorce, how I put him up when he was going through his divorce, how he saw me as family. I can't go weeping to Granny, she's had more than enough of that. Who is there who will listen?

It comes to me as I make my way home. There is someone uninvolved, someone who won't judge me, someone who has somehow brought joy and warmth when I've thought the world had run out.

The bounce in Betty's word play isn't all there is, though. There's also honesty and resilience, an openness of heart and inspiration too – a dose of Life Goes On could help me work out what I need to do with my life. Would it be too much to write it all down for her? She asked me about fatherhood, and perhaps it can be a way of seeing my feelings and trying to understand them.

At the very least, it'd be like talking it through with someone. And I'm so very short of someones.

I get in, go straight to the workshop, open the stationery drawer and take out a letter-headed sheet of A4 and then pour myself onto the paper.

72

The Repair Guy
5 The Mews, Tunbridge Wells, TN2 5FD
07954 240981
www.therepairguy.com
therepairguy@googlemail.com

Dear Betty,

Congrats on Life Goes On – I imagine it to be fabulous, dynamic and creative, much like yourself. And naturally, in high fashion, inspired by your trip to Venice, no doubt.

Do you miss London at all? And how are you finding it back home? You probably can't move for people walking their dragons or waving daffodils in your face.

It's similar in TW with top hats and bonnets everywhere. They're dashing, of course, but there are drawbacks aplenty – it's easy to forget you're wearing one. I can't tell you how many times I've got mine wet in the shower.

You asked me about parenthood. It's been the most wonderful thing ever to have happened to me. I've never known love like it. There was no slow burn or getting to know one another – it was instant and enormous, possibly ginormous, and I knew from the second I met Maud that I would do anything to protect her. Some say it's overwhelming but it completed me. Most incredible of all is that it arms you with superhuman skills. For how else could you change an evil nappy on two hours' sleep and still coo? (Breathing through your mouth also helps.)

Take today, when Maud was bawling. The books

*tell you it's because they get overstimulated and miss their optimal sleep window but I wonder if they're raging at having strangers stick their faces too close to them or reliving the trauma of a cuddle with an overperfumed and possibly gin-soaked great aunty.*

*Anyway, Maud was in a state and she wouldn't settle, so I picked her up. How it felt to have her in my arms is how it feels to be a parent: there's a myriad of feelings in that contact. There's fear that something might be wrong, anxiety is wired into you, and you can feel your inner caveman on the lookout for a marauding sabre-toothed beast. There's the urge to comfort, to want to do anything to make it right. And there's the bond, the invisible tie between you, that pulses as it passes endless and unconditional love from you to them. It's true when they say you'd die for them.*

*On a lighter note, it's funny you say you eat coal for breakfast. It's making a comeback in this neck of the woods in hipster cafés. I've yet to try it but gastro-lovers are raving about smashed lumps on sourdough toast.*

*Finally, thank you for your thank-you. But I raise you a thank-you because you've helped me more than you know.*

*Best,*
*Guy*

# 9

## Betty

Three minutes to nine and it's dead at Life Goes On.
Through the grubby shop window, it looks like a
morgue for clothes and bric-a-brac.

Maybe I'm being harsh – I've hardly slept, I needed
two goes at putting on my lippy because my hand was
shaking so much and I'm a soaking-wet bag of first day
nerves from the rainy walk when I jumped at every car
and still got splashed to boot.

'We're not open till nine, so you'll have to wait.'

I get shoved to one side by a woman in a drenched
parka who opens up and slams the door in my face. I take
a breath then go in and open my mouth to speak. The
stench is so vile I end up coughing and the woman comes
at me with a broom.

'I told you, lady, we're not open yet.' She glares at
me through a dripping thick black fringe and begins to
sweep at my feet, which are pooling with water.

'I'm the new manager, I start today,' I say, hearing
myself and still not believing it. But it'll feel real when
she gives me a gushing apology.

'Good luck with that, then,' she says.

I'm so thrown by her hostility I even imagine the
hideous beige – and naked – mannequin with a wonky

75

tangled blonde wig in the corner is giving me the eye.

Every inch of me screams that I should get out. But I can't move. I'm stunned into silence by her obvious agitation. It's boiling in here, yet she's dressed in a baggy jumper, drainpipe jeans and biker boots, which make me feel hot with panic. I'm still fighting off nausea too so the jumble before me, which is actually worse now I'm closer up, matches the state of my brain. I give myself a pep talk, reminding myself that once upon a time I was the very model of professionalism, therefore I must not vomit on my shoes.

'I'm Betty Hopkins, so you must be the retiring manager,' I say and immediately wonder how she could be retiring when she's barely twenty, if that.

'She's owed holiday, so she's not coming in.' She must hear my heart stop because she swivels round and leans back against the counter with her arms crossed. A smirk slithers onto her face. 'Didn't Mrs Hughes tell you?'

'No.' She bloody well didn't.

'So it leaves muggins here to show you the ropes.' Resentment pours off her and I delve deep into my toolbox of experience. Amid the cobwebs I remember when Sami and I first met at Banta. He'd gone over the top on his expenses with one hundred too many bar tabs. Ahmed wanted to make an example of him so no one else took the piss – and it fell to me to rein in his nephew's spending. So I do what I did then, what Sami has always referred to as my nut-cracking moment, which was unfair, really, because I did not take a sledgehammer to his balls. This has to be delicate but firm.

'So what's your name, then, and your role here?' I say in an even voice that's kind and interested.

'Mrs Hughes didn't mention me?' She tuts and splutters. So much for my management technique. 'After everything I've done here?'

The chip on her shoulder is large enough to feed the village. But it identifies the problem.

'I'm guessing you've been very valuable here and earned your place.'

'Earned? I'm a volunteer; I get nothing and yet I come in, day in, day out, and I've practically run the place singlehandedly because your predecessor hid out the back, stuffing herself with cake, talking to her mates on the phone.'

The penny drops. She wanted this job and didn't get it. And the one who did, the grapevine says, is damaged goods. No wonder that hurts.

'That must have been so hard for you. Tell you what, why don't we have a cup of tea and you can tell me the issues here and we can work on a plan?'

My management skills feel rusty but I realise the creative side of me is bursting at the sight of the sub-jumble sale: clothes hang half-drunk off hangers, shoes are unpaired in what looks like a lucky-dip tub, books are here and there rather than together and the usual vases, pans and trinkets are stacked three-deep, which gives nothing any breathing space. 'We need a bit of a revamp. There's too much going on at once.' Too much of a hideous and confusing mess. 'So any ideas?'

I get a huge yawn in response. I need to wake her up and bring her along on the ride.

'We could make it exciting! Create a catwalk with whole outfits, jewellery and bags! Maybe we can style up different zones, so ...' I'm looking around and ideas fizz up inside me – 'that pine chair, the white picture frame and the chunky knit throw could make it a Scandi living zone. Then next to that we could lead on to a library, with all the books and games, and that cerise sequin jumper could be where we stick everything bright and wacky! What do you think? That could improve things.'

'Improve things?' she almost shouts. 'What's wrong with how it is? They said you'd make it all la-di-da London,' she tuts.

So I was wrong about the rumour mill; the gossip has instead focused on where I've come from. I'm accused of the worst crime of all around here, of forgetting my roots.

'It's true I worked in London. But I'm from here, I was born in Pant Bach,' I say with steely eyes. 'I've done my time on the sticky floors of Merthyr Tydfil's nightclubs, I've watched every episode of *Gavin and Stacey* three times, I can sing the national anthem backwards and I've heard every sheep gag going. I can assure you there will be no la-di-da London here.'

She drops her chin very slightly. It must mean she's found a grain of respect for me so I tone it down.

'All I'm saying is we need to give people a better shopping experience, to draw them in so they wonder what we'll have done next, to try to get the till ringing. Not for me to be the Big I Am, but for those kiddies who've lost a parent.' It feels like I've won her over so it's time for a peace offering. 'Let's start again, eh? But first things first, I'm gasping. What would you like? A tea or coffee? The café next door is my sister's. It's on me, or on her, if I can wangle it. And please,' I say with a smile, 'can you tell me your name?'

Surely she's on board now.

'I'm Megan King and I'm twenty,' she says politely. But then her glare is back. 'And just so you know, I was one of those – what you called "kiddies",' she says it thick with sarcasm, 'and I'm bringing up two more of them, my twin half-sister and half-brother. We lost our mam two years ago. I was going to go to college to study retail. But if I hadn't stepped in, they'd be in care. I got sacked from my last two jobs because if I have to go, if they're sick, I have to go. But I can if I'm volunteering. It's also my only chance of getting any work experience. And I happen to like it here, I owe Life Goes On a lot.' She sniffs hard and starts work, tidying around the till, which I see now won't ring because it's an ancient manual cash register. 'I'll have a large latté and a full Welsh on white with a can of Coke and an almond croissant for afters.'

She's torn me to pieces. Another boss might take umbrage at her tone. But I feel humbled by her and foolish at barrelling in. It's not what I can call a win but at least I know her attitude is down to me rather than a sign of complacency at the job.

I drag my tail behind me into Hoffi Coffi where Nerys gives me a huge cheery wave through the steam from the shining silver coffee machine.

'How's it going?' she sings then sees my face. 'Oh. Megan playing hell, is she? I meant to tell you to tread carefully.'

'No, it was me, I buggered it up. I said all the wrong stuff. Went in too gung-ho.'

'It's your first day, presh.'

'I thought the old professional muscle memory

79

had kicked in. The dealing with people bit, and being switched on. But I got it all wrong.'

Nerys gives a sympathetic nod.

'And yet the weirdest thing is that I had no trouble with the creative bit. Like, I can see exactly what needs to be done.'

'Well, that's good, isn't it?'

'Since when, though, did the left-hand side of my brain overrule the right?' I ask her before I reel off my order. And as she busies herself getting it ready, I wonder again. How can it be? The words in Guy's latest letter pop up into my head – he called me fabulous, dynamic and creative and I was taken aback when I read that. How could he say it when he's a stranger? More tricky is why I would take it on board from him. How can I feel seen by him? That's the unsettling truth. Until now, like every-one else, I considered myself more of a well-oiled robot. But what's reared its head instead is my imagination, as if the break from work allowed it to resurface.

'What are you smiling about all of a sudden?' Nerys says, presenting me with a takeout paper carrier.

I hadn't even realised I was. Before I can stop myself, I tell her the story of how I met this bloke just before the accident.

She listens, hooked, laughing at the hankie bit, then a frown falls when I tell her about our letters.

'Why are you looking at me like that? What are you thinking?'

'What am I thinking, Betty?' she says. 'I think you should steer clear, that's what I'm thinking. He's married with a child, and he's lapping up the attention!' She is bristling with scorn, something I only ever see if there's a threat to her tribe.

'But there's nothing suggestive.' I say it more defensively than I wanted to. 'And he's head over heels with his daughter.' Seriously head over heels. I was so moved, not just by his expression but by his devotion. It's so far from what my father feels for me.

'Hello! A married man loves his kid but you know what'll come next? My wife doesn't understand me! What do you think he's after? Not a second-hand jumper! And I don't want to be insensitive but I'm not sure this is the right thing for you after what you've been through.'

'It's a no, then?' I snap, feeling thoroughly patronised. He is decent and a gent, I'm sure of it.

'Oh, Bet. I'm sorry. But come on – Steve would agree with me, he's very protective of you.'

This small-minded small-town attitude is what drives me mad about Pant Bach.

'Have you told this fella about your accident? Where you're working?'

I deflate like a blow-up bed. I haven't but it's not out of shame, it's just that when I met him, none of the bad stuff had happened and he doesn't feel sorry for me. And it's an escape to think I'm living my dream.

'It's just … we have a connection,' I say, sounding hollow.

'Listen,' she says, kindly, 'if you're back on the market, then why not better the devil you know, eh? Because I reckon you go for blokes that you can keep at arm's length, like with Jude; you could avoid settling down because of his age, you never thought it'd last the way it did, and this one is the same, he's far enough away for you to keep at bay. You don't want to get hurt, like Mam did with Dad.'

What? She must have thought a lot about it to rattle it off like that. And without ever telling me. This is all a bit too much to take in on a tea-break on my first day. 'Hang on, Nerys, who says I'm on the market? That whole analysis of my relationship history is a bit heavy, you know how sensitive I am about what happened with Jude. And what's it got to do with Dad?'

'Well, you remember him going. I don't. That's why ...' She shrugs as if it's obvious.

'That's why I'm on the shelf, is it?' And she's a smug married.

'I just don't get why you're bothering with him when there are thousands of men around here. Brody Burns, for one. I'll get Steve to invite him round for a barbecue.'

She sees me startle. The hottest boy in school, whom Nerys and I nicknamed Broody Buns, was my schoolgirl crush. He had green Irish eyes courtesy of his mother and was the unlikely but delicious combination of hunky captain of the rugby team and in-touch-with-his-feminine-side artist in my A Level class.

'I told you I don't want a bloke.' Not one from around here who would treat me differently either because of the accident or they think that I'm up myself.

'So you don't fancy this fella?' Nerys narrows her eyes.

'I'd like him for a friend, that's all.' I ignore the fact that I dodged her question. 'He saw a side of me I'd forgotten existed.'

'Oh, lovely girl. You can't go back, you know that. And you can't trust what he says. You don't know him.'

'He's hardly a threat, he repairs things! Christ, he even carries a hankie!'

'Dear God, Betty, there's a weirdo klaxon for you. What's the point in looking back, eh?'

It irks me that I'm supposed to be the big worldly sister. But she's seen how low I've been and she's only trying to look out for me; reluctantly, I can see where she's coming from. Bottom line, he has a wife and baby after all. I nod slowly, pick up my takeaway and say goodbye.

What was I thinking? Guy's been useful for helping me get my act together but what kind of person would carry that on? There's probably no point replying to him. I need to concentrate on what I have to do here so I can get out as soon as I can.

Back in the shop Megan is putting the phone down and scribbling in the diary.

'I've been thinking,' I say. 'The best way to do this is for you to treat me as an idiot. Like I know nothing.'

'That won't be hard,' she says. 'Old lady rang, wants a house clearance, it's in the diary.'

Then she grabs the bag and heads towards a door marked stockroom without a thank-you. She hates the sight of me. In an instant, my intention to stop contact with Guy is undone. If I can't have a mental escape during this nightmare I won't get through it.

I brace myself for the rest of the day, which will have to start with getting a scented plug-in the size of Chernobyl. But I seek refuge in my imagination and in my head I draft a letter to Guy that I'll write later about the life that I wish was mine. Not as an intentional act of deception but a fortifying fantasy, which even includes a doting dad rather than a waster. The memories too of a trip to

Venice that I never actually made, but easy enough to conjure up I've googled it so often. Plus a hashtag blessed career as a designer who splits her time between here and London, just as the Before Betty could've gone on to do. Guy doesn't need to be dragged down by my miserable reality. The chances are we'll never meet and the act of writing is cathartic so what's the harm of telling him a few white lies?

Dear Guy,

I could have done with your hankie when I read your letter. Your description of fatherhood was so moving and it reminded me how much my dad thinks of me. Having a loving father is so important for a child's self-esteem and it sets the bar for the rest of your life when it comes to love and basically everything else.

Maud – cute name and I can imagine she is a peach in her bonnet – will grow up feeling treasured, self-assured and confident and that's the greatest gift a dad can give to a daughter. Your wife is lucky to have you so involved. Is married life bliss? And you must be so excited at the prospect of becoming the main carer, if that's still the plan.

You're spot on about my project being influenced by Venice. What a fantastical spectacle the place is! So much so it sparked the inspo to quit my job and work on my own label.

Getting there sets the tone. You go by train from the mainland and the railway track thins until you're seemingly cutting through the lagoon with the sea within touching distance. There's no soft landing when you arrive at the station – suddenly you're in the midst of the city. Smack bang in front of you are water taxis, gondolas and people, so many people, and the ornate buildings soar up high in a spectacular stone-and-marble mishmash of Gothic, Moorish and Byzantine styles, boasting arches and geometry, golden domes and stained glass.

It's like stepping onto the set of a film – in fact, it's so immersive it's like being in a film. And all built on stilts on water around an s-shaped canal. What a ridiculous place! But it's oh such a beguiling work of art.

I fell under its spell immediately and spent the days exploring. You were right – it was exactly like a fantastic giant puzzle of canals and bars and pizza to get lost in. Filled with street art, street food and street performance, everywhere I turned revealed something to gawp at. Living statues, modern sculptures, the Rialto Bridge – be still my beating heart! – St Mark's Square and on and on. I walked and walked, through wide plazas, peeking through passageways, creeping through alleys that hugged your body, stopping off for tiny coffees and slabs of calzone for sustenance.

That, you'd think, would be enough. But add in the carnival and it hit an even crazier level. Processions on water, parades on the ground, regattas, acrobats, fire-eaters, live music and then the chance to take part yourself – I did a make-your-own-mask workshop followed by a costumed night out complete with a hoop-skirted emerald-green ball gown of lace and silk and an extravagant Marie Antoinette wig. I was positively pedestrian compared to the dolled-up churchmen, jesters, princes, butterflies and highwaymen in half-masks, feline masks and beaks, adorned with gems, feathers and gold leaf.

*Mind you, Merthyr is just as enchanting with all its dragons and daffodils. Although I could do without my sister trying to set me up with a Valleys boy. I adore her, Nerys is so positive and capable, but because she tied the knot with her first boyfriend and has never wanted to leave Pant Bach, she thinks it's the answer for everyone. I suspect she's already planning the barbecue she's threatened to hold to bring me and Brody Burns together. Having said all that, I'm curious to see if the school hottie remains on fire or if he's been extinguished by the goldfish bowl of village life. We shall see!*

*As for London, I don't miss it at all – because I spend half my time there! I get the best of both worlds. I can design and sew up prototypes in the peace of Wales and then chase my contacts and fill my boots on life in the smoke. It's early days for Life Goes On but I am loving it. I often think back to our hideout – it helped me see things a bit differently.*

*I should thank you but we've kind of done that a lot already. I'll say it in Welsh instead.* Diolch.

*Love,*

*Betty xxx*

# 10

## *Guy*

'Fancy a road trip, Thelma? Or you can be Louise, if you like? Your choice.'

I've popped in to see Granny before I head off for a few days on a delivery run.

She turns to me from the jigsaw seat and says straight-faced, 'Driving off a cliff would mean I miss jazzercise tomorrow. Otherwise I would.'

'Shame, because I'm off to Wales via a few drops on the M25 and M4.' I sit down beside her. 'Pack a bag! Come for the ride! You can be my tour guide. Bit of sightseeing, bit of jigsaw-hunting in the charity shops, food ... tempted?'

'It sounds lovely,' Granny says, patting my arm. 'But you know Bobby isn't a good traveller. Very territorial when he's out of his comfort zone; he'll go for someone at the services, no doubt about it.'

'All right. But if there's a next time, you'll have to come. Or we can just go anyway!' I would love to take her back after everything she's done for me.

'I must admit I'm envious as I haven't been to see my brother and sisters in quite some time. Perhaps I'll give them a ring, see if there's any room at the inn in Bethlehem soon.'

She swivels back to work and I join her. This puzzle is called Raining Cats and Dogs and the box shows a riot of paws and whiskers, tails and ears falling from the sky. Some have landed already on the roofs and trees, the cats, of course, on their feet, whereas a few dopey dogs are splayed out upside down on the pavement. Granny has this one half done but she invites me to have a go at the complicated far-right corner where a distant downpour features specks of fur.

'Do you remember when we'd go to Bethlehem for Christmas?' Her hand swoops down on a piece, she pats it in place and sighs with satisfaction.

'Bits here and there.' There's a fuzzy sort of retro cine-cam feel in my mind to the hills and wellies, sheepdogs and relatives' kisses.

'The live nativity at the farm when one of your second cousins ran off with the baby Jesus and was chased by a goat?'

I guffaw. 'I so wish I remembered that! But I have a recollection of a long line of people – were they posting their Christmas cards?' I'm not sure if this is a memory of mine or a memory of being told about it.

'Yes!' Granny claps with delight. 'People came especially to get a Bethlehem postmark! In their thousands, from all over the world. They still do, apparently, although the post office has gone, it's in the old school now, so Gladys tells me.'

'That's one of my deliveries! Bryn the Bear is homeward bound.'

'Well! Give her my love, won't you! Make sure you tell her you can't stop or she'll have you stuffed with Welsh cakes and you'll be done for, stranded for days.'

I spy a tortoiseshell blob on a very dark grey piece and it slots in perfectly.

'I think there may be a missing one in this section.' Granny taps a hole where an easily identifiable green cat's eye should go. 'I've looked everywhere.'

I reach for the box and take a snap of it and of the gap where it should sit. 'Leave it with me, I'll rustle you up one when I'm back so you can make sure it's complete before passing it on. There's nothing worse than a missing piece, is there?'

'Thank you, cariad!' She elbows me gently. 'I think it'll do you good to get away after all this ...' She throws her hands in the air, dismissing the black clouds we've lived under for weeks.

She's a woman who keeps her emotions in check but when I told her about Charlie being Maud's dad and then how I had to step in to soothe Maud, she looked on the verge of tears. It's been hard for her too in her own way, thinking she had become a great-grandmother. Sarah's mum was first to visit at the hospital and Granny gave her a respectful hour alone with Maud. 'I remembered holding you for the first time; there's nothing like a grandchild coming into your life,' she'd said, 'nothing, that is, like a great-grandchild.' She's been stoic, keeping her grief private but I saw her dabbing her eyes with a tissue when she was putting away the lemon-yellow matinee jackets she had knitted for Maud.

'Yeah,' I say, 'that's why I'm going in person. I feel lighter at the thought of it, you know. I'm not over this yet.' My dreams have been filled with Maud and I've been worrying about how she'll cope with nursery. And, I admit, I still love Sarah. It's a grown-up kind of love, understated but, I thought, solid. Replaying our happiness before all of this has made me long for the three of us to be together again. Yet will I be able to trust Sarah? Just when I need Charlie the most to chat to, I can't. 'I just want a break, a few days, that's all, because I'm fed up of feeling like a victim. I want to take back some control, be my own master, if that makes sense?'

'Absolutely.'

'And think of something else, for a change.'

Granny takes my cue. 'So how many deliveries do you have? Any pick-ups too?'

'Lots of both. My inbox is clogged.'

'Well, it's good you're not overwhelmed by it but rather see it as a kick-start.'

'Actually, I can't take the credit for my get-up-and-go.' Dare I say it out loud or will it make me sound like a madman? But then I can always and have always been able to share inner stuff with Granny. Other people's parents would jump down their kids' throats out of fear and instinct to protect them, whereas Granny being one generation removed was always more level about things, like experience had taught her to trust me to find my way. Plus, I suspect, she knew how she had to get it right: my maternal grandparents couldn't help in bringing me up; mum's mum was in a home and her dad had already passed away.

'No?' Granny tilts her head to me and her deep brown, almost black, eyes search mine.

'No. It's strange, but it's down to the return of a hankie, actually.'

'How very intriguing!'

'Not really. But on my stag do, I gave it to someone

who needed to mop up a G and T and it's made its way back to me.'

I find I'm smiling as I explain. 'There was a letter with it, we'd had a chat, you see, and it said, "I hope you're well. Scrub that, I'm sure of it" and it inspired me, sort of reminding me that there was a time when I was happier and capable. So we've been writing a bit. There's lots of banter but it's also helped me process things. It's different talking about stuff with someone uninvolved.'

Betty's latest, where she talks about her father, Venice and having feet in both London and Wales was so honest and thrilling. While we're technically strangers, it doesn't feel that way; it never did on that day in February. We seem to be able to read each other. Apart from the misunderstanding about me being Maud's dad. Yet in my heart I still feel I am. And Betty has obviously thrived from having an adoring father. My heart squeezes that I could do that for Maud because Charlie isn't capable. If Maud's the most important person in this shit show, then could I do it for her? As for her question about married bliss, it had been before – if I can forgive Sarah, it could be again. It's not as if she'd been a serial cheat; believe it or not, she had always had such high standards because of her feckless father. I even have moments of pitying her; one mistake and it ended up being catastrophic and she will be full of self-loathing.

'So where does this ... where does she live?'

There's a twinkle in Granny's voice and I feel myself blush. I realise with embarrassment that I'm gazing into the distance with a grin so cheesy it could be a lump of Brie on a radiator.

'She – she's in Wales, funnily enough. But that's not

why I'm going. I'm not going to see her! That would be ridiculous! It's just chance that I've got business there. It's a business trip. A trip for business. She's just a pen pal, that's all.'

Suddenly the jumble of pieces in front of me are very interesting and I focus on them hard. Never mind that they're dancing before me because I can't seem to concentrate.

'Well, why don't you see if she's free?' Granny says it as though it's the most natural thing in the world.

'Because, Granny, that would be weird. Thanks for my hankie, it's pure coincidence but I've travelled four hours across the country and would you like a cup of tea? I'll look like a stalker. And she thinks I'm happily married and have a child.'

'But you're not.'

It's like a bolt from the sky. That is the truth, that's where I am. Maybe I could suggest it? I'd love to see her again and I could do with a laugh, not to mention a new friend. I can tell her face to face how things have really worked out. It propels me up.

'Right,' I say, 'I'm behind already, I've got to get to Guildford to return a repaired vintage lawnmower to a hipster who has sworn me to secrecy that he has artificial grass. After that it's Reading, where there are three drops: a typewriter that needed – and I swear to God this is the truth – new A, R, S and E keys, which belongs to a woman who wants to write her first erotic novel; and a battered old suitcase with a lock that needed replacing and I'm sure the owner is a retired spy. Then it's Swindon to collect a Lego Death Star that I have to glue together, that's three thousand pieces plus, because the woman's dog smashed it with its waggy tail. Over the border, there's a broken jukebox in Cwmbran. I'll get to Gladys in Bethlehem after that, which is the furthest west I'll go, then double back to stay near Merthyr Tydfil, where I'm returning an old desk globe that needed a new Australia because his grandchild had felt-tipped the word "boobs" on it.'

I get to the front door and the world's most incompetent but cutest guard dog ambles up the hallway to my ankles.

'Oh, Bobby, sorry mate,' I give him a stroke, 'I'm about to go, I think we need to get you some hearing aids.'

I kiss Granny and she waves me off, giving her pug a consolatory cwtch, and I start the engine and pull away, mind buzzing with my to-do list.

But around the corner I stop. There's something at the top of that list that I want to do most of all. I scribble out a note on a jotter, find an envelope in my work satchel, grab a first-class stamp from my wallet and drop it in the postbox.

Then it's behind the wheel where I resolve not to think about the past just for a few days. The only looking back I'll be doing is in my rear-view mirror.

*Dear Betty,*

*Wow, Venice!*

*We never got to have a honeymoon due to the baby, but if the opportunity ever arises, I'm sold on that place. Mainly because I want to wear a Marie Antoinette wig myself. I suspect I'd look more like Rod Stewart. But I bet Brody Burns could pull it off.*

*Anyway, I'm taking a leaf out of your book by doing some Life Goes On of my own.*

*Would you believe that means a delivery run to Wales. I realise it's a big country – you don't happen to know Tom Jones, do you? – but I'll be in the south for a few days.*

*So if you're not in London and fancy a cup of tea, it would be my pleasure.*

*In case you chucked my last letter with my contact details, here's my email should you want to contact me:* therepairguy@googlemail.com

*Best,*

*Guy*

# II

## *Betty*

I press the doorbell and get a blast of 'If You're Happy and You Know it, Clap Your Hands'.

I'm not, so I give a defiant up yours to Nerys's front door just before it opens, thinking I've got away with it.

But my niece Poppy's ice-blue eyes are agog. 'You did the finger!'

My sister is struggling to hold a straight face. 'Naughty Aunty Betty!'

'I was scratching my nose,' I say weakly. 'Have you got your invisible X-ray specs on, Pops?'

Nerys snorts. 'No. We have a new wireless thing with a camera, don't we, Popsicle? You know how Steve loves a gadget. And this one here has worked out how to programme it so the tune changes every five minutes!'

Caught out, I hang my head in shame but Nerys pulls me in for a hug and in an instant Poppy forgives me for my sins. She throws her arms around my waist and it's just what I need after a third awful day at Life Goes On. A cry goes up – someone's feeling left out.

'Baby Daisy wants to see you!' Poppy says, leading me along the hall, which is a portrait gallery of the family's story so far. Running the length of both walls, white-framed photo after photo captures their most joyful moments: Nerys and Devoted Steve on their wedding day, grainy baby scans, pregnancy bumps and the girls as they grow. We get to the kitchen, where the door frame is marked with Poppy's increasing height, and I take in a delicious lungful of cooking and clean washing. By the time I swoop up Daisy from her high chair I've decompressed from the stress of work. When I had recovered enough from the accident, I started coming here once a week for a family tea and it's been one of those things that's kept me going. Being with my tribe and getting to know my nieces takes me away from my worries – you can't dwell on things when a little girl insists on hopping onto your lap and wants to do your make-up while gazing up at you in adoration. Yet as I blow raspberries into Daisy's neck rolls and suck in her little breaths, I feel something shifting: it's a bitter-sweet taste of 'what if this never happens for me?'. Guy's description of parenthood echoes inside of me and I ache with longing.

But Poppy comes to the rescue, ordering me to put the baby down. She clambers onto me, her white-blonde pigtails swinging, and begins to tell me about her day. She's five but going on fifteen with her tales of who's fallen out with who in her class and the scandal of who lost their playtime at break.

I see there's an extra place set. Suddenly, I have a mad idea that Nerys has invited Brody. I mean, she couldn't have because this is our inner sanctum. Yet when I watch Nerys draining the pasta I see she's almost dancing and it's like she's got something up her sleeve. I flush with panic. I'm looking haggard from the battering of Megan's bruising company at the shop and I swear I've developed a whole new set of wrinkles from the rules and regulations

I'm learning on the job. I don't actually know if it's real or a phantom stench but I get a whiff of damp – I need to up the air-freshener count in the shop – and wonder if it's my hair. Then, ludicrously, there's a hint of a flutter in my stomach because actually, if Brody does turn up, I know he would be completely unfazed by the setting. Valleys men have a macho image but they've grown up in a community of big, busy families, having free rein to go from one house to another, embraced and raised by their villages, where mams are adored and obeyed. Still, if it is him, I wish Nerys had warned me.

'Who else is coming?' I say, trying not to sound bothered.

'Ah! Wait and see!' She gives me a wink with one of her fake eyelashes. 'He won't be long, Steve's bringing him.'

'Nerys! Why didn't you say? I could have at least got changed. If it's Brody—'

She stops mid-stir of the tomato sauce. 'Oh, so you are interested, then?'

'No!' I cry. But I am lonely. I don't say it out loud because it'll only stoke her match-making mission.

Her eyebrows shoot up at my high-pitched protest. 'As long as you've ditched the creepy married man.'

I give her the evils – she's so blinking traditional sometimes, like thinking men and women can't be friends. I don't tell her I wrote back to him and I definitely don't say I found myself writing about the life I want rather than have.

'It's not Brody,' she adds.

I actually feel a bit disappointed because, beyond family, I have no one else here. My contact with school friends petered out and when I'd come back I didn't have time for catch-ups.

'You know I'd get you to scrub up a bit if it was!'

'Charming.'

'Listen, don't worry, our guest won't care about that.'

I'm curious but the warmth of her grin suggests it's nothing bad so I allow myself to relax. There are footsteps and Poppy jumps down and runs out to greet her dad. He carries her in the crook of his arm like she's the weight of a fairy and he's so big he takes up most of the doorway.

'How's my baby button?' Devoted Steve gets a squeal from Daisy who jiggles her legs with excitement at his kiss.

'Don't wind her up, she needs her tea!' Nerys playfully scolds him as they cuddle and press their lips together like they've been apart for days rather than since breakfast.

'All right, Bet? Good day?'

'No!' I say but with a smile because when he's in the room it's impossible not to feel calmed by his strength and balance.

But it turns out it is when the guest follows behind him.

'Grampy!' Poppy says, wriggling free from her dad.

'Princess!' my father booms. My body actually flinches from the shock.

Their intimacy stuns me – I had no idea they were this close. I feel as if I'm in the audience – as if this is being played out before me. He's swinging her about – only an idiot would do that in a kitchen when there are hot pans about. It shows how much he knows about parenting. Then, with so much sadness, I realise he'd already left by the time I was Poppy's age.

This is the first time I've seen him in – what, two years last Christmas? He asked to see me after the accident but I refused and have ignored his requests ever since. I can't stand the sight of him, I don't want to look, but it's like when there's something grisly that has some kind of pull over you and I can't help but stare. I feel myself curdling inside and physically recoiling in my seat at his tragic appearance. Whenever I think of him I see an image which was everywhere in my childhood: handsome, charismatic rugby hard-man Dai Hopkins in full flight scoring a try on his debut – and only – game for Wales. The sports photographer caught the bounce of his thick black curls and glistening biceps and it was Sellotaped to walls in the pubs and rugby club. For a while my dad was the pride of Pant Bach and even I felt touched by his magic when he'd show up out of the blue at Mam's. But it was never for long; he always had somewhere to go. Then it soured. He could've had it all but he threw it away, believing his own hype, and putting more into being a playboy than a player. Now his appearance shows it: his hair is thinning and a greasy grey, his eyes are baggy, he has a red nose and his belly is swollen from beer. The only thing that's the same is the red Wales shirt he's wearing as if to remind everyone, and himself, of who he was.

There's still a grace to his movements, though, as he twirls Poppy round.

'Careful, Dad, I'm dishing up,' Nerys warns.

He catches my eye and it sets light to my anger and I stand, seething at this set-up, seething at my sister and at the man who's acting as if he deserves to be here. Nerys clocks my defensive, crossed arms and glares at me to behave. Who does she think she is?

'What's he doing here?' I whisper violently above the kids' chatter.

'I thought it was about time you two got talking.' She goes over to him and they give each other a peck.

'Without telling me?' My voice is taut and could snap into a scream any second.

'You wouldn't have come otherwise, would you? Dad agrees. He wants this too.'

I look at my father who at least has the decency to offer no words but a nod of the head. But then I'm raging that he's sitting back and letting Nerys do the talking.

'And to be honest, you know, we're getting busier and busier with clubs after school and so we thought it'd be good if we could do one tea a week together rather than two separate ones.'

'You mean, he comes once a week too? How long has that been happening?'

'If you'd ever let me talk to you about Dad, you'd know it's been happening forever. But because you're so uptight about him, I can't ever mention him. And I've had enough of pussy-footing around.'

'Right, I see.' My pulse is pumping and I want to run but Nerys commands everyone to sit up.

We all do as we're told. I think if I did try to leave, my legs would give way.

'Veggie pasta, garlic bread, salad and brownies for afters. Dig in!'

There's a clatter of cutlery and Nerys asks her husband about his day, the girls are oblivious to my discomfort and I'm grateful because whatever my feelings are, they don't need to know the truth about him.

I go mute and my ears buzz as I try to keep myself

together, looking straight down at my plate but sensing the presence of a threat. He says very little to begin with, I know I'd criticise him however he behaved, but I'm outraged he's being so meek. He's a coward, an embarrassment, but this act of his makes him seem the child and me the adult. It's always been like this – any contact we have is about him trying to avoid confrontation rather than seeking to make amends and own his mistakes. Gradually, his throaty tone fills the room; he mentions the weather, and I think how lame he is, as he claims there's a storm on the way. But then he moves on to his grandkids and it becomes clear how up to speed he is with Poppy's ballet and Daisy's weaning.

We get through it and Devoted Steve takes Poppy and Daisy off for a bath. It's only then Dad dares to speak to me.

'So … how are you doing, Boo?' He says his nickname for me softly because he knows he's got to tread carefully.

Flooding with adrenalin, I begin to clear the table to avoid his gaze. 'Fine.'

'I hear you've got a new job.'

'Yep.'

'Come on, Betty,' Nerys says with gentleness.

'Come on, Betty what?' I explode. 'This man never showed any interest in us when we were growing up and now he's on his own he wants in. That's who he is, that's what he's like.'

'I know I wasn't a good dad to you … I still call you, once a week, every week,' he says to my stiff back where I've taken my position to wash up. Anyone who's close to me knows I'm not using my mobile. 'I want to make amends.'

I've turned on the taps and the Fairy Liquid is furiously bubbling like the blood in my veins.

'Well, you should've thought about that before you—'

Nerys leaps in. 'Mam has forgiven him, it's water under the bridge, he's said his sorries to her. She's moved on.'

'Aren't you heartbroken by what he did?' I say.

Nerys reaches over and stops the water which is dangerously close to overflowing.

'Because I am. Still.'

'This is what I'm talking about, Betty. You hold onto things.'

'Excuse me! I left as soon as I could get away from him. I left it all behind!'

'You took it with you, lovely girl. You escaped but it's still here,' she pats her chest.

It hits home that she's right. Nerys has stitched me up, but, I hate to admit it, she's given me the opportunity to have my say.

'Well, no wonder!' I slam the worktop to drown out the sniggers that haunted me as a girl. 'That man, our father, left us, left Mam, had it off with half the village and then had an affair with my teacher, my form teacher, when I was twelve years old. Everyone found out and every day of my life at school, someone would make a comment. "Is Miss Griffiths your mam? Did they do it in the classroom?" He crossed a line and it followed me everywhere I went.'

'Boo, I wasn't married at the time.' Dad finally reveals himself and I confront him face to face.

'You still think it's all right, don't you? You're still justifying it to yourself.'

He shakes his head. 'It was … I was wrong, I know that now.'

'But you think I should let it go, don't you? Like Nerys has. She got over it, so why can't you? I'm not her, though, am I? I was the oldest, you and Mam might have split up years before but she still had to go in and face the humiliation of parents' evenings and knowing people were talking about her yet again.' This is painful but weirdly pleasurable to finally tell him how he's hurt me. 'And … dear God, you have no idea how your shit show has affected my relationships with men.' Nerys takes my hand and even though I'm so cross she orchestrated this, I know she did it with good intentions. 'I sabotage them all, like I think I need to do it before they hurt me.'

Dad puts his head in his hands. Through his fingers he says, 'Don't you think I know all this? That I've caused so much pain?'

'Imagine if your granddaughters knew what you'd done. Although I bet there are a fair few others out there who do!'

He looks up, horrified, with piercing green eyes. 'I'm a lot of things but I'm not that. You two girls, you were the only kids I ever wanted, and believe it or not, you two have always been enough, more than that, everything. I stayed away because I didn't want to damage you anymore. Now you're home, for good, I'd like to try again.'

It's the first time he's ever displayed any kind of self-awareness about his behaviour. And while I'm nowhere near forgiveness or wanting to reconnect with him, it knocks out a brick in my defensive wall. It's unsettling because I hate him, don't I?

I decide to go, then and there, with his words hanging in the air between us, hoping he rereads them.

'I won't be here forever,' I say, getting my stuff. I mean it as a warning but there's a little girl inside of me issuing it as a plea to her daddy to rescue her.

Nerys comes with me to the door. 'I'm sorry I had to do this, presh.'

Sisters can be the most frustrating people in the world but they have the right, the insight and the history to help you confront your demons.

'You're not off the hook, Nerys,' I say, but then we cwtch. 'I understand why you did it. It's not you I'm pissed off with, is it? I've never said any of this to him before, I'm not sure I feel better but I do feel … some sort of release. Give those girls a bedtime kiss from me.'

I walk home and go over it all. There's light traffic but not even that gets to me because I'm so absorbed by what's just happened. Mam will be able to tell something's up but I don't want to burden her. So I keep strolling to try to make sense of tonight. It was a horrible moment when Dad appeared but it unlocked something in me.

I'm on my third lap of the high street when someone calls out my name.

'Betty? Betty Hopkins!'

It's friendly and so I turn around and my stomach flips. Brody Burns is waving at me.

'If you're doing a marathon,' he says, jogging up to me, 'you might need a drinks stop! Not that I'm asking you out.'

He steps back. 'Just if you fancied a catch-up?'

'Still a man of action, I see!' It's not flirting, it's just familiarity.

'I've wasted too much time in my life,' he sighs, perfectly comfortable wearing his heart on his sleeve. 'Great to see you out and about anyway.'

It's his way of showing he knows what happened to me and I'm touched. He holds up a carrier bag. 'My eldest only just told me he's got food tech tomorrow and we had no ingredients.'

His emerald eyes sparkle at me in the evening sunshine and the golden hour gives him a gorgeous glow. He's not as tall as I remember, just a head height above me, but he's as fit as he was, ageing well, and he's maintained his muscly physique. His short blond hair is styled and he's dressed smartly too, in a button-up short-sleeved shirt and chino shorts. I note he's in trainers not flip-flops, setting him apart from the Valleys boys who bare their toes at the first sign of sun in February. I feel about fourteen again. He was one of the few who didn't tease me about my dad. That's why I had a thing for him. It's then my face crumbles.

'I've just seen my dad.'

'Oh, Bet.' He touches my arm.

It feels so good to be understood. There's no need for me to elaborate because he knows my backstory. I wipe a tear and insist I'm all good.

'Want me to walk you home?' He always was so kind, he always had a depth to him, probably from the fact that he had three older sisters. It's lovely to see life hasn't ground him down.

'Thanks. But I'm fine.'

'Listen, here's my card,' he pulls one out of his wallet, 'pop the number on your mobile so you can't say you've lost it! Give me a bell anytime. Although you might have to shout up over my kids. Three boys make a lot of noise! Or pop by the rugby club, we're up there messing about most evenings and weekends.'

I take it and say goodbye, wondering if I will find the courage to pick up my mobile and call him. And I find I'm hoping I will. I miss Sami hugely, the distance makes it hard to stay properly connected, and Brody has an easy way about him. Surely I'm due a break? I tell myself off for being so self-pitying just as a breeze picks up my hair and thick warm drops of rain slowly start to fall.

## 12

### *Guy*

I drag myself awake from a nightmare I haven't had for years.

In that suspended space between sleep and consciousness, I'm trying to save my parents but they disappear behind huge falling trees. Edging closer to reality I realise the whoosh of wind and bullets of rain are, in fact, actually happening outside my window.

I sit up, my heart racing, drenched with sweat, blinking away the vivid dream that would come to me in night terrors as a kid.

It's as distressing now as it was then with the faceless figures of my fading mum and dad. Then Granny would soothe me back to bed. Now alone, I wonder why it's come back. Why now?

Perhaps it's been triggered by the ferocity of the weather that's rattling the panes of glass. Of course, I have no memory of the night my parents died. But when I was a teenager, I hunted down every bit of information about the Great Storm which hit the south-east of England in October 1987. I'd watch on repeat a forecast by weatherman Michael Fish who dismissed the fact that a hurricane was on its way against a cheery rainbow-coloured map of the UK. Technically he was right: the winds, which reached 122 mph in the UK, hadn't originated in the tropics, so it wasn't a hurricane – it was an extratropical cyclone. It was said to be the worst storm to strike England since 1703, with a severity that usually only occurs once in two hundred years. It left hundreds of thousands without power, ripped down fifteen million trees and claimed lives, including those of my mother and father.

I press down on my eyelids to try to unsee their smiling photo which was in every newspaper. Then I cover my mouth at the same time as a groan comes out of me, because suddenly I'm hollow with grief. I haven't had this feeling since … I don't remember, it's been so long. But time hasn't changed it and I recognise the familiarity of the intensity of loss; there's the disbelief that I'll never see them again, anger that I never knew them and a longing to have them a part of my life, to have got to know them. Granny and Grandpa would tell me stories to keep them alive for me but as I got older, I'd shut them down. How could I have a connection with a pair of strangers who became more distant with every birthday?

A boom from outside that's louder than the howling gale stops my navel-gazing. I swing myself round and put my feet on the wooden floor and remind myself where I am: in a B & B in Wales and, I check my watch, it's five past seven.

From my window I see someone battling to control what looks like a wooden panel of a small shed that's threatening to fly away. I throw my hoodie over my T-shirt and shorts and race down the stairs, almost bashing my head on the beams. I whip outside. A gust snatches my breath and, for a split second, I hesitate. I'm spooked. But the person I see is the landlady and I can't leave her to it. I step into the elements and stagger to her as the rain stings my face.

'Mrs Lewis!' My words are instantly drowned by the roar of a squall so I get to her side and grab the other end of what I now see is part of a chicken shed. Our movements are stiff, our hair is in our eyes, but somehow we make it across the field to a barn where we fall inside and recover. Immediately she cries out – because her hens have taken refuge inside.

'You clever girls!' she says, before she turns to me grinning, looking completely unperturbed about what's happened. 'I heard a racket so I came out and found the coop in pieces but I was getting blown to Ireland! If you hadn't come out I'd be in Dublin by now. I'll shut them in, they'll be safe here.'

She takes me by the arm, announcing she's in the mood for a big breakfast, then the wind pushes us back to the house where we shake ourselves dry in the kitchen like dogs.

'That's some storm, Mrs Lewis,' I say, feeling like I've been through the washing machine as she busies herself at the kitchen hob.

'I told you, son, call me Kay,' she says, over her broad shoulders. 'Right, so a full Welsh, is it?'

I wonder what on earth the difference is between that and a full English breakfast. Is there such a thing as poached leeks or dragon on toast? Somehow, even while Call Me Kay has her back to me and she's attending to the grill and three pans, she senses my confusion.

'It's the usual, bacon, egg, sausage, tomato and mush-rooms, all locally sourced and organic, bar the beans, which are Heinz, but they're from the village shop, so they count. But what makes it a full Welsh is cockles and laver bread, which is a kind of seaweed; it's lovely stuff,' she rattles off. 'And that wasn't a storm, it was just a bit of wind and rain,' she says, tying up her daffodil pinny.

Just a bit? I feel myself go pale at what it would have felt like in that cyclone of 1987. I can still feel the shock of being outside, as if I've been winded.

'Take a seat,' she says, pointing at the farmhouse table, 'won't be a minute.'

Two huge plates and a tower of toast are soon heading my way.

'This is a treat! I'm on my own, see, four kids have flown the nest, my husband Dewi passed away three years ago, so I enjoy the company. You can be mam,' Kay says, jabbing at the teapot and cafetiere with her knife. 'The tea is God's finest, Welsh Brew. I can't stand it, mind, went off it after my second was born. Been a coffee person ever since. I've had three cups already.'

No wonder she's a whirlwind. I do the honours and fill our mugs, then admire the spread.

I'm starving, I realise. I last ate well the night before last when I'd been coerced into staying with Gladys, having made the mistake of saying I hadn't booked anywhere. It was the least she could do after I'd made Bryn the smartest bear in Bethlehem. I could have taken a chance and toured the tiny village to find my long-lost relatives but they wouldn't know me from Adam – it made my mind up to bring Granny back to see them. The next morning I left Gladys and headed off through the breathtaking and sometimes breakneck mountain roads of the Brecon Beacons, stopping for views of peaks swallowed by clouds and a burger from a bikers' café. With bad-weather warnings on the radio, I decided to stop off near the M4 to make it easier to get home. Which just happened to be near Merthyr Tydfil. Near to Betty. I arrived too late for dinner, although Kay had offered to cook, but I shoved down a sandwich to get me through the night.

I go straight for the cockle-and-laver bread, which, with its oaty crust, resembles stuffing. And she's right, I can taste the sea in that mouthful.

'Delicious,' I say, 'this'll set me up for the day.'

She nods. 'Spare me those unsubstantial smoothies! If you're like me, chasing sheep on the hills, then you need something to line your rib cage. Can't nip back for a lettuce leaf when you're ten miles from home.'

That'll explain her no-nonsense resilience.

'So, just work you're here for?' Kay says, spreading her sourdough with at least an inch of butter.

I hesitate and then think why not tell her, I'll be gone tomorrow. 'Yes, but I had hoped to tie it in with meeting someone, a new friend, nothing untoward,' I say, at pains to emphasise it. 'But I've not heard back.' I'm a bit disappointed; Betty might be in London but also, these days, you have to be careful. 'It's easy to suggest something without thinking about how it'll be interpreted.'

'That's true, sad but true. Because anyone can see you're a big southern softy.' Her brown eyes are smiling but she definitely means it. 'What are your plans, then?'

'Well, I've got a long journey home tomorrow with a load of pick-ups, so I'm taking the day off. I'd like to have a walk and find a decent pub.'

'Sounds nice.'

'And if possible, if there's a shopping centre, I'd like

to get my granny a jigsaw of Wales; she's from here, you see, she misses it massively.'

She beams at the news of my genes. 'I knew there was something Celtic about you! Thought you were Hugh Grant to start with but now, now I look,' she peers at me, 'you're handsome and strapping, so it makes sense!'

No one has ever thought I was either Hugh Grant or Welsh; I'm pretty dark and I was mistaken for Portuguese on holiday in Lisbon once. But my host is very pleased and I wouldn't want to burst her bubble.

'Do you have any suggestions?'

'There's a load of leaflets in the lounge with various walks. My favourite is the waterfall loop. There's a lovely pub, The Prince of Wales, on the drive back here and when you head home you can call into Merthyr to get some souvenirs.'

'Great! Thanks, I think I'll do that, then.' I stretch my legs and take a deep breath as I relax.

'But you won't be able to today or tomorrow,' she says casually, dabbing her mouth with a napkin of the Welsh flag. 'Or the day after, I'd think.'

'Oh? Why not?' How can you shut a waterfall?

'It's just that we're flooded in.' Kay starts on another mouthful as if she hasn't just said we're flooded in. 'And the only road out is blocked by a landslide.'

'I'm sorry?' She can't mean it because she isn't looking worried.

'Probably be here for three days, I'd say. Entirely cut off from everything within five miles in every direction. We're in a valley, see.'

I freeze and then realise she's being funny. 'That's OK,

I'll hitch a lift to the waterfall on a passing inflatable unicorn, shall I?'

'I expect they'll be busy delivering sandbags and saving animals. More tea? Help yourself.'

I laugh out loud and this time she does stop eating.

'Don't believe me, then check your phone.'

I take it out of my pocket but see there's no signal. 'What's your Wi-Fi password?'

'No idea. But it's down. Everything always goes down when we get bad weather.'

'I'm beginning to think you're suggesting we're stranded, Kay,' I say, still unsure. I get up and look out the window and the fields just look a bit waterlogged, that's all.

'Go to the other side of the house,' she says, matter-of-fact, so I nip across the flagstones and then I see what she's talking about. 'Why do you think we called it Bryn Mawr Guest House? It means big hill; lucky for us we're higher up.'

She's right, it is higher here but I can see a lip of water that has swallowed the road. 'My God,' I say. 'This is insane. How come you're acting like this is no big deal?' My voice goes up a notch with panic.

'It isn't. It's life.'

'What about food? What if there's an emergency?'

'We have freezers, stocked to the armpits. Come in useful during the snow too. If there's any bother, a farmer will get a tractor out or the fire service comes. One of the two. Now come and sit down and finish your breakfast. We've got work to do.'

Her sense of calm is strangely reassuring. My panic goes, and there's no sign of my nightmare hangover either.

'So what do people do when they're flooded in?'

'Some daft beggars go kayaking or have a swim.'

'I mean about the damage?'

'Well, that's what we're going to do, you and me, help out.'

It seems the most natural thing in the world to agree to.

'We'll get our waders on. Dewi's are still in the garage so you can use them. We'll go and check on next door, half a mile away, then see if they need us at the landslide.'

'Right, of course. I hope it's all right for me to stay, then? I'll pay, obviously.'

'No you won't!' Kay gives me a hard stare and repeats it.

'Then let me do something. I'm quite handy, as it goes.'

She considers this and nods. 'There are a few things you could do. Now eat up. We won't be back till the afternoon, I wouldn't think; you've made a good effort so far, got your colour back, son. You were white as anything before.'

Her manner is so maternal it's like having my brow smoothed with a loving palm. 'I just had a bad dream, that's all.'

'Oh dear, dear,' she says so gently that it all comes out. 'The storm must've set me off. I lost my parents in one when I was a baby. In 1987.'

'That one where six of the seven oaks of Sevenoaks came down?'

'Yes.' I'm amazed she remembers.

'All over the news, it was,' she says, tutting. 'Well, no wonder it brought it back. And to think you came out and helped me anyway. I got you wrong, you're no softy. Look at you, you saved my shed, and you're six-foot-something gorgeous. That girl you wanted to meet, she's missing a trick.' She winks at me then touches my hand. 'Listen, lovely boy, you're safe here with me, right?'

The funny thing is, I feel it.

Within half an hour, the breeze has dipped and the rain has stopped and I'm hammering away at the shed while hens cluck around my muddy ankles.

The feeling of loss has gone, there's no resistance or doubt as to what I'm doing and where I am. It is utterly bizarre. I'm in a strange new world where I've had no choice but to surrender to the way things are. The devastation I'm used to, the ache for my family and the hole left by my best friend's betrayal, is no more; I feel a life-affirming happiness instead. What on earth?

# 13

## Betty

S he doesn't say much but at least Gloria the mannequin's icy stare isn't personal.

Ever since I gave her wig a brush we've reached an
understanding.

Megan, on the other hand, is showing no sign of
defrosting although she's really warmed to treating me
like I'm an idiot. I did ask for it but it turned out to be
a stroke of management genius – without her spelling it
all out, I would be lost. She knows the safety regulations
about selling used goods like the back of her hand, the
insurance details too, not to mention how to refill the
price-tag gun, the importance of remembering and dou-
ble-checking the size cube for clothes hangers and the
foibles of the volatile steamer. And she can drive, so I can
duck out of getting behind the wheel of the van.

Luckily, and this is how bad my phobia is, we've been
flooded in the last two days. Megan isn't in the shop
because her brother's and sister's holiday club has been
called off. With the water only now beginning to recede
and the landslide almost cleared, I couldn't possibly risk
the work vehicle. So I have an excuse not to even attempt
a collection today.

But I know how old folk worry. Megan took a phone

number but the lines are still down so I've decided to close for a couple of hours and head up to the lady's place to have a look to see what she's got.

'I'm off, then,' I tell Gloria, whom my former work best friend Sami has christened my new work best friend, much to his hilarity. 'I won't be long. Promise I'll glam you up later.' I've put an apron on her to cover her privates but there's something kinky-looking about it and I don't want a clientele of men in macs.

I lock up, my nose full of dust, but at least it's citrus-scented, thanks to the nuclear reactor air fresheners. I leave a note on the door saying, 'Back now in a minute' which is Valleys speak for 'at some point'.

Not that anyone will be banging on the door to get in. Trapped in the village, the Arcade has been buzzing with people coming to get essentials. But Life Goes On has been empty – when a crisis hits, there's not much call for Elvis LPs. It's meant I've been able to make a start on the mammoth task of reorganising what goes where: I've grouped like for like in different sections of the shop and kept back things that draw my eye for the window display. The shopkeepers are looking after their own: I've got bread from Nerys (who handed it over as a peace offering after the scene with Dad) and milk, spuds and leeks from the greengrocer's, Vic The Veg. Mam is stocked up so I'll give this lot to the lady.

In the high street, you'd never know we were cut off because the warmth of the summer has returned, burning off all the puddles. But as I go downhill out of the village, there are tidemarks of sludge, plastic bottles and unidentifiable bits of debris from the storm. It was a pretty bad one out in the sticks and I hear they're still stranded.

Kids here, though, are making the most of non-existent traffic by popping wheelies on the roads. It's only when I'm further along that I can see brown lakes in fields, half-submerged trees and sandbagged doorsteps. In the distance there's a car waist-height in water and someone using a stand-up paddle board to get about.

I find the lane where a huge barn has been converted into four properties with the de rigueur people carriers and transporters. This means there'll be a good haul for the taking. I bet there'll be a load of barely worn trends from last season, that's what people with money do. It makes them feel good and gives them an excuse to buy new.

An idea comes to me and it could help me get through to Megan. What if we put on a fashion show? Or, better, hold an auction? Jewels and treasure sparkle in my mind. I suddenly feel ashamed of my meagre food offerings for the lady. Whoever can afford to live in this stunning row will have heaving cupboards of Waitrose delights.

I knock on number one and up close this one is scruffier than the other three. They have smart arched double glazing and restored brick. This has small squares of thin glass, rotting window frames and crumbling walls. My heart sinks and I remembered Mrs Hughes mentioning grimy flea-bitten places – this is far more likely to be one of those.

A wizened lady two thirds my size opens up, holding onto a walking stick as gnarled as her hands.

'Yes? May I help you?' she says, in an unexpectedly polished accent which doesn't match her appearance. She has untamed white hair and is wearing a lilac jersey jogging set.

'I'm Betty from Life Goes On. You rang about a house clearance?'

'Yes, dear.' She raises her glasses, which are hanging on a chain on her chest, and looks past me. 'But you can't have risked coming here in a van, surely?'

'Not with the flood, no, but I'm here to say don't panic, we'll do it as soon as we can.'

'You came up here to tell me that?' The lady's bright blue eyes pop out at me.

'And to bring some food, just stuff for soup but we all need a hot meal once a day.'

'You must come in, then!'

'You sure?' I ask as my feet are muddy from the walk.

She insists so I take off my shoes and hold up the carrier.

'I'll take this through if you don't mind?' I don't want her struggling with a bag and a stick.

'Well, Betty, I must say, that's very kind. Please excuse me, I'm Helen, you must have a cool drink.'

'Only if it's no bother.'

'None at all. I can show you what needs collecting.'

She sets off at a snail's pace and I hang back, taking in the bare-brick walls and closed doors. It's sparse but it's clean and Helen seems chipper rather than vulnerable.

'Most of my things have already gone,' she explains, insisting I sit on one of two tatty wing-backed chairs by her kitchen log burner while she pours homemade lemonade.

'Where are you off to, then?'

'A flat, one of those serviced ones for retired people. I've lived here all my life.'

'Nearby or …?'

'Cardiff. I thought I'd make the most of my time left and live in the city. I've always wanted to. My children are appalled. They think I'm a little old lady. But the place I'm going, nearby there's a coffee shop, an art gallery, a little supermarket. Even a pub! I won't know I'm born.'

'That's exciting!'

'They think it's risky, I might get conned out of my life savings by a toy boy, or get mugged. But if I stayed here, I could fall over and not be discovered for days!'

'What about your neighbours? Don't they call in?'

'Too busy living their lives. I used to own the whole barn but bit by bit I've sold it off and I've decided now's the time.'

Helen carries a glass to me. I get up to get hers but she shakes her head. 'You've got to keep doing the little things or you sign your own death warrant.'

I take a swig and shut my eyes in bliss at the cold fizz and Helen continues.

'It's a brand-new flat, ground floor, my own little garden. No having to call out plumbers or wait for my children to sort out my Internet. It's all there, all maintenance included. Life's too short not to do what you want.' The 'you' settles on me. 'Things might seem risky but you have to go with your heart.'

She smiles at me and I see past the wrinkles and the stiff legs and fill up with admiration for her.

'So you're the new manager. I heard there'd been a change.'

It's not a surprise she knows; people love the village and feel a responsibility for keeping up to date with all its developments, no matter how small.

'I am, yes! I was supposed to have a week shadowing

the old boss but it didn't work out. So I'm kind of finding my feet really.'

'Thrown in at the deep end, then.'

'Yes, totally. It's a steep learning curve, there are a few issues.' My God, are there issues. 'But I need this job and I'm determined to do it.' If I nail it, it'll give me the confidence to re-enter London's atmosphere and it'll put a stop to my dad's nauseating bid to appease his guilty conscience.

'Well, that's a good attitude, isn't it.' Then she points at me with a shaking finger. 'You can't sit here all day, Betty, you're busy. I'll show you what I've got.'

We go back through to the hallway, her bedroom is on the left because she can't do stairs anymore, and she gestures for me to open up the next room. There is nothing but a sheet covering a pile of things, so we lift it back together – and my eyes go wide.

There's so much stacked up and it looks in good condition. No, not good, I realise, it's immaculate and top-quality vintage and some of it has to be antique.

'It's all original,' Helen says.

Greedily, my eyes run over the spoils. Clothes, belts, handbags, evening purses, furnishings, shoes, a standard lamp, art deco mirrors, jewellery ... my pulse is racing. I step forward and run my hands through the rail of dresses and women's suits, seeing labels through the dry-cleaner plastic covers and, beneath them, high-end heels with designer stamps. I'm dizzy. The decades are all there – the frills of the Eighties, flares of the Seventies, prints of the Sixties and cinched waists of the Fifties. Beyond them, costume gems sparkle at me from a bowl on a gleaming 1920s drinks trolley. There is a low rectangular retro sideboard without a scratch on it – imitations of those go for a song! A deep-brown Chesterfield leather sofa … a walnut Victorian ladies chair with a padded pink seat and curved legs … an oval dining table from the 1960s …

I'm staring at a fortune. But how am I going to sell it? How am I going to protect it? How can I get it in the shop? And I'm concerned Helen doesn't realise what she's giving away.

'You do know this is worth a lot,' I say. 'You realise you won't make a penny out of it. You could, you know.'

'I've led a charmed life. My grandparents were in the coal business. Those poor kiddies deserve the spoils of it.'

'Your children, don't they want any of this?' I'm incredulous.

'No. It's all junk to them. They prefer modern,' she says, raising her eyebrows.

I blow my fringe, my mind blown.

'I might have to get Life Goes On online, then!' I say, almost laughing. 'Go national!'

'Whatever you need to do.' Helen is serious.

I'm overwhelmed and come out in a sweat. But it's not the bad feeling I'm used to. This is naked excitement. 'We can make the necessary arrangements. Just quickly—' I can't help myself, reaching to an empire-line high-waisted white gown – 'was this …?'

'My wedding dress. The rising hemlines of the swinging Sixties didn't cut through to my world. You can touch it.' Helen nods at me in encouragement.

I run my fingertips over the long lace sleeves of ornate flowers. 'It's stunning.'

'And the veil, it's just behind …'

I sigh when I see it. Floor-length and so delicate. 'You must've looked beautiful.'

'I was twenty,' Helen says. 'Defied my parents' suggestions to marry someone they thought was more, shall we say, suitable. I was quite the rebel marrying Owen, he was in the mining business like us but he was a cleric, not grand enough.' She flashes a smile, letting me see for a second the daring streak that runs through her. 'But they knew really, we were head over heels in love and stayed that way for the rest of our lives together. I miss him terribly.'

She gazes at her simple gold wedding band and clasps her hands together as if she's holding him to her heart. In a flash, she's back in the room and thanking me.

'I'm very grateful for you coming today. Good people are hard to come by.'

I realise what an effect her appreciation has had on me. In London I'd be praised for finding budgets to cut, identifying promising succession managers and getting a buffet to a meeting on time. But this is a different feeling: it's like I've made a genuine difference to someone's day. Along with the freckles bursting on my nose and the gorgeous clear sky and air, I get to see that this experience doesn't have to be a drain on me. It may be short term but I'd be a hell of a lot happier if I embraced it. An auction could engage Megan too. Ultimately, if we can raise the cash, increase the footfall, it's a big if, then perhaps I can line her up for the job when I leave?

Helen has inspired me. What courage she's had, what courage she's got. What courage it takes to do something which those close to you don't believe in. Her words are taking root inside of me and they stay with me for the rest of my shift.

When I get home there's a letter waiting for me. Just seeing Guy's scrawl confirms what I know: he's a good person. I sensed it when I met him. And on paper we click. I can't explain how it's possible, I don't even really want to. Overthinking would ruin this special secret. I understand Nerys's suspicion, it means she cares. While she was right about my self-sabotage with my exes because of Dad, this communication is platonic. And the contents of this envelope will prove it.

I sneak up to my room, I don't want Nerys getting a scent of it via Mam. This thing I have with Guy is mine and mine alone, and somewhere I can escape and be my true self.

So I read his note. Immediately, I'm laughing at his Marie Antoinette wig joke – his self-deprecation is sweet and I love how he bigs up Brody Burns. Then I get a shock – he's in Wales and, oh God, he wants to meet for a cup of tea. This wasn't meant to happen. But then what did I think would? That we'd be pen pals and the subject of a face to face wouldn't crop up? I guess I assumed it'd fizzle out or at least if we did arrange to see each other, it'd be much further down the line. How can I see him when I've told him what I wish I am rather than the truth? But worse, I find myself wanting to see him. Do I dare? Am I being ridiculous? Yes, of course. Yet it's a nice change from being miserable. I mean, it'd only be a quick cup of tea. My sort-of-lies aren't a deliberate 'fake news' attempt to pull the wool over his eyes; they're just a harmless daydream version of myself. Nothing heavy will happen over a cuppa, it'll be a brief chit-chat and a laugh. And should he ask any awkward questions, I can skim over them, change the subject or maybe kind of explain that I'm not quite as far along as I said but working very hard on it. To be fair, he inspired it all, he believes in me, so it's not really a load of porkies. Is it? The temptation to see him makes my fingers tingle. It'll be a one-off, our paths won't cross again. I really like having him as a friend. A lunchtime meet, obviously nowhere near Hoffi Coffi, will be a tonic. Just the thought of it gives me a buzz and I want to grab this feeling by the scruff because I'm wholeheartedly sick of my new normal.

Good people are hard to come by, Helen said today. And like I decided earlier, I'm going to try to enjoy myself while I'm here so I may as well start with Guy.

To: therepairguy@googlemail.com
From: Bettyhopkins@gmail.com
Subject: Cuppa

Hi Guy,

As it happens I am in Wales at the mo!

As it happens, though, it's because we've been flooded in after a terrible storm and I couldn't have left if I wanted to. It also means the reception here is being temperamental so if this doesn't bounce back, I hope you get to receive it your end in time to meet.

Because I would love a cuppa. Let me know when you're free. Plenty of glamorous options available such as a Ye Olde Tea Shoppe (but the milk there is usually off) and a pub beer garden (currently shut due to water damage), so an al fresco one in the park would probably be best. I can bring take-outs or you could nip into the nearest Starbucks en route which is a mere thirty minutes away from here.

I have to say this is the strangest thing, to be writing to someone I met fleetingly. But it's a very nice strange thing.

Love,

Betty xxx


PS I don't know Tom Jones personally but my nan's sister's second cousin once went out with a bloke who went out with a girl who once snogged him after a gig at a workingmen's club in Pontypridd in 1960. So we're practically related.

PPS I can confirm I have had eyes on Brody Burns.

I've considered it and you're right, he could pull off a wig. But don't be so hard on yourself. The pair of you could form a Marie Antoinette—Rod Stewart supergroup.

# 14

## *Guy*

The floodwater's gone, the landslide's cleared and I'm a free man.

But I couldn't be more miserable. It turns out that being trapped in the muddy middle of Welsh nowhere with no contact with the outside world is better for the soul than a fortnight abroad. Before this I'd have put money on a sangria at sundown being the best way to recharge. Hard work seems to have been what I've needed.

The trouble is the end result is the same: I have to go back to real life. The one thing that's straightforward there is Granny. The rest, Sarah, Maud and Charlie, is complicated.

I've not had a chance to think about them until now as I walk to the village to buy Kay a thank-you present. I'm all packed and this is the last thing to do before I leave today.

The choice, it seems, is either stick or twist: attempt a reconciliation with Sarah, put my all into trusting her so that Maud has a father, and try to work things out with Charlie, or walk away quickly. That would mean I have to face up to getting a quick annulment rather than a long drawn-out divorce; we'd qualify no thanks to the painful truth that she was pregnant by someone else when we got married and our union was unconsummated. Then ditch Charlie and sell up.

Ripping off the plaster seems the right option when I'm here. Kay will laugh as I tell her how grateful I am to her for everything; she'll say, 'You're thanking me for what? For working for nothing, fixing fences, sluicing hallways and carrying sheep to safety?' But it's been about belonging and community. In Tunbridge Wells people don't always know their neighbours or the postie's name but here it's gut reactions and heart, with care and laughter during food deliveries, loans of dehumidifiers and tractors doing the prescription run.

But when I'm home, when Sarah contacts me, when she'll, say, send a photo of Maudie or I bump into them both, how will I be able to turn my back on love and responsibility?

Whatever happens, I just hope this experience has ramped up my resilience and courage.

The sunny walk to the village is bliss: the hedgerows are teaming with birds and butterflies and a mile on the decompression into normal life begins with cars and people.

I see a parade of shops but the high street has very little to it. There's a mini-supermarket, a chippie and a launderette. But I can hardly give Kay a battered sausage and washing powder. There's another option though; shoppers are going in and out of what looks like an undercover alleyway. I get closer and see it's an arcade with plenty going on.

With its peeling gates and blown Victorian lamp, it's shabby but well loved. Inside, it pulses with spirit. Yet as I wander up and down, there isn't anything instantly shouting gift shop. So I do a trawl of what's here. I buy Kay a bouquet from the greengrocer and two lots of chocolates and Welsh cakes from the sweet shop, so I can take Granny something back. There's a bakery and Kay has asked me to get some 'oolmeal', which, I assumed, was a delicacy but it turns out it's wholemeal bread.

It's a buzzy little place and I eye up a spectacular three-tiered showstopper that wouldn't look out of place under Paul Hollywood's nose. On impulse, I decide to get one for Kay.

'Is it possible to buy a whole coffee and walnut cake?' I ask the woman who's working the till while frothing milk and shouting orders into the kitchen.

'That's a bit greedy, that is,' she says, putting her hand on her hip.

I stare at her, taken aback. Then in a split second I realise she's joking.

'It's not for me, it's a present for someone.'

'That's all right, then. I've got one cooled out the back. Give me five and I'll ice it for you. That OK?'

'Perfect! A loaf of "oolmeal" too, please.' She nods and I feel like I've passed some kind of test.

'No problem! Let me get a pen, hang on.' She scrabbles inside her apron and produces one with a flourish. 'So your name?'

'Guy Slater.'

'I have to ask because I once gave the vicar a dubiously shaped cake that was meant for a hen do. Here's your order number.'

'Thanks,' I say, looking around but seeing all the tables are full. 'I'll pop back in.'

Next door there's a charity shop and I wonder if they have any decent jigsaws I could take back to Granny. I put my hand to the door and go to push when I notice something.

Jaded and joyless, the sign above says Life Goes On in faded hospital waiting-room green. Betty called her project by the same name – and she used initial caps in all three words. I suddenly wonder where I am. Kay and her friends simply call it the village. The cake receipt is in my hand so I take a look to see if there's an address. There is and it says Pant Bach. That's the same as Betty's village. Is this Betty's village?

Everything suddenly collides and stops.

Because I see her. I see Betty and she's behind the till.

What is she doing there? She's running her own high-end fashion business, isn't she?

What do I do? My fingers press harder against the door with excitement at seeing her. She's talking to a younger woman, her face is illuminated and engaged and her red hair dances as she speaks with her hands. Betty is even more vivacious than I remember. So many times in life you recall things and they disappoint you when you see them again. Not Betty. Then she moves and there's something off about it. Looking closer now, I notice too that she holds herself slightly differently to when we were hiding out that day in February. It's almost as if she's trying not to take up too much space. What's happened to her? I find myself longing to go inside and say hello.

But then I recoil. She never replied to my letter about meeting up. If she sees me now, she'll think I've tracked her down and am an absolute nutter. It's a horrific scenario – the truth that I've been stranded, and ignorant of where I am, will look flimsy, especially as I'll be so thrilled to meet her again. I feel sick at the thought of it and at the imbalance: that I've seen her when she's unaware of me. I back away, praying she doesn't look up.

I put my head down, go and collect the cake and speed-walk home, still in shock. My chest is thumping – I need to put as much distance as I can between Betty and me. I feel discombobulated when I hand the goodies to a gushing Kay but she thinks I'm different because I've got my work head back on.

'You take care, son,' she says, as I hug her goodbye, 'you're welcome back any time, you're one of us now.'

I plug in my phone, which I'd left to die because there was no signal. I'd given up on Betty anyway and I was too busy and engaged with life to even think about charging it. Then I pull away from the farmhouse, going over the letters between myself and Betty, wondering why she'd be involved with the charity. Maybe she's a volunteer or she was just shopping. But it didn't look it – I'm wildly overthinking this but the shop window with its energetic display of 'Summer Lovin' ', with a nod to *Grease*, and a yellow polka-dot dress, shouted Betty all the way. Have I misunderstood what she said about being a designer with her own label? I don't even go near the thought that she's lied to me – she seemed honest and up front in person and, anyway, why would she make something up? There has to be an explanation. Unless I've been completely gullible and lost my mad-woman detecting skills.

I climb up out of the valley onto the dual carriageway and see signs for the M4. My mobile starts going berserk with notifications. What am I doing, just listening to them go off? My head is in the clouds. I could be missing out on work or something important, an emergency, for God's sake. I'm angry with myself for getting carried away and thinking I had some kind of epiphany after mopping up filthy water.

I park in a lay-by and begin to scroll through a mass of messages and listen to voicemails from clients, plus one from Granny asking me when I'll be back, then I check my inbox which has seventy-four emails.

I don't believe it when I see her name. My stomach actually flutters. Then it lurches when I think somehow Betty might have seen me earlier and it's a warning to back off. I open her email with total dread, cringing with anticipation. But it's the opposite of that – I double-check, the date is two days ago – she's up for a cup of tea.

My heart triple-somersaulted at just the sight of her. And it's doing it again. Then I'm belly laughing at her tenuous Tom Jones joke.

I'm suddenly torn between what to do. She wants to see me, she's just down the road. Yet something feels strange about this Life Goes On thing. Am I asking for more bullshit if I turn around? Should I just carry on and go home and focus on what's waiting for me?

Resilience and courage, that's what I've hoped I've got out of this trip. Now's the time to find out if I've learned anything at all.

I turn on the ignition and pull out. I know exactly which direction I want to go in.

# 15

## Betty

Megan was absolutely delighted by my idea of holding an auction at Life Goes On.

By which I mean she didn't say no or roll her eyes. She's also following the outline of my rejigged shopfloor plan without a word of complaint, helping me to organise sections that run logically from women's clothing to menswear, teens to kids, toys to music and homeware to bric-a-brac, then books. And as for my first attempt at window-dressing, she hasn't slagged it off. Yet. It's not bad: the theme is 'Summer Lovin' ', where Gloria is Olivia Newton John in a full-skirted yellow polka-dot dress and 1950s shades with a diner-style backdrop made from a hanging sheet glue gunned with vinyl, and by her feet are various tenuously related items including a popcorn machine, a blow-up guitar, strappy silver stilettos and a pastel-blue dinner service set. But beyond that, I get more conversation out of Gloria. Still, it's progress and the atmosphere is more slow thaw than deep freeze. On reflection, anything faster would probably freak me out anyway.

How did I manage to spin so many plates when I was at Banta? It was effortless dealing with figures and reports, firefighting problems and managing people and projects at a multi-million pound company with thousands of staff. We take mere pennies by comparison here and it's just me and Megan, yet my brain is fried at the end of each day.

Sami says I need to be patient – it'll all come back to me as I get into my stride again. But it seems a long way off. My confidence is low because I have to keep asking for help from Megan, and when I walk home, everything hurts. I'd cover miles every day in London without getting a blister but a fraction of that now leaves my feet sore and aggravates my pelvis. I know it could be much worse – some people in my shoes are on long-term pain medication, suffer urinary problems and can't return to work.

I remind myself how lucky I am as I serve a lady who is thrilled at finding a cross-stitch kit of Barbra Streisand. The personal stuff isn't helping – the scene with Dad has brought back the disgrace I felt as a kid, and I overheard Mam talking to her fella about them 'getting closer' but they couldn't live under the same roof while I was here. It breaks my heart that I'm in the way. Last, but obviously very least, Guy never replied to my email.

I hear a ping from the work laptop and leap on it just in case. But it's Sami coming back to me after I filled him in on my foolishness last night.

To: Bettyhopkins@gmail.com
From: samirkhan@banta.com
Re: Oh God What Have I Done?

Can't believe he hasn't got back to you! The cheek! His loss, hot stuff. Maybe it's for the best – you don't

actually want to meet him if you've been feeding him
pie in the sky, do you? Imagine how awks it'd be if
you have to tell him the truth. Love you xxx

My toes instantly curl. Why did I think it was a good
idea to lie? I mean, it never felt dishonest because it was
about wanting to be who I was, where my destiny was
headed. But in the cold light of day it's clearly unhinged.
I'm wondering, too, if it actually is another act of self-
sabotage? I can't face Nerys being right twice. I physically
droop when I realise what a waste of time and energy it
is writing to a married man with a baby. What is there to
get out of it? I'm better off accepting he was there when I
needed him but it would be idiocy to continue it. It looks
like Guy has already come to that conclusion.

I look up when I hear a kerfuffle outside. The door is
open – it's my number one non-negotiable to improve
ventilation – so I can hear a child crying and there's
Megan, who's on her lunch-break. I go closer, wondering
if she's going to need some help, and I see a little boy
with black curls being comforted by a man as Megan
looks in her bag for something. The scene is so tender,
they have to be father and son. The dad is talking gently,
crouched right down at his level, and he's dabbing at the
lad's knee, which must be bleeding. I get a lump in my
throat out of nowhere – there are good fathers out there
when my own deserted us.

Megan showed me where the medical kit is so I grab it
from the storeroom and wave it at her from the shop door
because I can't leave it empty on a busy Saturday. She
takes it from me, uses an antiseptic wipe to clean the boy
up, then pops on one of those industry health-and-safety

compliant blue plasters. Then the boy gets up, his tears dry, and goes to hold her hand. Is that man the father of her twin brother and sister? If that was the case, wouldn't he be bringing them up rather than her?

'Thanks so much for catching him,' Megan says as the man stands up and I realise he was just a Good Samaritan. 'He'd shot off on his scooter and I couldn't keep up.' She looks quite pale, and the adrenalin of the chase comes out because she turns to me to explain. 'I popped home for lunch, my cousin's there with the kids today; they walked back in with me to go to the sweet shop. Here she is now with Nancy.'

Megan bends down and gives Alfie a peck, then whispers something in his ear, which makes him giggle before he goes off to his sister, who's as cute as he is.

'Be good, you two! I'll bring chips home for tea,' she says, blowing kisses. 'Love you.'

I feel as if I've had the tiniest of insights into Megan's life, how hard it must be for her to bring up two children when she's still one herself. She walks past me, dropping a quiet thank-you for the first-aid bag, and I wait to follow her in to give her some space. She's up against so much, this young woman; anyone can see how she adores those children and how they must treat her as a mum rather than a big sister. I've been thinking her silence is down to me; it must be, partly, when she so wanted my job, but there's a possibility, a real chance, she's being pressed down by the weight on her small shoulders.

I've got to help her, I think, when I get up from resting on the frame of the door.

But suddenly I freeze. Because I've just been hit by two things: the man who dabbed Alfie's knee used a pink hankie and when I leaned out of the shop to give her the kit, I got a waft of citrus. We have lemon plug-ins but they're not that powerful to extend beyond the doorway. Then I berate myself for even going there. What is this madness?

I shake my head and give myself a talking to then look up. And I'm staring my madness in the face. Right in the beautiful face.

'Hello, killer queen!' he says all bold but his shy smile gives him away.

Everything around him rushes back and out of focus and it's only him I see. His height, his olive skin and those dark-chocolate eyes. I feel giddy, my heart swells and a million shivers run their fingers up my spine. The obvious questions, what he's doing here and why, go off like popcorn in my head but I can't quite catch them.

'The Repair Guy!' It's all I can say as a flush of heat sweeps across my chest. How can it feel so familiar, yet so exciting?

'This is the strangest thing,' he says, quoting from my email, which leaves me speechless. 'But just so you know, I'm not a weirdo.'

I nod, appreciating him for ruling it out when it could look like it because he's turned up out of the blue. But that's manners for you because I have never told him to leave me alone.

'I was staying up the road, I got flooded in.'

Two nods from me.

'I came up here first thing this morning and I saw you, but I didn't know then that you'd been in touch.'

Then three.

'And that would've been odd for both of us. So I left

and was on my way home when my phone started going off, because it was being charged and I finally had some reception.'

I roger all of that, knowing how dubious coverage is here and at the same time I have the urge to laugh at this preamble.

'And then I thought—' he hesitates – 'oh … and now I'm saying this out loud I'm worried I actually do sound like a weirdo.'

The twitch of my amusement grows into a smile.

'But I thought that as I was here I might as well pop in.' He grimaces, he's doubting himself now.

I find some words to save him. 'Because if you hadn't, you'd have had to make a very long return trip just for a cup of tea.'

'Exactly,' he says, pleased I'm joining in. 'But if this isn't fine, then that's fine …'

'No, it's fine.'

He lets out a long breath of tension and grins.

'I've never met anyone "practically related" to Tom Jones.' His vital side, the one I saw in that bunker, comes out to play. But it's gone again as he composes himself. 'Anyway a cup of tea would be lovely.'

How can a man his size be so sweet? His wife is one lucky woman.

'I can't wait to hear about you and everything …' He gestures at the shop and I suddenly want to puke. In all the delight of seeing him, I completely forgot where I was. My panic alerts my imagination and all of a sudden I'm talking.

'Everything's great! I'm here mentoring for the day. You know, having made it and all that, I wanted to give something back and charity shops don't always have the right "look" to them, if you know what I mean?'

Guy nods deeply. 'I thought it'd be something like that. When I saw you earlier I assumed you worked here! But of course, why would you? You're a designer!'

I let out a laugh that goes on a fraction too long. Then, nightmare. Megan calls me because Life Goes On is filling up.

'I'm going to have to go, Guy. Are you heading home now?'

He frowns. Even though I'm squirming because I could so easily be rumbled and I'm faced with what the hell I'm going to say to him if we do have a cuppa, I am crushed because, obviously, he can't hang around when he's got a long journey ahead of him and a family to get back to. But then he scratches his nose and looks bashful.

'Um ... funnily enough, I'm not, no. I've just remembered I have a job to do that I couldn't finish so I'd be staying anyway.'

I manage to resist punching the air. 'Your wife won't mind? As long as you won't miss your baby too much!'

He looks up to the ceiling – it's clear how hard it is to be apart from them. 'It's just something you get used to,' he says misty-eyed with an adorable wobble in his voice.

'I'm off tomorrow, are you free?' I say. I don't suggest tonight because I'm treating Mam and Cliff to a Chinese. 'Although if you're working ...'

'I'll sort it. Shall we go next door?' He points at Hoffi Coffee. Where my sister would see and know I went against her advice. Thankfully, it's not open on Sundays.

'It's shut. Such a pity.' Then I have an idea because I

don't want anyone getting wind of this. 'How do you feel about flasks of tea? We could go on a walk.'

'I have very positive feelings towards flasks of tea,' he says, breaking out into a grin. 'What about – there's a waterfall hike near here, I'd love to do that.'

'Yes!' I haven't hiked for years. My hobble will turn into a limp. And I'm still not happy being in a car. But how can I say no to this man who is so kind, decent, empathetic, sensitive and funny and ... attractive. I can take the opportunity to explain myself to him then.

'Great! Email me tonight to sort the details.'

He ruffles his hair and I go hot. This isn't what friend-ship feels like. I put it down to the surprise. Yet I don't want to say goodbye. But then I can't risk him finding out at this moment that I'm not some worthy philanthropist.

So what do I go and say? Something from the heart, that's what, that reflects the marvel of us meeting again and our mutual joy.

'This is the strangest thing.'

'But it's a very nice strange thing,' he says, stepping backwards.

I watch him walk away. He has an easy lope that begins in his broad shoulders and drifts down his hips and, yes I admit it, peachy backside all the way down to his muscular calves and sure feet. I get the urge to chase him to tell him I may have embellished the facts. But then I recall his reaction to the idea that I worked at Life Goes On. He didn't scoff, he doesn't seem to look down his nose at anyone, but he said he thought it was un-likely. I feel a mix of shame that I've hidden it from him and a jolt that he believes I'm what I want to be. He'd be disappointed – and what would he make of it when I said he'd inspired my success? Sorting through bin bags and gagging on the contents would be an insult to him. Of course, it is a big deal that I'm even out of the house, but would he understand? He's given me so much – he's given me the fuel to come up with an exit strategy to get back to London. I just don't know what to do.

Enjoy it for what it is, I decide, ignoring the fact that I'm crazily attracted to an unavailable man and that could land me in a whole heap of trouble.

To: therepairguy@googlemail.com
From: bettyhopkins@gmail.com
Subject: Flask of tea

Dear Guy,
   Lush to see you today! The forecast looks amazing tomorrow, still up for a flask of tea?
   Love,
   Betty xxx



To: bettyhopkins@gmail.com
From: therepairguy@googlemail.com
Re: Flask of tea

Dear Betty,
   The walk, definitely. The flask, that depends.
   Best,
   Guy



To: therepairguy@googlemail.com
From: bettyhopkins@gmail.com
Re: Flask of tea

On what? Is there a Code of Flasks of which I am unaware? Is this an English thing? Or a Repair Guy thing?
   Yours,
   Mystified xxx

To: bettyhopkins@gmail.com
From: therepairguy@googlemail.com
Re: Flask of tea

Dear Mystified,

The Code of Flasks stipulates that a flask should:

a) be metal and not plastic, otherwise it tastes of grey and the 1980s;

b) contain black tea with separate vessels for milk and sugar/sweetener;

c) be warmed first with hot water for maximum heat retention;

d) be big enough for at least two cups each.

Hope that clarifies the situation.

Regards,

The President of The Code of Flasks


To: therepairguy@googlemail.com
From: Bettyhopkins@gmail.com
Re: Flask of tea

Er ... obvs. What kind of monster do you take me for?


To: bettyhopkins@gmail.com
From: therepairguy@googlemail.com
Re: Flask of tea

Thank God. Resorting to the Conciliation and Arbitration Service over a Code of Flasks dispute is a route I very much did not want to go down.

Would you like a picnic too? Any special requests?
Also, will we be swimming?
(I refuse to crack a joke about packing my Speedos.)


To: therepairguy@googlemail.com
From: Bettyhopkins@gmail.com
Re: Flask of tea

I love a picnic. I'm veggie so feel free to choose from
anything at the crap Pant Bach SuperShopper such as
a two-day-old baguette, a packet of vinyl cheese slices
and an enormous bag of crisps (get two of those). Two
weeks ago it was rumoured they had started stocking
hummus so keep an eye out.

There will definitely be swimming. If not
intentionally, of the horizontal kind, then absolutely
the vertical kind because you can walk behind the
waterfall and if you don't want to do that, then how
can we be friends?

(Even the word S****** makes me feel sick. For
health and safety reasons, they are only to be referred
to as budgie smugglers.)


To: bettyhopkins@gmail.com
From: therepairguy@googlemail.com
Re: Flask of tea

Wait! What?
We can walk behind a waterfall? As in stand on a
ledge and there's a curtain of water? That will be the

fulfilment of a childhood dream. I'm serious.
    (Said dream has never featured budgies.)


To: therepairguy@googlemail.com
From: Bettyhopkins@gmail.com
Re: Flask of tea

Yes, yes and yes.
    It is very cool.
    (Good.)


To: bettyhopkins@gmail.com
From: therepairguy@googlemail.com
Re: Flask of tea

I am so excited. What time shall I pick you up?


To: therepairguy@googlemail.com
From: bettyhopkins@gmail.com
Re: Flask of tea

Me too. 9.30 a.m.?


To: bettyhopkins@gmail.com
From: therepairguy@googlemail.com
Re: Flask of tea

On the dot. I know where you live. Oops, that makes

me sound like a gangster. What I mean is, I have your address.

To: therepairguy@googlemail.com
From: bettyhopkins@gmail.com
Re: Flask of tea

You forget I saw your 'killer instinct' when I found you hiding at paintballing.
   See you tomorrow.

To: bettyhopkins@gmail.com
From: therepairguy@googlemail.com
Re: Flask of tea

Good night.

# 16

## *Guy*

I hear it before I see it and the thundering sound of the waterfall echoes my heartbeat.

My pulse is working hard already from the heat and the hike. But it's mainly from being with her.

Betty is leading the way beneath a canopy of trees down steep rocky steps which are fringed with ferns. We're taking it slow, as we did in the van because Betty had a bout of travel sickness – she was white and nauseous but insisted she was fine to do the walk.

And so far she's looking good. More than good. Because everything about her is perfect: when she turns to me to point out something or make a joke, my stomach flips. Her bluebell eyes crease with amusement, her huge open smile uncovers a drop-dead-gorgeous gap in her front teeth and her hour-glass figure stops me – and time – in our tracks. She was 100 per cent the Londonista when I first met her but there's something different to her now, as if she's part of this environment of a million shades of greens and browns. Her long hair is the colour of berries. Her creamy skin is kissed with freckles and her floating sage slip dress makes her look like some kind of woodland nymph. I'm so bewitched I nearly bump into her when she pulls up at the start of a natural pathway.

'After you,' she says, stepping aside to offer me pole position for the final descent. 'You should see it first.'

'Tell me, what's its name again?' I say, raising my voice over the roar of water.

'*Sgwd yr Eira.*' I could go into raptures over Betty's rich tone, there's a huskiness too. Carried away, I hear myself repeating her.

But while I'm knee deep in the romance of the Welsh language, she's snorting at me.

'What?' I say, an absolute sucker for her teasing.

'It's the way you say it. *Squiddy-Eye-raaah.*' And just in case I don't get it, she emphasises the 'rah' bit again, like I'm some raging toff.

'That's how you said it!'

'Stick to the English, lovely boy,' she says, hamming up her accent. 'It translates as the "Falls of Snow". You'll see why.'

It almost comes out: when she visits me in Tunbridge Wells, I'll have some fun at her expense. That's how easy it is to be around her. But what am I thinking? Why would someone as driven and talented and spectacular want to visit me? I know how pleased she was to see me but she hasn't got a minute spare, what with designing, mentoring and travelling between Wales and London. We're getting on now, but that means nothing. When I'm gone, when it comes to priorities, I'll be way down the list. Yet if we are to keep in touch I need to tell her about Sarah, Maud and Charlie. Soon. Like today. But I need to do it carefully – breaking it to her now when we're in the sticks and alone might freak her out, like I'm some fantasist and she could feel unsafe. I never actually wrote that I'm loved up, it's more that she presumed it, but I do need to correct her at the earliest opportunity. Inevitably, though, she'll pity me and that'll upset the dynamic. But pity or not, I have to tell her. Just not yet. I let myself fall back into the moment as Betty waits for me to move.

Like a fairy tale, it's spongey underfoot from a thick blanket of pine needles, ivy trails hang like curtains from trunks furry from moss, the humid air is steamy and shards of August sunshine fall in hazy strips. Then as I come to the clearing, the waterfall suddenly appears like it's on a cinema screen as if Disney did nature.

Wide and tall, the torrent thrashes down fifty feet like a blizzard of sparkling snowflakes. Mist rises where the water crashes on the green plunge pool and then I see the ledge behind it and I'm so excited I feel like a kid.

'What do you reckon, then?' Betty says beside me and the fuzzy sensation of us almost touching makes the hair on my arms stick up.

'I'm going to tell everyone I know how rubbish Wales is. So no one else comes and it stays like this. How have we got this to ourselves?'

'Oh there's plenty more about. The waterfalls where they filmed one of the Batman films are up the road; that's the one that gets all the visitors, though I've never been myself.'

'*Batman*?' My voice goes high as if I'm a seven-year-old dressed in a cape with my underpants over my trousers.

'They filmed *The Dark Knight Rises* at Henrhyd Falls because it's even bigger, nearly ninety feet,' Betty says, casually, while I gawp like a comic geek. 'I'd race you to the ledge but I'm no mountain goat. Feel free to go ahead.'

There's no way I'm dashing off. 'Let's do it together.'

We kick off our trainers, dump the backpack and silently pick our way across the stepping stones. I go first, testing the rocks, and as we get closer, cold water foams at our toes making them more slippery. As we fight to keep our balance, thrown too by the tremendous wall of sound, our hands find one another, both at the same time and fitting perfectly. We don't let go of each other when we reach the ledge and I'm in such a trance I only realise how wet we are already when I see drops of spray dotting her nose and cheeks. It's impossible to speak so we pull 'wow' faces and walk the length of the cave. The energy is colossal; it's like we're in a car wash but with no windscreen. My skin stings, my eyelashes are drenched and I see Betty start to laugh. I join in, and my open mouth gets a battering. Our eyes meet and suddenly the mood has changed to something different altogether; it's as if we're alone in our own private shower, shielded by the falls. Our clothes are stuck to our skin, outlining our naked shapes, we're joined at the hip in this confined space and we can feel each other's sultry breaths.

I reach out my hand and move a tendril of her silky red hair from her eyes, and we drift into each other, feeling the pull of our chemistry, which melts into desire as our lips meet.

Except, of course, that last bit doesn't happen. And I see her shiver. What am I thinking? The water and the cave are chilly so, quickly, I tug her to the end and we find a sun-bathed rock where we can dry.

'You warmed up yet?' I ask her.

'I wasn't cold.' Betty is gazing at where we've just been. 'Not once.'

'You shivered!'

She looks down quickly and I gulp. Was she shivering because she felt what I did? Could that imaginary kiss have happened between us? Is she, like me, conflicted by what's happening here, that we want to be friends and yet we can't deny there feels something beyond? I need a reboot and quick. We have to get across the pool either the long way around the sides or … I'm soaking already, so why not? I slide down into the water, and almost hear my longing hiss as I cool down.

'Guy!' Betty says, wide-eyed. 'You should've brought your budgies!'

I hoot with laughter; the aftershock of the cold has turned into euphoria. 'I'm just going the most direct route for a cup of tea! Come on! I can touch the bottom. It's glorious!'

Betty hesitates. 'What's it like?'

'Freezing!' I start to swim in a circle when I hear a splash behind me.

She's in and gasping and giggling and coming towards me with the broadest smile.

'This is mad!' she says and we bob for a couple of minutes, asking each other if this is all really happening, before reality hits. 'I didn't bring a towel. Did you?'

'Nope,' I say, as we enter the shallows and shake ourselves off. 'But I have got some two-day-old baguette we could use?'

In a patch of sunlit ground we devour our picnic of crisps (two packs), hummus, grapes and breadsticks and I inform Betty she has satisfied the Code of Flasks for a cracking couple of cuppas. Then, still damp, we head back the way we came; Betty is slower now and every so often her gait changes, as if she's in pain.

'You OK?' I ask, not wanting to make it obvious that I've noticed it.

'Fine!' she says but when I find a big stick to help her balance, she doesn't refuse it.

I should have got myself one because when we're on the last stretch that leads to the car park, down an uneven slope of scree. I slide and land on my right ankle. Betty's there, her arm round me, asking what's up.

'It's nothing!' I say, but it isn't.

'Sure?'

Even just flexing my toes makes me wince. 'Honestly, I don't think we need to involve the air ambulance.'

It's me with the hobble now as we go hand in hand, which works amazingly as a painkiller. We get to the van but when I press the clutch down, my ankle screams.

'Betty, there's no way I can drive with this.' I turn to her. 'Not safely. If it was just me, then I'd have a go but ...'

In less than a second, her face has gone from glowing to panic-struck and she holds her throat and shakes her head.

'I can't,' she announces. 'No way. Absolutely not. We'll have to ... maybe I can ring my mam. Are you with the AA?'

'I'm not sure I'm covered for a twisted ankle.'

'Give me your phone.'

'Mine's got no service. Where's yours?'

Betty's shoulders crumble and then they shake and she's heaving for air.

'Hey, hey, Betty, what is it?' I start to inhale and exhale slowly and she joins in, calming down after a while.

In a small voice, she tells me about an accident when

154

she was run over by a man who died at the wheel. 'I haven't used my mobile since ... I wasn't paying attention, I was on it and that's when I got hit. Never mind the police report that said I had checked the crossing was clear. I should've kept checking. Not that they said I'd have had a chance to get out the way. But still, what kind of idiot crosses a road on their phone?'

Now I come to think of it, I've not seen her with one today, nor yesterday. It's so unusual for people not to carry them, especially on a day like this for the obligatory selfies and Insta pics. Odd too when she was stuck to hers that day we met.

'And being in a car never bothered me before.'

'So it wasn't travel sickness ...'

'No. And driving in London traffic never bothered me, but now ... I don't want to, in case I do the same thing to someone else.'

I'd be buggered without wheels and a phone. But this is where her trauma shows itself in something so essential to having a normal life, to being free.

'You know you won't, though, don't you?' I say gently. 'Or at least the chances are miniscule.'

'But it happened to me,' she says.

'So in all probability it will never happen to you again. When did it happen?'

'A few months ago,' she says. 'I got a fractured pelvis and ... you might've noticed it still shows every now and again with a bit of a limp.'

'A limp? That's nothing compared to mine!' It's a moment of light relief and we share a watery-eyed smile.

'But it's no wonder you're so shaken up. Crash scenes are always really unsettling. How humans survive the impact ... like, the day of paintballing, when we left and went to the tube, there was a car that was completely totalled. People were just driving past like nothing had happened; we walked off too and forgot about it. Isn't that awful that someone somewhere is probably still affected by it?'

Betty's breathing quickens. I've brought it all back to her, I'm such an idiot.

'Listen, you weren't to blame when you were run over. How could you be at fault? Holding onto bad stuff is so pointless. Letting go takes less effort.' It's a revelation to myself – perhaps I can do that too?

'The Repair Guy,' she says, sniffing, 'fixes people as well as stuff.'

'Hardly! Not my area!'

I suddenly think this might be the time to tell her. But then I'd be taking this away from her and I don't want to make it about me. Yet the temptation is there because it feels a leveller; I don't want her to think she's alone in her damage.

Be brave, I think, and I draw a breath, beginning to walk the path towards the truth. 'Holding onto this, here, now, walking behind a waterfall, that's the thing to hold onto, isn't it? That's what I want to do, believe in the wonderful, not the awful, that's how I want to live my life because—'

But Betty has swung the passenger door open and is walking around the bonnet and is now at my window.

'Out you get,' she says, determined, 'come on, meter's running.'

It would be selfish of me to offload now when she's found the courage to do this. I shift across the seats.

'I'm insured, right?' she says, getting in.

'Yep.'

'Right. Belt up.'

I don't know if by that she also means for me to keep quiet, but I do because she needs to do this uninterrupted. She rolls the seat forward, tilts the wing and rear-view mirrors and revs up. Easing the van out with an iron grip, Betty puffs her cheeks and keeps it together – not just when she turns onto the country lane, or when a pair of bikers overtake her, or when she has to turn right across a road, and not even when she comes across a zebra crossing. She's meticulous and careful all the way and only when she's turned off the ignition and we're back at hers does she relax with a huge sigh.

But then she's got her hands in the air. 'Why did you let me come here? How did I think you were going to get home? I'm so stupid! Don't worry, I'll drive you, then I'll walk back.'

'You're not going to believe this, Betty, but my ankle feels a bit better.' It genuinely does, as it happens.

Her head twirls round in a flash. 'You what? Have you been faking it? Did you do this on purpose?'

'No!' I cry, 'I wouldn't do that!' I do my best offended frown. 'But anyway, look what you just did!'

Her brow lifts and she nods at me slowly then stops. 'But it was more what you did, what you said.'

'You're the one who drove.'

'You were wrong,' she says softly, twisting her body to mine, leaning against the headrest. I do the same and it feels so intimate it's like we're looking at each other from a pair of pillows. 'Fixing people is definitely in your skill set.'

She laughs – she's empowered and she's beautiful. I hear thunder in my ears but this time there's no waterfall, it's entirely the booming of my heart.

I'm desperate to share myself with her. If only I had more time. But I have to get back to Kay's for supper. And then I'm leaving first thing tomorrow. Now is not the right time. Betty is bursting with happiness – there's no way I want to bring her down with my sob story.

# 17

## *Betty*

'You did what?' Nerys says as I peel back the plastic on the cucumber with a firm stroke.

My grip instantly unfurls at her disgusted tone, which is accusing me of committing an act of the highest indecency. I prepare myself for one of her hairdryer moments: man has tried and failed to take on her indignant chest as she draws for breath. Over the years Devoted Steve and I have worked out it's always better to let her blow herself out.

'You agreed to a cup of tea,' she begins, with nostrils flaring and hand on hip as she turns her kitchen into a courtroom. 'He turned up without warning in person. You went into the wilderness with him, a stranger, a married one.' Her other hand is jabbing a finger at me with each point. 'By yourself, without telling anyone, and you swam in your clothes. And he has a baby. My God, Betty, what's got into you?' Her palms rise towards the ceiling, she's at the splayed-fingers section of her outrage.

She exhales like a dragon, then goes back to the salad, albeit with some energetic chopping. I think she's done, so I'm safe.

'He also cured me of my driving phobia, you missed that bit.'

It turns out she isn't done, and I'm not safe.

'Because he faked a twisted ankle!' she cries, waving her knife in the direction of her framed Hashtag Be Kind poster. 'Maybe he's a fake, Betty!'

'Nerys! You're going way over the top.' It's my turn to get my hair off.

'Am I now? Am I? Right, let's get Sami on speaker-phone, let's see what he has to say.' She gets her mobile out and punches the screen.

'How have you got his number?'

Nerys rolls her eyes at me. 'Remember the time, or should I say times, when I tried to call you about Mam's back, Poppy's birth and Daisy's colic? When you didn't answer because you were in meetings and then you gave it to me so I could get him to get hold of you in emergencies?'

It's a horrible flashback to how consumed I was in London and it means she wins this tussle.

'Nerys!' Sami says when he picks up. 'How are you, darling?'

'Great! The sun's shining so we're having a barbecue, just getting prepped.'

'Nice! How's Steve and the girls?'

I go slack-jawed at their chit chat – it makes me feel like an eavesdropper.

'Yes! We're all fine, presh, it's just a friends-and-family barbie.'

This sounds ominous – I thought it was just us, so I butt in, 'Dad's not coming, so who is?'

'Broody Buns!' She claps her hands and I am fuming. 'He's the local hottie, Sami.'

'Why do you keep interfering?' I hiss, while being

grateful that I've put on some make-up and a violet polka dot halter-neck tea dress that gives me a waist because I do have standards.

'Because you don't know what's good for you, that's why.' She is unbelievable. 'Anyway, Sami, the reason I'm ringing – it's about Betty.'

'Betty Blue Eyes! Did you ever hear back from that mystery man of yours?'

Nerys launches in. 'So you know what she's been up to, then!'

I ignore her and speak up. 'Yes, Sami. I did. In person. Turned up without warning, he did.'

'Ooh!'

'Ridiculous, isn't it.' Nerys wants him to agree with her.

I will my best friend to be on my side.

'It sounds harmless.'

I smirk at my sister.

'But he's a family man.' She goes back to cross-examining me. 'I suppose he told you all about his wife and baby, then?'

Balls. She's got me here. 'Not really, we just kind of chatted about whatever came into our heads.'

'Red flag, Betty, if his other half and their sprog weren't in his head.'

'Hang on,' Sami says. 'Maybe he and Betty are friends. Give her a bit of credit; she'd hardly fancy someone who's into jigsaws!'

Nerys performs imaginary semaphore and I jump to Guy's defence.

'Actually, jigsaws are quite hipster these days.'

Sami snorts.

'And I don't fancy him, all right? Nothing happened.' I suddenly get a whoosh of heat at the memory of locking eyes with him a few days ago behind the waterfall. 'He's just really nice to talk to. He doesn't see me like everyone else does. As damaged goods.'

'Oh, Bet,' Sami sighs. 'I'm sure he's great. But maybe he doesn't see you like everyone else does because you told him you're a designer and you'd been to Venice ...'

Nerys gasps. 'You never! That is seriously nuts.'

'I did tell him about the accident, though!' I cry. Not specifically when it happened, because that would've opened Pandora's box and revealed my codswallop. 'Listen, right ... I did say I'd set up my own label and I'd made it to Venice but I did it as a way to cope with this ... state I'm in.'

The air fills with sympathy.

'I didn't do it to tell lies, I did it to kind of put it out there in the universe, that that's what I want to do. Nerys, you're living your dream. Sami, it's so hard to hear how your life is carrying on. You're both sorted, you have security and certainty. The stuff I've told him, it's been an escape and a coping mechanism and he believes I'm capable of it all – there's no doubt in him, he treats me like the Betty I was and, you know what, that's what I need. If you were me and you could go back to before it happened, you would. To change how things turned out. Is that so wrong?'

'Oh, lovely girl,' Nerys finally gets it and comes at me.

'And I might've said I've got a great dad too,' I say into her hair as we cwtch. 'He's so adoring with his baby that I wanted to feel that too.'

'I hope you're giving her a hug,' Sami says.

162

'On it, Sami!' Nerys says. 'I just want you to be careful, Bet.' She releases me and wipes away a smear of my mascara. 'This fella sounds great and all that but you need to protect yourself. Maybe it feels like friendship now but you might develop feelings.'

I worry I already have. We've had no contact since and I'm fretting when I didn't before all this.

'I think Betty knows that if she does it'd be like a crush, because you don't know each other, not really.' Sami says it kindly and he's got a point. Then I realise something with horror.

'Nerys, is this me doing that sabotage thing again?'

'Could be,' she says, gently, which translates as hell, yes. 'Except this one, there's not even a hope it'll go anywhere so nip it in the bud, yeah? It's meaningless, babes. He'll spin you some tale about his wife, that they're on the rocks and then, fast forward when you've fallen for him, he won't leave her, they'll rekindle their love because anything is possible when kids are involved. Better to work on building a relationship with Dad, eh?'

'That's a whole other conversation,' I say, weary. 'I think we've covered enough for today.'

After a flurry of 'love you's, we end the call and Nerys tells me how fab Sami is.

I can't resist pointing out he's a bloke, therefore it is possible to have male mates.

'That's because he's gay, though, isn't it?' she says, matter of fact, and it sets me off – she really doesn't understand at all.

'His current partner is a woman, Nerys,' I say. 'Not everything in the world is black and white, you know.'

She doesn't understand why I've gone sour, that I'm

not happy at calling whatever is going on between Guy and me as meaningless. He does something to me that makes me feel completely myself, untroubled and brave, happy and confident. I just want him in my life for now.

The door goes and Poppy runs in with a packet of ice creams for afters. She collides into me, hugging my legs, and then showers her mother in love. Devoted Steve appears in the doorway with a sleeping Baby Daisy in a chest carrier; he cradles her protectively with his arms.

'Hi, Bet!' he says. 'Heard about our VIP guest?'

'Yep.' I still feel spiky.

'It was my idea, by the way, not hers,' he says, nodding at his wife. 'We've done some business together and it's a thank-you to him. He runs an outreach youth scheme where he pairs disadvantaged kids with apprenticeships and he's had a few good ones come to me. So no pressure, yeah? It's just a bit of food, a nice afternoon.'

I feel the load lifting and a surge of sisterly affection for him. And a new respect for Brody's choice of career.

'You're in that area, aren't you, Bet, helping children, so you'll have something in common.' Nerys is pulling an innocent face so I let her off.

'And he's divorced, so no grey areas,' she adds. 'With three kids.'

What is she getting at?

'So … you know …' she says softly, 'there's no pressure on you baby-wise. If it came to that.'

My eyes immediately prick. Nerys is attempting to be supportive, she isn't needling me this time. She's unaware she's being insensitive – she's just trying to help me find happiness. Where my anger was before there's now sorrow: the desire to have my own family is a luxury that could cost me dear. It could dominate every decision I make with no guarantees it'll come my way. I've resisted her way of doing things, to fit into her neat and tidy world.

Perhaps the reason I've failed to find someone is because I haven't tried it her way? It's worked for her after all.

The doorbell chimes with Poppy's latest favourite tune – 'We Don't Talk About Bruno' from *Encanto* – and the household bursts into song. Devoted Steve hands over Daisy to his wife then goes to answer it. Brody walks in wearing an ironed stone-coloured T-shirt and crease-free navy linen trousers with the ease of a man used to the madness of this way of life. He hands Nerys a bunch of flowers, coos at Daisy and places a bag of food and drink on the side, then gets down on his knees to give Poppy a comic. Then he looks up at me and gives me a smile that feels like a secret because no one else can see it. He bobs up and presses his smooth cheek against mine, wafting a musky, manly scent my way, and I find myself relaxing, feeling safe and known with not a hint of the schoolgirl fizz I felt when I saw him the other night.

'Looking gorgeous,' he says to me, then to everyone, 'all of you!'

It's like he's always been here, he fits in so well.

'No kids?' Nerys says. 'They're invited.'

'They're with their mam today; it'll be nice to have some adult chats.'

Then devoted Steve calls for him to help in the garden. 'Time for man to make fire, mate!'

'Speak in a bit, Betty,' he says, grabbing a beer and joining him outside.

Nerys is peeking in the carrier. 'He's brought veggie stuff! He isn't but he asked if you were.' She gives me a knowing glance and I shake my head at her meddling.

'All right?' she says.

'Yes, not that it's got anything to do with you!'

She cackles. 'Good girl, that's the spirit! Remind me, who's that other bloke again? No one, Betty, no one when Brody Burns is in the house.'

# 18

## *Guy*

I carve my way down the lane, my aching arms arcing and my lungs burning after almost an hour in the swimming pool.

If this doesn't give me a good kip tonight, I don't know what will.

Sleep came easy in Wales but back in Tunbridge Wells it's trickier to catch than an eel lubed up with Vaseline. Then if I do drop off, my dreams aren't about Betty, even though just a few hours with her made me the happiest I've felt in months. They've become deformed, where I'm not just losing my parents but Maud too.

It's as if the effect of the magic of seeing Betty is just out of reach. No matter how hard I try, I can't grasp it. Instead, there's a low-grade buzzing in my head and I can't put my finger on it.

On the sofa bed during the long hours of the night, I relive my time in Wales to make sure the memories don't fade: meeting her again and feeling that instant spark when we couldn't stop smiling, getting over the charity-shop mix-up, her vulnerability when she trusted me enough to tell me about her accident and her bravery to get behind the wheel when she became determined and defiant as if she was wearing armour. There was laughter, in-jokes and discovery. Even the little stuff was fascinating during the chats on our hike. We share the same taste in food – carbs and savouries all the way. We aren't board-game team types of people – give me a jigsaw and her a needle and thread and we're in heaven. The cinema goes on too long, we prefer a box set – *Succession* is our number-one favourite. I keep thinking how mad it is that we know so little about each other but that it feels as if we've known each other for ages. We have the same values too when it comes to family and we both see the beauty and stories in second-hand things.

But the scene I play most of all is in the waterfall when I felt something beyond friendship for her. Maybe that's why I've come to the water? To reconnect with her when I feel an odd shyness, even a reluctance to write, because I don't want to spoil this precious connection or turn it into some fantasy that's impossible to live up to. But I want to know more, that's the trouble. Like I asked to see her designs and photos from Venice but, of course, she doesn't use a mobile. It only makes me more curious. There's also the need to be honest with Betty and tell her about my situation, but all at once? It could ruin everything.

The splash and thrash around me sets me off again. My mind slips back to being behind the curtain of the torrent. Then, underneath the surface, the calm takes me to the swim we had. We're rolling and diving like seals as our mouths get closer ...

I get a whack on the shoulder blade as a man butterflies past me. I've obviously slowed up because I was ahead of him at the start. It's a sign to get out and I'm happy to have achieved something, tired and hungry.

I climb up the steps, whip off my hat and goggles and pad along the tiles, passing the baby pool where a class is taking place to teach little ones to swim. A wave of sadness hits me because I'd planned to do that with Maud when I took paternity. I'd even got as far as buying her swimming nappies and some bathers patterned with dolphins. I curse the chances that there's an older woman who's dressed a ginger baby in the same costume and is bobbing her up and down on her hip in time with the instructor. In fact, is that Maud? My eyes are sore from chlorine and I double blink to check. With a fright I realise it is – who's she with? Where's Sarah? I look around, panicking, but she's not in the gallery. Immediately I get closer, the urge to protect her slams into me and my chest constricts. Wild thoughts hurtle in – has she been snatched? Then the lady gurgles at her, Maud beams and I see it's her nan, Sarah's mother. The wind goes out of my sails, knowing how I've overreacted. What's wrong with me? Every time I try to move on, there's a reminder of what I've lost. It's boiling in here but I get goosebumps as I watch with envy that life is going on without me.

The parents and carers are blowing air into the babies' faces now; it's something to do with the reflex that stops them taking in water. Maud's eyes widen then shut and she gulps then closes her mouth shut. Then, one by one, they're dunking them under with a little thrust and a metre later they bob back up in the teacher's arms. I should go. A grown man watching kids in a swimming pool is not a good look. But I just want to wait for Maud's turn. When it comes, my anxiety returns and I'm staring intently as she gets the countdown. I mean, how stupid, a baby can't count. Linda raises Maud above the surface and then slowly dips her under and lets go. Time slows down and the seconds pass like hours; Maud's blurry body seems not to be moving quickly enough compared to the others. My heart is thumping and I take a step forwards, thinking 'Come on, Maudie, come up now'. The others were quicker than this and I can't see any movement of limbs. I'm suddenly furious with Sarah for letting her almost-seventy-year-old mum be in charge. Then I'm running, not caring that my feet are sliding, and I get to the side and plunge in just as Maud comes up smiling. But the splash of an adult male jumping in, albeit to his thighs, sets off a huge wave and half the babies get drenched. The crying starts, they're scooped up, and accusing eyes are on me.

'Guy!' Linda gasps, pulling a screaming Maud close, with horror on her face.

'I thought she wasn't coming up – I panicked,' I stutter.

The instructor is immediately ordering me to leave and Linda is talking to him, explaining that I'm not a threat. But I feel a monster, not to mention foolish, and I back off with pure shame.

'Guy!' Linda calls, getting out and carrying Maud towards me. 'What's going on, love?'

We've always got on and she treated me like one of her own. She puts an arm on mine and I'm stunned at what I just did.

'I dunno, I just saw her and didn't recognise you at first and I panicked. Then—'

'It's just because you care. Look, Maud's fine, she just had a shock.'

'I'm so sorry, Maudie,' I say over and over. She cowers

and it's clear why – she doesn't recognise me anymore and I try to win her back. 'Daddy didn't mean to hurt you.'

We realise what I've just said and Linda's eyes reflect my own pain.

'How come you're here with her? Where's Sarah?' I say it, then pinch my nose. 'You don't have to answer that. It's none of my business.'

'She's picked up a sicky bug from Maud, who got it in nursery. Still working from home, though, because it's only her first week back.'

'She's back at work already?' I am ruined that mum and baby can't be together. 'Oh God, what timing.' My heart hurts. Maud is so tiny and so young.

'Tell me about it,' Linda says. 'Hardest job in the world, being a mum.'

My face feels like it's cracking and she sees it.

'But she's all right, no need to worry.' I get a reassuring smile.

'What about Maud's father?' I shouldn't ask but I can't help it.

'He's started offering to help, which is good. But at lunch times, when she's sleeping, or after work, when she's crotchety. He's never done it before so ... it's a change of mindset that he needs. It'll come, I'm sure.'

Will it? Will Charlie sort himself out? There's so much I want to say. I want to offer my help, see if Sarah needs any shopping or some meals. But it's not my place. And yet I still do.

'If there's anything – you know – if I can make things better for Maud.'

'This must be hard on you, Guy.' Linda's sympathy is going to make me cry. 'We all miss you, love.'

I can only nod. She sees me struggling and lets me go with a 'Take care, son.'

I head into the changing rooms where I sob in the safety of the showers. I don't know what this feeling is. Is it love or loss? If only I had Charlie to ask. What would he say? I don't know that I can trust him either way not to have his own interests at stake. 'Go back to them' gets him off the hook. 'Start anew', and he might just be wanting me out of the picture, so I'm not there judging him. Perhaps he'd ask if I still loved Sarah – and the truth is ... of course, but it's not the heady feeling when we first met; it's more complex and wrapped up with Maud's welfare. Is that loss, then, instead? That buzz in my head is growing.

I need to unpick the stitches to find out what I want. I need to start being honest with myself. And the only person who I think can help is Betty.

To: bettyhopkins@gmail.com
From: therepairguy@googlemail.com
Re: things

Dear Betty,

Very remiss of me not to write until now to send my thanks for the guided tour of Pant Bach and surrounding areas. The hike and scenery were incredible. Not so much my ankle – which I maintain still niggles if I put my entire body weight on it and sort of squish it down, just in case you were doubting me.

Most impressive of all, though, was your courage. To think you had an accident which broke your pelvis then got back up again and started your own label is testament to that. Then to drive a big white van and its man to safety was epic.

I've been thinking about this quite a bit. You must've felt a big loss not just of physical movement but also of freedom, choice and your future, to name a few. I didn't get the chance to tell you because of the circumstances but I too know a bit about loss myself. And it's reared up lately.

I mean, I should be over it by now – I lost my parents when I was a baby and never got to know them. My granny and late grandpa brought me up and I had a happy childhood, bar the odd bit of bullying about being an orphan. Typically Tunbridge Wells, it had to have a literary theme so the bastards called me Oliver Twist. Luckily, I wasn't alone; I had my wimp of a best mate – the one who was my best man – to come up with brilliant retorts that I could deliver three hours later when we'd thought of them.

But lately, a few things have happened that have triggered it again. That emptiness inside, that hole within you that's full of pain.

I won't bore you with the details but it's coming out in weird dreams about my mum and dad. It feels like I'm stuck between looking back and looking forwards. It probably won't make any sense to you but that's all right. The way you've handled things is a priceless reminder that this too will pass.

Must dash, it's stiff-upper-lip time. I'm under orders to finish repairing a miniature boat made out of matches that an ex-sergeant major had accidentally set light to when he was smoking his pipe. He inherited it from his father who crafted it in the trenches and he needs it back by seven o'clock this evening to take to an exhibition of war artefacts at his ex-servicemen's club.

My job is completely ridiculous. But I love it.
Best,
Guy


To: therepairguy@googlemail.com
From: bettyhopkins@gmail.com
Re: things

Dear Guy,

I'm so sorry to hear you lost your parents at such a young age.

174

Nothing I've been through can compare to that trauma but any loss can leave you feeling at sea without an anchor. There's a whole spin-off of emotions, I imagine, beyond grief, such as feeling disconnected from things, shame, guilt – as well as empty.

I completely relate to that state of being stuck between the past and the future. People say 'don't look back' as if the future is all shiny. But you can't always go forward if you have troubling things behind you. I'm in the same space as you so don't be lonely, we can sit there and wonder and try to make sense of it all together.

Surrounding yourself with the good people in your life will help too – there's your granny, wife, best man friend and, of course, Maud. And get stuck into your passions.

Love,

Betty xxx

PS Delighted to hear your ankle is on the mend. Bear in mind that when anyone puts their 'entire body weight on one and sort of squishes it down' it will hurt regardless of whether it's been twisted.

PPS I too had nightmares after my accident. I'd wake up in terror, think I was OK, then fall back into it. I conducted extensive research into this phenomenon and discovered that a quick cup of tea and two slices of toast gave me just enough time to shake it off and go back to sleep. But then, a cuppa and carbs is my answer to everything.

PPPS I'm so glad you enjoyed your trip here. I'm so grateful you conned me into driving. And I'm flattered you think I'm brave, even though I really am not. So thank you.

PPPPS Did you meet the seven o'clock deadline?


To: bettyhopkins@gmail.com
From: therepairguy@googlemail.com
Re: things

Are you suggesting I am making a meal out of my ankle? A cuppa and carbs is life.

Yes, I got the boat back to the ex-sergeant major just in time. Amazing how focused I can be when the threat of a jolly good beasting is hanging over me.

PS While we're sitting in this space suspended between looking back and moving forwards, how about I bring the snacks and you provide the entertainments?

PPS I hoped you'd understand. And you've completely got it.


To: therepairguy@googlemail.com
From: bettyhopkins@gmail.com
Re: things

That's not fair. Snacks are easy. I have no party tricks

at all. Oh hang on! At my sister's barbecue the other day I showed off my After Eight act. You stick one on your forehead and gurn your face until it gets to your mouth and you can eat it – all without using your hands. No one else managed it. And Brody Burns was impressed.

To: bettyhopkins@gmail.com
From: therepairguy@googlemail.com
Re: things

Brody Burns will never look at After Eights in the same way again. That works for me. We could form a human circus because I have a wealth of irrelevant and useless skills with which I can amuse us such as playing Peruvian-style Andes music by blowing into bottles (with my nostrils, if I'm in the mood). Oh, and I can wiggle my ears.

So we could just divvy it up between us?

To: therepairguy@googlemail.com
From: bettyhopkins@gmail.com
Re: things

Sold to the lady at the back with a melted After Eight on her cheek.

## 19

## *Betty*

**M**egan's Back-to-School window is a total winner.

In fact, her idea of 'flying' ties and shirts hung with fishing wire, bins of pencil cases and dictionaries and a colourful collection of backpacks and lunch bags is such a draw we have a queue, an actual queue, down the Arcade out onto the pavement.

'You've done brilliantly! Does this happen every year?' I ask her as we work side by side at the counter, where I'm on the till and she's folding and bagging up.

'First time.' If she's chuffed at the praise she isn't showing it.

'What? But there're so many people, it looks like it's some kind of annual date in the calendar to me.'

'If only.' Megan says it sourly and I remind myself not to take it personally. She might not be annoyed at me, there could be something else wrong. Maybe she reads my mind because she carries on but tones down her contempt. 'The manager before you, her sister runs the uniform shop in Merthyr and there was apparently a conflict of interest.'

'How principled of her.'

Megan glances at me. 'I know, right, people who want

new will always buy new. But for the rest of us, when kids grow so quick, we can't afford to do that. And why should we? It's better to wear stuff out than constantly replace it.'

She's opened the door to me a crack and I see how deeply she feels about the issue.

'Too right. How come we've got all this stock, then?'

Megan does a big huff. 'You'll only go mad.'

The door slams but I'm not going to give up on her.

'Hang on, tell me, then I'll decide if I'll go mad.'

'So I put a call out on Facebook asking for spare uniforms that we could sell.'

'Why on earth would I go mad at that?'

'Because I didn't ask your permission.' She throws me a scowl. 'I'm just a volunteer, aren't I?'

'So? It was a stroke of genius! Look at how much we're making for Life Goes On.'

'Serious?' Megan keeps her eyes fixed on folding a pair of trousers before handing them over to the customer but there's a vulnerability and a disbelief in her voice.

'Yes!' I turn to her, taking advantage of the brief break in the line as people browse. 'Ideas and action are what we need! We can't save this place if we sit back!'

'Save it?' She hisses it at me and I realise I've made a massive mistake. I don't want a master-and-servant dynamic here, I want her to feel an equal, but I've divulged something too big for someone who isn't paid to worry.

'Not save it, strictly. That was the wrong word. What I mean is, you know, how we need to keep up the good work.'

'Oh please. I'm not a dummy. I'm not Gloria.' She

knows back-pedalling when she sees it. And she has the right to know what's happening since I put my foot in it.

'Right, so I'll be honest with you. Mrs Hughes mentioned the shop is at a critical point, not because it's a failure but because the charity sector as a whole is being affected by lots of factors – I mean, there's a lot of competition out there for us, plus people are feeling the pinch as ever. I've looked at the figures and it's not great. The charity's income has tanked in the last ten years. I suspect fast fashion is playing a part. In my day you'd come in and spend your Saturday-job wages in the high street but the chains, especially online, offer so much cheap stuff with free delivery, it's hard to compete.'

'It's evil, fast fashion. Sweatshops, pollution, all that waste going to landfill.'

'But, Megan, and I truly believe this, I think the tide is turning. I think consumers' attitudes are changing. It means we have an opportunity. And you're already making it happen. The Facebook call for uniform was inspired. And if we can do the same with the auction, then—'

But I see Megan hugging herself. 'I can't lose this.' Her big eyes are cautious, checking me out to see if she can open up. 'This is my link to my mam. It was where she used to come, to potter about, when she could still go out. I was almost eighteen when she died and as soon as I was, the charity helped me apply for legal guardianship of Alfie and Nancy. I owe Life Goes On everything. This is why I'm here too, to repay them. And it's not just me that's benefited, there's the Christmas party we put on for all the kids, presents every year until they're sixteen, legal help and grants.'

So this is why she cares so much. Her passion rings a bell inside of me and I have a brainwave. But the punters are back so I run through it in my head while we work. And it seems doable.

I have an excuse to ring Mrs Hughes; she emailed yesterday to say I'd passed the trial period. I gush on about how much I'm loving it so she doesn't think I'm trying to bail already, then sell her my idea, hoping she'll at least consider it. When she agrees I can't quite believe it. But then, as she wrote in her email, takings are slightly up and shoppers appear to like the new layout. I'd like to think she believes in me but there's a definite suggestion to her voice that it's my decision and on my head be it. I wait until we close to approach Megan.

'Listen, I've got a proposal for you.'

She nods glumly, which shows how little she expects of people.

'You'll need to check out whether or not it's compatible with your benefits, that's if you even want to accept, but how about a job share? I'll cut my hours so you can up yours and on the days you're boss, I'll be the volunteer and vice versa. It makes sense for there to be two of us running it, businesses plan for succession and so should we. This will give us cover for holidays too.' Previously, the shop would always close when the manager took time off. 'And you should be rewarded for what you do here.'

Her mouth has flopped open. 'What? Like joint-manager?'

'Yes, exactly.'

'But what about the money?'

'I'm renting out my flat in London. I can manage. It's not as if I'm on the rampage much, having weekends

in Dubai and champagne for elevenses, is it? And ...'
There's another reason too – something so obvious that
I've somehow missed it while it's been staring me in the
face. 'I could do with some breathing space.'

'What for? You're not looking to leave, are you?' Her
mistrust is another sign of how life has treated her.

'I will eventually.' I can't lie but I also don't want to
mention London because she'd doubt everything I've
said. She seems content with that. 'I just have something
I want to try.'

If we're job sharing, I've got the time and if I don't do
it now then perhaps I never will. If it takes off, then I can
pursue it back in London. Haven't I been wanting to do
it forever? Didn't I tell Nerys and Sami about my dream?
And then there's Guy, the one who rebooted my desire,
reminding me who I really am; I said he should get stuck
into his passions and I've realised the same applies to me.
It'll be a positive thing to do and a distraction.

My courage gets stage fright in front of Megan. 'I
want a side hustle,' I say, full of nerves, 'I want to design
clothes, nothing big but a kind of niche thing, making
stuff from factory leftovers or dead stock or whatever
I can get my hands on.' Her eyes widen. 'Or is that
mad?'

She shakes her fringe at me then pulls her hair up and
she's wearing an amazing pair of earrings. 'This is what
I do. And I hope it's OK but whenever we have broken
bracelets or necklaces or anything sparkly, I put them
together and make new jewellery. So for these, I used
gold chain links from an old bracelet and threaded on
yellow beads from a plastic chain.'

'They're great!' Maybe we have more in common than

182

we thought. 'I can see it now, a collaboration of ours on the catwalk!'

She gives me the slightest trace of a smile.

'So what about the job?' I remind her.

'What does Mrs Hughes think?' Megan bites her lip.

'It's my decision. I'm the manager.' I don't say I suspect she's agreed on the basis of 'whatever it takes'. 'It's a goer, if you want it.'

Megan takes a breath and then the corners of her mouth turn up and joy tiptoes all the way to her eyes. 'I do, Betty. I do.'

It's a massive breakthrough for me, for her, for us and the charity.

'Thank you,' she says, holding her chest, 'I'm overwhelmed.'

I'm thrilled – we could be the dream team with our mix of experience, insight, imagination and heart.

'Our first priority, then, what do you reckon?' I say, as we close. 'The auction?'

'Defo. I've got some ideas on how we can run it,' she says. 'Online, it's the only way. We'd never be able to reach people if we did it in the shop and there's no space.'

'Exactly. And I'm thinking about how we can make it look. The stuff's all in my mam's fella's garage and I reckon we could turn it into a living room, like an art installation.'

Megan stops as we get to the arcade gates. 'Thanks, Betty. It's the best thing that's happened to me in ages.'

She heads one way and I go the other, wearing a smile for a change. The evening is a gorgeous one, an August classic with the sun still beating away in a cloudless blue sky.

The roads are quiet; there's hardly anyone around in the village because on a night like this everyone congregates in their gardens to eat, drink and watch the kids in the paddling pool. I hear the buzz of lawnmowers and smell cut grass and there's a sweetness to the air as summer reaches its ripe crescendo. In London it will be crowded and sweaty with people spilling onto the pavements from pubs, blowing cigarette and vape smoke into the already heavy muggy atmosphere that is thick with exhaust fumes and horns and rotting rubbish. It's the first time that I feel happy about being here rather than there. Perhaps it's because I've had a good day with Megan and come up with a plan to get my life back and I find myself dreaming of how satisfying it could be to split my time between the warmth of Wales and the stimulation of London. I could have the best of both worlds.

I take a detour via the rugby club so I can see the mountains minus chimney pots and roofs. The wide expanse of the pitch kneels at the foot of the hills, giving a picture-perfect uninterrupted view of the land, lush with ferns and heather.

It's busy here but not rammed as children practise their kicking and parents imagine they're watching a Wales player of the future. Among them is Brody, who is taking on three boys who must be his. Carrying the ball, he darts past the tallest, swerves past the middle one and then lets the smallest tackle him to the ground. They all dive onto him and their laughter is infectious. He sees me and rolls to a standing position, telling them to be good while he trots over. Brody is vital and alive, glowing from the exercise and fun.

'I'm still hoping to be selected for the under-sevens!'

he says, bashfully, rolling his eyes at himself and putting his hands on his hips to catch his breath.

'I hear you. I've just heard I haven't qualified for the playing horsey world cup.'

He laughs at the memory of me being on my all fours with Poppy on my back at Nerys's barbecue.

'You could always fall back on being a model though,' he says wryly.

It's a reminder of how my niece had given me two red circles of glittery blusher and orange lipstick and it's my turn to guffaw. 'Poppy was rather enthusiastic with my makeover, wasn't she?'

'The things we do for them.' He shakes his head and then tilts it at me. 'You can tell how much you love those girls. That must be a bonus being here, to see them growing up.'

My heart blooms into a blossoming rose. 'They are the sweetest.'

'You're a natural with them, trust me, I know with those three running me ragged.'

I feel the underlying pang of wanting my own babies but the knowing it might not happen and that my chance has already been and gone throbs inside.

He hears a scuffle behind him and turns to tell them to behave. The smallest delivers his last word in the form of a punch to the biggest's thigh.

'Little sods.' Brody smiles. 'Feel free to borrow them!'

It's a joke but there's truth in it; of course, I'm not projecting myself into their life but it could end up that my only chance of motherhood is with stepkids.

'So … fancy coming over?'

The question is innocent but it makes me wonder if

this type of family life wouldn't be too bad. A partner and an instant brood couldn't stop it but could appease my biological clock. Getting involved with someone like Brody could give me what I crave but also the space to focus on my career and my fingers are itching to start designing and researching.

He sees my hesitation. 'Come on, if you do, there's more chance of Connor, Liam and Declan being on their best behaviour. You'll be doing me a favour and it'd be nice to have some adult conversation. I'm going to the bar now,' he thumbs towards the clubhouse, 'get them some pop and crisps, myself a pint, want me to get you anything?'

I'm really tempted. There is something between us, perhaps it's just being of the same soil, but I would like to explore it. Yet inside the squat grey building behind Brody, my father will be holding up the bar and holding court.

'I'd love to,' and I mean it, 'but my dad . . .'

Brody nods. 'I get it.'

I'm so pleased I don't have to spell it out; if he saw me sober he might hold back but there's little chance of that. There'd be the fuss, the chat and then his eyes would go glassy and they'd wander to find someone to buy him his next drink. I've had enough of being humiliated by him.

'I've got your number still,' I say, 'how about we get something in the diary?'

'Perfect!' He grins. 'See you soon, then, Bet!'

I watch him walk into the club and I can see it now: he'll see an old pal or two, there'll be some man hugs with the mates he's known since school, with whom he had his first drink, who have each been each other's ushers and best men, who have so much history and such a bond that they'll always be there for one another. It doesn't matter if one has made it or another is on his uppers; wealth and status mean nothing to them. It's all about heart and everyone is equal.

On my way home, I get a lump in my throat because I know it's all there on a plate for me, not necessarily with him but with someone local. How would it feel? Would I finally understand the pull of being here or would I get claustrophobic?

Mam is waiting with a cold bottle of Prosecco and we go out onto the patio where she's set up some nibbles and we sit down on her recliners.

'I've had a right time of it with a broken machine at the launderette,' she says, delivering today's headlines. 'Cliff's a grampy again; he's got a new grandson, Gareth.'

Wales is the only place in the world where no one bats an eyelid if you call a baby Gareth.

'They've decided on the theme for this year's bank holiday bash. It's Bingo, Beer and Bopping.'

When everyone will get Bladdered, Battered and Blind Drunk.

Our row of houses all have their back doors open and I can hear next door's telly, a load of laughter further up and, on the other side, Tom the trumpet from the brass band practising away. Coming home is like landing in a nest of feathers.

My mind drifts to Guy and I imagine him now, sitting on a rug on the lawn blowing bubbles, which pop on Maud's nose while his wife watches them adoringly. For the first time I feel unsure about him. Why is he turning to me to talk about his loss when he has them? Why has he confided in me? And at what point will I realise that the communication between us could be inappropriate? If I was happy with someone I wouldn't need to reach out to a stranger. Does that mean he's not telling me something? Or am I reading into it, and developing some kind of dependency on him because of the way he makes me feel?

The things I've kept from him, too, are a sign. We're just friends, maybe not even that, maybe we're each other's soundboard. But what is the point of it? Am I going to hear what Nerys said would come – that his wife doesn't understand him?

Today has been a good day. I feel stronger than ever, empowered by my plan and bringing Megan on board. I haven't thought of this before but occupying that space between looking back and going forwards also means I'm in the present. As well as grounding me so I feel solid and secure, it gives me a reality check. I raise my glass to the sky, and I'm raising it to Guy, too, in farewell. It's time to focus on where I am, not where I've been or where I should be.

## 20

## *Guy*

It's my turn to cook for Granny and tonight I've gone all out on the ultimate in comfort food.

What else can hit the spot other than a homemade lasagne that's bubbling away in the oven, turning the mozzarella brown, when it's raining?

It's been squally today, one of those reminders that while it's still officially summer, autumn is coming. But it was the perfect excuse to whip up my favourite meal – except this time I've gone veggie. There's still the thick passata laced with red wine, garlic, onion, black olives and herbs, a deli counter of cheese and layers of pasta and béchamel, but Granny's grow-your-own in the greenhouse has gone bananas with courgettes and aubergines and my fridge is beginning to resemble a supermarket shelf.

The timer pings and I grab a tea towel, all dark waffle-grey to Sarah's taste, and put the dish on the hob. Then I get a teaspoon because you have to check it's cooked, right, and I dig in. I'm actually salivating as I raise the mouthful that stretches with perfectly oozing mozzarella like a decadent, yawning cat. A quick blow and wow, it's delicious. I stop myself from another go, otherwise there'll be none left for Granny, and pack it into a jute bag, find my phone and keys and drive over.

The van fills with the steam of supper and my stomach rumbles in anticipation.

'Ooh!' Granny says when I arrive, sniffing the air with pleasure. 'Let's take it into the kitchen, keep it warm. The garlic bread is just doing and there's salad too.'

'All your own work?'

'Not the baguette! That's from Mr Sainsbury's, but my tomatoes, cucumbers, spring onions and lettuce are freshly picked!'

'Lush!' I say and she gives me a big smile.

'There's a Welsh word if ever I heard one!'

'Yes! They use it for everything. I can see why, because it's such a glorious word to say.'

In unison we both do an extravagant drawn out 'luuush' and Granny stares into space. 'One day, I've always said, I'll go back.'

'I've told you, give me a date and I'll take you.'

'I mean to live.' She plays with the rings on her fingers, deep in thought.

'So what's stopping you, G?'

She weighs it up. 'Oh, perhaps it's better to think of something as it was. What if I got there and it had all changed? And what about my life here. And you.' Bobby wanders in as if to say 'don't forget me', so I bend down to give him a chin rub.

'Me? Don't stay here because of me.' Nothing would make me happier than her happiness. 'You'll have tons of friends there in an instant, old ones too. And, not to be rude, but Bethlehem didn't seem like it had gone hurtling into the twenty-first century. I didn't see any spaceships or robots walking dogs. If that's what you want, then go for it.'

'But it'd be a burden on you, knowing I was there. And when I'm old,' she winks, 'you might think you need to help me and I won't have you racing up the M4 if this silly old fool starts having falls.'

This prompts me to say out loud what I know is a possibility. 'Who says I'm going to stay here?'

'Well, why would you leave?' Her intense dark eyes search mine.

'What have I got here? Only you and my business. And I can move that, no problem.'

She realises with delight that I'm serious. But she wants to test me. 'You sure it's not an excuse to be nearer Betty?'

'Very funny. I'd hardly uproot for someone I've spent a few hours with.' I suddenly imagine walking down the street and bumping into Betty and my heart leaps. But I've been thinking about her and us – while she is so re-assuring and understanding, there's no way it can become anything. All it would take to break the illusion of our friendship would be an unanswered letter or email. Who would chase up a silence, asking what's gone wrong, when the foundations of it could be built on sand? She's a woman going places and there'll be a line of admirers; for one, there's her schoolgirl crush.

'I haven't told her about my situation anyway. She knows about Mum and Dad but what's the point of going into the rest of it? This isn't to do with her.' That's the truth. 'It's about me needing to decide whether or not I stay and try again.'

'Something will happen and then you'll know. And, in

the meantime, we could have a look on Rightmove! It's my guilty pleasure, to spend a rainy afternoon looking up properties in Wales on the iPad. Not that I did anything of the sort today.'

She gives me a look which says she so has.

'Besides, I'm not sure I'd get a mortgage at the age of seventy-four!'

'I've always said I'll help you!' Before I bought my house, I'd seen somewhere with a granny annex but she told me off for even thinking about her future.

'I couldn't take money off you!' She gets some glasses and the subject is clearly closed. 'So, what are you drinking? Red? White?'

'Whatever's open.'

My phone goes and it's Sarah. I've been dreading hearing from her. Her mum will have told her about me jumping into a baby pool to save Maud. The humiliation of it makes me feel hot – what an overreaction, what a sign that I can't let go. Sarah knowing about it could give her false hope and it makes me feel vulnerable.

'Hi, everything all—'

'I am so, so sorry to call you, Guy. But I need your help,' Sarah cuts in, breathless, and because she was always so together before this, I know something's wrong.

'What's up?'

'I wouldn't ask but Maud's just got off to sleep and I need some Calpol – and I've run out.' She speaks quickly with worry and, her brain whirring, she preempts my next question. 'Mum's out, Charlie's not picking up. I've called in a lot of favours from my friends and it's just – after what you said to Mum – if there's anything Maud needs.'

I can hear the desperation in her voice. It is so tough on her having to juggle everything. I could waste time raging at Charlie but that would not be helpful and he could have a genuine reason for not answering his phone.

'Don't worry. I'll get some and bring it over now.'

'I've also got a prescription – she's got an ear infection and I need to double-check with the chemist about the dose because I can't remember what the doctor said. I should go. Is there a chance, would you mind, but could you just sit here with her for ten minutes while I go to the late-night pharmacy? I hate to ask, I know it's not your problem.'

How can I say no? And I wouldn't dream of it.

'I'll be over now.' Granny has been listening and nods. I'm already walking to the front door with my keys.

'Thank you so much.' Her relief floods down the line. 'We're back in my flat. The tenant left early, so come here. You don't have to see her, she's in her room; you can listen to the monitor, if it's too ... difficult.'

I wince and then pull myself together, for she is only trying to be thoughtful. I drive over, park and buzz Sarah, who answers in a split second.

'Come in,' she says and when I turn the corridor, she's on her marks by her open door. When I get to her, she whispers a thank-you and brushes past my body to go.

Inside the lounge it's a mess of boxes and suitcases. The clothes horse is covered with Babygros and vests and the kitchen sink is full of dirty bowls and pans. The coffee table is stacked with files and papers from work and, outside, the security light flashes, revealing shadows in the courtyard and an overflowing black bin. My throat is dry at this picture of how hard life is for her, God

193

knows what state her brain is in. Sarah is trying to support Maud with everything she's got and it looks like she's drowning.

A snuffle on the monitor becomes a yelp and I dash to Maud's door and listen, holding my breath. I fight with all my might not to go in – what if I woke her up and couldn't get her back to sleep? And what if she howled in fear because she doesn't remember me? I step back and go to the kitchen where I wash up because I might as well do something.

Within twenty minutes Sarah is back, immediately asking if Maud has woken. I say no and she thanks me profusely and offers me a drink. But it's out of politeness and she looks exhausted.

'I don't know what I'd have done without you,' she says. 'And I know I really shouldn't have brought you into this. It's just … I had no one else. But I wish with all my heart that I didn't need anyone else, that I had you here with us.' How quickly she gets to the point shows how little time she has for herself. ' I love you, Guy.'

I wish with all my heart that I could feel this way too. I pull her into me and she wraps her arms around my waist, burying her head into my neck. I feel her soften but she's wiry from the stress.

'I still love you both, Sarah, but I'm so torn.'

She lifts her head and stares up at me. 'Have you thought about coming back?'

'Yes, all the time. But I'm still broken from it all, and I don't think that's the basis for a decision. Whatever happens, though, I'll always care about you both. I'll always be there.' I rub her back and kiss her forehead.

'This is torture,' she says, 'How long do I have to wait?'

Then she drops her head. 'I shouldn't ask, I'm sorry.'

'I can't put a timeline on it, there's stuff I need to sort out before I can get there.'

I go quietly, feeling the gravity of the situation. Anger and tears would demean what's just happened and I know I need to get a move on with a decision. It's not fair on either Sarah or me. There's also someone else involved.

A mile down the road, I'm knocking on his door.

'Foxy,' Charlie says quietly, pale as anything. He's not wearing what I'd expect, either a suit or training gear. Just a simple black T-shirt and jeans.

'I'm not here for a row,' I say, feeling strangely calm. 'Can I come in?'

His eyes, Maud's eyes, are wary but he steps back and lets me shut the door behind me.

'Can I get you anything?' He hovers in the hall, his hands trembling as he wipes the sweat off his top lip.

'No, I won't be long. I'm on my way to Granny's.'

We go into his lounge but the bachelor-pad look I'm used to seems even starker. I haven't been in here since before Maud was born. Perhaps it's because I've had a taste of fatherhood with its soft toys and fabrics but the black leather L-shaped sofa looks more imposing and the widescreen TV with its PlayStation console and headset more laddish.

Charlie waits for me to say why I'm here but it's obvious something is wrong.

'Are you unwell?'

He takes a breath and holds his chest. Then he crumples. I watch him sob his heart out but I can't console him. Not yet.

'I'm – uh ... I've been having panic attacks.' He says

it with shame because his adult life has been devoted to forgetting he was a wimpy kid. 'I've been signed off work for a fortnight. I thought I was having a stroke or a heart attack; I was in a meeting and I couldn't breathe and all of a sudden I'm in an ambulance and having tests. Turns out I'm fit as a fiddle, but it's – er, anxiety, apparently. I've been signed off for a fortnight and the company's providing counselling. I had my first session tonight.'

'That's why you didn't pick up Sarah's call.'

He nods. 'I called her just now. She said you helped.'

'How do you feel now?'

He puffs his cheeks and leans forward, resting his elbows on his knees. He rubs his head. 'Embarrassed, a failure, useless, incapable, a let-down. No change there, then, right?' he says.

'What?' Because he's breezed through life. His divorce was his biggest test; it was hard when his wife Rachel left him because he was 'just a big kid' but he accepted he was to blame for not being always there for her. I know because he moved in with me for a while. He's your classic happy chappy, but the man in front of me is like a different person.

'Because of what I've done.' His lips thin with self-loathing. 'Because I've lost you. My best mate.' His chin is wobbling. 'Because ... and this is the hardest bit to admit,' he says, gulping, 'I don't know how to be a dad. You got it straight away, you didn't even have a dad to show you.' This doesn't upset me one bit, we always used to talk this frankly. 'But me, with mine, you know what a great bloke he is. So what's wrong with me? Why can't I get my head round it? It's like I need to punish myself for ruining everything with you and Sarah.'

I swore I wouldn't ask him – I have my pride. But it rises up – I need to know. 'So why did you? Why did you sleep with her?'

'I . . .' But he shakes his head.

'What?'

'I won't use it as an excuse.' He holds his face in his hands.

'Tell me.'

Charlie looks up. 'Sarah didn't say?'

'Sarah just said she started it. Jesus, Charlie, don't make me do the hard work here.'

'All right.' He stares at his hands. 'The night it happened, us three were meant to meet in the pub. Then it all blew up. She asked to talk. I'd called you, asked if you wanted a pint, remember?'

I nod. 'You put me first, I get it.'

His eyelids flinch from the dig. 'We got pissed. I told her not to throw things away. I was going, I swear . . . then Dad called . . . he told me Mum had cancer. I said I'd go over but he said no, he was all positive that it'd be OK, caught early, all that, chances are good. But I was . . . terrified. Sarah got me a brandy. I walked her home, we had more. I was reeling, man, I needed a hug. Then things changed and I . . .' He grits his teeth, then his nostrils flare with emotion. 'Fuck, Guy, I didn't want to use my mum as an excuse. I was stupid, I was drunk. I should've got up and walked out.'

I loathe what he's done but I feel his pain. I know how much he adores Pat; how, of all the brothers, he's closest to her. And I know if my mum was alive, if it was Granny, I'd be knocked for six too.

'But then wishing I had left seems grotesque – because

197

even though it's fucked us, it made a human being and all I can hope is that we can make something good of it. But I hate myself.'

That's it. I can't watch him like this. 'Shit happens, Charlie,' I say, getting up and going to him where I crouch at his side and put an arm around him. 'There's nothing we can do to change what's happened. It's been fucking awful. Maybe I forced the situation, maybe we should never have—' I'm about to say 'got together' and it shocks me. I've never considered that maybe we weren't right for each other. 'That we should've communicated better.'

I can tell Charlie won't even consider that anyone else was to blame. But he will.

'You know, that thing about turning back the clock, I've thought it but then that would mean no Maud, no wonderful, smiley baby Maud. Your daughter. How can I wish that away? And it sounds like you've got this block; you can't feel anything for her because you feel so bad about yourself. But trust me, it'll come.'

'I just don't know how to do any of it. The basics. Nappies and bottles and—' His breathing starts to falter and I know how to stop this. But am I prepared to do it? Can I put aside my own issues? It'll mean putting his betrayal behind me and letting him back in – but, most of all, it'll mean Maud comes first.

'I'll show you, mate,' I say, patting his back. 'How about that? Would that help?'

It's like a shock curing hiccups and it does the same job with his panic.

His eyes fill up and he nods. 'Yeah,' he says, gulping, 'I think it would.'

198

Charlie doesn't need to say any more; getting to the nub of it is the way we've always done things.

'I have to go,' I say, 'but maybe let's get that WhatsApp group going again? I'll leave you to chat to Sarah, she should know. It ain't going to be easy, not at first, but we'll get there.'

I ring Granny on my way back, telling her to pour me a large glass. She's waited for me to eat so she'll get everything dished up. I'll fill her in over supper. But even before I've done that, there's one thing that's patently clear. There's no way I'm going anywhere, not for a while.

And I get a sudden fright – it means I won't see Betty again any time soon.

I had clarity earlier today about us keeping in touch. The logic in my head understood how fragile it is. After tonight, though, I've got a deep gut feeling that over-powers all rationality: I don't want to lose touch because I don't want to go through this without her.

But to do that I need to tell her everything.

*Dear Betty,*

    *How are you?*

    *I'll get to the point. I wondered if you fancied
a trip to Tunbridge Wells? You showed me Sgwd
yr Eira and in return I would like to show you
our watery wonder of the world. It's a bit feeble by
comparison.*

    *But the Chalybeate Spring in The Pantiles has
attracted visitors for four hundred years, including
Queen Victoria, who come to 'take the waters', owing
to its iron-rich content which reputedly cures all sorts
of ills. (I've nicked this from the tourist website.)*

    *As you can see on the card, to this day, merry
wenches in bonnets, who go by the name of dippers,
still ladle the water in a genteel fashion for people
to try. On the whole they find it tastes like a rusty
spanner. (I wrote this bit.)*

    *I'd love to see you.*

    *Apologies in advance but I made the mistake
of telling my grandmother that you're Welsh
and inevitably she'll make an excuse to 'pop in'.
Apparently, she says, you'll understand.*

    *Best,*

    *Guy*

# 21

## *Betty*

It comes to me at the end of one of those days. Have I bitten off more than I can chew?

It started first thing when I was putting the finishing touches to a window display of clothes incorporating the whole rainbow to celebrate Pride's annual big weekend in Wales. Just as I was admiring it, Megan broke the news of an email from the board informing us that Life Goes On had signed up to an environmental pledge to promote wearing a jumper rather than whacking up the heating.

Absolutely worthy but hardly smelling the air when we're having a last blast of sunshine. It was agreed, though, before I joined, after several years of late August turning dismal. Surely, as someone who worked in fashion which decided on trends months in advance, I understood? I got my own back by sticking colour-coordinated cardigans, knits and hoodies onto my existing run of red wrap dress, orange Hawaiian shirt, yellow T-shirt, green leggings, blue jeans and indigo and violet nightie. But even looking at jumpers made me hot. I went to get a breath of fresh air after that but couldn't get out the back door. On investigation, the alley had been piled up overnight with a mountain of donations and when we went through them it was more of an act of fly-tipping junk.

Then I had a row with a customer who informed me that his ten-pound buy of a rusty tea caddy was in fact vintage and four Seventies pottery coffee cups were by an obscure lusted-after designer and would go for ten times that when he put them on on eBay. Why would you do that? Why would you take money away from the kids? I asked. 'Do you want my money or not?' he said, with a smirk.

Megan consoled me with a reminder that money is money and the guy was just trying to make a living. She's right, I think, as she says goodbye on her way out to pick up the twins and take them for haircuts at Jack of all Fades. My frustration is out of proportion – I would count this stuff as shrapnel, were I in London. But it shows how far I have to go to get back there. I have half an hour left until closing and I use it to give the shelves a clean and mop the floor. I'm feeling sorry for myself and it's not like I'm doing what I promised I'd do – living in the present, not comparing this life with that life and using the empty time to let my mind wander.

The trouble is, my mind has come to a dead end. When I sit down of an evening to sketch ideas for designs, nothing comes. Why, when it's the only thing that's given me a boost lately? I've been so excited putting out feelers with local factories asking for quotes on dead-stock material. But the one reply I've had so far says it's not worth their while, it's less hassle sending it to landfill or the furnace. Never mind being in the present – I feel like I'm treading water at best. And all this happens when I'm missing Guy and trying my hardest not to.

Just when you think you're turning a corner, you find you're stuck in a maze.

I have two minutes until I can go. Sod's law means someone is going to come in and spend fifteen minutes browsing and then leave without buying anything. And sod's law is taking the bloody biscuit, as my dad appears at the door.

'We're closed,' I say, busying myself with unnecessary tidying of pens at the counter and straightening the vases behind me.

'Says two minutes to on my watch,' he says.

I spin round and see him proud and barrel-chested with a ridiculous pair of luminous green shades perched on that greasy scalp of his. And he's grown himself a goatee. All the irritation I've been sitting on comes up and out at him.

'As if you've ever been bothered about the time!'

He says nothing but holds out a carrier bag to me.

'What's this? A donation?' I say it sharply, because he's a taker, not a giver.

'As a matter of fact, it is. Heard about your auction and I was saving it for you girls, when I pop my clogs, but I thought you might think the charity is a better cause.'

I take it off him and inside there's a faded red jersey, a battered pair of boots, some kind of a hat and a rugby ball. Then I look up at him. 'Why on earth would this help us out?'

He shuffles now and looks embarrassed. 'You don't know what it is?'

'Your sweaty old kit, by the looks of it.'

'Not just any old sweaty kit.' He says it in a whisper, as if it's the holy grail. 'It's my Wales cap, my shirt, boots and the ball from the day I scored that try.'

An ache unexpectedly hits my throat. I get a wave of

sadness that this is the most precious thing he owns; it's who he was and it represented his potential, his moment of fame and achievement, and by offering it to me it's a kind of sacrifice.

For the first time ever I feel something for him, for my father who is trying to make it up to me.

'It might not mean much to you, granted – but it might do to someone, a collector or a fan. Of course, it might only get a fiver. I could sign them, if that'd help?'

But something in me shifts – is this gesture more about him than the cause? This is my father, of course it is. I snap at him. 'You could model it, maybe? Do a meet-and-greet the great Dai Hopkins?' Meet-and-greet the one-cap wonder who shagged his way around the Valleys, missed training after too many beers the night before and ended up a bit of a joke. Oh and he was a feckless father with no morals whatsoever.

He swallows hard at my sarcasm.

'It was just a thought,' he says, his head dropping.

I suddenly feel ashamed of myself. Because aren't I doing the same as him through my lies to Guy? My dad is harking back to the time when he was somebody. I'm doing exactly that, pedalling my imaginary success to conceal my demise.

'And maybe it's time to let all that go.' He waves his hand back. I realise with horror that this is him acknowledging his failure and accepting he can't live in the past. Yet I'm still pretending.

'You know, my greatest achievement – it's you and your sister.'

I'm winded by his words. Of course Nerys deserves the

acclaim with her success at life. But me? How can he be proud of me?

'This is looking good, Boo.' Dad surveys the shop. 'You've come a long way since . . . what happened.'

'How do you know?' I say, throwing my distress his way.

'I speak to your mother. I know what it's like to feel worthless, and shame, and it was all my own doing. But you, there's no need, it happened to you and—'

Enough. I don't want him assuming he understands me.

I tell him it's past closing now and he goes, leaving me holding his bag of bones. I shove it under the counter and as I lock up and leave, the tears begin to flow.

I no longer feel like I'm treading water. Instead, I'm slipping under, unable to get a purchase on anything to stop me. All this effort to get myself better, when I thought being here could be enjoyed rather than endured, all the momentum has crumbled. I have the urge to run, but a phantom pain screwdrivers my pelvis and I'm gulping for oxygen. I can't breathe here, this place, its walls are closing in on me. So are the lies I've told Guy – I need to stop the fantasy and confront my reality.

I stagger into the house and find I'm home alone. I feel bad but I'm relieved. I don't like to tell Mam how Dad gets to me; she says he's made it up to her by being there for Nerys and – archly – trying to be there for me.

A note in the kitchen confirms she's out with Cliff and she says to call her if I want her to bring me back a curry from the restaurant. But what I'm craving is what Mam would make if Nerys or I needed cheering up.

While the oven chips are cooking, I do a hoover of the downstairs and then run up to get into my scrotty tracksuit before I return to heat up some baked beans, make a cuppa and fry a golden egg, which reaches the perfect runny stage when the alarm pings. I chuck it all on a tray to carry it to my room.

But as I go past the dresser, I see a postcard tucked beneath Mam's Princess Diana commemorative plate from 1992 when the Princess of Wales visited Merthyr and Mam took us to wave daffodils at her in the street. I balance the tray on the edge and almost end up with egg on my feet when I recognise Guy's scrappy handwriting. Just when I have decided to forget him he comes back into my world.

So much for saying goodbye to him. Then my stomach drops – what if he's been thinking the same? What if this is goodbye and good luck? Because we haven't had any communication for days now and haven't I had my doubts? It would be natural for him to have them too. If it was a breezy thing, he would've emailed – he's the type who would feel it right and proper to 'end' this situation how it began, on paper. Hungrily, I read it, unable to wait to put myself out of my misery and my heart begins to pace because, thank God, it isn't the end of me and him. He's like my own cheerleader, who helps me through the bad stuff. If we're to stay friends, I need to be brave, out of respect for him. If this is to continue, it's time I honoured his support with some truth-telling of my own.

To: therepairguy@googlemail.com
From: bettyhopkins@gmail.com
Subject: Water Feature

Dear Guy,

Don't diss your watery wonder of the world! The spring sounds enchanting, particularly as I'm partial to a regency bonnet, if that's part of the dipping experience at all?

I would love to visit – I'll find myself a place to stay so I can suit myself when you're with the family. I could kill two birds with one stone and meet an old work friend in London either on the way there or on the way back.

The problem here, deep breath, is that I haven't been quite honest with you and I would like to be.

OK, so no beating about the bush … I haven't left the Valleys since February. I also haven't travelled alone. The reason for this is because that accident I told you about happened when I left the paint-balling place. I had to come home to recover. And I've never made it out. Which means Venice didn't happen either.

I didn't intend to lie – it was more of an escape from how things are and, believe it or not, your letters have kept me going. I apologise for not being true to you and while this sort of thing is best done face to face, I feel it's important to fess up now. Besides, this has always been how we've communicated in the main, so it doesn't feel too horribly a shocking and weird way to do it.

Oh and my dad, he's an arsehole who doesn't know my birthday.

So you see, it might make the train journey a bit tricky. Especially if all this has terrified you, you feel used and you've suddenly moved house and changed your email address and blocked me.

Love,

Betty xxx

To: bettyhopkins@gmail.com
From: therepairguy@googlemail.com
Re: Water Feature

Dear Betty,

Still here. I understand completely. It's not as if we've had an awful lot of time or opportunity to open up. And it's all the more impressive that you've managed to set up your own label without being able to get to London – but everything can be done remotely these days, can't it!

I'll help you.

Best,

Guy

To: therepairguy@googlemail.com
From: bettyhopkins@gmail.com
Subject: Water Feature

You're very forgiving! Thank you. The trouble is it feels a bit *Mission Impossible*.

To: bettyhopkins@gmail.com
From: therepairguy@googlemail.com
Re: Mission Impossible

Your mission, Agent Betty, should you choose to
accept it, is looking impossible where you are now.

But your fear about these 'obstacles' are a
reasonable reaction to what's happened to you.

If you wanted me to meet you somewhere, maybe
halfway* or take you door-to-door, then I will. Unless
I can get hold of Tom Cruise, that is.

Does the bank holiday weekend suit?


*Just googled and the midway point between us is
somewhere I've never heard of in Oxfordshire. So
let's say it's London Paddington.


To: therepairguy@googlemail.com
From: Bettyhopkins@gmail.com
Re: Mission Impossible Code Name: Water Feature

Sigh. You'd better book me a bonnet, then, Agent
Guy.

I'll look into train times. But under no
circumstances are you to involve Tom Cruise – he's
far too excitable for a nervous traveller and I can't
have us kicked off when he starts jumping on the First
Great Western seats.

I will arrange to meet my friend Sami on the return
leg so I've got one confidence-building journey under
my belt. And I will sort my phone (eek) and message

the mobile number on your website, if that's the best
place?

To: bettyhopkins@gmail.com
From: therepairguy@googlemail.com
Re: Mission Impossible Code Name: Water Feature

That would be best, yes. As an international spy, I find
it difficult to keep on top of all my burner phones.

To: therepairguy@googlemail.com
From: Bettyhopkins@gmail.com
Re: Mission Impossible Code Name: Water Feature

So where's the best place for me to book to stay?

To: bettyhopkins@gmail.com
From: therepairguy@googlemail.com
Re: Mission Impossible Code Name: Water Feature

I have something to tell you myself and it happened
before we got back in touch and I should've
mentioned it sooner but, again, there hasn't been the
right moment.

My wife and I separated a couple of months ago.
I have plenty of room at mine, if you are OK with it?
That's not to say I wouldn't have invited you if I was
still with her. I would have, of course, but we are
where we are and it's whatever you feel comfortable

with. Wherever you stay, be warned my grandmother
will hunt you down. She's like that with the Welsh – I
call her the polar bear for that.

By the way, if this changes things, I would like
to thank you for helping me through a terrible few
months and wish you happiness because you deserve
all of the happiness.


To: therepairguy@googlemail.com
From: Bettyhopkins@gmail.com
Re: Mission Impossible Code Name: Water Feature

Oh, right, wow, I'm so sorry to hear that and I'm sure
you've had a really difficult time of things. And, of
course, we've not had the chance to really share much
so, yes, I'm fine with it.

We can talk when we see each other, that's
probably the best thing.

Over and out.


PS Please tell your granny I would love to meet her.


To: bettyhopkins@gmail.com
From: therepairguy@googlemail.com
Re: Mission Impossible Code Name: Water Feature

I read you loud and clear.

PS Granny will be thrilled to meet what she classifies
as a 'full-fat Welshie', because the only contact she

has with her countrymen and women is through her Tunbridge Wells Welsh Club and they're semi-skimmed at most.

I never use emojis but here's a Wales flag for you.

To: therepairguy@googlemail.com
From: Bettyhopkins@gmail.com
Re: Mission Impossible Code Name: Water Feature

PS

*I told you a few days ago I'd do it and guess what? I've done it, I'm using a mobile! Although I don't know if you can read this because my hands are trembling. But I get into London at 1.15 p.m. tomorrow. Would you be able to meet me at Paddington? Love, Betty xxx*

*I can just about make it out. I'll be there. And if you feel funny at any point on the journey, call me.*

*OK, will do. Might need a bit of help. Only when I get on at Merthyr, and possibly when I have to change at Cardiff, then when it stops at Newport, Bristol Parkway, Swindon and Reading, just in case I try to get off.*

*My tip: don't move from your seat. Barrage yourself in with train snacks. I suggest a fortress of Scotch eggs.*

*Train buffet already sorted. Mam has got me egg and cress sandwiches, a Grab Bag of salt and vinegar crisps, chocolate buttons, a fruit salad and water. Then, once I'm in Cardiff, I can get some more for the rest of the journey.*

*You're bossing this phone thing.*

*Sort of: I couldn't face using my old one because there'd be a million notifications and old photos to brood over. I've got a basic Smartphone so I can start again.*

*A master stroke.*

*So. See you tomorrow. GULP.*

*Copy that.*

*Cool. This message will now self-destruct.*

# 22

## *Betty*

The screech of the braking train goes right through me as it comes to a stop at the platform.

It echoes my scream inside, the same one that came in my nightmares in the first weeks after my accident.

The commotion of doors opening and people surging around me crushes my chest and I slam my eyes shut to block it all out. But I'm hurtling back in time, jolting from the impact of the car and flying and my clenched body prepares for the concrete crash landing. I'm losing balance so I jerk back to reality where I'm breathless and on the verge of tears but everyone else is in a state of normality.

I can't do this. I can't do it. I suddenly wish my mother was here to soothe me and to agree that maybe I should try again another day. A million ants are on the march on my skin, drumming out the threat of what's out there beyond the precipice: uncertainty, risk and danger.

The crowds are thinning and doors are slamming and I have to decide. I can't do this. I can't do it. But I have to. Otherwise I'll be confined in a cruel comfort zone of my own making, where I'll never leave. And it'll be a slow suffocation. I feel it now and the sensation of fighting for air forces me to count my steps of progress.

For every 'first time' that I've broken through a self-imposed boundary, there's been huge discomfort – when I've left the house, walked alone, returned to work and driven.

The latest, using a mobile yesterday, was a battle of wills between past and present. I'd immediately blamed myself for the accident and it became my default. Yet no one has ever accused me of any wrongdoing; everyone has said I was unlucky – I was simply in the wrong place at the wrong time. As I passed the phone from hand to hand in my bedroom, I weighed it up. Why haven't I listened to them? Why have I wanted to see myself as the guilty party? Was it my way of trying to make sense of something out of my control? If I was at fault, there was a rational reason for it happening. That tipped the scales and then, by thinking of Guy's advice that it took so much more to cling on, I found I could let go.

And I've survived and my life is richer. This is just another one of those firsts. And I need to remember that, actually, they're only 'firsts' in my post-trauma world. I have done one or other of those things every day of my adult life.

A whistle blows and my throat clams up and I know that to be able to breathe freely I have to go. Pant Bach is where I want to hide but I can't stay within its confines for ever. And as I climb into the carriage with my heart hammering, I give myself an out should I need one: I can get off at any of the stops, change trains and go home.

I just make it when we start to move. I steady myself with a hand on the compartment door but the greasy, grubby glass along with the sway turns my stomach. I find a forward-facing seat, plonk my bag beside me to keep foes at bay, and exhale and tell myself 'well done' for making it this far. As my adrenalin fades, the lull of motion begins to soothe me and my senses come out of hiding, seeking familiarity to reassure me. The teal and white fabric of the seat has the same slightly spiky feel. There's the murmur of talking, the tinny beats from someone's headphones and bursts of laughter coming from a hen party. And in minutes my eyes settle into that soothing soft-focus gaze at lush green countryside out the window. Each time we stop, when we stop, I check myself: am I OK? And, miraculously, I am. But once we leave the Valleys behind and we enter Cardiff, the nerves build again as we pass back gardens, depots and then high-rise buildings. On arrival, I'm swallowed up and spat out and I have to double, triple check my platform and maybe it helps, but the inter-city is waiting with open doors and I slip inside on auto-pilot and go to the quiet carriage so I can recharge my batteries for the onslaught of London.

To my surprise, I enjoy this part of the journey: it's cleaner, air conditioned, less stop-start and the rattle on the rails is now a space-age hum. I feel so good and so safe I eat my sandwiches, flick through some glossy mags Mam bought me – but find myself puzzled by the fashion pages, when I used to snort them up – and then get out my phone. Like a normal person. I get a buzz from that thought – that I've rejoined the human race – and my fingers swipe and type and I remind Sami that he's sworn to secrecy about this: I've told Mam and Nerys I'm visiting him for the weekend. I sent him Guy's address and number and I've agreed to message him regularly. Of course I filled him in that Guy's separated. I had a grilling, as any decent friend would do, but I found my voice, reminding him I'm a grown woman. Even so, Sami's on standby should I need him and so I reassure him I'm fine.

Ha! I'm fine! Who'd have thought? I decide to message Guy to let him know.

> Hiya! I'm on the train. I always used to cringe when people answered their phones and said that. But now I want to shout it at the top of my voice! Love, Betty xxx

> Oops, forgot to say I'm on time and the Scotch egg fortress is working. Look at me showing how at ease I am with my mobile, haha!

I lay it on the table and marvel at the landscape that's been whizzing by; we've left the farmland behind and we're in the urban sprawl of factories and estates and as the graffiti builds I realise we're beyond Reading. I didn't even notice we'd stopped, which means I didn't even consider getting off. Now I can start to get excited about seeing Guy and I'm so glad he's meeting me at Paddington. This has been enough of a test today and I'm confident that having him beside me will see off any anxiety. I won't actually get to walk the streets of London if everything runs smoothly, it'll be an underground to Charing Cross, then a train to Tunbridge Wells, and once I've done all that and enjoyed my visit, I'm sure I can muster up the courage to meet Sami in Soho and have a celebratory lunch.

I'm smiling at the thought of us clinking glasses and I check my phone to see if Guy's in position, imagining

218

some gag to put me at ease. Yet there's nothing. My messages have been delivered. But he hasn't replied. As far as I think I know him, and I feel I do quite well now, it's not like him. Why hasn't he got back to me? He definitely knows to expect me today, I recheck our chat and yes, he said he'd be there. I wish we'd arranged a specific rendezvous. Paddington is a big place. What if he's held up? What if we miss each other? What if he's run out of battery, or his phone's been nicked and I'm there alone? Do I wait or do I go home? I feel really warm all of a sudden, and then cold as a chill descends. What if he's not coming? What if he's changed his mind?

It's not as if we revealed our shoe sizes to each other. I'm still head blown at what he's had to go through and he'd be a saint not to feel the same. Maybe if he's begun to think we told each other lies rather than half-truths, he might be having second thoughts.

I scroll back and reread our conversations: there's nothing but support and understanding. Yet people can change their minds. Just twenty-four hours and I'm already feeling that mobile-induced anxiety of why hasn't he returned my messages?

Panic begins to snake its way around my body and its squeeze grows in intensity.

People are beginning to stand and collect their bags and the train is slowing, brakes screaming again, and the sunlight is snatched away as we enter the terminal where the filthy walls come at us.

I hear my sister telling me Guy's a creep and a fake and Sami's warnings to take care. Only Megan wished me well, and I sucked that up because she's met him albeit briefly. Yet what does she know about men? Then there's

Guy himself – separated from his wife and baby. It did throw me, as any bit of turbulence does; I mean, he let me believe he was happily married, but why? Then again I can hardly talk. He hadn't had the chance to explain – and how devastated he must be, which will always make the words dry up. Whereas I, on the other hand, have committed a worse sin by embellishing the truth – and I still haven't come clean about where I work. My mind is a mess and, I admit now, Guy's a stranger; people are in the main good but is there a chance I'm stepping into something complicated or possibly unsafe? What if he's not who I thought? There's a chance he could ghost me too.

We've stopped and I'm frozen in my seat, then I'm alone as an announcement informs me this is the end of the line. What if I get up, leave the train and find he's not there? What if I don't and I stay where I am and wait for the train to go back the way it came? I stare hard at my phone to think.

My lies have been about wanting to get back to the person I was before, when I was brave and capable. They've also showed my fear of failure.

It's time to work out who I've become.

## 23

### Guy

Finally, the tube train moves and everyone whoops and applauds. Except, of course, they don't, because this is London. In fact, no one does anything. To do otherwise – like, for example, talk to a passenger you don't know – means you are a psycho. There are some fed-up faces; I risk a look but eye contact is a no-no too, so I watch my knee bouncing with impatience.

Being stuck for fifteen minutes means I'm late for Betty and I've had no way of telling her because in the bowels of the capital my phone has no reception.

So when we get to Paddington, I jump off and leg it through the labyrinth of tunnels, my mobile in hand, which buzzes with messages. I can't properly read and run but a glance shows they're from her. I curse everything, rushing to get through the barriers, then take the stairs two at a time and emerge into the light of the huge glass-domed terminal.

Damn it, I'm so late the Cardiff train has dropped off the arrivals board, so I don't know which platform she came in on. I read her messages and if I'd have got them, I'd have reassured her I'd be there. But I didn't and I wasn't there waiting for her. I call her straight away as I turn in a slow circle to see if I can see her through the busy moving mass of people. But it rings out and I start to panic. Where is she? Did she leave when she saw I wasn't there? The thought of her getting all this way by herself, expecting me to be waiting by the platform barrier and then seeing I'm not is crucifying. Where would she have gone? Then I wonder if she actually made it to Paddington at all? She sounded fine in her messages but what if my not replying threw her and she's heading home? Maybe she thinks I've got an ulterior motive? That I've deliberately reeled her in with the soppy dad thing so I'm no threat but then, wallop, I tell her I'm separated, but it's made her feel uneasy? Some blokes are like that. I need her to know I'm not. I redial but there's no answer. Again. The customer service desk will tell me which platform she came in on but there's a queue. My only option is to do a check of every single one.

I start at the first, scanning the gate and benches for red hair and I imagine how overwhelming it would be for her to land in this swarm of people all walking at each other balancing hot coffees and wheeling bags. At the second, third, fourth and fifth my hope begins to fade and by the time I get to the twelfth, I've lost it completely. I drop to my haunches and command myself to think. What would Betty do?

Exasperated, I say it out loud up to the pigeons perching on high, 'What would Betty do?'

'Betty,' says a very familiar voice that makes me leap to my feet, 'would ask where the hell you've been?'

I swing round and see her frowning, with her arms crossed and tutting.

'Betty!'

'Calm down, I only popped to the loo!' She smiles,

222

dropping the act. 'You told me not to leave my seat! The Scotch eggs were unsurpassable!'

We burst out laughing and I begin explaining but she kind of glazes over and sags a little. Any reticence either of us might feel about the new information we've learned about each other disappears as we go in for a hug and I notice how we fit, like jigsaw pieces.

We pull apart and I take her bag and we head to the tube. On high alert, she's wary and quiet on the journey underground and I notice her limp is back. As soon as the Tunbridge Wells train departs, she falls asleep and her head lolls onto my shoulder. It should feel awkward and complicated but it just feels natural.

'Sorry to wake you,' I say quietly into her silky hair that smells of coconuts and happiness, 'we're nearly here.'

Betty comes to as we slow to a stop.

'I was tired out! All that nervous energy, I think,' she says, still looking delicate as we get off. 'So what's the plan?'

'Entirely up to you. If you're chomping at the bit to see the dippers, we could do that?'

She nods enthusiastically but she's let down by her endearing, flaring nostrils as she fights a yawn. If that was me, I'd resemble a horse but somehow she remains gorgeous.

'But if you'd prefer to save that for tomorrow, you can anticipate it even more, and we could get food or go home? You've been travelling all day and it's almost four.'

'Let's drop my bag,' she says, 'then see what happens.'

And what happens is we don't make it out the house again.

She gets a tour, pleased with her en suite room in the attic, then asks to see 'where the magic happens' – her idea, her words, not mine, because I assume women would die laughing if I offered to show them my workshop. But she's almost reverential in there as she pours over my shelves of nails, nuts and bolts, trailing fingers through sawdust as if it's fairy dust and taking in lungfuls of the smell of paint and varnish. She asks about each repair that I'm working on, marvelling that I'm able to fit a new lock and key on a jewellery box for a poorly little girl who is in and out of hospital and attach new mirror tiles to a disco ball owned by a ballroom champion. But she's most touched by a man in his eighties, a friend of Kay's, who's entrusted me to mend his rusting ancient tin opener that's lost its bite, preferring to spend more on repairing the wedding gift from fifty years ago than buy new.

Now we're in, we decide to stay in. I cook a veggie pasta while she showers, then we shovel it down with wine at the kitchen island. We chat, she gushes about her nieces, and I tell her how I dream of a big family. She mentions an auction she's working on with Megan, the woman whose half-brother fell in the Arcade, but when I praise her about mentoring and ask about her label and designing, she says she needs to talk to me.

The garden is the place for that so we curl up on cushions on the giant day bed I made from pallets, beneath a wooden pergola threaded with jasmine, which exhales its heady scent as the warm night falls. Silhouettes of wildflowers line the edges of the lawn as moths dance around low solar lanterns which line the sleeper steps to the workshop.

She goes to speak but I hold up my hands.

'Let me go first, it's important you know the score, you deserve to hear it, when you're on my territory. And I think you're amazing for getting here, and I understand why you didn't tell me about the whole timing of the accident. I saw how traumatised you were by it ... remember, I saw the crash scene afterwards. So let me open up to you, OK?'

Betty nods and listens in perfect silence while I explain how Sarah and I broke up because I wanted kids and she wasn't ready, how she slept with my best mate, how she came back to me saying she wanted to start a family, how she was pregnant and never once thought to tell me it might not be mine. And then the final heartbreak of hearing Maud wasn't.

'I've never said this to anyone before but, on top of everything, and I'm embarrassed to say it because I sound like a Neanderthal, it kind of emasculated me. When all I've ever wanted to be is a dad.'

'Oh Guy,' she sighs, 'I can't imagine the torture you've been through. It makes my stuff seem so insignificant.'

'No, no. Please. Talk to me.'

She shakes her head. 'Another time, because what happened to you must have been so much worse as you'd lost your parents.'

I fill her in on the Great Storm of 1987. 'So,' I say, deadpan, 'I pretty much win at "my mum and dad are dead" competitions.'

She gives me a sad smile. 'It must be difficult being a father one minute, then the next, kaput, no more.'

'It's not that simple.'

Betty blinks slowly at me. 'What do you mean? Because you're not involved anymore, are you?'

'Well – you don't switch love off like a tap, do you?'

'No, of course not. I mean on a practical level.'

'So I'm not doing nappies anymore, obviously, but it hasn't been a clean break, put it that way. Sarah and Charlie kind of need support. I know it sounds like madness, but Maud was mine for a while, you know? There've been a few problems and I've been there to help, that's all.'

Betty bites her cheek and says nothing.

'I've banged on for too long,' I say.

'Not at all.' She touches my arm.

'Your go.'

She takes a deep breath and considers it. 'My problems are small fry, honestly. How about instead,' Betty says, lifting her glass for a top-up, 'I tell you about Venice?'

I laugh, reaching for the bottle, while she reaches for her phone.

'Addicted already?'

'Don't! I do worry I'll get attached to it again. I'm just messaging Sami, otherwise he'll ring if I don't let him know I'm still alive.'

'Of course.' I let her finish and then ask her, 'So, are you OK?'

Something shifts between us and her eyes travel around my face which makes my heart beat faster.

'Yeah. I am. Are you?' Betty plays with a strand of hair and I have to look away, she's so beautiful.

'Yeah,' I admit, pulling at a thread on my shorts.

'Don't tell me there's a but.' I think she's teasing me yet there's no way I'm going to run with it.

226

'No buts at all.' I lift my face to hers because I want her to see I'm genuine. 'It's so nice to have made a friend in you.'

'Same,' she says, now shy. 'It's gorgeous here, Guy.'

I watch her take in the darkening sky and the first twinkle of the stars and I see her shiver.

'Oh Betty, are you cold?' I say, getting up. 'I'll get you a blanket.'

She hesitates then takes my hand and she's warm to the touch.

'No. I'm not cold.'

'This reminds me of the waterfall!' I say. 'You claimed you weren't cold then! What is it, do you Welsh pride yourselves on not feeling the chill?'

'Guy. I wasn't cold in the waterfall and I'm not cold now.'

I'm getting definite vibes off her but she's vulnerable. I mean, I am too. Both of us have been broken and if this goes somewhere – I get a wave of desire as she shuffles ever so slightly closer to me. This is going to piss all over our chips but I have to ask her.

'OK, so you're either impervious to the cold,' I say, dropping my eyes to watch her fingers play with mine. 'Or maybe you feel what I do?'

If I put myself out there first, at least it gives her the chance to double-check herself. And if this is the only chance I get to tell her, then I can't wonder 'what if?'.

Her eyes go heavy and she tells me, 'I do.'

I can't believe my luck. I need to clarify this. 'Look, just to be sure, you're OK with this … now … because this isn't why I asked you to visit. Bottom line, if you only want to be friends, I'll take it.'

'Guy, shall we live in the moment and be brave and be all the things you and I need and want to be?' She says it with that huskiness that makes me want to abandon myself to her.

'What if it goes weird?'

'It already is,' she says, moving towards me as our finally undeniable chemistry pulls us together and our lips meet. It's hot and slow, sexy and deep, and it's like nothing I've ever felt before.

The thump of my heart, the flow of my blood. Her growing intensity. Our tongues entwining. And our hands exploring one another. She's smoother and softer than anything, her curves have me swooping and rising and her touch sends me further into her.

But I stop and come up for air because while the want is there, there is no need to rush.

'Just the truth from now on,' I say, as we snuggle into each other.

I feel her taking a breath and wait for her to talk. 'You can tell me anything, you know. It's about trust, isn't it?'

'Despite my giant whopper about Venice.'

'Shush! I get it.'

'I almost didn't get off the train, you know,' she says quietly.

'Really?' I wince. 'Oh God, I hate to think of you waiting to hear from me.'

'It was more because – well, my sister has this theory. That I sabotage things … with people … just in case they go wrong. Like I didn't want to turn up and find out you'd sacked me off.'

I cringe at the thought of her returning home. 'I would never have done that.'

'My sister says it's my philanderer of a father's fault, basically. Low self-esteem, low expectations.'

'I won't let you down, Betty. Anything else to get off your chest?'

'There are some things but we're tired and – I do have something to ask you.'

'Anything,' I say.

'Can we sleep out here, it's such a nice night. Can we do that?'

I hear her yawn into my neck and suddenly I'm as exhausted as she is. But I can think of nothing better.

'Yep, of course.'

'All night long?' she says.

'What, is Lionel Ritchie coming too?'

She elbows me and it is thoroughly deserved.

'All night long,' I confirm. 'Or as long as we can get before next door starts on his naked sunrise salutations. He can be quite grunty.'

She laughs and I tell her I'll be as quick as possible getting some bedding. And I'm fast, I'm that excited about sleeping al fresco, but not fast enough, because she's out for the count when I get back.

I put a pillow under her head and then cover us up and in seconds I join her sleeping under the stars.

# 24

## *Betty*

We wake up cosy in bed after the dawn chorus and dew forced us inside.

'Well, that escalated quickly,' I say to Guy, who's the big spoon to my little spoon, and he laughs quietly as he pulls me in even tighter.

'I reckon ...' he says, whispering numbers as his brain whirrs, 'we've spent probably less than twenty-four hours together in total and here we are.'

'There have been a few letters and postcards in-between, mind; I wouldn't want to think of you as someone who's loose with his morals.'

'Hardly! I'm such a stud muffin I've had a single one-night stand in my life. I'm what you call a serial monogamist.'

I squirm and he reads into my silence. 'You, on the other hand ...?'

'Yeah,' I admit, 'a few – with unsuitables.'

'The sabotage thing again?'

'Exactly. But it's more obvious in the longish-term boyfriends I've had. Take my last, Jude, who I assumed wouldn't want to settle down because he was younger than me but he did and...' This is short version of events and I'm not ready to tell him everything. '...it wasn't right so off I went. This, though, might be my worst.'

'What? Why?' He's taken aback.

'Because you're married and I have always sworn never to go there, m'lud.'

'It's a technicality. Would I be introducing you to my granny if I were a cad, your honour?'

He's not a player, I'm sure of it. OK, last night I was thrown by his involvement with Sarah after what she did to him. But then his devotion to Maud is obvious – is loyalty such a bad thing? I know doubt and insecurity will come, as it always does when you make yourself vulnerable. And I need to tell him about my job, but it wasn't right to do it just when he'd opened up so bravely. But right now, when I want to savour something good after the shit show of badness, I'm making the most of being cuddled up with Guy. I wriggle my back even closer into his naked, warm chest and he throws a thigh over mine as if he's claiming me. I'm obviously a passionate feminist but there is no denying the pleasure of feeling wanted. And there's physical proof he wants me and I more than match his desire. But without having to say it, we both know to go slow: his boxers and my vest-and-pyjama-shorts set have remained on throughout.

Hunger gets us up and out for a gorgeous sunny brunch on The Pantiles which, after Guy told me, will forever be known to me as The Panties with a silent L. When it's time to meet Myfanwy, my nerves come at me.

She's not just Guy's grandmother, she's also his mum, his dad, his everything now, and I imagine a matriarch with pince-nez glasses.

'She'll love you,' he's said more than once, 'and you'll love her.'

231

But, understandably, she'll be very protective of him. I get it; I remember my late nana telling me and Nerys every teatime when Mam was working that if anyone ever so much as looked at us funny she'd give them a bunch of fives.

Yet from the moment we say hello with a flurry of 'how are you?' and 'lovely to meet you!' and she opens her arms wide for a giant cwtch, I realise she's as warm as a Welsh cake bakestone without a hint of dragon about her.

And, my God, she's a total queen with cropped silver hair, chunky jewellery and a long, belted, floaty palm-leaf kaftan.

'You know, it's true what they say, isn't it,' she says as if we're continuing a chat of old, 'when you hear a Welsh accent outside of Wales you can't help but get excited!'

'Oh yes, I'd practically combust when I'd come across one in London, it's that feeling of belonging! And you haven't lost yours at all!'

Myfanwy clutches her chest as if I've granted her the elixir of life. 'Thank God for that! You worry it'll go, it's been so long since I've been home – last time was, what, three years ago, Guy?'

He nods with a faint look of bemusement on his face.

'He's promised me a road trip. I'm from Bethlehem, my brother and sisters are still there, so I'm hoping it won't be too long. And, fingers crossed, I'll get to move back one day.' Quite clearly it is too soon for me to be thinking of my future feelings for Guy but my heart leaps that he could be visiting her and perhaps popping in to see me – that's what happiness does and my imagination never needs much encouragement. 'So tell me, Betty, how are you finding Royal Tunbridge Wells?'

'Er, can I interrupt the love-in for one second?' Guy says, stepping towards us and I realise we are both still holding hands across the lounge.

'Excuse me!' Myfanwy says, her eyes twinkling, 'It's not often I get to commune with a proper Welshie!' Then she winks at me and we let go of one another because, frankly, we are being a bit exclusive.

'Coffee, G? Betty?'

'Yes, cariad.' Then she turns back to me and we walk through to the garden.

'Ooh, before I forget, I've got something for you,' I say, taking a seat and handing her a bag.

'What's all this, then?'

'Open it!' I say. 'It was in the charity shop.' I remember just in time not to mention it's my place of work.

I get a gasp of approval and she calls to Guy, who appears with a tray.

'It's a jigsaw of love spoons, Guy!' she cries. 'Love spoons of Wales, it's called.'

'What the hell are love spoons?'

I tut at his ignorance while Myfanwy explains. 'They're carved out of wood, traditionally given to ladies by a suitor to show romantic intent; the spoon idea is the wish to feed someone, to support them, the one you love. But these days you can get them for friendship, anniversaries, that sort of thing. And the carvings are of symbols. See, here—' she points to the cover – 'horseshoes are for luck, locks for security and twisted stems mean a coming together. Your grandfather made me one, Guy, for our engagement.'

'I've never seen it!' He says it disgruntled – it's a sign of how close they are, that he's annoyed there's something he doesn't know.

'It's in a drawer somewhere, battered beyond. I'll dig it out for you. I'm so very touched, Betty. Thank you!'

Then Myfanwy asks again what I think of the town.

'It's lovely! Very refined and leafy.' Expensive too, like London in parts, and the charity shops are a bit more upmarket than Life Goes On.

'Where has Guy taken you, then?'

I immediately think 'heaven', then wonder what's got into me and quickly move on.

'I was too tired to do anything last night,' I glance at Guy and we exchange a heated look which threatens to throw me off. 'But we've just come from The Pantiles; it's so olde worlde, like something off a period drama. We mooched about, had some tapas. It's been lovely.'

'And did you take the waters?'

This puts an end to my longing and I guffaw. 'I did! Guy went first and pulled a hilarious grimace and I thought he was messing about but when I had a go – ych-a-fi!'

'Ych-a-fi!' Myfanwy claps with delight.

'Uckavee?' Guy echoes.

'It means yuck and disgusting,' I say.

'It is an acquired taste.' Myfanwy smiles. 'I know exactly the face you mean that Guy pulls; he was like that as a toddler, didn't like something and he'd look like he was chewing on a wasp!'

I roar at his obvious embarrassment.

'Know what, I get the piss taken out of me in Wales, I thought I was going to be getting my own back on Betty here! But nope.'

'Quite right! Now pour the coffee!'

*

After a long goodbye, which is a Welsh tradition that involves a few new conversations interwoven with promises that this time I'm really going, we leave to pick up my stuff.

The mood alters between us. My glow has become an ache because my train leaves in an hour. He's gone quiet too and I hope he feels the same. His phone has also been beeping on and off for the last twenty minutes and I wonder if it's a Repair Guy thing and this is his work face. But as we walk to the station he remains distant. Suddenly, I worry that I've been too casual with the mention of seeing him again and all the bed talk runs through my head as if we have been too intimate too quickly.

'You OK?' I ask, as we swing hands.

'Mmm,' he says, 'You?'

'All right.'

That gets his attention. 'What's up? Are you worried about London? Sami's meeting you at Charing Cross, isn't he? Bit of food, then he'll take you to Paddington, isn't that what you said? And your mum's getting you from Cardiff, so you won't have to do the last leg. That's good isn't it?'

Remarkably, I wasn't thinking about any of that. I was thinking about how much I'll miss him but I have to keep it buried because the bubble has burst.

'Yeah,' I say just to shut it down. But I know Sami will prise it out of me, this unfamiliar feeling of pining for a man while he's still by my side and how quickly I've gone from feeling adored to needy: worrying if he'll kiss me goodbye or if we're back to being friends and he just hasn't told me. Because there is a lot to worry about. The distance, when we'll be together again, and his ex, who is still clearly in his life, not to mention the fact that I still haven't told him the truth about Life Goes On. Plus, there's the fact that he wants, as he called it, a whole brood of kids when I might not be able to … I stop myself. I'm being irrational rather than in the present. I need to be jolly and gay and make him wish I was staying. Tits and teeth, kid, I tell myself.

'So this is me.' I smile as we get to the redbrick Victorian railway station.

'This is you,' he says, taking my face in his hands and turning me to mush and it feels like I have him back.

He strokes my hair and starts to move towards me with a waft of lemon scent and all the desire I have for him rises up inside of me. I want to press record to save this forever. But a bellow of 'Foxy!' goes up and Guy flinches.

He steps back from me and his face goes sallow. There's a man coming towards us with a pram and Guy's jaw sets while his Adam's apple bobs up and falls in a gulp.

What the hell is Foxy all about? His surname is Slater.

A rumble comes from behind me, it's my train pulling in but it might as well be the brakes on my heart.

I look for a clue from Guy about what's happening but he seems to be in a trance.

'Guy, I've got to go,' I say. His eyes don't register me and I tug my bag off him.

'He's early, for fuck's sake,' he says.

'Who?'

'Charlie. I repeatedly messaged him to meet me here in ten minutes.' That's who he was communicating with that made him withdraw. 'Once you'd gone.'

'Right, so? What's the issue?' I could take offence at that – was it that Guy didn't want to be seen with me?

They might not be best mates anymore but he told me today his oldest friend had been a brother to him.

'He's got Maud with him. He's not doing great and I kind of offered to help him with her, to sort of build his confidence and show him the ropes.'

'Oh.' The truth feels like a slap on my cheek; I didn't realise this was what he meant about being involved with Maud. I thought it meant he missed her. An alarm begins to ring.

'It's fine,' he says but he looks distinctly unfine.

'I can get a later train, if—?' I offer in case he needs me.

'No. No.' It's a definitive answer and it catches me in the windpipe – as intimate as we've been, this is something he can't share with me. In the meantime, people are streaming out of the ticket office; I need to get a move on. I can't wait any longer.

Stuck in his emotion, Guy kind of gropes through the air at me but it's more an absent gesture. I have to go. Then I'm gone, through the barrier, onto the platform and into the carriage. I'm dizzy as I fall back into my seat.

The train kicks forward and as we go through a tunnel so black I can't see my hands, I get a glimpse of a feeling that perhaps I've totally misjudged what's happened between Guy and me. I've let down my guard, believing we have some deep connection, that this thing is meaningful. He makes me feel like I'm the centre of the world. But he could be like that with everyone; I dropped off his radar completely just now. Could I have been taken in by him? Not that he's deliberately misled me, but have I read this and him all wrong? I'm damaged, and so is he. Yet he presents as normal. Have I missed any clues?

Has my heart overruled my head? Falling for a man so troubled when I'm struggling myself could be madness.

As we emerge into the light, I understand I need to pull the reins on my feelings for Guy.

But it won't be easy. Because when I'm with him they run and run and run free.

## 25

### *Guy*

I thought I'd be OK with this, I really did.

But with Charlie coming towards me, I'm suspended, physically rooted to the spot and emotionally stunned.

Because Maud is in that buggy, the one Sarah and I picked out from a million of them for its safety features and travel capacity.

Through the railings behind him and his daughter, I see the back end of Betty's train disappearing and I feel helpless and hollow. And the biggest idiot going because I didn't get to say goodbye to her; I let her go without telling her how happy she makes me.

I get a stab of anger that I was robbed of that moment. Robbed again by Charlie. What is it with him? He takes my wife, my baby, my life and now my future. But I can't live like this, I can't allow the past to rule me. I exhale slowly and deeply to get rid of what I can of the poison. I was the one who said Maud had to come first. Who offered to help Charlie.

I raise a hand to him and he lifts one at me but then slaps it back down onto the handlebar just as quickly, like he's a child learning to ride a bicycle. This is the man who was the first to volunteer to do a bungee jump or a sky dive on lads' holidays back in the day. His idea of good fun is skiing down a black run or hurtling down an extreme mountain bike trail at breakneck speed. Even when it comes to food he's fearless: he's sampled grubs Down Under, fried crickets in Bangkok and his favourite curry is a vindaloo. Yet this is the most uncomfortable I've ever seen him.

'Sorry about all the messages earlier. I was panicking I'd get Maud then you'd be late or … and I'd be alone with her.'

In that instant I want to shout at him to pull himself together. Instead I nod. 'So what's the plan?'

Charlie's face goes panicky. 'What do you mean? I don't know. I thought you'd have one?'

I realise we're not even at the starting line with him. I look down on Maud, her eyes are sealed tight and she's clutching Peter Rabbit. I remember how I'd watch and wonder what dreams she was having – were they of light and shade, or colours or of our faces? But the one I'd settle on would be of bob-tailed bunnies in waistcoats.

'How long do you have her?'

'Sarah said two hours.'

'OK, so maybe take her to yours? Because you need to get her used to being there.'

'Right, yes.' He's not embarrassed – it's worse, he's bewildered.

'Sarah OK?'

He shakes his head. 'She had a bad night.'

This information is too much. Charlie hasn't a Scooby, Sarah is struggling and Maud isn't my responsibility.

He gestures for me to take the pram. But that's not going to help him. I stuff my hands in my pockets.

'Let's go to yours. Have you got Maud's stuff?'

Charlie slaps the cross-sling nappy bag that's hanging against his hip. At least he's got that.

'And have you baby-proofed the house?'

'What's that? How do I do that?'

Maud starts crying and Charlie almost jumps.

'Don't worry, we'll do it later. Just start pushing, the movement will soothe her. And talk to her, let her know you're there.'

It takes us a long ten minutes to get to Charlie's, as he makes a meal out of kerbs and checks the empty roads and glances anxiously every few seconds at Maud, who looks like an angel as she sleeps.

Inside the house, I run through the potential danger zones – she'll be crawling soon, pulling herself up on furniture, sticking anything and everything in her mouth. Charlie follows me around with a pen and paper and scribbles every time I mention he needs covers for the plugs and pointed edges on tables and a guard to go round all the wires and the telly and a baby gate for the stairs. When she wakes up, he looks at me as if to say 'what next?'. It tips me over the edge and I can't help it.

'You've got four nephews and nieces, mate, have you never held them?'

'Briefly, you know, to say hello when we were introduced.' His language is stilted, like he's describing meeting an acquaintance. 'But then, you know, parents are protective, they want them back or the baby cries and then I couldn't always make the family lunches, and if I did go, there'd be this joke about me being in nappies still.'

It all makes sense. The youngest of three boys, he was considered the baby; his mum certainly was softer with him than with the other two. Maybe she was hanging on to keep him little for as long as possible? He was also the joker of the three and when you get a role in a family, you tend to be stereotyped into it forever.

'I'm much better now with them being older. It's easy to play and chat and be Uncle Cheeky Charlie. Eddie and Tommy thought I was taking the piss when I told them I was a dad.'

I don't feel sorry for him though – I just feel impatient with him. Meanwhile, Maud has been silent and watchful as if she's sizing him up.

'Right,' I say, sighing at his ineptitude, 'so pick her up, support her head as you do it, then cuddle her.'

His movement is cautious and slow, but he gets the idea that he needs to reassure her. Charlie gingerly reaches in and it's this moment that's the hardest of all.

Maud stares at him, there's no recognition there, but there's also no complaint. Then as he begins to lift her, she mirrors his smile as if she knows.

'Hiya, Maudy Moo,' he says, so gently, 'it's Daddy.'

His words go straight through me; his knowledge and experience are non-existent yet it's clear he has instinct in spades. He's come up with a pet name for her and he's owning fatherhood. It's moving and it's agony. I turn away because I have tears in my eyes.

Somehow I talk him through a nappy change, a feed and a story. I suggest he shows her the house and where her room will be. An hour ago, he'd have freaked at this. But now he's settled into it and disappears upstairs. I should call to him to say goodbye. Yet, heart-breakingly,

I'm surplus to requirements now. I don't belong here anymore.

But he hears me opening the door and comes down, looking a different man.

'I didn't even ask who you were with at the station.'

'Just a friend.' My heart bursts at the thought of Betty, her vivacious life-giving spirit and her voice, the way she laughs at me, how I bathe in her attention, and her body, which has the softest, most sensual curves.

'Weird, she looked familiar.' I don't tell him he would've seen me returning with her as the two winners at my stag do. He doesn't have the right to know anymore. 'Anyway, thanks for today. It means a lot.'

'No problem. You'll get there. You're already getting there.'

'Reckon?' He beams at me. 'Good job, really, seeing as I've knocked that Glasgow position on the head.'

About bloody time, I think. 'So ... best count me out from now on.'

'Oh,' Charlie says, as if it hasn't occurred to him that we are no longer pals.

I realise I have no one to rage at about this – Charlie would've been my go-to in times of need before but he's the source of it. It makes me want to shake him, tell him 'what the fuck did you expect?'. Ask if he thought I was going to be chaperone for the rest of his bloody life.

I slam the door on the way out, seething at him holding my daughter. I'm an outsider in my own life. My entire network has gone. That smug social circle of new parents collapsed when Sarah and I split up – separations can be catching after all. I know a million people but when you pour everything into your business and family, when you drop out of five-a-side and stop going to the pub, you become isolated. The only person I have to talk to is Granny.

I panic. That makes Betty even more important. I bash out a message to her to apologise and ask her to let me know how the journey and her day goes and to say how happy I was to see her.

I have to concentrate on calming down and I use the walk to Granny's to do some thinking.

She's at the jigsaw table making a start on Betty's gift.

'See her off OK?' she asks. 'Want to find the straight bits?'

I sit beside her with a huge sigh but don't join in. She hands me the cover of the box and it has masses of love spoons of all different shapes and sizes decorated with hearts and dragons, daffodils and harps. But it swims before my eyes. 'I've just been with Charlie and Maud.'

She puts her arm around me. Then finds the right way to reach me – I take it back about pitying myself for only having her to lean on.

'I found the love spoon Grandpa made me.' She reaches inside her pocket and hands it over. I turn it around in my hands, surprised it's not heavier because it's solid and the length of a Christmas cracker. 'It's seen better days, but you can see the carvings, the bell means marriage, the heart is love. He made it from a tree back home, in his father's orchard, a few miles from here.'

'It's beautiful, G. I'll buff it up for you, if you like?'

'Lovely!'

'What do the two small balls mean here?' They're perfectly round and tucked inside the heart.

'That represents how many children we wanted to have. We had your father, then there were a few miscarriages and I decided enough was enough.'

'And you ended up with me, poor thing.'

'No, no! You were a blessing. You still are – you keep me young!'

It's my way in – her youthfulness might make her more flexible.

'I wanted to talk to you actually, Granny.'

Immediately she looks up at me. 'It's a yes from me! She's wonderful!' She widens her eyes to emphasise just how wonderful.

'I didn't mean Betty but – yep, she is.' I kick myself again for messing up our goodbye.

'I can tell how fond you are of her. She's cheered you up no end too. You go very well together, I must say. Do you think it'll lead to anything?'

'It already feels like something but I don't know what we do from here because of the distance. And, well, this is what I wanted to talk to you about.' She moves her body around to give me her undivided attention. 'I'm thinking about putting my place on the market. It feels right to let it go.'

'Good on you. You can stay here until you decide what your next step is, if you wish? You could go anywhere! Imagine that!' Her eyes widen at the possibilities.

'But what about you?'

'What about me? I have a home, thank you very much.' Bobby wanders up and paws my hand for a stroke.

'I can't leave you. Bobby isn't very good at conversation, is he?'

'So what do you suggest? A granny cage where you can

stick me on a rocking chair?' She shakes her head softly at me.

'That is exactly what I mean, us going together.' My heartbeat bangs with approval. 'Apart from the cage and rocking-chair bit. I was going to go round the houses before saying it, but now you have. Why not?'

Granny gapes at me.

'It's just you and me now. And Bobby. We're the only family we've got.'

'There's my lot in Wales! Don't forget them.'

'So what if we went to look for a place nearby? You're always saying you want to see them and you miss Wales.'

'Is this Betty related? Because I know how much you like her but—'

'No. Not at all. And I mean that. It's to do with everything here, there's no anchor anymore.'

'You can't run away from life,' Granny says, kindly.

'But what if it's not running away but building a new one? I'm tired of worrying about bumping into Charlie and Sarah and the baby. And to be honest, as much as I like Tunbridge Wells, it's not – it doesn't make me feel alive. It hasn't for a long time. I feel stifled here by the past. But, more than that, wouldn't it be good to have an adventure? While we still can, together?'

I see something shift in Granny's eyes and she plays with her necklace.

'I suppose ...'

'Yes?' I get up and throw my hands out at her.

'There's no harm in looking.'

'Seriously?'

She takes a big breath. 'I don't want to be a burden on you, that's my main concern. I don't want you to feel

246

you have to look after me. Because I have years left in me.'

'I know and you're not a burden. But, actually, I do have to look after you. The way you looked after me.'

'I have some savings.'

'We'll be able to get somewhere decent with the money from my house. But whatever you insist. We'll get it all drawn up legally. We could have a place with some land. Cover Bobby's ears, G, we could get another dog. I can have a new workshop, you can build that summerhouse you've always said you wanted. Rolling hills ...'

'Fields of sheep and a community hall – a village, I think, with its own heartbeat, where people care and you can't walk down the street without bumping into someone you know. Yes, I miss all of that, I always have.'

'I'll get on it straight away.'

'Well, that's settled, then!' She laughs with astonishment. 'I thought I was going to live out the rest of my life here. But all of a sudden, well,' she says as her voice cracks, 'it looks like I'm going home.'

I have no idea why but I know how she feels.

# 26

## *Betty*

There are tears when I get to Sami.

But this time they're happy ones and they're accompanied by hoots and honks of laughter because our reunion is a ridiculous slo-mo run towards each other straight out of a cheesy film.

'My God, Betty!' Sami cries, as we embrace on the concourse, 'I love that boho dress, it really brings out your inner bumpkin. You look amazing! Not as good as me, though, obvs.'

'Obvs. How on earth can I compete with a tux, silver sequin belt, shorts and cowboy boots? I had no idea the Wild West James Bond look was in.'

'It never went out, darling.' He speaks with the authority of a London-born and London-bred designer. We squeeze each other again and then he slips his arm through mine. 'How are you? You Soho-ready?' His tone becomes soft and he pulls me in. 'We won't go berserk. I've got to get you on a train in one piece. Besides, I'm all grown up now.'

'Pffft!'

'None of that, thank you. Now, it's completely up to you where we go and how we get there. Whatever, wherever, I'm with you.'

He's as buoyant as ever and it lifts me and gives me the extra shot of confidence I need to face the city.

'With you, Sami, I am forever Soho-ready. Let's do it,' I say, 'let's walk those streets paved with gold.'

We step out of Charing Cross and it's like that blast of heat when you get off an aeroplane in a hot country. Except the blast is noise and neon and it takes my breath away. You forget how intense it is, how formidable the buildings are, how fast the cyclists go, how huge the buses are and the endless march of people and pigeons. Horns are blowing and pedestrian crossings are beeping and the smell is of exhausts and food. My heart is going; how could it not when I'm back where I was when I was hit by a car. And I stop for a second, holding Sami tightly, to compose myself. It won't happen again, I tell myself, just as Guy did when I had to drive. I was unlucky, that's all. Still, though, it feels like I'm about to step onto a merry-go-round and I'm frightened I'll fall.

'One foot in front of the other,' Sami says, patting my arm, and we start to walk along the pavement. We stick to the side furthest from the traffic and it's going OK until we encounter a zebra crossing to get to The Strand. There's no need for me to revisit the exact one where it happened, that would feel ghoulish. This one, any single one in London, will do and I'm feeling sick as we approach it. Fortunately, we're in a thick crowd, we're near Trafalgar Square and it's heaving with tourists. I don't even have the time to think about it because we're swallowed up and swept along across the path of traffic and it's that, how matter of fact it was, that tells me I'm not cured but I'm in a place of acceptance. All the months of fear and worry have given me so much pain

249

that I've caused extra suffering for myself. I can never change what happened or be grateful for it but I can give myself permission to acknowledge it. If I allow it to be, then maybe it'll shrink and become a distant memory.

'OK?' Sami asks as we reach the other side.

'Yes! I actually believe I am!' And instead of thinking of myself and what I've lost, I work out how far I've come – and I find I'm asking myself whether I'm ready to live in London again.

During the heart-soaring twenty-minute walk to our old haunt, passing the National Gallery and Chinatown, he fills me in on the Banta gossip and naturally I'm delighted to hear that Sami's uncle Ahmed is still holding out for me to return. I laugh at how different things are as co-manager of a charity shop to a company PA. But Sami's no negative Nelly, and he sees what I'm doing as resilient, as giving something back, and that I'm one of a new breed of people who combine a work ethic with ethics. Everyone should have a mate like him.

'You look well on it too. More ruddy-cheeked!'

'There's a lot of fresh air at home. But I guess it's because I'm able to be both organised and creative. In fact, I've done some sketches on the way; I'll have to show you.' I'll mention my label idea another time because it's only right Ahmed should know first if it becomes a thing – I could always cut my hours, there's always a way round things. 'We're having an auction, too, of fabulous vintage gear. Which, by the way, I need some help with.'

'Of course!' he says, as we arrive in the narrow lanes of Soho, 'I'll give it a shout on all my channels. But now let's get down to business.'

Once we're on the rooftop of our favourite bar,

speckled in shadow from the palms and giant pots, he gets to the point.

'I want to hear about your dirty weekend.'

I've never been one for spilling the beans because it's pretty sleazy and I still feel the resistance of opening up. So I sidestep the question.

'Nerys is going to kill me.'

'Nezza doesn't have to know!' It's a lovely reminder he's my friend first and foremost. 'My lips are sealed.' He zips them, then realises he needs to rewind to put in our order. I'm expecting Filthy Beasts, our trusty drink of choice.

But to my surprise he orders a sharing plate of nibbles and a mocktail. 'Sorry, Betty, but I'm taking my girlfriend out for dinner and I can't turn up steaming.'

'My God, you have grown up! Make that two of those, then, because I don't want to fall asleep on the train and end up in Carmarthen. So it's serious, then? Because I know not who this sensible Sami is!'

'It is, yes. Cara and me, we're moving in together in October when our leases are up. Funny, because we've only been together six months – in fact, that was who I was meeting when you shot me at paintballing. Except I never got to meet her that night; I cancelled when I heard it was you who'd been in the accident.' Sami shudders. 'We'd seen the remnants of the crash when we came out of the activity centre, the ambulances had been and gone. Is it OK for me to say this?' I nod because it's not just my trauma. 'It was awful. Shattered pieces of plastic from headlights, the crushed bonnet and the police cordon. I could never unsee it when I found out it was you. I went straight to the hospital.'

I never knew this and it brings a lump to my throat that he came to visit.

'But because I wasn't family, I couldn't go in. I rang Nerys and she kept me updated. I was so worried. I hope all this doesn't bring it back.'

'No, it's actually lovely to know you cared. I mean, you even blew someone out for me!'

'But Cara didn't take it badly, you know, like she trusted me when I said my best friend had been hurt. I mean, we've all heard the "so sorry but my dog's just die" excuses. Except she messaged later on and the day after and … here we are about to, as they say, co-habit.'

'Living in sin? What do your mum and dad think?'

'Delighted, would you believe. But then they're just happy I'm not with Christian anymore.'

I shake my head at him. 'I just can't understand how a parent can be bigoted regarding their own children.'

'Bigoted? Nothing to do with that! They just thought Christian was a bit of a wanker! Which he was, of course. But now I have my Cara. She's definitely The One.'

'How do you know? All I've ever known are blokes who are definitely Not The One.'

'Well, we just click. No games. We laugh and talk and she makes me feel good about myself. We bring out the best in each other. Nothing like what you're up to, having a bit of meaningless fun! You know, conquering your fears to visit a man halfway across the country, that's the definition of meaningless fun, right?' He puts a finger to his chin, suggesting quite the opposite.

'All right, you win,' I say, because I have no one else to confide in. And I feel a dreamy smile cross my face and forget all my doubts. 'He's lovely. What you say about

Cara and you, that's how it feels with Guy. I really like him.' It feels so nice to admit it, I say it again. 'As in really, really like him.'

'But ...?' he asks pointedly. He knows me so well.

'There's too much stuff involved.'

'Oh I see, so you're planning its demise already? Signature man move, Betty!'

'No, this is different. This one I want to be with, actually. He's truly lovely and funny and genuine and—'

'Shmexy?' He strokes his sideburns with his fingertips, like he used to when we'd be out and he'd spy that night's soulmate.

'Super shmexy. But we haven't done much, I'm not ready.'

'That's not like you,' he says archly before taking an innocent slurp through his straw.

'Ha ha. I mean, come on, I had a pelvis injury and—'

'Go on top, then,' he says and shrugs.

'Thanks for the tip, Karma Sutra Sami. And I was about to say that if we do have sex, I'll fall for him.'

'So he's into you, yes?'

'I think so.' I feel a burst of euphoria. Then it plummets back down. 'But as I said, it's complicated. He's separated from someone who I suspect doesn't want to let go. He hasn't said that, exactly, but he's still kind of involved. And he wants loads of kids.'

'Oh how dreadful!' He rolls his eyes at me. 'So, the baggage, which we all have, aside, the problem here is that you like him and he likes you?' Sami shakes his head at me in disgust.

'It's not that clear cut. It might just be that we've been

253

there for each other when we've needed to get out of a rut, but maybe that's all it will ever be.'

'That "met for a reason" crap? You're overthinking it and I know it's hard, but Betty—'

'But we're from different backgrounds too. Maybe I'd be better off with the devil I know?'

'You have more options?'

I tell him about Brody and how we both know where we've come from and what the vocabulary means.

'Oh ditch Guy quick, then!' he says sarcastically. 'Here's an idea.'

'What?'

'Nothing, just keep on keeping on, get to know Guy more, reconnect with Brody, something will happen, something will force it and when it does, you'll know.'

'That's just it,' I say. 'Maybe I already do.'

'And why would that be?' He pulls a cynical face ready to knock my reason down.

'I mean that, maybe when it comes to the crunch, Guy won't be capable of a relationship. He's still stuck; he lost his parents when he was a baby, I saw one photo of them, one, and that was in his workshop, not in the house, it's like he's in denial, and it's all compounded by fatherhood being ripped from him so brutally. To be honest, I think I'm just a stepping stone. Or it could just be I'm a temporary diversion and, like Nerys said, anything can happen when kids are involved, like Guy and his ex will rekindle their love because of Maud. And how much time do I want to waste if I want to have children one day? If I can, that is?' Sami takes my hand because he knows my past with Jude inside out. 'Plus, he lives miles away.'

'Just see what happens. What if you two are meant to be?' he says, kindly.

'OK, so tell me, Sami,' I say, 'how relationship-ready do you think someone is when our goodbye was interrupted because he saw the baby he thought was his and I saw his heartbreak before my eyes? He'd agreed to help his best mate, the one who went behind his back with his woman, to teach him how to change a bloody nappy. I mean, come on!'

His jaw flops because the penny's dropped. I know what that means – not even Sami can polish that turd.

Finally home! Thought I'd let you know. All fine and thanks again for having me. Love, Betty xxx

Phew! I've been wondering all day. And sorry again for the dreadful farewell. How was London?

Great! V. tired now. Going to bed.

So I've decided to sell up. Have convinced Granny that we should up sticks and go somewhere new.

Betty is typing ...

I think meeting you made her miss home.

Betty is typing ...

I'm doing a drop-off next week so I'll pop by, if that's OK? Let me know if not.

I can barely keep my eyes open. I've realised how much I need to do for the auction – I'm going to have to put my all into it. So if I go quiet, that's why. Night, night.

## 27

### *Guy*

'Another delivery to Wales?' Granny says when I turn up with the missing piece of her jigsaw, which I've made. 'I thought you had a courier?'

'All booked up,' I lie, 'but it means I can go and scope out some properties too, so two birds one stone.'

'And, what a coincidence, you can see Betty!' She says it with glee like she knows what I'm up to.

'If I'm passing,' I say as casually as possible when I have a new sign I've made for Life Goes On, plus my toolbox, because she might need some help with repairing the lots in the van on her auction.

I hand over the puzzle piece – the green eye of a cat from Raining Cats and Dogs.

'You clever thing! How did you do that?'

'Scanned the images onto my laptop and used a nifty bit of software to get the measurements right, printed it off, then stuck it to cardboard. Easy!'

'Sounds anything but,' Granny marvels.

Then I'm off with a vanload and after a slog of drop-offs, I get to Evan Evans's house just outside Pant Bach and knock on his door.

'You came all this way to return my tin opener?' White-haired like a wizard, he booms it out in a gravelly sing-song voice that, Kat tells me, was once part of the big bass sound of the men's choir.

I've convinced myself all the way that it's an entirely rational thing to be doing. But when he questions me, I feel a prod of doubt.

'Personal service is my thing,' I say to his raised bushy eyebrows, 'and I'm in the area anyway.'

'Well, such kindness is a rarity these days. Just to see a friendly face and have a chat means the world to me, see, because I've been on my own for years now. My wife and I, we'd use this tin opener for our tinned salmon sandwiches that we'd have on a Sunday teatime, every Sunday without fail. We couldn't have children; our dogs, Welsh collies, they were our babies. They'd both get a bit each too. Happiest days of my life.'

He wipes a tear and goes in to get his wallet but can't find it.

'It's fine, pay me later,' I say. I couldn't take a penny off him with a sweet story like that.

Kay breaks the spell when I get to hers.

'Back again for more of that Welsh cake you're so keen on?' She gives me a knowing look.

I feel completely exposed – I haven't told her who but she knows there's a girl – and the confidence I had at my idea to come now drains from me in sweat.

'I'm having second thoughts about Welsh cake,' I admit, as I grab my bag and we go into her kitchen. 'Not that I don't like it, I do, it's – uh – delicious and moreish. But what if the Welsh cake has gone off me?'

Looking at the messages from last week, when I said I'd pop by, I realise Betty didn't answer me. I'd told her to let me know if it wasn't OK – and she hasn't. Betty also said she'd be up to her eyes in work. I'm not entirely confident now. Have I made a mistake? Yet it's all there when I think of what we've got going on between us. We came so close on her visit, we know so much about one another, everything personal, anyway, and the rest we learn naturally when we're bouncing off each other. I don't want to let that slip out of my fingers.

Also, this time it's not weird that I'm here. She didn't tell me not to come and the bottom line is we have a kind of relationship going on. But, more than that, if Granny and I find the right place to live, then I need to stake out the market and make contacts. That is what matters here, I decide, that is what I can control. And I want that fresh start and to give something back to the one person who's held me together.

'See, the thing with a Welsh cake is that it stays fresh for a while. You don't have to gollop them down all at once,' Kay says maternally.

She's right. I'm here and it would be odd if I didn't contact her.

Kay puts the kettle on and I reach for my phone to message Betty.

> I'm around as in here, up the road, if you're free over the next day or so?

I don't expect to hear back from her yet so I put my mobile on charge in my room while I share a cuppa with Kay, who's drummed up business for me with a list of who needs what doing to which heirloom. I have a shower and then see Betty has been in touch.

259

> I'm so sorry I haven't messaged. I've been super busy sewing into the night, mending clothes for the auction. Anyway, I'm helping out at the charity shop do at the church hall from 7.30 p.m. but we could meet after that? Love, Betty xxx

She seems genuine and, honestly, I can't be doing with analysis – I want to see her and if it's gone off the boil and we're to be just friends, I'd rather know. Whatever happens, my mind is made up to leave Tunbridge Wells and bring Granny home. If this fizzles out, I know it'll suck. But there'll be an hour's drive from here to the Bethlehem area and what's more of a barrier between us than an entire national park of mountains and valleys, lakes and hills?

After being fed until I'm fit to burst, I roll my way to Pant Bach and decide to surprise her at the church hall, where the door is ajar. I can't go in because it's all quiet, people are in their seats and I catch sight of Betty. Her limp is now completely gone and she's looking breathtaking in a black-and-white-stripe wrap dress which makes her red hair pop. She mounts the stage and I'm in awe at how giving she is when she has a big designing job.

'Ladies and gentlemen, boys and girls, trustees, sponsors, everyone, welcome to the Life Goes On and On event!' she says, in command and sure of herself.

'Our chairwoman has sent her apologies; she's unable to make it tonight, due to a commitment in Cardiff, but she sends us luck and asks everyone to dig deep wherever they can, no matter how small, for the raffle. There are some great prizes: we've got rugby tickets, a hamper from Vic The Veg, treat boxes from The Sweetie Shop and afternoon tea at Hoffi Coffi, not to mention lots of bottles of bubbly and bubble bath donated by all our friends. Tonight is about raising money for our beloved charity's Christmas kids' party but also to give you a heads up about a very special auction which we'll need your help with to spread the word.'

Again I marvel at how involved she is with Life Goes On, at how much she knows about it when she is only a volunteer.

She pauses and her tone changes. 'As you all know, Life Goes On has helped many people.' A wave of nods ripples around in a show of understanding. 'But there's someone far better qualified than I am to tell you about that, someone who has experienced Life Goes On's support first-hand – my co-manager, Megan King.'

Co-manager? Why did Betty say that? Unless ... she is co-manager of a charity shop. But if she is, why didn't she tell me? Has she lied about it, is this why she didn't ask me to come tonight but to see her afterwards? I'm confused and then I question myself, asking if I've misunderstood, but no, she quite clearly told me she was a mentor. Then I wonder why she wouldn't have told me – could it be embarrassment or shame because she thinks it's lowly compared to her previous life? Or, and I don't want to believe this, but it has to be considered, is she a liar? I hate to think it, but she didn't tell the truth about Venice. I stop myself there, remembering she's been through hell. Perhaps she thinks I'd look down on her, which isn't a generous portrait of my character. I feel the ground shift beneath my feet, I shouldn't be here. I deliberate whether to leave when the woman whose half-brother I picked up in the Arcade joins Betty.

'I'm not one for talking, usually,' she says, barely looking up at the crowd, 'but there is one thing I will always speak up about.' She lifts her face to the audience, shaking back her fringe, and begins to make eye contact with people. 'Life Goes On. I used to hate it when people said that to me because when Mam went, I didn't want it to go on. I wanted the world to stop turning because it felt the same awful loss that I did, that the world should feel as angry and sad as me because she was our rock; didn't they know that too?'

She might be speaking quietly but her voice has filled the room, which is silent and gripped. Me included.

'I'd rage at that, because people were carrying on as normal and not feeling what I was feeling. And it wasn't just me either; it was the injustice that my twin brother and sister hadn't had enough time with her and how they'd grow up without her.'

I hardly know her but her simple words and raw emotion have such power that my heart feels heavy.

'But now, two years on, I'm grateful everything didn't stop because, if it had, then I wouldn't have had the charity to turn to, to guide me through the funeral and the forms. I got counselling, too, and then, when I was eighteen, they helped me to apply to be the legal guardian for my brother and sister, Alfie and Nancy.' She waves at two heads peeking up over their chairs. 'The fact that the world carried on, meant that I've been able to be like a mam as well as a big sister to them. But so many children aren't that lucky. So many don't get to open up.' Suddenly Megan clocks me at the back and it feels like she's talking to me. 'They're more likely to bury things, avoid them, suffer bad relationships and carry the trauma of abandonment for the rest of their lives.'

I hear her explaining their Sale of the Centuries auction which alone could fund the entire charity for the next year, such is the wealth of treasure in their catalogue. To bring in the big bucks they need the publicity to spread far and wide. 'Facebook shares and word of mouth, especially to any rich relatives and friends, would be the best support you can offer.'

There's an explosion of clapping and then the tissues are out and a buzz of positivity sweeps across the throng. Somehow it doesn't reach me and I feel stunned by what I've just heard. I mean, I knew the cause was for children whose mothers and fathers have died, but I hadn't in any way related to it. Why would I when I'm an adult and I was so fortunate to have loving grandparents who could step in? But even so, listening to Megan has sent me back to my childhood, when I was teased for being an orphan. Once 'Oliver Twist' had run out of steam, the little shits called me 'Harry Potter', and I was held down in the toilets while they drew a scar on my forehead. Tears burn my eyes because I can't even imagine my mum and dad in the flesh. I have no memories of them, only photographs and videos, and other people's ideas of them. When I was small, those stories were enough but now they feel like fiction.

Suddenly Betty is standing before me, pale as anything. 'Megan said you were here. How long for, exactly?' she says, gingerly.

I could lie but where would that get us? 'From when you gave your speech. Listen, Betty, I'm sorry, I didn't mean to sneak up on you, it was meant to be a surprise.'

She shuts her eyes briefly. 'So you know, then ...' Her

shoulders drop and her voice is flat. 'I'm not Betty the big-bollocks designer but the co-manager of a charity shop.'

I search her face to understand. 'Why didn't you say so?'

Her eyes turn desperate. 'I'm sorry, I meant to tell you.'

'All right. But I just don't get why you let me think you were doing something else?'

'Because ...' She looks around her and escorts me outside into the balmy evening. 'I ... this is going to sound mad, but it's kind of that I wished I wasn't here doing this, not that it's beneath me, but that I was still the person you met before the accident. Before everything went wrong.'

'The way you did with Venice?'

'Yes.' She cringes, then sniffs. 'The way you did, too, with being married with a baby.'

Is it a dig? Or maybe it's embarrassment?

'I'm not judging, Betty.'

'Well, I'm judging myself.' She crosses her arms and shuffles her feet.

'Isn't it that we both wanted what was taken away from us?'

Betty looks up and she exhales deeply. 'Yes, that's exactly it.'

She gives me a small smile but then her brow furrows. 'So where does that leave us?'

'How do you mean?'

'Well, that we've not had the best start, have we? And neither of us are who we've claimed to be.'

'Isn't it that what was happening in our lives didn't

match up with reality? Not that we're frauds, or we've been deliberately misleading each other to hurt one another – doesn't that make the difference? I mean, we're not going to turn it into an obstacle, are we?'

Betty's considering it when she gets tapped on the shoulder and she turns to a man who leans in for a kiss on her cheek. I step back, I feel like I shouldn't be here, that I'm intruding on her professional life.

'I've convinced myself that you've lost my card, that's why you haven't rung,' the man says with the most charming smile I've ever seen. And his eyes, oh God, they're greener than a lagoon. Even I'm dazzled by them.

'Hi,' Betty says. 'As a matter of fact, I was going to call.'

'Really? I can do any night of the week.'

He is making it clear he's not here to talk business.

'About a collaboration between your project and the charity,' Betty says, correcting him.

He groans and I realise he's after her and suddenly I feel green-eyed myself with jealousy.

Betty smoothly brings me in with introductions.

'Guy, this is Brody, Brody this is Guy.' So this is Broody Buns. Disaster. 'I've known Brody since school; he runs an outreach scheme for disadvantaged children.'

Glass-half-empty me isn't reassured by the things they have in common, but if the glass is half full, then it explains his easy familiarity. But he does give me a strong handshake and it brings me to my senses: I have to tell her how I feel. Because she didn't get to answer my question that things were good between us. I wait to hear how Betty will explain me.

'And Guy is a very good friend of Life Goes On.'

265

It's not as bad as some introductions, which include a total spanner, a complete tool and a handyman, delivered with innuendo eyebrows. But it gives me no clue as to how she feels.

Brody makes his excuses and she's all smiles and I realise I shouldn't be here.

'Listen, you need to work the room,' I say, as I rifle in my wallet. 'Here's twenty quid for the raffle, no point in putting my name on the stubs, put them down as my landlady Kay Lewis at Bryn Mawr Guest House.'

'Maybe we should leave it tonight?' Betty says.

She's right. She still looks awkward after I found out what she's really doing for a job. And I want to process it too. I've no doubt she's meant no harm but it's another moment that needs to be allowed to breathe. Like I said, I'm not judging but the heart can be a right dick up against the facts – I'm falling for her big time. Better to play it safe and think it all over.

'Yes, course. I can pick you up tomorrow, say six p.m.?'

As soon as I've said that though, I regret it – that heart of mine is banging on my rib cage demanding to make my feelings for her known. Admitting I want to be with her full-time. And it's obvious I've got a love rival. But I can't declare myself here and now. But I can't declare myself here and now.

'OK,' she says, and while I yearn to pull her into me and kiss her possessively on the lips, I step back instead, cool as you like. And off she goes, taking my heart with her.

## 28

### *Betty*

'Not yet, Betty!' Guy says as he steers my shoulders from behind me. 'And no peeking!'

'I'm not, I promise!' I say, sensing we've moved inside but it can't be completely indoors because it's still spongey underfoot. I can smell the countryside and hear birds and I'm dying to know where he's brought me on this loveliest of Indian summer September evenings. Although I wouldn't complain if this continued for another minute – I'm secretly enjoying being at his mercy with his big hands on me. So much for me doubting him, so much for my reservations about how damaged he is; they come when we're apart but as soon as we're together, something else takes me over.

'OK, stop here. You can open your eyes now,' he says, and I drop my palms and gasp.

We're in an open-sided barn with a cloth-covered table and throws on chairs all made from the blondest of hay bales. There's a huge wicker hamper and then I see stairs up to a loft and there's even a sign saying '*Bathroom*'.

'How did you find this?' I thought I knew the hinterland, it's only a thirty-minute drive from the village, but this is new to me.

'Friend of a friend. Man got contacts,' he says, with

just the right amount of swagger that makes me gush. 'And it's all ours. Look,' he says, taking my hand and leading me out into the meadow, then down three stone steps to a beautiful infinity lake where the water merges seamlessly with a mountain landscape, 'we've got our own private pool and there's a bottle chilling in the water.'

'It's amazing, Guy. Seriously, how did you find it?' And, I want to ask him, why? Because there's something different about him tonight. As if he's on a mission.

We take off our shoes, feeling the warmth of the jetty's wooden slats, and sit and dangle our feet in the cool shallows beneath a setting sun.

'I was online and ended up down a rabbit hole, as you do,' he says, swishing his toes. 'Thought it would be fun!'

'Especially after last night's not fun.' While he's been asking if I'm OK, alluding to my humiliation of being rumbled at the church hall, we haven't spoken about it. 'I just wanted to say that you're right. We both wanted to be living our best lives,' I cringe at the term but it pretty much sums us up. 'I never lied to deliberately deceive you.'

'Same here,' he says.

'Even so, I had to wonder if it meant if we were truly being ourselves, if pretending to each other things were better than they were, was a good foundation for . . . this.'

'And what did you decide?'

I turn to him. 'Because if someone lies to you, if you lie to someone, you may worry about trusting them or being trustworthy in the future. I mean, we could say how little we actually know of each other—' Guy looks worried – 'but, actually, these half-truths have in the end kind of meant we've had to be brutally honest instead, if you know what I mean?'

A smile dawns on his lovely face. 'Yes, absolutely.'

There's something I need to clarify too, which has been troubling me since Tunbridge Wells and here's my opportunity. 'And things are definitely finished with Sarah?'

'Yes! Completely. I swear.' He sounds and looks sincere.

I realise the irony that neither of us have a good track record with honesty. But really, all we've been doing is lying to ourselves.

'You said last night we shouldn't turn what's happened into an obstacle. And I agree. So maybe we should keep doing what we're doing?'

'Definitely. And we can keep doing what we're doing with me up the road, if you like . . .' Guy says, mysteriously.

'What?' I say, leaning in for the goss.

'My place went on the market today. Granny has her heart set on coming home.'

'To Wales?' My heart stops then swells because this means more than him ruling out a reunion with Sarah. It shows he isn't stuck in the past like I thought he could be. This means he's thinking ahead, of a new future. 'That's brilliant news!'

'Phew!' he laughs. Then he holds up his hands. 'Because I don't want you to get freaked out that it's for you or anything, that I'm upping my life and holding you responsible, because it's not that at all. You know, that right? I want to get away from all the stuff that's happened. It's not an escape, it's about starting afresh.'

It makes perfect sense.

'I mean it's gorgeous here, right? Who wouldn't want to live here? And it's to give my grandmother what she's always wanted but wouldn't dare have done if I hadn't suggested it. She's always said that when I've lost two parents, she wouldn't make me go through it again, which is the measure of her, really. But it's about time she was rewarded for her sacrifice; she says it never has been one, but, you know, I want her to have her dream and I've nowhere else to go, or want to be, so why not here?'

'I get it, it's not sudden at all, then, is it? If you've known this for a long time.'

'All my life, Betty.'

'Then it must feel so good to be finally doing it. Especially when it means leaving where you were born and your connection there with your parents.'

He drops his head. 'There's no connection there with them,' he says. 'Not really.'

I want to ask more but he's jumped up to standing. 'Anyway, let's enjoy this!'

I don't want to spoil it so I join him and we hug. 'So what's the deal with this place?'

We pull apart but he doesn't let go of my hand, like he needs to have some kind of physical contact with me. I won't lie – I'm loving it. 'I don't have to give the keys back until tomorrow,' he says, softly. 'That's not to say I'm presuming anything.'

I tut at him. 'Taking advantage of me like this – you know, if you'd told me, I'd have at least brought a tooth-brush.'

He laughs. 'I've got a spare. Just in case.'

'Just in case? What do you take me for? A slattern? You're a fast mover. Is that why your nickname is Foxy?'

'Oh God, that,' he groans. 'No! It's because I'm double-barrelled. Fox-Slater.'

'Ooh! There's posh!'

'Precisely why I don't use it. Listen, talking of names, I want to know what this is between us, now that we're being honest. I don't want to be unsure. I don't want to be just friends.' My heart loops the loop. 'But if you do, then of course, that's—'

I let go of him and put a finger on his lips. 'How about we call it "not just friends anymore and seeing each other"?' I am so happy I feel delirious.

'Or Colin? We could call it Colin?'

I belly laugh hard and he suddenly remembers something and his face turns serious.

'What do you think about signs, Betty?'

My stomach pops with anticipation. 'Like, as in us meeting each other that day and me sending back your hankie?' It feels so great to get it out there and to be able to talk about us.

'There is that, yes.'

'Or do you mean star signs? Because I'm a Libra. What are you? How do I not know when your birthday is?'

'Scorpio. Shush, no, I mean I've made you a new sign for the shop, if you'd like it? Shall I show you? It's in the van.' His shyness makes me melt.

'That is the sweetest thing! I can't wait to see it!' I squeeze him and rest my head on his chest. 'Why do we always go off on tangents?'

'Because – well,' he says, murmuring into my hair, 'we just want to know about each other, if that makes sense?'

'Oh yes,' I say, feeling myself begin to simmer.

'What would you like to talk about now, then?' he says.

I lift my head and turn up the heat. 'Maybe we should stop talking?'

He says nothing but his eyes say everything. He lifts me up and sits me round his waist where I can feel how much he wants me. I wrap my legs around him and we push hard to get as close as possible as he carries me to the barn where he lays me down on a blanket on a bed of straw.

He kisses my neck and my shoulders and the well of my throat as I pull at his T-shirt and he unfastens my bra. We go topless and simultaneously groan at the sight of each other. His chest is broad and brown, soft with hair but taut with muscle, his nipples as dark as his eyes and he gazes at all of me, breathing hard before he sinks his mouth onto my breasts. This time neither of us have to check if the other is OK with this because we're both ready, we're both slowly taking off the rest of our clothes, never once breaking apart.

'I want you, Guy,' I whisper as we begin to move as one.

'I've never wanted anyone as much as you, Betty,' he says, tracing his swollen lips down my stomach, which makes me shiver. But there's something I need to say before we go on.

'You need to know, Guy, that I haven't been with anyone since my accident.'

He comes straight back up and strokes my cheek. 'I'm happy as we are, Betty. We don't have to do anything.'

'Such a gent,' I whisper. 'But I want to.'

'Sure?'

'Positive. Just let's take it slow.'

He kisses me on the lips then traces his finger down my body to my scar, making me feel beautiful all over, even and especially the damaged part of me. And then he rises back up and puts on protection, and we begin gently, ever so gently. I'm afraid, of course I am. But he's so tender and careful that I'm able to take the lead. It's a sublime slide and then we plunge down into the deepest velvet where there is only us, nothing more, and we stay there until the waterfall is crashing down around us, and it feels, finally, that we've found each other.

Afterwards, we stay entwined, panting at the alchemy of our coming together. Guy rests his forehead on mine to recover, taking in gulps of air, but he still has the strength to squeeze my hands which are beside my head in an act of total surrender.

'I feel as if I haven't eaten for days,' I say.

'I've got loads, even SuperShopper hummus.' He collapses around me, still holding onto my palms, drawing them in to my waist.

'I don't mean that,' I say with a shuffle to try to get every possible inch of skin on skin I can.

'What do you want, then? Barn room service?'

'I have no complaints whatsoever about barn room service.'

He laughs and I join in. It was incredibly cheesy of me but I don't care because I am the most absolute version of me ever. Because of him. How can I feel so safe but so alive?

'What I mean is I've been starved for so long I didn't realise how hungry I really was.'

'Good job Colin's on hand, then, to cook up some veggie skewers and halloumi.'

'Thank God for Colin,' I say.

'Who'd have thought a hankie would lead us here? Imagine if you hadn't sent it back.'

'I guess if I hadn't had the accident, I wouldn't have bothered.'

'And you'd be shacked up with Giovanni the gondolier dining out on Italian sausage every night.'

I snort. 'I'm veggie remember. Where would you be?'

'Lost without you,' Guy says, seeing my cheese and raising it to a very ripe Stilton. Which I happen to adore.

We share a grin but I'm so post-coitally dehydrated my teeth stick to my lips. 'I could do with a drink first if Colin's got any?'

'A nice chilled one?' Guy says, 'I know just where to get one.'

I gasp. 'Shall we go in naked?'

Guy honks with laughter and we get up without a sliver of self-consciousness. He grabs two glasses and we kind of tiptoe, giggling all the way, until I slip down off the jetty and Guy dives effortlessly into the lush depths of the lake.

Dusk is falling, the pinks of the sky are fading into purple and the peaks beyond have turned to silhouettes. The peace around me matches the peace inside of me and it's here, just a few miles from where I was born.

Suddenly I realise that all those years in London, when I was achieving, I thought I was happy. Yet now I see it was more of a race to outrun myself. The busy, busy was a way of distracting me from the fact that I was on the wrong path. And I don't think I want to go back.

Seven months ago I thought my life was over. I believed the accident had robbed the essence of me. But looking back, I'd lost my sense of self way before then. It was only when Guy gave me the space to talk in that paintball hideout that I had an inkling I needed something to change. Of course, I'll never be counting my lucky stars for the accident. But as I tread water and wait for Guy to surface, I realise that hitting rock bottom exposed the true me. In amongst the rubble I found my creativity and I remembered my dreams and I learned to live in the moment.

Guy bobs back up for air and as we swim towards each other with big goofy grins, I realise how far I had to go to understand that what I've been searching for has been right under my nose all along.

## 29

### *Guy*

'You again!' the woman at the coffee shop says to me when Kay produces her raffle-winning afternoon tea voucher.

'How on earth do you remember me? I was literally here for three minutes!' Then turning to Kay, I explain that this was where I bought her the coffee and walnut cake after we were flooded in.

I look from one to the other in amazement but they're already snorting with laughter.

'No offence, lovely boy,' Kay says, 'but you do stick out a bit. With your Englishness.' As an afterthought she adds, 'And being so handsome, of course.'

The pair of them begin to discuss openly how 'strapping' and 'manly' and 'lush' I am. Kay moves on to reveal 'he's not just a pretty face, he's a whizz at fixing things, got his own business', which her cohort approves of but she tuts when she hears 'he's taken'.

'Dear God, I'm not a piece of meat, you know!' It's a feeble attempt to cover up my embarrassment. All it does is make them howl and they continue doing so while we're shown to a table.

'Have you quite finished with the hen do, Kay?' I ask as she wipes her eyes.

Immediately she peers into my face and says, 'Someone getting married, then?'

'Behave, I still am.'

'Better get that sorted, then, if you're as into this girl as you say you are. Still not going to tell me who it is?' Kay puts on her glasses as if she's heading an inquiry into my love life.

'Nope. And I bet that's the most annoying thing someone could possibly do to you. I'm not saying anything because it'll only whip around the village and I don't want her to be talked about.'

'Ooh, who's that, then?' The woman is back with a wheelie trolley flashing me a huge encouraging smile which makes me laugh.

'What is this? Good cop, bad cop?'

'He's not for talking,' Kay says to our hostess, who's filling the table with towering sandwich and cake stands, tea pots, tea bags, dainty china cups and saucers, knives, forks, serviettes and, finally, a bottle and two flutes.

'Well, lucky lady, whoever she is,' she replies. 'Not that you're my type.'

'Great, thanks for clearing that up,' I say, amused.

'My Steve,' she pats back her blonde waves and stares dreamily into space, 'he's my world, he is, has been ever since school.'

'Same with my Dewi, God rest his soul. We were like a jigsaw puzzle, his bits fitted into my bits perfect. The only man I've ever been with.'

Dewi's bits fitting into Kay's bits aside, their drifting off is touching and it's a chance to ask if what I feel for Betty is anything close. 'What does it feel like, then, to be that in love?'

'Just feeling so comfortable with them, you know, how they make you laugh,' Kay says. 'Support you whatever. Inspire you too.'

Tick, tick, tick and tick.

'How waking up with them is a joy, that feeling you're so blessed they've chosen to be with you, every day,' the woman says.

Instinctively, I know this is it with Betty. I felt exactly that when we woke up this morning with hay in our hair in the giant double in the barn. And I'm cringing when I think this even privately but it wasn't sex with her, it was making love. It's frightening, in a way, to admit that I have never felt like this with anyone; Sarah was all wrapped in what I was set on in my head. But with Betty it's heaven. I know she feels a lot for me too but the fear is that she'll leave me. And that I'm guessing that's because of what Megan talked about that night at the church hall: she named it, the fear of abandonment, and it made me realise that there is a part of me that feels like that no matter how loved I am by Granny. I imagine Betty not being mine and it hurts. At least I think we've named it and claimed it, even if we do refer to it as Colin now.

'Oh look at his face, Guy's gone all gooey,' Kay says, pointing at me.

The woman inspects me and nods to confirm it. 'He's got it bad!'

Usually I'd be mortified but the growl of my stomach moves them along.

'Now, this here is the luxury afternoon-tea-for-two package,' the woman says, 'so you've got smoked salmon and cream cheese, roast beef and horseradish, egg and cress, cucumber and prawn and mayonnaise. Then there's Welsh cakes, scones with clotted cream and jam, mini eclairs and coffee and walnut cake. Choice of teas there, and a demi of fizz. So enjoy and give me a shout if you need any extras.'

We dive in and it's delicious but I pass on the booze because after this I'm off home. There's far too much, so Kay insists I take it with me for the drive. She's tiddly by the end and totters over to say thank you and I hear them exchanging see-you-soons. I get her bag and as we leave, the woman gives me a very cheery wave.

'Lovely, that one, wasn't she,' Kay says as I pour her into the van. 'Two kids, both girls, it's her own place, that.'

'How is there someone here that you don't know?' I wonder.

'I'm a blinking farmer, I don't have time to go coffee-ing and gossiping, do I?'

'Whatever you say, Kay.' And we sit in companionable silence until I get to hers, share a hug, and then it's time to leave.

Betty and I said our goodbyes in bed this morning but I can't go without seeing her again. Plus I've got the excuse of fitting the new sign. I rock up with my toolbox and Megan gives me a hello smile.

'She's out the back, I'll go get her. There's a ladder out there that I'll fetch too,' she says and turns to go.

I call her back. 'I just wanted to say how brave you were for talking about your mum the other night.'

'Oh thanks.' She bites her lip and then tilts her head at me. 'Have you been affected too? Because I saw you looking a bit—'

279

'Ha, yes, you did make me cry! I lost both of mine.'

'I'm so sorry.' She wrings her hands in sympathy. 'It never goes away, does it, that feeling of loss?'

'They died when I was a baby, though, so I don't have much – in fact any – memories.'

'That's hard.'

'I think I'm pretty OK with it, I'm used to it, bar the odd ghost haunting me.'

'Oh.' She examines me. 'Ghosts? Is that how you see them? I think of my mam as very much here, within me, she's my heartbeat. Don't you ever wonder how it would feel to carry them with you? I'm doing my best to keep her alive for the twins too. I've made them each a remembrance album for when they're older, of all the things they got up to with her. Maybe knowing where they've come from will help them at crossroads in the future.'

'I'd rather keep it in the past.'

'Trouble is, unresolved grief has a way of rearing its head again.'

She goes off to get Betty and I think of the suitcase of Mum and Dad's stuff that Granny made up for me that I've never looked through and I wonder. But life is going so well now, compared to what it was, that there's no need to go through it. There's been enough trauma in my life and now I want to seize on this happiness I have.

'What are you doing here?' Betty hisses from the back doorway but she has a massive smile and beckons me to her.

'You ashamed of me or something?' I joke as we hug and kiss and rub noses like a sickeningly loved-up couple in the privacy of the stockroom.

'No, no. No! Of course not.'

But does she protest too much? Something is off and she reads my mind with a sigh.

'It's just my sister works next door and she doesn't know. I didn't want to say anything until Colin turned up and I haven't had a chance.'

Next door? It all becomes clear.

'I think I've just met her. With Kay; she won the afternoon tea.'

'What?' Betty does the scream emoji face.

'So after I dropped you back to yours this morning—'

'Yes?'

'And after I went to Cliff's garage to fix the furniture that you mentioned needed doing—'

'Yes?' She's getting impatient. 'Sorry! Thanks for helping!'

'That velvet pink Victorian lady's chair needed the most work, but I got it looking perfect.'

'That's my favourite!' she says, temporarily forgetting where we are. As is our way when we chat. 'Anyway, yes?'

'I went back to Kay's and she told me she'd won the afternoon tea voucher and she wanted to take me.'

'To Hoffi Coffee.'

'Yes. I didn't know it was your sister's place! Nice, though, isn't she, Nerys?'

'Did she know who you are?'

'No, but why worry?'

'Because – she's got opinions about what I should be doing.'

'Eh?'

'As in I set myself up to fail by going for the wrong men. I should shop local.'

It lands in my stomach like a rock.

'For someone like that bloke at the charity do?' I say it with a prickle.

'Guy! Are you jealous?' Her blissful blue eyes widen and I feel ashamed.

'No!' I say. But I can't lie to her. 'A bit. At the time, but not now.'

'That's funny because I had that about you,' she says.

'Jealousy is an abhorrent waste of an emotion. But is it wrong for me to feel the very slightest bit of satisfaction? So why would you have been jealous about me?'

'It's just – don't worry, I'm being silly.'

'Come on! I told you mine, you tell me yours.'

My phone buzzes in my pocket between our bodies and we both snigger at the sensation like juveniles. 'I'd better check, it might be Kay saying I've left something behind.'

Betty looks on as I unlock my phone and then I see a message on the Maud WhatsApp group. Suddenly I feel exposed but I can't hide it from Betty or she'll suspect something. It's a photo of Maud sitting between Sarah and Charlie and the words read 'Never thought we'd get here, thanks, Foxy'.

'Is that—'

'Yes.' My voice is clipped and I shut it down as if it's not important. But the Happy Families snap cuts me in two. I don't want to be there, of course not, Betty's made me realise that. And I can't complain that Charlie has embraced fatherhood; I just thought I'd feel ready to walk away from Maud when it happened. But what if this is just another Charlie cock-up? What if he gets bored or meets someone and abandons her? I also feel something else: self-pity that I'm no longer needed. When things were rocky I could still delude myself that I was needed.

'That's good, then, that they're getting on, isn't it?' Betty narrows her eyes, waiting for my reaction.

I'm well aware I've gone quiet. Just then Megan's voice floats through. 'Betty, Nerys is here!'

We immediately jump away from each other.

'She can't see you in here!' Betty whispers.

'But what about me fixing the sign? I've got time to do it.'

'Too risky. I'll ask Devoted Steve to do it.'

Footsteps are coming. Betty shoves me towards the back door. 'It goes out into the alleyway, turn left and left again and you'll know where you are.'

I step outside, realising too late that she didn't kiss me goodbye. That bloody photograph distracted me. I feel robbed of the moment and I make a vow. When Betty and I have parted before, I've never felt sure of what's been happening. This time I leave knowing that only something truly monumental will tear us apart. And there's no way I'll let that happen.

To: bettyhopkins@gmail.com
From: therepairguy@googlemail.com
Re: Colin

Dear Betty,

I made it home last night after a dreadful drive. I meant to message you but fell asleep. How are you? Just wanted to check in on Colin.

Best,

Guy

To: therepairguy@googlemail.com
From: bettyhopkins@gmail.com
Subject: Colin

Dear Guy,

Colin is a man in demand. Devoted Steve put up the sign – I love the rainbow lettering – and now Nerys wants one for Hoffi Coffee!

What the hell should Colin do?

Love,

Betty xxx

To: bettyhopkins@gmail.com
From: therepairguy@googlemail.com
Re: Message for Colin

Tell her Colin is open to a brief, if Nerys is sure. He can bring it up on his next visit.

It won't be long before I'm back – someone has already put an offer in on my house for the asking price. And I've accepted. The market is crazy here but then it is commuterville. The quest to find a new place is now biting at my heels.

To: therepairguy@googlemail.com
From: bettyhopkins@gmail.com
Re: Colin

Great. I'll tell her.

I'm not surprised that your house went so fast – it's absolutely lovely.

So what's the plan going forward?

To: bettyhopkins@gmail.com
From: therepairguy@googlemail.com
Re: Colin

Hopefully I can find a pair of cottages for Granny and myself or a bigger place we can split into two.

To: therepairguy@googlemail.com
From: bettyhopkins@gmail.com
Re: Colin

Sounds ideal!

If you need a solicitor for that or anything else, I have one.

To: bettyhopkins@gmail.com
From: therepairguy@googlemail.com
Re: Colin

Anything else? I'm probably being dim, so feel free to extrapolate.


To: therepairguy@googlemail.com
From: bettyhopkins@gmail.com
Re: Colin

Just about your situation.

Because *bosom hoik* I've always said I'd never have a thing with a married man.


To: bettyhopkins@gmail.com
From: therepairguy@googlemail.com
Re: Colin

Aha, I see. It's a bit late for that though. Funnily enough, it's on my things-to-do-tomorrow list.

The process is I apply to the court for an annulment, then a decree nisi, then six weeks after I have that, I can apply for a decree absolute. Then it's job done. Hopefully, all within six months, if it's straightforward.

To: therepairguy@googlemail.com
From: bettyhopkins@gmail.com
Re: Colin

If?


To: bettyhopkins@gmail.com
From: therepairguy@googlemail.com
Re: Colin

It all depends on Sarah.


To: therepairguy@googlemail.com
From: bettyhopkins@gmail.com
Re: Colin

She can't contest the facts, though, can she?


To: bettyhopkins@gmail.com
From: therepairguy@googlemail.com
Re: Colin

No. But she could drag her heels.

To: therepairguy@googlemail.com
From: bettyhopkins@gmail.com
Re: Colin

What do you mean?


To: bettyhopkins@gmail.com
From: therepairguy@googlemail.com
Re: Colin

Unfortunately, Sarah doesn't see things the way I do.
Not now.


To: therepairguy@googlemail.com
From: bettyhopkins@gmail.com
Re: Colin


???


To: bettyhopkins@gmail.com
From: therepairguy@googlemail.com
Re: Colin

I should've said this before now – perhaps I need to
get a T-shirt with this printed on? And I'm a total idiot
for not saying it sooner. But Sarah doesn't want the
annulment. From the start of the split, she has asked
me to go back to her and Maud.

To: therepairguy@googlemail.com
From: bettyhopkins@gmail.com
Re: Colin

Not now? As in you had considered going back?


To: bettyhopkins@gmail.com
From: therepairguy@googlemail.com
Re: Colin

Before you.


To: therepairguy@googlemail.com
From: bettyhopkins@gmail.com
Re: Colin

Oh. I see.


To: bettyhopkins@gmail.com
From: therepairguy@googlemail.com
Re: Colin

Betty, I swear to you that it would never happen.

To: therepairguy@googlemail.com
From: bettyhopkins@gmail.com
Re: Colin

So you need to tell her, then, maybe? To rule out that you're not just hedging your bets.


To: bettyhopkins@gmail.com
From: therepairguy@googlemail.com
Re: Colin

I am going to tell her.
I'm not sure what you mean by hedging my bets.


To: therepairguy@googlemail.com
From: bettyhopkins@gmail.com
Re: Colin

That you have only decided to leave her for good because you have me.


To: bettyhopkins@gmail.com
From: therepairguy@googlemail.com
Re: Colin

It's not an either or. It's only by being with you that it has given me total clarity.

To: therepairguy@googlemail.com
From: bettyhopkins@gmail.com
Re: Colin

But you had thought about going back to her!


To: bettyhopkins@gmail.com
From: therepairguy@googlemail.com
Re: Colin

For Maud, yes. Sarah thought if we had a baby of our own we could make things right and I could have the family I had wanted.


To: therepairguy@googlemail.com
From: bettyhopkins@gmail.com
Re: Colin

If that's meant to reassure me …


To: bettyhopkins@gmail.com
From: therepairguy@googlemail.com
Re: Colin

Look at the tense: the family I had wanted. Not what I want now. With you.

To: therepairguy@googlemail.com
From: bettyhopkins@gmail.com
Re: Colin

And what is it you want to have with me?


To: bettyhopkins@gmail.com
From: therepairguy@googlemail.com
Re: Colin

Forever.

## 30

*Betty*

Like a bridesmaid, I smooth the puddle train of the wedding dress and then stand back to see if my finishing touch has pulled it all together.

But my gut already knows the answer when I take in the auction installation in Cliff's garage.

The look I wanted was a show-stopping sophisticated segue of decades going from one side to the other as if it was one continuous glamorous soiree. Instead, it's too cramped and too dark and resembles a junk shop.

Nothing has space to breathe. OK, a bit of camera trickery could improve things – after all, this is just for the website; very few people will be actually coming to view this. But it's all too busy – I'd need the wizardry of Edward Scissorhands to crop this lot into shape.

I feel exhausted as well as defeated. Three nights in a row I've been here, coming straight from the shop with just a curled sandwich to keep me going to get everything ready. I have pored over floorplans, changed my mind a thousand times over what goes where, and my back is broken from dragging the Chesterfield sofa from left to right and left again before deciding it needs to go centre. My fingers are sore too from the fiddly fishing wire that I've attached to garments to give them life, and they were already pricked to death by hand sewing on buttons and repairing hems on the outfits. Countless times I've manoeuvred standard lamps and mirrors to try to get some more light in and on many of them I've accidentally set a vase wobbling with an elbow or knocked something, and I've watched in horror as the domino effect wreaks carefully positioned hats on shoes and jewellery balanced on bags.

Megan arrives to find me with my head in my hands.

'I meant to come sooner but the sitter was late,' she says, assuming that I'm cross with her.

'I don't expect you to come and help me with this stupid idea of mine. What was I thinking? It's all too squeezed in.'

'It looks good! It can't be that bad!' she says, grabbing the work camera and looking at it through the shutter. But then she sees the problem. 'Hmm. Maybe we just need to rearrange some stuff?'

'I've tried every configuration going,' I wail. 'It's like doing a Rubik's Cube except being unable to do a Rubik's Cube.'

She chews the side of her mouth to think. 'There has to be somewhere else we can use.'

The prospect of the upheaval is too much to contemplate. And yet I would be so unhappy if I didn't do this haul justice. I have promised to let Helen know when she can come and see it all when it's ready and I desperately don't want to disappoint her. Worse, if it isn't presented properly, then the charity won't get the best possible price.

'I know it's not ideal but what about the back hall of the rugby club?' she says. 'Do you know anyone there who could help?'

'Ha, only my useless bastard of a father.'

'Wow, you're lucky you know who yours is!' Megan says and we burst out laughing.

It relieves some of the tension and I have to agree at this short notice it is our only viable option.

'Shall we go up there?' she says and it's then I notice something different about her. She's looking softer somehow.

'Your hair!' I cry.

'What?' She puts her hands to her tresses.

'It's gorgeous. You've had layers put in and I love the fringe, it suits you being above your eyebrows! Where did you go for that? Was it that new salon that's opened?'

Megan blushes and I gasp. 'No! Have you pulled yourself a hairdresser? I am so jealous!'

'Not pulled, no!' She only gets redder. 'Dylan from Jack of all Fades came round and did the kids for me and then he persuaded me to have a change.'

It's obvious she's embarrassed so I stick to complimenting her about her new look – and I mean it.

'It's OK, Betty, you can ask.' Megan fiddles with the rings on her fingers and I understand this is a big deal to her. To open up to me.

'So are you a thing? Is he nice?'

'Very.' She smiles. 'Early days but he's fab with the kids. Not like one of those who want you to ditch them to go out. Like he includes them in our plans.'

'What a sweetheart!' I can see them together, her with her Goth look and him with his rockabilly hair.

'Yeah, and he's just really nice. Like, I don't really have anyone close apart from my cousin.'

'And family's great and everything but sometimes they're a bit much.'

We nod in symphony.

'Exactly. I was the weirdo at school with my piercings. But Dylan isn't just a bloke, he's like a friend too. And all of mine have left here, gone to Cardiff and away for work, to get out. I don't blame them, I wanted to do the same.'

'So did I. But look, I came back.'

'You didn't want to, though, not really, did you?'

'Know what? I always had the ambition to come home once I'd made my name. But it didn't work out like that.'

'Wish you were still there?'

'Sometimes.' It's a big change from July, when I'd have cried yes at the top of my lungs. 'This place, it's not so bad, is it?'

We stare at each other and I realise this is the most intimate conversation we've ever had. I suddenly wonder why she's here.

'You didn't need to come up,' I say. 'If you've got other stuff to do.'

'No. But I wanted to.'

It's then I realise she's here because she has begun to see me in a way other than her workmate. She's been lonely, so have I. And I have a huge burst of hope that we could become actual friends.

'And I'm so glad you did! Shall we lock up and then head up to the rugby club?' I feel much bolder with her beside me.

When we're done, we make a start along the hedge-rows of the country lanes and the chat flows again. 'So – uh – what about you and that fella, then? Guy? He seems nice.'

'He is. He really is,' I admit. 'Like I'm proper into him and that's a first for me. But I have doubts.'

'What about?'

'Whether I can give him what he wants. If I can make him happy.' I need to tell him about the chances of me being able to have a baby. When I know how much he wants a family, it feels wrong to keep it from him even though it's early days. His face, when he received a photo from Charlie of him and Sarah with Maud, worries me too – he isn't acting like he's a free man. Then the emails; he said he wants forever with me but it's easy to pluck that out of the sky – is that one word enough to cope with the stress if Sarah strings out the annulment?

'He spoke to me about his parents.'

'Did he?'

'Yeah, he said I'd made him cry with what I said at the church hall.'

A thought occurs to me. 'Megan, I'm wondering something about him. It's complicated and everything but he told me he doesn't have any connection with his parents, like at all. Is that odd?'

'It happens when you have no memories; he was a baby, all he's got is what people have told him, probably along the lines of "how alike you are" and "you're just like your mam or your dad" and I guess he accepted that when he was small, but now he's wondering if people just said that to make it all easier.'

'See, I think there's a lot inside of him that he hasn't reconciled.' Perhaps the will he has for a family hasn't been the cause of his troubles but a symptom of something deeper?

'It's highly likely. I said to think of them not as ghosts

but as with him, in his bones. Burying it all isn't the best way to live with that kind of loss. I said, more or less, that you can run but you can't hide.'

Is that what he's doing coming here, I wonder? To get away from his loss. And to put distance between himself and Sarah, so he doesn't crack? Because as much as I believe him when he said he would never get back with her, the offer of them having their own baby hit me hard. I feel the gut punch again because we didn't get the chance to talk it out. Telling him I might have trouble conceiving could change everything. You hear of couples splitting up all the time because of fertility issues. It's one of those non-negotiable things for some people. I mean, if it didn't happen for me, I'd be gutted. But I'd rather be with someone who made me happy than suffer a bad relationship to have children. Forever is a long time, after all; would there come a time with him where he'd feel that longing from his past in his soul? Yet even knowing all that, I miss him madly. Like, massively, as in feeling a constant ache. And I've never had that before.

We reach the club and I realise all this talk of family and fatherhood affects me too. And hey presto, there he is at the bar, as usual.

'Betty!' he cries as if he's been waiting for this moment all his life. He doesn't bother getting off his stool and that's fine by me; he only ever stinks of booze. 'Have you come to see your old man?'

A bolt of anger goes off inside me – he's on the committee that makes decisions about things like this. It grates that something so important will partially rely on him.

'Hi, Dad. I'm after a favour.'

The words taste bitter. I've never asked him for anything in my life because of the fear of being let down.

'Anything for my princess!' He says it loud enough for people to hear.

I explain what I need and he agrees on the spot, emphatically, without hesitation. 'I'll get the boys to help set it up; you won't have to lift a finger.'

His tone reminds me of the same promises that he ended up breaking over and over throughout my childhood. It pains me to thank him because it means I owe him one when he's in debt to me.

When we leave, Megan says to me, 'That was easier than I thought!'

I feel no satisfaction though. 'It's for the good of the charity, the space will work. But in the run-up to the auction, I won't get a wink of sleep. He is the most unreliable man on the planet. What if he's double-triple booked us and we end up having to share it with someone's eighteenth birthday or a bloody wake?'

'Think positive!' Megan says. 'We all have to trust in someone at some point, don't we?'

This time I do. But I so wish I didn't have to.

## 31

## *Guy*

Sarah breezes into the café looking so much brighter than the last time we met.

'Hi!' she mouths, finishing off a business call as she makes her way to the counter before joining me.

'You look great,' I say, getting up, 'back to work suits you.'

She looks very professional in a crisp white shirt and pinstripe trousers. 'It's nice to be able to have a cup of tea while it's still hot!' she says.

I remember that, making one, then having to do a nappy change and then returning to find it stone cold. The little things still have a power to them and I lean into Sarah, who air kisses me. Already it's a different vibe; it feels we're on a more equal footing.

'How are things?' I ask when we sit down. I would've preferred to have done this via the solicitor but I wanted to see how she was. Mainly for my own interests because I want this to go smoothly – I need to prove to Betty I'm a man of my word — but also, I guess, on a human level because we were together for so long.

'Good. Busy!' She laughs and to my relief it's genuine. 'I think you got off lightly, actually. You'd have been doing your paternity now, up to your eyes in baby groups and weaning.'

Her comment stings. I doubt she meant it to – it's just me being oversensitive.

'How is Maud?' It would be ridiculous not to ask but also I can't help myself.

Sarah grabs her handbag and produces an envelope. 'I got a couple of prints for you. If that's OK? I mean, I don't know how you feel about her anymore ...'

'It's not a tap, is it?'

'No, of course not. That's why I thought you might like to have some pictures. I dunno, maybe that's weird of me?' Sarah looks unsure and places the envelope on the table between us.

'Actually, I think it's incredibly thoughtful. No matter what's happened, Sarah, I'll always want to know how she's doing.'

'You've always been loyal, Guy. And I'm just so pleased that we can do this.'

My tension washes away and I reach for the photos. My heart soars when I see her latest milestones: she's crawling and clapping. 'Four teeth already!'

'And she's sleeping so much better now she's on solids. She's crazy about toast although she just kind of sucks on it, bless her. But bananas, rice cakes, scrambled egg, cheese, broccoli, she's not fussy.'

The pang of hearing about her development is still there. As is wanting to be reassured about her safety.

'All good with Charlie?'

Sarah gives a wry smile. 'He's learning the ropes, put it that way! We're working up to overnights, so it's just day time at the moment but he's involved with nursery and things, which is good. A few glitches, mostly health-related; he's taken her to the doctor twice because she had a couple of spots and he was terrified it was smallpox.'

'At least he's aware of that stuff.'

'Yes, completely, and you get into the groove of things, don't you. But sharing her means I can earn and have a little bit of a life outside of being Maud's mum.'

Sarah's cappuccino arrives and I pop the pictures in my wallet.

'So what about you?' she asks, hugging her mug.

'Same as you, really. Busy. But good. We seem to be doing OK, the both of us, eh?'

Sarah offers her cup to mine for a cheers and I realise I have nothing to worry about.

'So about the annulment – it's probably time to get that moving, isn't it?'

'Yes, definitely,' she says. 'I've sorted the birth certificate so that's done. Your name's off the paperwork.'

Again I feel a stab in my chest. But again she's spoken with no malice and this is just something that was always going to make me feel tender.

'I've sent the nullity form to the court and you'll need to respond within eight days for it to kick in. It should only take six months if there are no obstacles.'

'Of course,' she says, 'then, after that, we'll be completely done. There'll be no need for us to stay in touch at all; you'll be rid of us!'

'Well, no, not exactly. Like I said, I'll always want to know how Maud is.'

'You say that!' Sarah says. 'But you'll meet someone and have your own family. It's natural. You won't remember us at all!'

The thought of that is shocking – that's not how I've assumed it'll go. I wonder if she's doing this on purpose. Then I tell myself to stop being so selfish – she's here, isn't she, agreeing to the annulment? Yet I feel really unsettled; I hadn't thought of this angle at all.

'In fact, Charlie let it slip the other day that you're with someone now.'

I can't protest because I am – he saw us cuddling at the station before Betty left. But it all feels out of context, that because I've got her, I'm unable to keep up with Maud.

'Yes, I am,' I say, hearing myself strain, which makes it sound like I'm playing down what I feel for Betty and that horrifies me. 'But that doesn't mean I won't care for you both.'

'Guy, you have to face it. Our lives are going in different directions now. You'll get to have the children you've always wanted. You'll feel more for them because they'll be yours. I don't want Maud to feel she was a stop-gap and then get dropped.'

'I wouldn't do that, you know that.'

'Maybe not intentionally. And is it actually right for us to keep this up? Maud will be ever so confused when she finds out you're "the man who's not her dad". I'm so sorry to say this ... but I think it might be best if she doesn't have any contact with you at all.'

I feel a bomb going off. The way she's putting all this is coming across like some kind of threat or, at the very least, a nod to 'you can't have your cake and eat it'.

'Especially as Charlie says you met your girlfriend at your stag do.'

Oh shit. He obviously remembered Betty after all.

'I mean, it's all water under the bridge and I know when we were on a break that I was unfaithful. But it does hurt that you're now with a woman you met before we got married.'

'Nothing happened!'

'It's OK, you don't have to explain.'

Something in me snaps. 'No, you're right. I don't have to. But I did nothing wrong. It was just a random meeting; we were both hiding out during paintballing.'

'Paintballing. Your stag do. Even more inappropriate.' Sarah wrinkles her nose like it stinks.

'So how did you get back in touch with each other, then?'

'I can't believe I'm having to justify it to you. We had a G and T, she spilled her drink, I gave her my hankie, she sent it back. By which time you and I had separated.'

'Did you ever think about her before she got in touch?'

It's like she's digging into my heart with a knife and I, in turn, lash out at her. 'Did you ever think about Maud being Charlie's before you married me?' The air is sour now and instantly I regret how this has turned out. 'Sarah, this raking over everything isn't going to do us any good.'

She stays silent.

'I don't want us to part ways like this. I mean, won't we always be tied up in each other's lives because of Charlie? We might not be best mates anymore, but I hope we'll have some sort of relationship. No matter where I go.'

She takes a deep breath. 'So where are you going?'

I realise before I even say it that this is going to go against everything I've just said about being there.

'Wales.'

'Wales?' she says as if it's next door to Australia.

'Granny wants to go home. It's the least I can do.'

'And I don't suppose your girlfriend lives there too, does she?'

I hear the lid slamming shut on my coffin. 'Yes. She does.' I could protest and tell her that my priority is my grandmother and it's a happy coincidence that Betty will be nearby. But Sarah's made up her mind about me. And, really, I don't have a leg to stand on because Maud isn't mine.

Stiffly, Sarah gets up to go.

'What, so is this it?' I hear myself panicking.

'Yes. Why would I want you and your issues around my daughter?'

'What issues?'

'Your obsession with family. I get it, you've never had one. So you idealise it, you create this perfect world and only that will do. Except it doesn't exist. It puts so much strain on everyone. And the saddest thing is you'll end up making the same mistake with this new woman. You're in denial. What we could have had isn't textbook, but you could look back and regret not trying again with us. What if this is your chance? What if the happy family you have in your head never happens for you? What would you do then?'

Then she hacks through the last thread of the bond between us. 'My solicitor will be in touch.'

To: therepairguy@googlemail.com
From: bettyhopkins@gmail.com
Subject: Wales calling

Hello, England!

How is the househunting going? You do realise before you're allowed to move here you need to sit a citizenship exam?

Love,

Wales xxx

PS I'm sorry I didn't get back to you about forever. The auction is imminent and I'm rushed off my size fours.

To: bettyhopkins@gmail.com
From: therepairguy@googlemail.com
Re: Wales calling

Hello, Wales!

Don't worry, I'm already revising Bonnie Tyler, how to count to ten in Welsh and funny comebacks when England lose to Wales in the rugby.

Househunting involves not doing searches for Bethlehem properties because there is only one thing for sale online and that's a field. Having to broaden things with a million-mile radius. We're liking the look of somewhere in the Brecon Beacons. Granny has decided she doesn't want to live too near to her brother and sisters because they'll only call over every five minutes. Any suggestions?

Best,
England

PS The auction is important. Just to say the paperwork
is in for the annulment.


To: therepairguy@googlemail.com
From: bettyhopkins@gmail.com
Re: Wales calling

The Beacons? That's where the SAS train. Oh God,
you're not signing up, are you?

PS That's great. How did it go with Sarah?


To: bettyhopkins@gmail.com
From: therepairguy@googlemail.com
Re: Wales calling

That's classified.

PS As predicted.


To: therepairguy@googlemail.com
From: bettyhopkins@gmail.com
Re: Wales calling

*nose tap* I'm sure the DIY department of the SAS
would be delighted to have you.

PS Bad, was it?


To: bettyhopkins@gmail.com
From: therepairguy@googlemail.com
Re: Wales calling

Well, someone has to make those cut-outs for shooting practice, right?

PS No, in terms of her agreeing to it. Yes, in terms of what she had to say before said agreement: I'm obsessed with the idea of a perfect family because I've never had one, I'm in denial about the impact of losing my parents so young, she and Maud are my only guaranteed chance to have a family, what if I never get the chance again? Oh, and I'm to have no further contact with Maud because when I have a family of my own – she knows about us, Charlie remembered you from paintballing and told her – I won't give a toss about her because I'll have my own real children. So I went the long way home and smashed a greasy burger and chips. Telling you this for transparency. It's all poppycock, obviously.


To: therepairguy@googlemail.com
From: bettyhopkins@gmail.com
Re: Wales calling

I suspect there are a fair few wonky canteen tables that'll need repairing too.

PS I really don't want to be that person who slags off an ex. I don't know the whole situation. But I think you did marvellously well to only have one greasy burger. Now I want one. Especially as I still feel dirty from when I had to ask my dad for a favour to put the auction installation on at the rugby club where he's on the committee. Who'd have guessed a dilapidated garage wouldn't work out?

I have never asked him for anything. Now I'm depending on a feckless fool. He's thrilled because he thinks it gives him a chance to make things up to me. It's making me want to run back to London.


To: bettyhopkins@gmail.com
From: therepairguy@googlemail.com
Re: Wales calling

London? Just as I move to Wales?


To: therepairguy@googlemail.com
From: bettyhopkins@gmail.com
Re: Wales calling

Don't worry, it's not as if I have a history of self-sabotage, is it?

To: bettyhopkins@gmail.com
From: therepairguy@googlemail.com
Re: Wales calling

Just hold on for a few more days. I've got some
viewings booked, I'll drop Granny at her sister's in
Bethlehem, then I'll be there. We'll get through this.


To: therepairguy@googlemail.com
From: bettyhopkins@gmail.com
Re: Wales calling

## 32

### *Betty*

'Now is this supper or dinner?' Guy asks my mam, 'because Betty says I have to pass an exam in Welshness to qualify to live here.'

'It's tea!' she cries. 'Dinner is lunch and supper is what we have before bed.'

Mam is beside herself with glee at me having a 'man friend' over. I did warn Guy that she'd treat him like a saviour for taking me off her hands. I don't mind her excitement, she's entitled to it because she remembers how damaged I was.

Luckily Nerys couldn't make it – or rather I told Mam to not invite her. I need to pick a good time to break it to my sister because the facts are a bit stark. She's a traditionalist and my biggest protector – she could flip when I tell her. Yet surely she'll see how happy he makes me?

That's the craziest thing: the stakes are high – not least with an ex who may be difficult but whose tirade has me worrying. Is she right Guy's in denial about losing his parents and that's made him 'perfect family' obsessed? Megan said how important it was for bereaved children to understand their loss. Worse is Sarah's jab that she and Maud are like an 'oven-ready' unit, not least because I might be unable to give him what he wants. Her projection that he'd have kids with me only highlights his priority. Yet despite all of that, when we're together, it feels like we can take on the world. I can't help but believe it as Mam smiles and Guy's sitting with his knees tucked up by his elbows at the table because he's far too big for this terrace. While he sticks out a mile, he also fits in. They've nattered away about fixtures and fittings and he's already repaired a cupboard door and put up a picture for her. It also helped that he arrived with a bouquet of sunflowers and a new oyster-coloured silky M&S dressing gown because I'd told him how the sight of her in her threadbare one had been one of those small but major moments that had got me up and about after the accident.

'Nothing fancy, I'm afraid, Guy,' she says, bringing in plates of sausage, mash and peas. 'But filling.'

'Smells amazing, bangers and mash is my all-time favourite.'

'I didn't know that!' I say, marvelling at the host of things I have to learn about him, then realising how soppy I must sound.

'I'm a deeply fascinating person, Betty,' he says. 'There are plenty of nuggets of gold you are yet to discover about me.'

'Ketchup? Or HP?' I ask. 'Because the answer to that could change everything.'

'Oh, please. Brown every time.' He applies a hefty splurge to his plate, the classy gold-rimmed ones Mam has for best.

'Thank God,' Mam says, joining in, 'he's one of us! Now tuck in. You sure you don't want meaty ones, Bet? There's plenty more.'

'Mam, you've been asking if I want meaty versions of things since I was sixteen. When are you going to understand I'm veggie?'

She ignores me. 'Betty won't even have turkey at Christmas, Guy!'

'Actually,' Guy says, 'I'm considering going veggie because of Betty.'

'Seriously?' I say, pleased I'm rubbing off on him.

'Yes, easier if we're eating together.' I love the casual commitment of his words, the belief that this is going to continue. With Jude, with every other three-month wonder, I would have shuddered. 'And anyway, Carol, she's got a turkey full-time now. Me.'

'Ah, there's lovely,' Mam coos.

'Not ready to go veggie now, though?' I ask him as he prepares to mouth a forkful.

'That'd be rude after what your mum has rustled up.'

'So how many places you looking at?' Mam asks.

'Five tomorrow, across the Brecon Beacons.'

'Your granny must be so excited.'

'She was fit to burst when I dropped her and the dog in Bethlehem.'

'There's no place like home! Betty says you're staying just outside the village.'

'Yep, at a guest house. Kay's put me up a few times now and it feels like I'm seeing family when I go.'

'I might go there tonight,' I say, 'if that's OK?'

'Bloody marvellous! In fact, Cliff's on his way now!'

'Not that Mam's trying to get rid of me or anything!' I laugh.

But that was where it all started: wanting to give her her life back is the catalyst that's led to this exact moment.

'So how's it all going with the auction?' Mam asks.

'Fine, apart from having to rely on Dad.' I pull a face at the prospect.

'Oh Betty! I know you're not his number-one fan, but give him a go. He's as pleased as punch to be helping you out. He said so the other day when we had coffee.'

'Coffee? How can you be so ... fine with him?'

'He's your father.' She carves into a sausage with precision. 'Can't change it. I learned a long time ago to accept that. It makes life a lot easier. You should give it a go.'

Guy nods slowly and I look at it from his point of view – he'd love to have his dad around. And wouldn't it be grand if I could accept mine for who he is? But it's a big if.

We finish up, too stuffed for afters. Guy washes and I wipe, in between hot kisses and soapy cuddles, that is, and then Cliff walks in.

'How do!' he booms and we perform the introductions.

I've met him a couple of times but never in these circumstances when I know he's going to stay over. I could be appalled at the old codgers but actually I'm chuffed to bits Mam has someone. Especially as he's a bit of a silver fox with that full head of hair and the way he obviously adores her. He'd have to, to have stuck around while I was in the loony bin and spoiled all their private time.

'I'm so sorry the garage wasn't right in the end, Cliff,' I say, feeling bad I put him out.

'Don't worry, I did think it was a bit off the wall to use it. But you arty types, you have visions, you see things, don't you!'

'Well, I loved the garage,' Guy says, reaching out to shake hands. 'Incredible workspace in there, great sorting system, I saw.'

Mam and I exchange wide eyes in joke-horror that we've ended up with a pair of geeks who have moved on to discuss power tools and the case for and against cordless appliances.

'I'm sure you could talk all night, Cliff, but they're on their way out.' Good work, Mam, I think, and he takes the hint. I get an overnight bag and we leave.

'Where to, then?' Guy says, 'Back to Kay's or do you want to go somewhere else first?'

'You've been driving all day! How about – how about I take us somewhere, just for a bit of fresh air?'

'Yeah?' His surprise and delight is obvious.

'Yeah! I've been doing trips here and there, to keep my hand in, ever since you faked your ankle—'

'I did not!'

'Whatever.' I turn the ignition, feeling no panic. 'Right, I've been saving this place for you.'

He rubs his hands with excitement and on the way, we chat about a work idea I've had but when I pull up to a lay-by he looks dubious.

'Wait and see!'

With the hills soaring, I lead him up a path and at the peak the world stretches out before us – and beneath us, because the enormous lake reflects the vast sky. It's so still, the pure blue water holds a perfect mirror image of cotton-wool clouds turning pink edged by the mountains which are gold with fading ferns.

'Wow,' Guy says, 'this is incredible.'

'And so quiet.'

We sit down on the bank and he comes behind me and puts his arms around my waist, and we gaze, captivated, at the view. The air is warm and rich with the smell of the land and there's only the sound of us breathing it all in.

'So I've been thinking, and I don't want to ruin this,' he murmurs, 'about what Sarah said. About me wanting the two-point-four-children thing.'

I find I'm holding my breath.

'The house teeming with kids and the dog and sitting round a noisy table – it was all to fill a hole, I think, left by my parents. And it was a huge hole to fill. But then I met you, Betty, and you've filled it and – it's weird to say it, but having tea at your mum's, talking about nothing, just being there, that's actually better than anything I've imagined.'

'Serious?'

'Yep.'

It's a breakthrough of sorts. But it still leaves the question of kids – is it a deal-breaker for him? This is the moment to tell him he isn't guaranteed that with me.

'But what about when Sarah asked what you'd do if it didn't happen.' My rib cage is still tight with worry.

'I mean, it's all I've ever wanted but—'

I wait, knowing this will determine what happens between us.

'Because I wanted it so badly, I think I overlooked the fact that she and I weren't meant to be. I've never said that out loud to anyone, Betty. That won't happen with us, because what we have already is just … everything else will come. You see—'

I need to tell him and I need to do it now. I go to speak but Guy hasn't finished.

'What I'm trying to say, Betty, and it's bizarre how our worlds have become one after that – what – fifteen minutes in goggles—'

The moment has gone and, while I could stop him, I'm weak at what's hinting at. We turn our faces to each other as the sun dips beneath the horizon.

'—is that I'm falling in love with you.'

I'm dazzled and dazed and just like the water and the sky, our smiles shine back at each other. His is so radiant and magnetic and his eyes are pools of tenderness. It's lucky I'm sitting down because there's a danger I might swoon.

His face turns shy. 'I hope that doesn't frighten you; it's not to change anything, we've always gone at our own pace, haven't we?'

'We have. We don't live according to BST but BGT, Betty and Guy Time.'

He laughs.

'And I feel the same, Guy.' My resolve to tell him has vanished; another opportunity will come. 'I'm falling in love with you too. And it makes everything that's gone on before seem so dull and lifeless.'

We kiss and sway and as the darkness creeps in from the east, we head home.

A note from Kay says she's having an early night.

'Oh bless her,' he says. 'I finally told her who you are and she's being tactful, for once.'

'Shall we have an early night as well?' I say, just wanting to curl up with him.

He takes my hand and leads me up the stairs.

'I've brought you something,' Guy says as we reach his

room where a huge king-size awaits, 'but you're not to open it until I'm gone.'

'Ooh! Why's that?' I say as we collapse onto the glorious fluffy duvet.

He scrunches his hair in his hands. 'Because I don't want to see your face if you don't like it.'

'Why wouldn't I like it, you ridiculous thing?' I wrestle his palms away and make him roll to face me.

'Because it's meaningful. Like, it's a gesture – for the future.'

'How mysterious! I don't get you – but I got you. I promise I won't look.'

'Good. Now come here,' Guy says, his eyes simmering as we merge into one and he whispers into my ear, 'I'm so glad I found you, Betty, because you're my missing piece.'

# 33

## *Guy*

I managed to avoid an inspection when I dropped Granny at her sister's yesterday.

But today there's no getting out of it.

'Look at him, Myfanwy! Look at him! He's yuuuge!'

That's Great Aunt Miriam, who's creating a sound far greater than the sum of her tiny parts, which echoes off the stone cottage walls where she's lived all her life. She packs a punch of a hug too. While Granny is taller, and the eldest of the clan, there's no denying they're siblings; both have eyes like coal, their hair is cropped silver and their manner is playful.

From behind me comes another shriek.

'Come yuuur, you! Come and see your Great Aunt Mali!'

Resistance is futile so I get another squeeze, just as hard and by a woman very similar to the other two. And then a third voice launches at me.

'Well, if it isn't young Guy!' My hand is gripped by Great Uncle Morgan who threatens to yank my arm out of its socket.

'That's who he gets his height from!' Granny says as if it's breaking news. Like, wouldn't she have recalled her brother was tall?

The rest of them chorus their agreement and I get it – this is what families do, comparing and contrasting relatives, finding resemblances and black sheep. I've never been part of that, not in my adult memory. Because, since childhood, I haven't come when Granny has visited Bethlehem. It's a fantastically warm atmosphere and my grandmother, in fact all of them, are more youthful for it.

'Are you all psychic or something? How are you all here at once?'

'Oh Guy,' Granny scolds me, and I notice her accent has been turned up to the max, 'I've told you, they all live next door to each other.'

'In a row!' second-eldest Miriam adds.

'Like ducklings!' third-born Mali chimes.

'See what nonsense I have to put up with, Guy?' Morgan says wearily. 'I'll be glad of the male company when you move here.'

'Oh shush!' Granny says to him. Then to me, 'The baby loves it really, Guy!'

'Sixty-nine, I am, and they still call me the baby,' Morgan booms.

'We'll have to have a big party when you're settled,' Miriam decides. 'You can meet all the cousins. There's hundreds of them!'

'If I were you, I'd be busy that day,' Morgan suggests, rocking on his heels and wiggling his white eyebrows towards the exit.

'Talking of busy, we've got some houses to see, G.'

We escape to get on with five viewings dotted around the Brecon Beacons. It's a stunning few hours as we cross valleys, pass waterfalls and wild horses. The first four are straight no's – one is too remote, another needs too much renovation, the next is beside a river that's prone to flooding and the fourth is north-facing, dark and gloomy. As we move on to the last, I check on Granny's mood to see if she's having second thoughts.

'Not a bit of it! It's magnificent here,' she says, pointing at the spine of the looming mountain range. 'We'll find somewhere. It just makes me all the more determined. How I love Wales! You can feel it in the land, the spirit and the poetry of the people. And to be back with my brother and sisters is wonderful. I stick by what I said, mind, I don't want to be reliant on them, I'm independent, too, but I shall love being a short drive away from them.'

The sat nav announces we are at our destination and I pull into a gated driveway which resembles the pictures in the property details. I remember now why I booked this last viewing – it's £35,000 over our budget and a pipe dream. But I couldn't resist having a look. The estate agent waves and we crawl along the gravel and take a right and see a beautiful pair of converted barns at either end of a shared flagstone patio nestled in a clearing surrounded by ancient woodland.

We play it cool but the second the agent has gone we both know this is The One. Even though it's out of our price bracket, we get carried away, deciding who should have which barn, where the workshop would go, and the place for a veg patch.

By the time Granny's back with Miriam, we've agreed to try an offer. The property's been on the market for a while and it needs some work. But nothing ventured, nothing gained. I promise I'll make the call when I get to Kay's but I'm distracted by a message when I get there.

> The hall at the rugby club is free a day early and one of the boys can help me shift the auction stuff from the garage. That's where I am now, almost done. Want to meet me at the rugby club? Love, Betty xxx

I start up the engine again and head towards the H-shaped goalposts that you can see from pretty much everywhere in the village. I spy Betty bossing a team of burly sixteen-stoners who are lifting the lots from a van into the building.

I watch her, amused by the way someone so small can command men the size of giants. When she sees me, she runs over.

'My dad's here. You're going to have to meet him.' She's wide-eyed and flustered.

'OK,' I say, 'I'm fine about it.'

'But it bothers me. It's the dysfunctional bit of my family. I'm worried it's going to put you off.'

'Like I'm so functional. Maybe this is him trying to make amends? Maybe he's changed and you haven't been open to it. Give him a chance?'

She considers it. 'You might be right. He jumped at helping me out. But I'm scared about him letting me down. All over again.'

She glances back and then groans at a man heading towards us.

'That him?' I ask and she nods.

He looks all right, a bit rough around the edges, but I can see how, back in the day, he would've had the stature of a scrum half. He has a pint in one hand and his phone in the other and he's talking and laughing with someone. When he gets to us, he's still chatting and even though he's stopped, he hasn't, technically, because he's side-stepping on the spot, never still, as if he's ducking and diving. I look for Betty in his face but she's like her mother, a redhead with porcelain skin. Mind you, if there were any similarities it'd be hard to see beyond his crooked nose, which must've been broken several times over. There's nothing threatening about him and he has an easy way with words, cracking jokes, and signing off with a 'ta ta, mate'.

'My princess!' He opens his arms wide to Betty. Is he offering a hug? But he'd know she wouldn't get that close to him. He might be announcing himself then.

'Hi, Dad, thanks for the call earlier. Better to get it all inside tonight rather than tomorrow, so I can spend the day on it. Will there be someone to let me in at eight a.m.?' She doesn't wait for him to answer. 'Actually, maybe I should do it all tonight.'

'It'll be fine! Don't worry! You worry too much!' Then to me he says, 'She's a right worrier, this one, everything has to be just-so.'

'Well, I like to be self-sufficient. You can't always rely on people, can you?' she says, pointedly.

He stretches a hand out to me. 'David Hopkins, Dai these days, or Number Nine, a reference there to my playing days. I'll answer to most things as long as it's not one of the ex-wives calling!'

He's coming across as charmless but it might be nerves.

'I'm Guy. A friend of Betty's.'

'Just a friend? That's a shame. She needs to get a

hurry-up because I'm after a rugby team of grandkids, I am!' He winks at me as if I'm a man and I'll understand. I get it, though; he's a bloke of a certain age and that's how some of them are.

'I have other things on my plate, Dad,' Betty says, looking wounded. Then she goes on the attack. 'Like work and getting a business plan together for a new venture. Which you'd know about if you'd ever asked. But then again, you wouldn't understand what responsibility is, would you?'

I want to tell the pair of them to take a deep breath and start again. But it's not my place. Betty wouldn't thank me for ploughing in when I haven't earned the right to interfere.

'All work and no play, Betty,' Dai says, oblivious to her anger. 'Then again, you've never been the type to settle down, have you?'

She is struggling to contain herself, her eyebrows have turned white, she's that furious. But rather than ask her if she's OK, he's draining his pint and shouting at someone across the field; he says he's wanted and then jogs off with a wheeze.

'Oh Betty, I'm so sorry,' I say.

My phone buzzes in my pocket and I curse the timing of it. As I pull it free, my wallet falls out and lands open on the grass. I'm fumbling to get the call now and it's a number I don't recognise. It could be Granny or something to do with her so I answer with a hello.

'It's me,' she says.

'Sarah?'

'This is my new work mobile.'

Betty is staring at the ground and I follow her gaze.

The two photos of Maud from Sarah are lying beside my wallet. Then she looks up at me with pain all over her face. She gulps and takes a step back and then she turns away from me and she's gone.

# 34

## *Betty*

I don't know where I'm going but my feet are moving, following orders to walk away.

The heavy grey sky presses down on me and the hedges of the lane close in, the overgrown tendrils blowing into my path, making me claustrophobic.

I should've known. It was there gnawing at the edges of my gut and I chose to talk it down. The doubts I felt now feel like facts: Guy will never commit to me truly; there will always be the lurking shadow of what he's lost and we will never be able to shake it off.

The single certainty I have, the one solid thing I possess, is what I told my dad – that I can only rely on myself, my work, my capital, and no one else can make anything happen for me apart from me. I feel a fool for letting myself believe that love conquers all. And how stupid I've been to think my father's absence hasn't touched me. The one time I've had to rely on him has made me sick to the core.

There I was perceiving I'd made some great comeback and life was going to smell of roses. Instead, my heart has been pierced by thorns.

Angry tears are streaking down my cheeks, my vision is blurred and I have nothing but my hand to use to wipe them away. Damn that bloody hankie, damn that thing. Sheer desperation meant I based my entire recovery on one moment. I pinned everything on him, I can't actually believe I've been so blind. The backstory of his loss and mine, our lies, which revealed we were chasing ghosts, the pain we've been through to resurface, it was obvious that there would be an aftershock. And this is where we're at: we're two lost souls who helped one another to grope through the darkness but now the lights are on the bodies are exposed.

I hear footsteps thundering up behind me and instinctively I swing round with my arms in front of me to protect myself.

'Betty!' Guy shouts, his face full of angst. 'Betty, wait!'

He pulls up next to me but there's a chasm between us. 'What is it? Tell me.'

The thorns begin to draw blood. 'I just can't compete with your past, Guy. Every time we move forward, you get dragged back and I can't see an end to it.'

'You don't have to compete,' he says, holding his pleading hands out to me. 'It's all over.'

'Is it? I understand how hurt you've been, I know what that feels like, but you haven't truly let go. The photos. Of Maud.' I see them again as I shut my eyes: her beautiful smile and bright eyes. 'You carrying them in your wallet – it's just so very sad. I sound crazy, as if I'm jealous of her. I'm not, I swear; it's what they represent. There has to be a time when you commit to the now. With me.'

'I'm moving here, Betty. The photos were from Sarah when I met her to tell her about the annulment. I stuck them in my wallet without thinking, I forgot they were there,' he says, pleading.

'And why did she give them to you? Because she wants you back! That's what my jealousy has been about – her!'

'No. She's going ahead with the annulment, that's what she rang to tell me. And to apologise for – as you just said, trying to manipulate me. She's not a bad person, she was just lashing out. She's said she's sorry. And she said Maud's fine and—'

'Enough!'

My shout stuns us both and we stand there with heaving chests.

'Guy, there's something I haven't told you that could change everything.'

'What? What on earth could there be that would change how I feel about you?'

The wind picks up and I feel the force of it pushing me to tell him.

'I might not be able to have kids, Guy.' I throw my hands in the air. 'What do you think about that?'

His mouth falls open and he's scrabbling to understand, so I spell it out.

'The accident – my injuries – they said from day one I might be unable to conceive and delivery could be dangerous.'

I see devastation in his eyes. I look away because I can't bear to see his gut reaction.

'And, anyway,' I say, as spots of rain begin to dot the tarmac, 'even if that wasn't going on, I don't know if I could carry a baby full-term.' The final thing I've kept from him, the most painful of all, which I've buried so deeply as if to keep it from myself too, rushes out. 'With Jude – I had a miscarriage.' The memory comes hurtling back at me: the panic, not the joy, when I found out I was pregnant.

'Oh Betty,' he says, his fingertips reaching for me.

'Don't. Because—' Guy will hate me after I tell him this – 'I was glad.' The guilt suffocates me again, the guilt I felt as Jude cried when I told him we'd lost the baby. 'Because I didn't want to have to be with him because of a child. Like my mum did with my dad.'

I see myself crying in the bathroom of my flat, overwhelmed by physical pain and the ordeal of miscarrying at six weeks, and then the tears of pure relief that I wasn't going to be trapped with a man I didn't love. I asked Jude to leave the very next day.

I face Guy, holding his gaze to tell him, 'This is me', not the woman he thought I was.

But he's shaking his head slowly, wincing at what he's just heard. 'That must've been awful, to go through that.'

'In the depths of it all, I felt like the accident was my punishment.'

'No,' he says, firmly, 'that's just you wanting to punish yourself. And that life is over now. Just because what happened doesn't mean you can't have kids, does it?'

'That's just it, though, isn't it? I can't promise you anything. All you'll have with me, for definite, is me. And that won't be enough, will it?'

He hesitates for a split second too long before he speaks. 'Who knows what's coming every time we make a decision or take a step? Don't give up.'

'But you'll always hold out on it. And I can't do that to you.'

He crumbles and falls to his knees. I can't stand to see

him so upset, so I go to him and embrace him until he stops sobbing.

'It's you, Betty, that's what I want. And we can face this together, and whatever happens, if it doesn't happen, if we don't have a family, then we'll survive.'

'I'll forever feel a failure.' My chin wobbles and my throat aches and my tears start to fall. 'And the cruellest thing is, after the accident, I started to see kids in my future; I'd breathe in my nieces and imagine I'd have my own baby one day. As awful as it would be, I would cope if it doesn't happen for me. But it'd be unbearable to deprive you of being a dad.'

Guy holds me tighter.

'The lies – the things I should've told you – I said all this had made us stronger. But really, it's torn us apart.'

'Betty,' he says, pulling back to take my hands, 'I'll do whatever it takes, we'll do whatever it takes, we'll find the best care we can, see a consultant, a hundred consultants, if that's what you want.'

'But maybe it's better not to even try? Because imagine that, imagine wanting something so much it becomes the only thing holding us together. And if we lost a baby ...'

'Listen, no one can guarantee anything ever but there's always hope.' His eyes flame with it.

'Hope – it's the hope that kills you, isn't it? And this is so important to you, like I can see how much you think parenthood will fix you.'

Guy stares at me, then he lets me go and drops his head into his hands.

'So what do you want me to do? I beg you, Betty, this can't be over. I'll do anything.'

'But the bottom line is you want to be a father.'

He looks up at me, his eyelashes beaded with drops of his pain. 'I do, Betty. Yes.'

Finally, he's admitted it and the rain starts to sting my skin.

'I love you, Guy. With everything I am. I know you love me now and here – but I might not be enough forever.'

'So what are you going to do? Are you going to go back to London?'

'I genuinely don't know.'

Guy lets out a noise of frustration that sounds almost animal-like.

'Is that the truth?' he sobs. 'Or maybe you've got your bags packed already? You've outclassed yourself with the self-sabotage this time.'

I flinch and immediately he takes it back. 'I'm sorry.'

'Maybe you don't trust me, not really,' I say.

'Maybe you don't trust me either.'

The pair of us are still stuck. Our clothes dripping, we both begin to cry. I get up and pull him to a standing position and we kiss each other, tenderly and delicately, our lips tasting of tears as we cling onto each other. We've seen so many beautiful things which reflected our happiness, it seems fitting that this awful moment is on a rainy back road nowhere special.

'We're exhausted. Let's go, let's go back to Mam's, have something to eat.'

'What, for a last supper?'

His voice is flat, there's not a drop of humour in it. I can't answer him. I don't know what to do. So I say nothing and hug him instead in the downpour.

'Let's just go,' I say, because while my feet know the way home, they have no idea of the future.

## 35

### *Guy*

'Come and help me with the jigsaw, Guy, it'll take your mind off things.'

Granny is only across the room but her voice sounds distant. It's no wonder, I'm still there with Betty, hundreds of miles away, replaying the moment when we laid our agony bare.

I see haunting snapshots from the lane where it all began to unravel: her hair blown by the wind onto her wet cheeks; her eyes dulled as she told me our love was doomed; how she had carried the burden of not knowing if she could have children and the torment and guilt of her relief at miscarrying because of her circumstances. What we had, what I thought was solid, instantly became flimsy. I thought the walk to her mother's was misery as we held each other up, but there was worse to come. Looking back, I should've ripped the plaster off and left Betty at her doorstep. We were both so stunned, though, that we fell into the house. It was slow torture sitting around the table, clucked over by her mum, who knew something had happened but didn't pry, then lying with Betty and talking it over until the early hours. She promised to think things over and I agreed to look into myself.

I left to collect Granny from Bethlehem before dawn but I left no note for Betty; what more could I have said?

Anger bubbles beneath the surface – at the injustice of her assuming she wasn't enough. And at the dot-to-dot conclusion that I can't go forward because I lost my parents. She's the one who's given up, not me.

'Cariad,' Granny says, calling to me again, beckoning me to sit beside her at the table.

I get up with legs of lead and see with a pang that she's working on the love spoon puzzle. I think of the gift I've left with Betty and cringe at what she'll make of it now.

'Have you tried contacting Betty?' she says, poring over the box and then the pieces, tutting at how hard it is to distinguish one bit from another.

'No. What's the point? She's made her mind up. Once I admitted that fatherhood was what I wanted, even though I know it's not a given for anyone, just the fact that I said it made her put a thick black line through us. First Sarah saying I'm tunnel-visioned because of my past, then Betty pretty much saying the same thing, as if I'm stunted and … Granny?' I can ask her, she'll be honest. 'Do you think I am?'

'It's not what I think, it's what you think.'

'Which means you do.' I get up and go to the fireplace where a photo shows my parents crouched and laughing as they beckon me to walk to them, but I'm resolutely sitting on my backside. Refusing to walk. Is that me now?

'I think,' I say as a revelation, or at least another possibility, comes to me, 'I need to do something for myself.'

'How do you mean?'

I'm struggling to understand it – how do I put my finger on something I've only just considered?

'I need to …' I search for the idea and it finds its way to me – 'complete my own jigsaw puzzle.'

Granny tilts her head towards me in curiosity.

'So there are lots of pieces to me, G. Lots are already in place; there's you, of course, and all the family in Wales.' The image begins to build. 'Maud's with her parents now. Betty, well, I'm hoping I can still slot her in, right in the middle, alongside me. But there are a few bits that I haven't sorted through yet that need to come before her.'

'I see. And do you know what they are?'

I take a deep breath because it's going to take courage to forgive him.

'I've got to make amends with Charlie. I know what he did was wrong and all along I've said I wouldn't let him back in. But bottom line is – I miss him, especially now. He'd understand. He's family to me. If we can reconnect, then maybe he can help me with the last part, because he's like my brother.'

'And what's the last part?'

'Mum and Dad. Because … they feel like strangers.'

'Strangers? But they're your parents!' Granny waves at the framed pictures on her shelves, of them on their wedding day and my dad as a boy in shorts. 'They're in your blood. Why have you never said?'

'You have your memories of them, you feel they're alive in here,' I tap my chest, 'but I feel numb. They're faceless to me. I have no memories of my own; I know only the things people have told me, and I'm grateful for that, but now I'm a grown man, they seem like a fairy tale, they don't feel real.'

'Oh Guy. How long have you felt like this?'

'I suppose since I lost Maud. As a kid I had all the stories to hold onto, then when I was at uni and building my business and meeting Sarah, it wasn't on my radar. Life was happening. But that feeling, of being untethered, came when it all failed.'

'You were all at sea.'

'I lost my balance. I need to get it back.'

I look at my dear grandmother who has been my one true north and I need to tell her. 'You and Grampy gave me everything, I'm so grateful. But—'

'I'm not your mother and it's not the same. I know, Guy.' She rubs her wrist and stares at the wall. 'I'd brought your dad into the world in a different era and then I had you to raise and all the parenting advice and the approaches had changed. There was a pressure to do right by your mum and dad that would keep me awake at night, worrying if I was too indulgent with you or if Grandpa was too strict. And then there was my own grief. No parent should have to grieve for their child; it's not the natural order of things.'

'It sounds unbearable.'

'And yet I consider myself fortunate to have had those years with my son and your mother.'

'That's what I mean; you can look back and remember, but when I do that, all I see is a big black hole.'

'So where will you start?'

'At the beginning, Granny.'

'And do you think that will help you deal with things if you and Betty can't have children?'

This is the crux of the matter. 'I pray it will. I have to be able to feel whole if I'm going to support her, whether she decides against trying or we do and face disappointment while handling my own. I have to come to terms with that if we are to be together. Because, and I hate myself for feeling this, I've always wanted children and I have to make peace with myself, in that I might not be a dad. And really feel it.'

'If there's anything I can help with, anything you want to know ...'

'I'll ask, G, I promise.'

This, though, has to be my own discovery.

'We've got other stuff to sort out together anyway,' I say, 'like finding a house. If only I'd called straight after the viewing instead of the morning after—'

The situation with Betty had made me forget all about ringing the estate agent.

'What difference would it have made? It went to a cash buyer for the asking price. We couldn't have competed with that. When it comes to houses, these things are always meant to be.'

'Maybe we should look again at what's in our price bracket? The places we dream of are thirty grand out of our league. Broaden our search too?' I don't want to look further afield but it might be out of my hands.

'But then what about Betty?'

'What if she doesn't wait for me? What if I've seen her for the last time?'

'I refuse to believe it. The way you are together. Listen to me, Guy, there's something about you two that has forever written on it. You have to keep the faith.'

There's a knock at the door.

'I will, G,' I say, getting up to answer the door as Bobby wanders in to say hello. 'I'll give it my best shot.'

I open up and a man in a suit is standing with a

briefcase. He introduces himself but I don't catch his name – I'm too busy staring at the gnome in his hand.

'The late Mr Cummings, he wanted you to have this.' It's Gordon, the little chap who was his life companion. 'There's also something else, if I can come in?'

*Dear Guy,*

*Today there are no jokes. There is just honesty. I
love you so very much. From the second we met, I
felt as if you'd shone a light on me. When we began
to write, you fired a spark inside me. We came face
to face and you made me feel alive. When our lips
touched and we became one, I burned with happiness.*

*At every stage I've felt seen by you; in your belief
and love, in your touch and laugh, you understood the
essence of who I was and it inspired me to become the
truest version of myself. Love should be equal but how
can I ever match your devotion? If we stayed together
I'd be taking away from you the one thing you wish
for most in the world. I couldn't live with myself if
we tried to have a family and failed. So I've come to
a very painful decision, one that I'll regret every day
of my life. But I'd rather regret that than know you
sacrificed yourself for me. And that means I have to let
you go. It hurts so much to set you free but it would
be far worse if your dreams died with me.*

*When we met that day in London, it made me
realise how unfulfilled I was. Yes, I had the job, the
flat and the lifestyle, but I didn't have fulfilment.
If we were to commit to one another, you would
ultimately feel unfulfilled and I can't stop you on your
journey to find that peace.*

*I went to the waterfall to paint this card for you so
you would have a memory of a perfect day before real
life had to reveal itself. And I wanted to write all of
this rather than ring, because that's always been our
way. But I wanted to write too so that you had it in
black and white – there is no room for doubt of how*

338

*much I adore you, how much I wished I could have guaranteed you that joy of fatherhood. Too much longer together and the unhappiness we both feel now would be far, far worse. It's better to pull apart before we fall even deeper. Because what I've realised, when I've thought about you day and night, is that the only way for you to heal is by having a child. I have absolutely no doubt you will and I know you will be a wonderful dad.*

*As for me, the lie I told you about where I was going in life, I'm going to make it real because of you.*

*Thank you for everything, Guy, and goodbye.*

*Love,*

*Betty xxx*

# 36

## *Betty*

The lights go down and a hush descends. The stillness here at the unveiling of the auction is similar to my own, when the noise inside of me finally stopped and was replaced by the relief of a decision. My heart is broken but it's nothing to what I'd feel if I had to live with Guy's silent hurt in years to come.

My own regret is already aching at my sides, but if I hadn't released him the torment would've been a thousand-fold. And the knowledge that I have done the right thing by him is strangely soothing. It's probably the shock, too, from cutting him out of my life; I'm prepared for the inevitable despair, but for now I'm numb.

My card will have arrived and it will go unanswered – he understood it was goodbye.

Having a family would've been a while off, of course, and no one goes into a relationship with twinkles in their eyes. But knowing what I know, it's the best way before our lives became entwined and entrenched. Solutions would be out there if I was unable to have a baby but, by then, we'd be a long way down the road. I know he loves me enough now to risk it and to live without a family but as time passed things could change. A long, slow unravelling of our love and his search for someone

340

new could mean he never has the chance again.

Maybe pregnancy would have happened easily and quickly. But, if not, the issue would have dominated our relationship, always bobbing on the horizon, our decisions based on what-ifs. I can't live like that and I know it would kill him.

That's why there have been no tears – this is the least worst outcome. I've cried a lifetime since February, anyway, and there comes a point when it's too exhausting to keep on. My own grief at giving up the one definite chance to try to become a mother is something I have to live with. One day I will stop being childless and I'll be childfree; I know how time can heal. And I am surrounded by love.

The youngsters on this film Megan and I made to trail the auction – they're my focus now.

And here they are, talking to camera about the difference that Life Goes On has made to them. The little ones are excited and breathless about the seaside trips where seagulls steal chips and are in wonder at just how Santa knew what they wanted for Christmas. The older kids refer to the support they've had accessing services and the practical help when they've had trouble at home or school. Everyone here today, at the official launch of the Sale of the Centuries, already knows how important our work is. This promo is to accompany the lots on the website which we hope will be shared far and wide to pull at the heart and purse strings.

It finishes and the lights go up as people dab their eyes. Within me, there's pride at what Megan and I have achieved, and drive to make sure we fundraise our butts off for these kids. There's my own fulfilment too that perhaps everything that's happened to me so far has been leading to this point.

'Aunty Bet!' Poppy flings herself at me and I reach down to hug her tight. Over her shoulder I see Baby Daisy coming towards me, taking bandy-legged steps while she holds onto Nerys. I get the most gorgeous smile and just then she breaks hands with her mammy and we all hold our breaths as she takes one, two, then three little lurching stomps and falls into my other arm.

'She's just walked for the first time!' Nerys cries as Mam and Devoted Steve applaud.

'Did you just walk to your Aunty Betty, Baby Daisy?' I say into the fluff of her curls.

'That's typical, that is!' Nerys says. 'I do all the hard work and then she does it for you!'

Maybe I'll get the best of both worlds now, I think, having all the joy but none of the worry.

Another two faces are level with mine – Alfie and Nancy, who drop to their knees to join the little party. Poppy is entranced by the twins, who take her off to play Hide and Seek, while I pass Baby Daisy back to Nerys.

'This is so fab, Betty, I hope you're proud of yourself. When you said you were taking this job, presh, I did wonder if you'd get bored and you'd be itching to leave us again.'

'Who says I'm not?'

'Oh, don't tell me, this is your swan song?' My sister looks so disappointed.

'I need to have a long, hard think.'

Even if this auction is a success, the money will run out. Finding another haul like this is unlikely. The whole shop needs something more – I could certainly do it but

342

now would be a natural time to hand it over to Megan. Because I've found myself again and I'm at the stage where I could return to London, to that old life I so desperately wanted back.

'While you're doing that, then, can you also chase that Colin about my new sign?'

My face falls. 'Oh him, yeah, I'm afraid he's really busy at the moment.'

'Such a shame, well, never mind.' Being my sibling, she sees something in my eyes. 'Are you OK? Like, you've been really up and bouncy lately and now you seem more . . . well, less like that.'

'There is something, yes.' I can tell her now that it's all over – that she was right about getting involved with a married man. 'But another time.'

'All right, just as long as you're OK?'

'I'm where I need to be, Nerys.' Then, through the crowd, I catch Dad kissing Mam.

'How is it you've forgiven Dad?'

'Because I let him in, Bet. I let him try to make amends. The girls ... he's been able to be there for them in the way he wasn't for us.'

There's a tap on my arm. I tell Nerys I need to mingle, and turn to Megan.

'Guy not coming?' she says as Dylan appears with love hearts in his eyes plus the twins and Poppy in tow like he's the Pied Piper of Pant Bach.

I shake my head. Because she's been here on this journey with me I tell her the truth. 'He won't be coming back either.'

'No!' She breathes it out in a whisper, which makes my heart squeeze.

I find I can't speak, so I swallow and take a big breath. Megan understands – it shows how in sync we've become – and she knows to change the subject.

'OK, so it's nearly seven p.m. I'll go and press the button, shall I?' Megan says. 'I've scheduled posts all over the place, so if I get the website to go live now, then we should start seeing some traffic.'

'You do it. Brilliant job, Meg,' I say. 'Right, tits and teeth time, tits and teeth.' And I go off nervously in search of two very important people coming tonight who have let this happen – Mrs Hughes, the chairwoman of the trustees, whom I'm still to meet, and Helen, who donated the treasure trove. I look around for them but it's impossible to see through the crowd of villagers.

Instead, I turn back to admire the installation, which has worked very well indeed. It's exactly as I wanted it, with the outfits alive, as if they're human amongst a backdrop of the most exquisite antiques.

'It's marvellous, Betty, congratulations!'

It's Helen, with styled silver hair, swinging pearl ear-rings and in an olive three-quarter-length coat, looking like she's modelling some of the lots.

'You made it!'

'All the way from Cardiff. Without a walking stick! I can't stay long, I've got to get back to my toy boy who's in the process of stealing my life savings.'

'Ha ha, sounds like you're having fun. It certainly suits you!'

She taps my arm. 'You've really done it all justice. I love the movement of the wedding dress, it takes me back, and the velvet chair, it looks like new! Congratulations. When will we know how much it's all raised?'

'In a month or so – we wanted to keep it going for maximum reach. Although one lot will go tonight for a bit of drama.'

'I'm sure it'll be a success.'

'It needs to be. This'll be a short-term win for us but we'll need to bring in a few changes to keep the charity going long term. Not that you heard that from me.'

'I'm sure Mrs Hughes will agree wholeheartedly.'

'Oh, do you know her, then?'

'I do,' Helen says. 'Very well. Because I am Mrs Hughes.'

I stop dead and rewind what I've said. I have just indiscreetly divulged the fact that Life Goes On isn't out of the woods – she could've been anyone. Worse, she's Mrs Hughes.

'I should never have said all of that. It was very unprofessional of me.' I want to kick myself – I should have recognised her voice.

'Not at all. I can see how much you've changed things for the better and I'm very pleased you're thinking ahead.'

I could burst with happiness. But there's one thing I need to know. 'Can I ask, when I came to see you during the flood, why didn't you say who you were?'

Her eyes twinkle. 'Well, I suppose I wanted to see you as you are, not as who you thought you had to be. Very unfair of me, I know, and I thought about it that day when you came to my house, but you were so very charming I didn't want you to feel on edge around me.'

I laugh, then she asks what my plans are for the shop.

'I need to talk to you about that,' I say, 'and about my future. I'll call you in a few days, if that's OK? Shall we just enjoy this?'

She considers it, goes to speak, but then stops herself and simply nods her agreement.

Just then, out of the corner of my eye, I see someone I know watching me from the back of the room. He gives me a big grin and beckons me over.

'Betty,' he says, with a lightness to his voice that makes me feel warm, 'I thought we'd come along to have a nose.' Brody puts his arms around his green-eyed trio. 'Say hello, boys.' Connor, Liam and Declan give me sweet smiles before they get back to jostling one another.

'Ah, so nice of you!' I say. 'Anything caught your eye?'

'Lot number nine,' he says. 'A few of us want to chip in. Thought it'd be good for the club to have a slice of local history.'

I'm really touched. 'You're just in time.'

'Great,' he says, and as he goes to leave, I feel I owe him one.

'That drink, shall we do it on Friday? I could say I'll phone to arrange it, but you know what I'm like with a phone.'

'Yeah,' he says, 'yeah, why not?'

I get a proper Brody Burns beam that makes me laugh and then I tell him I will definitely, definitely give him a shout.

Club chairman Ray Watkins is on the stage and he raps his gavel on its block and announces the sale of lot number nine. Nerves dance in my stomach as he introduces Dai Hopkins to polite clapping and I brace myself for whatever my dad has planned.

But when he steps up, my breath catches in my throat. He's in a suit and tie, complete with rugby ball cufflinks and shiny shoes, he's clean-shaven and he's had a haircut.

And he refuses to take the microphone because he's intent on holding up the framed shirt and cap while standing paternally beside the glass box containing his boots and the match ball.

I'm staggered by his dignity as the sale begins. Bidders go up in increments of pounds and it's painful to watch. Still, he holds his head up high and I see him searching the audience. His eyes come to rest on mine and he gives me a small smile.

I don't know what comes over me, but I weave my way to his feet and he crouches down. I whisper to him and he takes my hand and squeezes it before relaying the message to the chairman, who looks at me to check. I nod and he declares, 'Going, going, gone' as he whacks the hammer down with a resounding thump.

'Ladies and gentlemen, we have had a bid of a substantial figure which would make your eyes water. So I'm delighted to say, sold to the lady at the front, Dai's very own dear daughter.'

Applause breaks out as Dad makes his way down to me and I can feel tears coming, so we cross the floor and head outside to get some air.

He starts to thank me but I shake my head at him. It's time for me to move on. I asked Guy to get some closure and I need to take my own advice; maybe this is his gift to me.

'You were there for me today, you didn't let me down.'

His chin wobbles and his big arms take me into his chest. He smells not of alcohol but of washing powder. He pats my back and the little girl inside of me who craved this all along becomes an adult comforted by our reconciliation.

We part and then he rubs his hands. 'I don't know about you, but I'm feeling thirsty.'

I roll my eyes at him – I was waiting for that. 'I'll get them in, then, shall I? Pint, is it?'

'No. I'll have a short, I think.' He coughs and then adds, 'An orange juice, please.'

'Just an orange juice?' I say it evenly because showing my shock could undo him.

'Yes, Boo.' He loosens his tie. 'Knocking it on the head for a while. It can make me ... a bit of a big mouth, you know, insensitive ...' He searches my face, waiting for me to add a few more adjectives to his list but every bone of contention of mine has crumbled in the face of his humility and my chin wobbles. 'It means I can be around to help out if you needed anything? With the charity or ...? Just a thought.'

I nod, unable to speak. But hasn't that been my trouble with him? Only by opening myself up to him can I make a start.

'That'd be fab, Dad. Thanks.'

He gives me a Dai wink, then walks inside, straight-backed and determined.

And just before I join him, I savour the scene: I'm looking back at the hug of people I love and while it'll take a while, while my heart will need to heal, I know I'll be OK.

# 37

## Two Months Later

### *Betty*

I've dreamt of this moment my whole life and it's featured slow-motion clinking of champagne glasses and fireworks.

The reality, though, of realising my ambition stars Prosecco in a mug and sneezing at dust – and I couldn't be happier.

'You did it, presh!' Nerys says, passing on the fizz but stuffing ginger biscuits. She's pregnant with her surprise third baby and while we both cried at my loss, we decided it was our gain and I'm thrilled I'm going to be at the birth without having any of the pain of delivery myself.

Besides, I've got a new baby myself.

'My own shop!' I say, still stunned that it's happened, particularly as it's all worked out exactly as I'd hoped. It's the empty unit next to Life Goes On, and we're going to knock through and rename the place Betty's Life Goes On. It's been a ferocious couple of months selling my London flat, getting everything signed and sealed with the charity, buying this space as well as sourcing dead stock material from a local factory and turning the designs in my sketchbook into new clothes. A percentage of their sale will go to Life Goes On and I'm looking to expand into funky retro homewares too. It means the charity shop remains the go-to for shoppers after a bargain but there's also a place for vintage finds and it's all still about reusing what there is rather than creating more waste.

'So I'm thinking the tea dresses should be the first thing people see when they come in.' They're the brightest and best of my collection, singing with animal prints and lightning bolts and blowsy floral blooms. 'The changing room and measuring-up area for bespoke orders can go there in the corner, then – Megan! Hi!'

'Had to have a quick look, didn't I!' she says, peeking round from next door.

'What do you think? How about we do a bench of your upcycled jewellery in here too?'

'Serious?' she says, 'That'd be amazing! Give me a shout when you're all moved in! Enjoy the rest of your week off!'

She doesn't just mean moving in here, but upstairs. Because the time has come to fly the nest and give Mam her house back. The flat above isn't in the best nick but it's airy and runs the length of the Arcade, so it fits a bed-room, lounge-diner, bathroom and box room, which will be my sewing emporium. And it's still bigger than what I had in London. Plus the commute will mean a trot down the stairs and I have views across the mountains, so I'll get a sense of space.

'Steve is free to help with any decorating. He doesn't know it yet, mind,' Nerys says.

'Dad's volunteered!' I say. 'Probably to make sure I do hang up the framed shirt in here, like I said I would!'

We've been having tea once a week with Nerys and trust is growing between us, particularly as he's sober.

'That's great!' Then, tartly, she adds, 'Such a shame there isn't someone you know who's properly handy.'

'Don't start that again.'

Because, incredibly, when I told her about Guy, it turns out she realised she'd met him not just once but twice.

'But he was lush, Bet.' She gives me pity eyes.

'Now you change your tune!'

'Well, I didn't know that the weirdo oddball you had your eyes on was him, did I? You should've said!'

'You would've shot me down if I had.'

'It's just because I care! And—'

I glare at her.

'It's not too late, Bet.'

'I broke up with him for him, Nerys.'

But how I miss him. Not an hour goes by without me thinking of him or, when things happen, how he'd laugh or what he'd say. I refresh his website every day to see what he's up to, I write emails I never send, and I generally feel I've lost a limb. And this is all when it's been so hectic – love doesn't conquer all, it bloody well smashes you into pieces.

'Well, I bet he's as miserable as you,' she says. 'It's all such a shame.'

'You forget you got excited when I met Brody for a few drinks!'

'That was more out of wanting you to move on. But I could tell you weren't into him. I mean, he's no Guy, is he?'

We went out a couple of times but I was in no way

wanting anything to happen. While we had an easy way with each other there was no chemistry. And there were no hard feelings, he's moved on, we're still friends and we're working on a funding application for a joint project.

'Right, I'm going back to the grindstone. Good luck with the unpacking!' Nerys disappears just as Megan pops back in, this time with an envelope.

'I've just totted it all up, the total from the auction. Thought you might want to see. There's a list there of who won what. I've highlighted who I've contacted and who's left, just so you know.'

I might be off work but she knows I'm desperate to find out how we did – we certainly had a lot of interest, helped by Sami, who spread the word to Londonistas and beyond. I stick the envelope in my pocket, then go to the door, which takes me up to my new home.

The stairs are dark, so when I reach the flat it looks amazingly bright. It's November and I can see the peaks of the mountains are dusted with snow, even though it's a sunny spring-like day. I wade through the boxes I've brought from Mam's to find the kettle to brew up and open the envelope.

And I gasp, because we've made masses more than I expected! I run down the list of lots, oohing at the money people paid for individual items and aahing at their addresses, there's Brighton and London and Cardiff and Chippenham – and Tunbridge Wells.

I double-check and check again but it's there, Guy Slater is down beside the velvet ladies chair. And Megan has ticked off every single name apart from his. My heart immediately gallops. This is her telling me to act. She has the right, having listened at length when the shock finally gave way to tears and she blew out Dylan for me when I needed a hug.

I can't believe he bought the chair – he knew I loved it. Is it some kind of memento or a sign that he wants me to get in touch?

I just don't know. I've heard nothing at all from him – I didn't expect to, but a piece of me always jumps when the post arrives, my inbox pings or my messages beep.

I pace the flat, wondering what to do. And then I see a package at the top of one of my boxes – and I know it's the present he gave me that I never opened.

It all happens in a rush, my fingers tremble, and I'm all thumbs trying to untie the string. I end up just ripping at the wrapping, which is made up of sheets from the Tunbridge Wells *Courier* newspaper. My eyes prick and then I'm crying when I hold it in my hand.

It's a love spoon, an old one which has been varnished up. There's a bell for marriage, a heart for love and two balls, which I know signify children, and he's carved a *B* and a *G*.

A cardboard label is attached to the handle and it reads: *B, this was Granny's love spoon from Grandpa. I put our initials on the balls because this is about us, not our hopes or what might be. Love, Guy xxx*

I remember what he said when he gave it to me: it was meaningful and a gesture for the future. He was saying he wanted me, just me, and he didn't even know then that I might not be able to have children. I notice too that it's the first time he ever left kisses on a note.

I'm hit by a huge wave of panic. What have I done? I lurch backwards, all the way to that day when I was at my lowest ebb and needed someone to believe in me and thought of him. Every time I had doubts about him, I was proved wrong. I've made the worst mistake of my life, I realise, because when he needed me to believe in him, I didn't.

I find a pen, rip a page out of my sketchbook and write.

*Dear Guy,*

*I'm writing to inform you that you are the new owner of a beautiful vintage ladies chair, thanks to your successful and very generous bid in the Life Goes On Sale of the Centuries auction.*

*In accordance with the T & Cs, delivery must be covered by the bidder. However, there are some extenuating circumstances in this case and I have come to the decision that I wish to deliver it in person. The reason is as follows:*

*I need to see you face to face to beg for your forgiveness and ask if you would take me back. Because I'm hopelessly in love with you. And I am lost without you. I thought I was doing the right thing, but I have just opened the gift you brought me, the love spoon which you altered to make it about us.*

*I'm incensed with myself for not showing the faith in you that you always showed in me – when you said you'd take me over children, if that were to happen, I didn't listen. All I could think of was denying you a chance to have a family. You said you'd do anything for me and I promise you now, finally, that I will do the same for you. Being too frightened to try and to let you down blinkered me – I didn't even give us a chance. When the time is right, I'd love to give us a go – whatever it is, whatever happens, we can do it together.*

*You have every right to be angry with me and to think 'it's a bit late now'. And I should've told you I felt the same that day, but if it's OK, if it'll convince you, if you can trust me again, you, Guy Slater, are my missing piece too.*

Love,
The Biggest Idiot on the Planet,
Betty xxx

PS Sorry about the state of this letter, I've just moved
and couldn't find any paper and I needed to write to
you straight away, so I ripped it out of my sketchbook
and the watery stains are from crying because I hurt
so much being apart from you.

PPS I could've rung, I know, or texted, or messaged,
or emailed. But I just wanted to do it the way we
have from the start.

PPPS If I've got it all wrong and you've moved on,
then there's no need to respond. I'll understand.

## 38

### *Guy*

'Oi! Foxy!' Charlie's voice bellows as I stand over the final suitcase.

'In here!' I shout as his footsteps echo on the hallway of my empty house until he finds me in the front room.

'Not too late to change your mind, you know,' he says, flexing his back, 'although if you did, I'd have to kill you because I'm never helping you move two houses again. Yesterday was a nightmare.'

'Think of the workout you got, mate. Next time you kiss your guns, you'll thank me. Anyway, I can't change my mind now, my entire life and Granny's is already halfway there.'

'And the G-meister, actually, hitched a lift with the removals people?'

'Yep, at the sparrow's crack. She wanted to be there to get the keys. Plus, they were happy to take Bobby, which I'm glad about because his farts are deadly, man.'

Granny locked up her place this morning and so all that's left to go is me, my sleeping bag, roll-up mattress, toothbrush and the van. Plus this battered old brown-leather bag.

'This it, then?' Charlie says, getting to his haunches to inspect its edges held together with gaffer tape.

I nod and feel the weight of anxiety on my shoulders. Two months I've been putting this off, two months. The day before Betty finished our relationship, I'd gone to see Charlie to ask if we could move on. I got a bear hug in response. And when I told him about my issues and asked if he'd be there when I opened the suitcase, he'd said 'in a shot, brother'. But then Betty's card arrived and the incentive to sort my head out disappeared because I was so devastated. That was when Charlie saved me because I could feel myself tipping towards utter despair. But he used it as a kick up the backside for both of us, getting us out training and eating healthily, when we'd spill our guts about love and loss. I went through it all: anger at her making such a dumb decision without talking to me properly about it, grief at losing the love of my life and then eventually a very sad acceptance that she thought she was doing the right thing. Granny said I should fight for her but Charlie sided with me: she had said goodbye and if that was what made her the least miserable, then I wanted to respect that. I don't think I'll ever get over Betty – she was never someone who was there for me 'for a reason'; if that bullshit was true I wouldn't still love and miss her so badly.

It made me even more determined to move – because doing nothing was what made it all worse when Sarah and I split up. Black clouds like a sitting target, so even though I was and still am brokenhearted, I've kept going, needing a new start more than ever.

But my departure means finally facing the past. The removals unearthed the case at Granny's and she dropped it here, telling me it was up to me what I did with it.

So here it is, looking entirely unimposing but

containing what could end up making me feel even more like an orphan. My greatest fear is seeing nothing of myself in there sending my parents further into the distance.

But then it's better to do this now. If it's too upsetting, I can dump it and drive off into the sunset.

'Ready then?' Charlie says, with faith in his eyes. 'Because I've got Maud in an hour, so, you know, no rush or anything.'

The joke would've grated once but now he's mastered fatherhood, I can see how seriously he takes his role as her dad. I haven't been around her at all; he realised that when Betty ended things, it could be a trigger situation. But he talks freely about her and, to be honest, the pain of losing her.

'I don't know what's in here at all,' I say, nerves jangling, as I lay the suitcase on its back and pull the stiff zip which releases the smell of old paper.

'I expect you'll find out your mum was a secret double agent and your dad was a Hells Angel.'

I laugh through my nose. 'They were a pair of teachers so yes, probably.'

But I'm so glad I'm doing this with him – Charlie instinctively knows to keep this as light as possible. I flip up the cover and have to take a breath.

'Come on, then! What's inside?'

There's so much stuff my eyes swim, taking in photos and fabrics, video tapes and a book, and my heart is thumping at what I'm about to unearth. I pray it's something to back up the stories I've been told – you're just like your father, your mother was such a happy person – because otherwise it will lead to some existential crisis that I'm nothing like them. I empty it all out into piles and find a long metal box with a handle at the bottom which I immediately open.

'My dad's tools,' I say, feeling as if I've hit the jackpot. I've always wondered if it was true that I got my handiness from him via Grandpa. It seemed such an easy claim to make when I had no proof otherwise. But here it is! And by the looks of the worn and rusty spanners and screwdrivers, they were well used. I pick up a hammer and feel how heavy it is compared to the modern ones and something inside of me clicks into place – my dad held this with his own hand and here it is in mine. I feel my heart whoop and my eyes prick with tears.

'If a hammer's going to set you off, Foxy, then you have no hope with that Babygro.'

'Jesus, this is mine?'

'Well, it wouldn't have fit your dad would it?'

I pick it up and at the same time I see a photo beside it – I'm wearing it while my mum cradles me against a pale green wall. 'This must've been my leaving-hospital outfit.'

'They had better taste than you've got.'

'And what's this?' I see a plastic bracelet and it has my name and birthdate on it. 'The tag from when I was born!'

'Mind if I have a look at some photos?'

'Go ahead, that's why you're here. To give me a heads-up if there's anything – unsettling.'

Charlie flicks through a thick wad and narrates as he goes while I find a heap of 'It's A Boy' cards Mum saved and a pressed flower from a bouquet she received.

'Look at your cheeks, Foxy!' Charlie says. 'You were a

right porker! Wow, you look so much like your dad here, same bushy hair, his eyes. But your nose is your mum's. You stand like that, you know, like your dad there, all laid-back and chill. Oh and this is a nice one, your mum is in a paddling pool with you. It says on the back ... "Mummy and Guy, summer 1987, a pair of waterbabies".'

'Show me that!' It feels like Christmas to know now why I'm so drawn to water. I take a snap of it, feeling an echo of my father because he was the one who took the picture.

'There's your first trip to the seaside too! In Wales, it says.'

And there's a christening gown, an incredible sketch of me sleeping that's signed by my mum – she really was a good artist, then, too – plus a little handmade yellow wooden boat which my dad must've made for me.

'How did all this survive?'

'The firefighters recovered as much as they could.' I imagine them risking their lives, picking through the debris, and I say a private thanks to whoever those heroes were who've given me an extra sense of who I am.

I'm drawn to the *Beatrix Potter Baby Book* and start at the beginning. Mum stuck a headshot of me looking fairly fresh out of the oven with a red wrinkly face and white eyebrows and she'd filled in the questions:

How I Felt When I Knew You Were Coming ...
Elated! But also nauseous because you gave me terrible morning sickness! But you were worth every dash to the loo!

What I Thought When I Met You For The First Time

... Like a lioness with a cub – I knew instantly I'd spend the rest of my life – and forever – loving you ferociously!

What It Feels Like To Be Your Mummy ... Roar!

How I Slept At First ... Bloody awful – you turned me into a zombie!

My Favourite Food ... Everything, the greedy guts that you are! But especially Granny's fish pie.

There's even a lock of my dark hair inside a tiny envelope.

She's so funny and sweet all the way through but then when it gets to My First Birthday Party, it all stops. I gulp at all the blanks on the page asking about my birthday cake, the guests and my favourite present. Mum and Dad missed it by just a few weeks.

'You all right?' Charlie says, as I go quiet.

'Yeah. Yep – just it's all so overwhelming ...'

'I'm so sorry.'

I turn to him and swallow hard. 'Actually, this has just made me so incredibly happy. To know I'm like them. It's weird, but just seeing these bits has made me feel more whole.'

I blow through my cheeks and repack the case. 'But I think that's enough for now,' I say. 'Got to drive in a bit, so ... and I'll look forward to watching those videos, I'll get the old VHS tapes turned into DVDs.'

Charlie looks at his watch and our time is nearly up.

'Thanks for coming,' I say as we face each other to say goodbye.

'I'll miss you, Foxy,' Charlie says before throwing

himself at me and we slap each other on the back, trying to cover up our crying noises.

'Me too. Come and visit any time.'

'I can't believe you're moving abroad,' Charlie says, shaking his bald head.

'Just remember your passport, OK?'

We clear our throats and the front door creaks.

'I hope you don't mind,' Charlie says, 'Sarah's brought Maud here.'

'That's fine,' I say, because I can't get aggro about a baby handover. And actually it feels right to see them with this chapter of my life closing.

'All packed?' Sarah says, half entering the room so I can only see the handle of the buggy.

'Bring her in here,' I say, because there's no need to hide her.

She's fast asleep and my heart bursts at the spidery eyelashes resting on her cheeks but, incredibly, the only pang I feel is a deep affection.

'We've got something to say to you, Guy.' Sarah smiles at me to reassure me there are no more skeletons. 'We want to thank you for bringing us together when we'd torn it all apart.'

'If it hadn't been for you,' Charlie says, looking more serious than I've ever seen him, 'I wouldn't have a daughter. It was really big of you to put everything aside, to make us put Maud first.'

Everything seems amplified by the emptiness of the house – the space seems so huge now. But I realise the emotion in here fills it to the brim.

'I'm just glad you're all OK. That we're all OK.'

We remain silent, taking it all in until Maud yelps herself awake.

She looks around, beams at her dad and then puts out her arms.

'If you want to have a cuddle, Foxy ...'

'Thanks but we've just had one,' I say, feeling my mum's spirit inside me.

He laughs and nods for me to go for it.

'Come here, Maudie,' I say, gently, and unbuckle her, lift her out and pop her on my hip so she can see her parents. 'You've put on a lot of timber,' I tell her as she examines me. There's no recollection on her face at all and that's all right – the fact that she isn't screaming is enough.

She pokes a chubby finger up my nose and we all hoot, which makes her jolt and cry. I hand her to Charlie and she stops straight away.

'So, I'd better get going,' I say and give Sarah a kiss and shake Charlie's hand.

'We haven't finished yet, actually,' he says. 'Because if it's all right by you, we'd like to ask you something.'

'Go ahead.'

'If it's not too weird, would you like to be ... an official uncle?'

I get a rush of warmth all over, thinking this isn't the end, really, not at all.

'We are weird,' I say, touched to my core. 'So I'd love to, mate. Thanks, Sarah.'

Charlie jigs his daughter, telling her, 'You'll love your Uncle Foxy! Yes you will! He's your foxy uncle!'

Both Sarah and I roll our eyes at each other and in that moment all the bad blood is washed away.

In a fuss of buggy brakes, bags and bottles, they disappear and I get my stuff together.

I pack the van quick sharp because it's a cold November day, then go back to lock up. I take one last look at the house that saw so much joy turn to misery. When I imagined leaving, when I was still with Betty, I thought I'd be glad to see the back of it because I had a future with her. Then when we parted ways, I expected to feel sadness, because I wouldn't be going to her. What's there is something I've never felt before – it's like I've found my balance. The final moments in here going through the suitcase gave me substance and resolution and my feet feel they're on solid ground.

I pull the door shut and drop the keys through the letterbox and I leave having found peace not just with Charlie, Sarah and Maud, but with myself. And I get behind the wheel and begin my new life knowing I can handle anything now I'm carrying Mum and Dad in my heart. Before I start the engine, I go to the photo of my mum and me in the paddling pool and I make it my new screensaver – it's the perfect replacement for the old one of Maud from the day she was born.

I turn the ignition and drive off, knowing a fire will always burn within me for a family but I won't let it rip through my heart and destroy me.

# 39

## *Betty*

'Confession time,' I announce with a deep sense of dread in my belly.

'Spill!' Sami says, his eyes popping beneath the sleeping mask on his forehead because he is forever gossip-ready.

Nerys leans in over my table ready to catch every humiliating word.

'So I wrote to Guy—' I push my breakfast away because suddenly I've lost my appetite.

The pair of them inch closer over their fry-ups.

'To ask if he'd take me back ...' I fiddle with a button on my nightie as they gawp at me, each other, and then back at me again.

'How did this not come out last night?' Sami pulls a dramatic face which turns into a grimace because he is feeling tender after he had a few too many homemade cocktails at my flat-warming pyjama party.

'Because ...'

'Yes?' Nerys says in a high-pitched voice, her fork frozen in mid-air.

'He never received it.' I'd hoped that sharing the humiliation and heartache would make me feel better but admitting it out loud for the first time makes me feel even more sad. Because, basically, I'm accepting that there's no hope left.

Sami slumps back with disappointment. But Nerys is furrowing her brow – she's clear-eyed because she had mocktails.

'When did you write?' she asks.

'Ten days ago.'

'Is that all? That's not long, he might still reply.'

I get up, find my coat and produce the envelope from the pocket and hold it up so they can read the words: *No Longer At This Address*.

'He's moved.'

'Why didn't he leave a forwarding address? Or get redirected mail?' Sami says.

'Because clearly he doesn't want to be found.'

'Oh.' Nerys looks on the verge of tears.

Sami is more pragmatic. 'Why didn't you email or text or phone, you fool?'

I throw my hands in the air. 'Isn't it obvious? Because that's how it started, writing to each other. And' – this is just as important – 'technology is so brutally instant. Like I'd know he'd received it or he'd seen it and to have him not respond would have been too final too quickly. With a letter you can let yourself believe for a while and then the let-down is more gentle.'

'I don't understand it.' Nerys shakes her head violently.

'It's just something I've got to accept. I've lost him because I dithered. That self-sabotage thing you've always accused me of – well, I've done it again.' A sob rises up and I can't stop it.

Four arms go round me and they rock me until I'm out of tears.

'I can't bear the thought that even if he's moved here, which I sincerely doubt, why would he even? I can't bear that if he is here he's under the same sky as me and I'll never be with him and I'll spend the rest of my life looking for him and my heart will jump every time I see someone that's like him. Like it is now, because hope is such a bell-end.'

I get up and go for a shower where I have another cry but this time it's louder because I can hide it under the sound of the water.

'I still believe, Betty,' Nerys says defiantly when I re-emerge. Then she looks as if she wants to say something.

'What?' I ask.

'I've got a favour to ask.' Devoted Steve is on his way to pick her up. She'll get washed and dressed at home and then they've got a family day out. 'A cake that needs delivering.'

'On a Sunday?'

'Yes, special late request – I made it yesterday and it's in the fridge downstairs in the café. On your way back from taking Sami to the station, could you drop it off for me? It's sort of on the way.'

'No problem.' I have the whole day to myself and all I'm doing is painting the shop.

She nips off and returns with a white box, cuddles Sami goodbye, then she's gone.

On the drive, Sami tries to turn the chat back to Guy.

'Don't give up, Betty,' he says in a strange voice which I take to be his hangover – he's wearing shades because his head bangs so much.

'Enough! I just need to focus on Betty's Life Goes On. Thanks so much for coming for the weekend. And for everything you did for the auction on all your social media thingies.'

I think back to the pink velvet ladies chair that's the sole uncollected lot in the store room and curse it for reminding me of Guy every time I see it.

'I'll do it again with your new collection, if you like?'

'Would you?' Because his Sale of the Centuries toots brought so much interest.

'Yes, of course! I do the occasional blog too. I'm thinking … "The queen of guilt-free fashion who's saving dead stock destined for landfill – and all for a good cause". How about that?'

'Perfect!' I say, feeling much more cheery as we get to the passenger drop-off zone.

'Just send me the links and some images and Sami's your father's uncle!'

'You're a darling,' I say, hugging him. 'I miss you already. Bring Cara next time, yeah?'

'I will. I just wanted to have you to myself this time.'

Then in a puff of kisses and love-yous, he's gone and I get that low of being alone after a lovely catch-up with my best friend.

I grab the cake from the back seat and pop the postcode into my phone and see with a start it's half an hour away. Nerys forgot to mention that bit.

But then maybe a road trip will do me some good. It's a gloriously sunny winter's day and I stop for a drive-through coffee to pep me up. The Heads of the Valleys road snakes the edge of the Brecon Beacons so it's a stunning journey and I marvel at how far I've come to be able to do this by myself. This time last year I was still in London, still in denial about what made me happy.

Here, now, as I soak up the soaring mountains and huge skies, is where I found my fulfilment. Guy was part of that, it's true, but I've never been one to put everything on a relationship. And I thank God for that. My life is busy enough.

The last stretch is narrow, with winding lanes, and a sign announces I've entered the Brecon Beacons. I get to the hamlet of Coelbren, where my sat nav tells me to take the next left, and then I've arrived.

I can't resist having a quick look at the cake. It's a towering coffee and walnut, Nerys's showstopper, with Maltesers arranged in the number thirty-seven. It's Guy's birthday today and I wince because it's yet another reminder of what I've lost. It won't be long before I'm the same age – and so begin the maudlin whispers that come every now and then about getting older. Before they can spiral out of control, they're drowned out by the sound of rushing water.

I realise where I am – beside the river which runs to Henrhyd Falls, the highest in South Wales, the one which appeared as the entrance to the Batcave in *The Dark Knight Rises*. Just looking at the ice-blue of the ferocious torrent makes me shiver so I put on my bobble hat and set off under the huge canopy of trees.

There's no name on the box, just the address, and there's only one house I can see, so I head for that, taking deep breaths of the cold, fresh air which smells of moss and green.

The sign matches the label – it's simply called Cartref, which is the Welsh for home. I crunch down the gravel drive and see a massive old country pile which is attached to a dilapidated coach house. A barn is tucked behind that. It's stunningly secluded with enormous lawns and views for miles. I get to the grand grey front door and bang the antique knocker, making sure to shut my gaping gob that's dropped in awe.

'Whoever lives here is blessed; it must've cost a pretty penny. There's no answer, so I knock again. I don't want to put the cake on the doorstep – all right, there's a gnome sitting there to keep watch but I can't see him fighting off a fox or a thief. I wonder if there's a safe place to leave it. But what if it rains? And I don't have a pen on me to write a note.

All I can do is call the number beneath the address and when I've punched it in, I hear the landline ringing behind the door. It goes on and on and on and I'm about to end it when someone answers.

'Hello?' a man says.

'Hi there – delivery! At your front door!'

'Oh, sorry! Have you been there long?' he says.

My heart jumps, because his warm, deep tone is like Guy's. I get a stab of frustration that this is going to happen and I have no control over it. Like now, when I hear myself tremor as I reassure him.

'No, no. Not long.'

'Good, I'm sorry to have kept you waiting,' he says, sounding as silky as the darkest, most sensuous chocolate, and my imagination and memory conspire against me; I'm seeing his full lips and remembering how it felt to kiss him. 'We've just moved and we're unpacking. It seems we're always as far from the door as possible.'

'It's fine,' I murmur, 'I'm in no rush.'

We hang up and I realise Guy and I never actually spoke on the phone together. The one, single most direct way of communicating when we were apart – and we never did it. I wish now I had called him rather than wasting time writing and sending a card – at least then I'd have heard his voice and perhaps I could have persuaded him. It's ridiculous, but I'm hit by a toppling wave of loss and I turn away just as the door opens.

I'm not prepared for what I see – the view in front of me takes my breath away. There's a gap in the trees and, through it, framed like a painting, is the waterfall in all its glory. The spray glitters with diamonds in a drifting mist which catches the sun and shimmers with a million rainbows. My hands go to my chest and I hear myself gasp at such beauty.

'Isn't it gorgeous?' the man says.

Again, my heart flutters as if I'm hearing Guy. And in another cruel trick of the mind I get the slightest hint of citrus. I need to get a grip. At least my eyes won't deceive me. But then I look back.

'Guy?' I say, shocked to the core. 'What the hell are you doing here?'

# 40

## Guy

'**B**etty?' My voice goes up at the end in pure disbelief. She pulls off her hat to prove it's really her and I'm mesmerised as her red hair tumbles down onto her shoulders.

'What am I doing here?' I repeat her question back because my brain needs time to catch up with what's happening. 'What are you doing here?'

The air between us feels taut, yet time seems to stretch as we stand there staring at each other.

'Delivering a birthday cake.' She says it robotically, then follows it up with a weak 'Happy birthday!' because that's what people do.

'Thanks,' I say, sticking to convention, never mind we're in a stunned stupor. I didn't recognise her voice on the phone and clearly she didn't recognise me either. How can that be when we were so close? But then we never communicated like that. 'You found it OK, then?' I ask like some old git, but it's because I still can't compute this.

She nods into the silence, then suddenly we both say each other's name at once.

'You go first,' I say because truly I don't know where to start. Because she ended our relationship and yet here she is.

'What are you doing here, then?' Betty says and any far-fetched hope that she's made it her life's work to find me and beg me to take her back vanishes. She hasn't been looking for me because nothing has changed in her mind and even if I stood here and told her I've made my peace with my parents, would that make a difference now?

'I live here.' I keep it short because I'm trying to protect myself; seeing her is making me ache with sorrow and love.

'Since when?' There's an edge to her voice and she's narrowed her eyes. For some reason it hits me where it hurts.

'Was I meant to inform you?' I cringe at myself for lashing out when I've squared this circle in my head. Or I'm supposed to have done.

Betty blinks quickly. 'Of course not, no.' She points at the box by my feet. 'So there's the cake. My sister asked me to deliver it. I had no idea it was for you.' She takes a step back and then, when I sense her withdrawal, I'm desperate to stop her going.

'Your sister? But who ordered it?'

She shrugs and I'm losing her.

'What flavour is it?' I gabble.

Her blue eyes pale, and Betty sniffs because she knows I'm grabbing at straws. 'Coffee and walnut.'

'Right,' I say, working something out in my head. 'So your sister took an order ... Coffee and walnut was the cake I bought for Kay and Kay knows I moved in yesterday and that it's my birthday ...' Am I barking up the wrong tree?

But Betty's head tilts. 'Actually, my sister has been acting weird since you and I . . . finished. Especially today. Like she knew something.'

'And Kay and your sister really hit it off when they met. Do you think they've …?' It feels such a big jump – and it could be because I'm willing it to be true. Kay knows full well how gutted I am to have lost Betty. Does it mean Betty's told her sister she's missed me too?

She's nodding now. 'Yes. Yes, I think they've set us up to meet.'

'Outrageous.'

'Devious pair of—'

I cut her off because something strikes me. 'But why would they do that?'

Betty stares at me and takes a deep breath like she's full of something to say. Then she flicks her eyes away to look around her. 'Give me a tour of the grounds?'

'Sure.' I'm torn between wanting this to be over and to keep her for as long as I can. 'So how are things?'

'Good,' she says, as we walk along the side of the house, 'I've got my own shop now, almost ready to launch my clothing range.'

'Wow. I'm really happy for you. I mean it, you deserve it.'

'Thanks. You?'

'Settled already. The barn there will be my workshop. I've already had a few enquiries.'

'And Myfanwy?'

'Absolutely loving it.' It comes to mind to tell Betty she can say hello but I feel the blow that we aren't in that position anymore.

'I'm so pleased it's all worked out. This place,' she says, 'it's beautiful, completely stunning. But it wasn't the original one you wanted, was it?'

It's all a reminder of how we've had no contact at all

for two months and I feel hollow that we used to be so connected.

'No. We lost out on that one. It was beyond our budget. But then, the weirdest thing happened; a lovely old fella I did a job for – a Mr Cummings – I fixed his gnome, Gordon, for him, well ... he had no living relatives, he never married or had kids, and he left some money to me. The rest was split between charities which fight loneliness. His only stipulation was that I looked after Gordon.'

'Gordon the gnome! The one at your door! Oh, Guy,' Betty says, 'that's so sad but so sweet.'

I clear my throat. 'It meant we could afford this. Granny's got the main section and I have the wreck of the coach house.' Once upon a time, maybe Betty would've come to call it her home too. 'And we've got our own private waterfall. Well, it feels like it with that view.'

Instinctively, we make our way to the path that leads to it.

'Have you seen it properly yet?' Betty asks.

'No. But—' I size this up. Would it be weird to see if she wants to go?

'Shall we?' Betty says and it's a bittersweet moment, knowing we still share a wavelength and it feels less like we're walking on a tightrope. Maybe we could still be friends? I wonder, picking my way down the rock steps. But when I turn to check she's OK, my heart rushes and I know there's no way we can be mates.

It takes ten minutes until we're being blasted by the force of the thundering falls. It's spectacular and the energy of this natural wonder takes our breath away. We back away from the ledge and find a slab of stone which is shielded from the noise and sit in awe as the water topples and twists and thrashes down ninety feet into the bubbling pool before continuing on its journey.

'God, it's humbling, isn't it?' Betty sighs.

'Hypnotising too.'

'All that movement in each single second over and over ...'

'It takes a lot to make me feel small but this certainly does.'

Betty picks up a stone and throws it into the whirls where it's sucked in and lost in the icy foam.

'Like life is made up of moments, isn't it? My accident, a split second.'

'My marriage, over like that,' I say, clicking my fingers.

'And then meeting you.'

I don't look at her because I don't want to be taken on a painful trip down memory lane. I've worked really hard to move on. In fact, what am I doing with her here now? If I'm not careful, I'm going to hurtle backwards. My legs are moving; I get up and tell her I have to go.

'Just one more moment, Guy,' Betty says, with passion. 'Please.'

'I'm not interested. I can't do this. I've made my peace with everything, with Maud, Charlie and Sarah. With my parents. I'm only going forwards now.' I make my way to the path.

'But there's one last thing you need to know from the past.'

She pulls out an envelope from her pocket and thrusts it into my hand.

'When I saw you'd bought the chair in the auction, I wrote to you and posted it to your old address but it got returned to me.'

377

The envelope is battered and creased and I'm torn between wanting to screw it up and rip it open.

'I've only just arranged to get the post redirected. The new owners haven't moved in yet, they've got decorators in; one of them must've put it in the post box.'

'I wondered if it had been you sending it back,' Betty says in a small voice.

'Why would I do that?'

'Because …' Betty swallows and her face is fearful. 'I told you I'd made a mistake.'

'About what?' The bastard, that is hope, jumps up to attention inside of me and I force it down.

She shuts her eyes briefly, as if she needs to draw on her strength. 'That I loved you.' Why is she being cruel?

'That I never told you … in you.'

All this talk of past tense is too much and the hurt tumbles out. 'That's just it. Why didn't you? Why couldn't you accept that I wanted you and that was enough?'

'Because I thought you'd had too much hurt. I was frightened my love would make you miserable.'

'So what are you saying, Betty?'

'I can't be glad that I had the accident, I can't be glad of the pain. But if it hadn't happened, I wouldn't have learned about myself and there'd have been no us.' She gives a shudder. 'I wouldn't have contacted you and… there'd be no letters or visits…and certainly not this.'

She goes into her other pocket. And produces the love spoon. 'I haven't put this down since I opened it. You made this about us, not about the future. About the moment. I get it now. I want to live in the moment with you.' Her eyes begin to plead with me. 'I want to live in the moment with you. Forever.'

It suddenly dawns on me that we're not talking about the past anymore. I can't compute it after all that's happened. I'm in bits, half wanting to go to her and half wanting to stay away to protect myself. Can I trust her? What if she gets cold feet again?

'Read the letter,' she begs, seeing my turmoil.

With trembling hands I open it up and see it's a homemade card with a simple but stunning sketch of the waterfall we swam in that day. Inside, she's written exactly what she's told me, but seeing it on the page makes it real. It's a risk to let her back in again. But the thought of never seeing her again is agony.

'I believe you, Betty,' I say and she sees and hears my caution. Her face falls and it hits me that I can make this better. 'If this happens . . .' I say, warily, 'It has to start and never stop again.'

Finally she breaks out into a smile that turns her eyes watery. 'I promise you,' she says.

'And when the time comes, when we get to that moment, I'll do anything to have a family. We can try, we can apply to adopt or foster, and if that doesn't happen we can get a whole pack of dogs or ... mates for Gordon ... a toadstool of gnomes or whatever the collective term is. Maybe we can do that anyway?' She's off on one of her tangents, our tangents, and it melts me. 'Because what you've taught me, Guy, is that love is love – it doesn't matter if it's blood or biological, it's about us having our own sense of family. All that matters is that love is there.'

I nod as tears come to my eyes. My hand falls to my side and I gaze at her with total adoration. She's still unsure if I mean it, so I have to tell her I do.

'You're not the biggest idiot on the planet,' I say, moving towards her. 'We can share that title because I am too, for not once ever picking up the phone to call you.'

'We can be joint winners, like we were at paintballing.' She beams, meeting me with open arms as we embrace, fitting together perfectly, each of us the other's missing piece. Finally, we're where we want to be.

'I was so scared I'd lost you,' Betty says. 'I was so scared you'd forget me.'

'But that's why I came here, why I chose this view. Because I didn't ever want to forget you.'

I take her in my arms and, for once, neither of us wants to break the spell with more talking. We let our lips speak instead as we kiss each other hello again.

And this time I know there will never be another goodbye.

# Epilogue

*Dear Myfanwy,*

*Venice was so worth the wait! The festival is freaky and fantastic, with all of its masks and carnivals.*

*I'm sketching like mad while Guy's having a go at smashing the world pizza-eating record. Hope you get to this in time before Cariad destroys it.*

*Tell her that if she's a very good girl, she'll have a special job, come the summer – to lead my bridesmaids Poppy, Daisy, Baby and Maud down the aisle.*

*Guy kept the decree absolute secret then popped the question on a gondola a year to the day that we met. There were a few tears – OK, floods – when he proposed with his mum's engagement ring. Thank you so much for keeping it safe for him in the suitcase all these years.*

*Right, must go; Guy's hungry again. Once he's fed, we're off to find you a jigsaw.*

*Love,*

*Betty and Guy xxx*

*PS Message from Guy: he doesn't want Bobby to feel left out – Charlie doesn't mind sharing the job of best man with him.*

# *Acknowledgements*

We were drunk on fresh air after climbing a mountain in the Brecon Beacons when we noticed road signs on our drive home advising 'essential travel only'.

That moment sobered us right up. But we had no idea how bad it would get. Death, distancing and darkness became the norm.

Our trip into the breathtakingly beautiful shadow of Pen y Fan turned out to be the final hurrah before stay at home became the law.

There were many sources of pain; the best of us, those frontline angels, had it the worst. Take homeschooling, when my son had to explain maths to me, while I shouted 'I do words! That's what I do! Not numbers!'

Then there was the daily walk, which quickly descended into the daily dragging our boy out and let's have a big row in public while we're at it.

Not forgetting lecturing my husband about the need to ration loo roll and then realising that as the only female in the house I was responsible for using most of it.

Far worse though was being apart from my family who live miles away in south-east England. I'd be caught sobbing (while not doing anything constructive, unlike everyone else who was decluttering and working out with Joe Wicks and learning how to train unicorns) and my son would wearily announce 'Mum's crying again'.

So I had the stir-crazy of staying at home combined with the ache of missing my tribe – and that's when I settled on the locations of the Brecon Beacons and Tunbridge Wells for *Love, Betty*. And it was a joy to escape in my head to my parents' neck of the woods and the Valleys. But this being a lockdown book, it wasn't easy. Trying to differentiate between the days without the usual stimulation sapped my creativity.

My energy was spent trying to differentiate between the days of the week and included camping in the garden, dancing on dog walks and swimming in the freezing sea (thank you, mermaids).

Eventually I got down to writing and I was lucky enough to have splendid people to lean on.

Lizzy Kremer, my agent, was as ever fantastic with her direction and advice, and her assistant Maddalena Cavaciuti expertly tucked in, unpicked the knots and got me to focus. Thanks too to the clever people at David Higham Associates, including Kaynat Begum, who do all the paperwork and finances.

Editorial director Charlotte Mursell was so enthusiastic from day one and gave me such encouragement as well as brilliant input. The Orion team, I salute you, and special mention to Sanah Ahmed for her *Encanto* knowledge!

I am very grateful to copyeditor Marian Reid, who raked forensically through thousands of words and spotted when I randomly changed a character's name to something else, and to Rachael Lancaster who produced a swoony cover I adore.

Thanks also to Jenny Braunton, Motor Accident Solicitors' Society membership coordinator, who put me in touch with Paul Lewis, partner and head of accident management at George Ide, who explained the legal process of a car accident to me in layman terms.

Naturally, any mistakes are mine, all mine.

The gorgeous author community, book reviewers and bloggers, booksellers and the Romantic Novelists' Association do so much cheerleading for contemporary novels and thanks to the gang on Twitter, Instagram, and Facebook.

Readers and library users, you are so very kind to pick me up and read me and I love it when you get in touch – your reviews are so important, so please, never stop! And the people who staff charity shops are wonderful, giving new life to preloved goodies, as well as giving me such joy when I come across one of my books on their shelves.

To the Barnfest Tribe, that reunion in the summer was a top-up for the soul, and I'll never forget eating outside, our crossword communing and failing hilariously at the aqua park.

My amazing, funny, wise, loyal friends, near and far, keep me going and I don't know what I'd do without you.

Last but forever first, my son, you make my heart burst, and my husband, you make my sides ache, and of course I must mention The Secretary who has no idea how much we adore him. The late Ancient Cat, my beloved Pillow, who was with me for nineteen years and responsible for many typos as she trampled my laptop. Rest in peace, you gorgeous girl.

# Credits

Laura Kemp and Orion Fiction would like to thank everyone at Orion who worked on the publication of *Love, Betty* in the UK.

**Editorial**
Charlotte Mursell
Sanah Ahmed

**Copyeditor**
Marian Reid

**Proofreader**
Clare Wallis

**Audio**
Paul Stark
Jake Alderson

**Contracts**
Anne Goddard
Humayra Ahmed
Ellie Bowker

**Design**
Rachael Lancaster
Joanna Ridley
Nick May

**Editorial Management**
Charlie Panayiotou
Jane Hughes
Bartley Shaw
Tamara Morriss

**Finance**
Jasdip Nandra
Afeera Ahmed
Elizabeth Beaumont
Sue Baker

Don't miss the gorgeously uplifting novel by Laura Kemp . . .

'The equivalent of someone pouring Welsh honey into your heart'
**Milly Johnson**

*One summer to change her life . . .*

Wanda Williams has always dreamed of leaving her wellies behind her
and travelling the world! Yet every time she comes close to following
her heart, life always seems to get in the way.

So, when her mother ends up in hospital and her sister finds out
she's pregnant with twins, Wanda knows that only she can save the
crumbling campsite at the family farm.

Together with her friends in the village, she sets about sprucing up
the site, mowing the fields, replanting the allotment and baking
homemade goodies for the campers.

*But when a long-lost face from her past turns up, Wanda's world is
turned upside-down. And under a starry sky, anything can happen . . .*

Charlotte Bold is nothing like her name - she is shy and timid and just wants a quiet life. When her job doing the traffic news on the radio in London is relocated to Sunshine FM in Mumbles, she jumps at the chance for a new start in Wales.

But when she arrives she discovers that she's not there to do the travel news - she's there to front the graveyard evening show. And she's not sure she can do it.

Thrust into the limelight, she must find her voice and a way to cope. And soon she realises that she's not the only person who finds life hard - out there her listeners are lonely too. And her show is the one keeping them going.

*Can Charlotte seize the day and make the most of her new home? And will she be able to breathe new life into the tiny radio station too . . .?*

'I loved it'
**Clare Mackintosh**

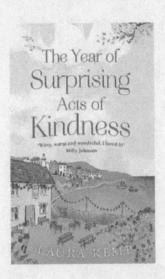

**Welcome to the Village of Love.**
**Where friendship flourishes and love blossoms . . .**

When Ceri Price arrives in the small seaside village in West Wales, she
only means to stay for a couple of nights – long enough to scatter her
mother's ashes, and then go back to her life as a successful make-up
entrepreneur.

But when a case of mistaken identities means she lands a job as the
barmaid in the local pub, she unexpectedly finds friendship, and
perhaps a chance at love.

But when the plans for a new housing estate put the local woodland
under threat, she fears the way of life here could disappear.

Then mysterious acts of kindness start springing up around the village
– a string of bunting adorns the streets, a new village signpost appears
out of nowhere and someone provides paint to spruce up the houses
on the seafront. But who is behind these surprising gifts, and can a
little kindness change all their lives?